The Battle f

# The Battle For A Home

**Book 3 in the
Norman Genesis Series
By
Griff Hosker**

# The Battle for a Home

*Published by Sword Books Ltd 2016*

*Copyright © Griff Hosker First Edition*

*The author has asserted their moral right under the Copyright, Designs and Patents Act, 1988, to be identified as the author of this work.*

*All Rights reserved. No part of this publication may be reproduced, copied, stored in a retrieval system, or transmitted, in any form or by any means, without the prior written consent of the copyright holder, nor be otherwise circulated in any form of binding or cover other than that in which it is published and without a similar condition being imposed on the subsequent purchaser.*
*A CIP catalogue record for this title is available from the British Library.*
*Cover by Design for Writers*
*Thanks to Simon Walpole for the Artwork.*

# Contents

The Battle For A Home ............................................................. 1
Prologue ..................................................................................... 5
Chapter 1 ................................................................................... 7
Chapter 2 ................................................................................. 18
Chapter 3 ................................................................................. 26
Chapter 4 ................................................................................. 37
Chapter 5 ................................................................................. 43
Chapter 6 ................................................................................. 56
Chapter 7 ................................................................................. 65
Chapter 8 ................................................................................. 81
Chapter 9 ................................................................................. 90
Chapter 10 ............................................................................. 100
Chapter 11 ............................................................................. 109
Chapter 12 ............................................................................. 118
Chapter 13 ............................................................................. 132
Chapter 14 ............................................................................. 143
Chapter 15 ............................................................................. 155
Chapter 16 ............................................................................. 164
Chapter 17 ............................................................................. 175
Chapter 18 ............................................................................. 187
Chapter 19 ............................................................................. 196
Chapter 20 ............................................................................. 204
Chapter 21 ............................................................................. 216
Epilogue ................................................................................. 224
Glossary ................................................................................. 226
Maps and Illustrations ........................................................... 231
Historical note ....................................................................... 232
Other books by Griff Hosker .................................................. 236

## Dedication

To my first grandson, Thomas Griffith Hosker. Have a good life and a long life.

# Prologue

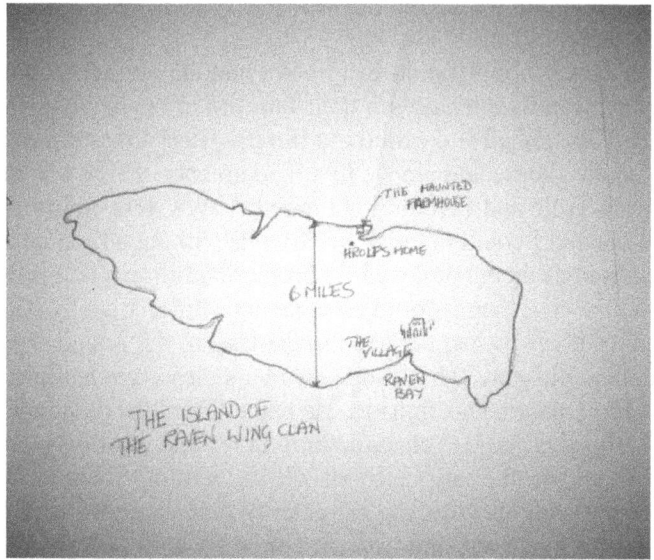

It had been almost half a year since we had returned from Dyflin where we had fought for Gunnstein Berserk Killer and defeated the High King of Hibernia. I had come back rich and with much honour amongst the warriors of my clan. I had thought that my life would have been better. In many ways it was. The slave I had freed, Mary, had become much closer to me and was now happy in my home. Gille, the Viking slave whom I had rescued, was growing into a fine warrior and he cared for my herd of horses well. We had started with three and now the two new foals meant we had five. I also had ponies we had captured. My life should have been perfect... but it was not.

It was, in many ways, my own fault. I had fought a Hibernian champion and defeated him. Ulf Big Nose had too but he had suffered a wound in that fight. He lived, like a hermit, in the western part of the island. He rarely visited the stad. When I visited the village all the young

# The Battle for a Home

men in the village went out of their way to try to fight me and defeat the Hibernian killer. After the third fight in as many weeks, I had stopped travelling to the stad where Jarl Gunnar Thorfinnson ruled. I had defeated the young men and there had been no blood but I knew that it would only be a matter of time. My friends and fellow warriors, Siggi White Hair, Erik One Hand, Arne Four Toes and Rurik One Ear had all tried to persuade me to return but I declined. I had no need. Now that Gille had grown he could visit to fetch more sewing for Mary and to trade for that which we needed. It was easier to stay at my home in the north and to keep conflict away.

In truth, it was not difficult for me. We had the brothers Sigurd and Skutal Einarsson who lived with their families in the bay below my headland. They fished and called me Hersir. Their wives dried fish and as Mary made cheese and ale we had food aplenty. There was much game for us. Gille and I would hunt together. We were comfortable but it annoyed me that I could not visit my friends without a fight ensuing. I was not afraid of them but the Jarl's brother had shown that if there was conflict in the clan then it could escalate and lead to tragedy. He and almost all of his crew had perished in the land of the Franks. I had rescued a handful only. That had been a harsh lesson to learn. It had changed Jarl Gunnar Thorfinnson. He had married the daughter of the jarl of Dyflin and that had changed him more. The most disappointing aspect of it all was the Jarl's attitude. He did nothing about it. He was now besotted with his wife, the daughter of Gunnstein Berserk Killer. She had given him a son and was with child for a second time. He dismissed the fights as unimportant. It was as though all that I had done for him and his family was for nought.

And so I would sit at night and look north to the land of the Franks. Could I find a home there perhaps? It was a dream. I had had the dream since I had visited the witch with Jarl Dragonheart and Aiden the galdramenn. It never left me. However, I knew that if I went alone then I would die. The Franks both loathed and feared us. If I went there I would need to go with others, like myself. I would need brothers with whom I could fight and protect a new home. Why should they leave this island which was like paradise? It was a dream only and one I kept to myself. When I had enough coin and treasure then I would travel to Cyninges-tūn and have Bolli the shipwright make me a drekar. When I had my own dragon ship then I would make my home.

The Battle for a Home

# Chapter 1

My days were filled with my horses. Gille and I worked hard to train them to the saddle. The ponies could be used to carry and pull but the horses were there to be ridden. Since we had used the stiraps I had begun to work out how to fight on a horse. It would be the secret to defeating the Franks. They used their horses to control large parts of their land. They could not defeat a well-organized shield wall but they could stop a war band from moving. So far I had two of us who could ride well, Gille and me. I dreamed of a time when I would have many warriors who could ride. We could still fight in a shield wall but there were times when horses would give us an advantage. A good warrior always sought an advantage. As far as I knew I was the only Viking who thought this way. We could all ride but we never fought from the backs of horses; there was just me.

It had been some time since I had seen Ulf Big Nose. The two of us had a special bond. He had taken me under his wing and helped me to become a skilful scout. I was not as good as Ulf but then, apart from Snorri and Beorn the Scout, of the Wolf Clan, I knew of no one else who was that good. I decided to visit with him. I could talk to Ulf and perhaps his age and wisdom might give me an answer. I saddled Dream Strider. He was my stallion and had been my first horse. We understood each other.

Gille asked, "Would you have me come with you, master?"

Despite the fact that he was free he continued to call me master. I could not shake the habit from his lips, "No, Gille. Mary has goods she needs taking to the stad."

As I mounted Mary came out of my hall. She had her own quarters within them. She had been the daughter of a noble but she was becoming used to our cruder ways. "Here, Hrolf." She had finally taken to using my name and, if truth be told, I enjoyed the sound on her lips. It was soft and pleasant.

# The Battle for a Home

"Yes, Mary?"

She handed me a wicker basket covered with a piece of linen. "If you are going to Ulf Big Nose I have some fresh cheese, warm bread and I pickled some fish for him. He must tire of game and wild berries."

"I do not think he gives it much thought but I know he enjoys your cheese and your fish. This was thoughtful."

She smiled, "Ulf is one of the few who was kind to me. I can count on the fingers of one hand those who like me."

"But the ones who do like you hold you in great esteem! The ones who do not... they are nithing!" I whistled, "Come Nipper." Nipper was my dog and a close companion of my horse. The two enjoyed running together. He was also the best ratter on the island and few of our stores were lost to those sneaky rodents.

I had not ridden Dream Strider for some days as we had been working with the two foals. I gave him his head. It was as much for me as for him. I rode due west knowing it would take me past Ulf's home. I would enjoy the ride. The sea, to the north, was grey and uninviting. It was still Gói and it would be some time before the sea became gentler. The Jarl had shown no signs of wanting to go A-Viking. We had returned from war both rich and better armed. That was another reason the younger men had taken to challenging me. Until the Jarl took a ship raiding then they would have no opportunity to either prove themselves or improve their weapons.

When Dream Strider began to sweat heavily I slowed down and turned around to find Ulf's hall. Hall was the wrong word for Ulf's home. We had recovered one of the hulls of the Frankish ships which had raided us and been sunk. We had carried it to Ulf's home where he had used six timbers to support it and then used sods to build up the walls. With just one door it was both dark and gloomy but it was warm and Ulf seemed to enjoy the stygian darkness. As he once told me he only used it for sleeping or when the weather was too bad to sleep outdoors.

I smelled the smoke from his hall as I neared it. He would have both smelled and heard me long ago. His nose and hearing were legendary. I reined in and dismounted to allow Dream Strider to cool down. Nipper raced off. Ulf always had some treat for him.

By the time I arrived Nipper was gnawing on a bone and Ulf was adding wood to the fire. He grinned when he saw me. "I smelled the bread some time ago. Tell me you have cheese and you are doubly welcome."

## The Battle for a Home

"I have bread, cheese and Mary's pickled fish."

"With dill?"

"With dill."

"Then I am a happy man. Come and sit. I have a brew here you might like."

I took off Dream Strider's saddle and allowed him to wander and graze in the lush grass close to Ulf's hall. As he went into it I saw that his limp was as bad as just after the fight. He would never move as quickly as he might wish.

He returned with a jug. It was a crudely made clay one and I suspected he had made it himself. He handed me a horn and poured some. It was a dark red liquid. "Wine?"

He shook his head, "Where would I get grapes? I used brambles and elderberries. I found that if you leave them for three moons and then strain off the liquid it is a warm and pleasant drink. I put the berries on my land and it helps the plants to grow. Taste it and tell me your thoughts."

It was more than warming, it almost burned as it went down but it was not an unpleasant taste. "This is an unusual taste. I like it."

He was pleased. I saw it in his eyes for his mouth rarely smiled. "Good and what brings you to visit this old man? You did not think to bring me cheese and bread. That was Mary."

"I have not seen you in some time."

"You have seen few save your own people for some time. Siggi White Hair came early in Þorri. He said you shun the stad."

I nodded. "Every young warrior wished to fight me."

"It came with your victory. You have a name."

"Dragonheart did not have young men trying to challenge him."

"Oh, you win one fight and you are a new Dragonheart!"

"I did not mean that but he won many battles. Why did no one challenge him?"

"They may have done when he was young, I do not know. We only sailed with him for a couple of seasons. You will hide away forever?"

"I do not know."

He topped up my horn. "You still dream of a land amongst the Franks?"

Was he reading my mind? Then I remembered that when we had scouted in the land of the Franks there had been no secrets. He knew of my hopes. "I do but I cannot see how I would manage to do so."

## The Battle for a Home

"You are oathsworn."

"I know and the warriors I would wish to take with me are oathsworn too. I cannot see how my dream will come true."

Ulf looked up at the sky and raised his horn. "That is out of our hands. The Gods and the Norns decide that." He looked away to the north as though remembering something from his past. "We all have dreams. Sometimes they are shattered and sometimes they come true. You need to see what the Norns have spun." He smiled, "The Jarl made us both hersir. The difference is I am hersir of this but you have the Einarsson brothers and their families. They are your people. Perhaps you are being tested to see if you can lead. You can learn to give commands. I know it does not sit well with you but if you are to have a home on the mainland then you will need men to do your bidding. You must learn to command."

Ulf was wise. I had not used my mind. I had been bemoaning my lot and that was not how I had grown up. I had dreamed of freedom and Jarl Dragonheart had given that to me. I dreamed of a home on the mainland where I could raise horses. I had to believe that I could attain that too. But Ulf was right, I needed to be ready.

"Do you have all that you need here?"

"I am comfortable. I was always the scout and always alone. You were the only one I could tolerate when I scouted. The day that you and I fought the Hibernians I knew that the Weird Sisters had twisted our threads together. When we raid again then you and I will scout. Until then I stay here and I carve bone."

I knew that he enjoyed the skill of carving. "What have you made?"

"I make combs to trade when I need supplies but I am working on this." He opened his leather bag and took out a horse. It was Dream Strider. "When you have children then your son can have this. It is far from finished yet." He gave it to me. It was beautifully carved and he had the details of Dream Strider in perfect proportion.

I put it in my leather pouch. "Children? I do not even have a wife yet!"

He laughed, "Of course you do! The whole of the clan knows it save you and perhaps the woman."

"You have lived alone too long Ulf Big Nose and lost your mind. I have no woman."

"And Mary? What is she?"

"We share a house."

# The Battle for a Home

"Yet she cooks for you. She cares for your animals and your stad when you are away. If you shared her bed then she would be your woman in every sense. Why have you not done so? She is fair. Most of the men in the clan would have lain with her long ago. Why have you not?"

For once I was struck dumb. I could not think of an answer.

He smiled, "This is your riddle and you must wrestle with it."

I stayed until late afternoon. It was good to talk with someone like Ulf. He told me stories of raids before I had joined the clan of how he and Siggi White Hair had protected the Jarl. I knew that he and Siggi were close but his stories told me that they had always been not only close but the protectors of the Jarl. Perhaps that was why he hid away. Like me, he had been ignored. He seemed to think that was a better time for the warriors had been fewer but they had been closer. "Sometimes I think we have grown too successful, Hrolf. It is not the same."

As I rode back to my hall I thought on his words. I knew why I had not done as he had suggested. Mary was still fragile. She was Frank and not Norse. She had been brought up differently. Her future had been to be the wife of a noble and not live in a crude hut with a barbarian. She had been so distraught that I had had to bring her back from a cliff where she had contemplated death. I did find her comely but I would do nothing about it. If the Norns wished me to then they would send me a sign.

Ulf had also given me a comb for Mary and she was overjoyed when I gave it to her. Ulf's work was always beautifully decorated. He had great skill. Mary said, "Why has he decorated it with a horse?"

"That is my sign. I am Hrolf the Horseman and I have one on my shield."

She frowned, "I thought you freed me. Is this the brand of a thrall?"

"If you think so then give it to me and I will use it!"

She shook her head and said, "No, it is a kind gift."

There was an embarrassed silence until Gille said, "The Jarl's new drekar is ready. He has taken the knarr to go to Dyflin with his wife, his hearth weru and some of the younger warriors. There are more men who wish to join the clan in Dyflin. They are close to Jarl Gunnstein and wish to serve his daughter and her husband. They will be the crew who will sail her."

"He does not take Siggi White Hair, Sven the Helmsman or Harold Fast Sailing?"

# The Battle for a Home

Gille shook his head. "They were unhappy about that. Erik One Hand said that since he took a wife he seems less interested in the warriors he once led." He shrugged, "It was only what I heard."

"What care you? We are happy enough here." Mary had regained her composure.

"He is the Jarl and I am still oathsworn to him. He is the heart of the clan and the clan holds us all together. If he loses the loyalty of his warriors then we are doomed. We are only strong so long as we stay together."

She shook her head, "I hear your words, Hrolf the Horseman, but I do not understand them. Do you Gille?"

"I am Norse and I do. Since I came here I have felt part of something and the master is right. We must be as one for the world hates all Vikings. We are surrounded by a sea of enemies."

The day had made my mind a maelstrom and I did not sleep well. However, Ulf's words had made me think and I went to see Sigurd and Skutal early the next morning before they went fishing. Our bay was sheltered and, often, they did not need to sail to catch fish. They had made fish traps which made their lives easier. They were able to catch them on the tide. So it was that I found them outside their huts gutting fish which they would either smoke or pickle. They both had fecund wives and there were now six children helping them.

They stood when I approached, "Hersir. Do you wish for some fish?"

"No Skutal, I just came to see you and your family. We live so close and yet I rarely see you."

"We are grateful that you allow us to live so close."

I nodded, "It was *wyrd*." I pointed to the mainland. "Do you see much of the Franks who live yonder when you fish?"

"They rarely come close to this island, Hersir. I think the bones of their ships and the haunted farmhouse make them afraid."

"But one day they may forget their fear and return. You and your families are close to the water here. If an enemy came then you would be in danger."

"But none do come, lord."

"But they may. I would have you and your brother help me to build a wall up there, by my hall, so that if danger threatens we will have a refuge."

"You would have us do this now, lord?"

## The Battle for a Home

"No. Laugardagr will do. Your wives will be busy and you could have your boys help us. We would need stones from the beach. I will bring my ponies to help us haul them."

Sigurd smiled, "They will like that. They enjoy watching your horses."

"I will see you then."

As I walked back up the hill I began to look at the land around my hall as though I was someone intent on harm. When the Franks had last come they had been stopped on the shingle slope. They had slipped as they had tried to charge and a handful of men had defeated them. We had been lucky. Had they come at night we would have had no warning. I had lived among the Franks and knew how they built their defences. They used ditches and stone. As I came up the hill I saw the haunted farmhouse first. We would not touch that. It would bring bad luck. I had built my hall on a slightly higher rise with a small bank behind for shelter. My horses were in a dell to the east of my hall. I could not build a wall which would be big enough for those too. I needed to protect my people. Ulf had shown me that I needed to be a leader. A leader thought of his people first.

Gille and Mary wandered over when they saw me standing there.

"What is wrong, lord?"

"Nothing. We are going to build a wall and dig a ditch. I would have all of us and those by the beach protected. They will come on Laugardagr to help us. We will take the ponies down to fetch stone."

Gille nodded but Mary looked fearful, "Is there danger?"

"There is always danger, Mary, but nothing that we know about yet. This is just a precaution. With the Jarl away in Dyflin we are more vulnerable. I am just being cautious. Come, Gille, we will mark out the ditch and begin to dig that."

We used old axes and our one mattock to break up the soil once we had removed the turf. Then our wooden shovels were able to pile up the spoil to make our bank. I was pleased that there were many small stones in the soil. They would make the bank stronger. We worked all day and by nightfall had a ditch forty paces long. Mary complained, of course, about the wooden bridge she had to use and the fact that we tramped soil into the hall. It was when she did so that I remembered Ulf's words. Perhaps I did have a wife and did not know it.

In the four days before Laugardagr, we managed to make a circle around the hall. The ditch was not deep enough yet but I could see the shape and proportions of my new defences. I paced it out and found that

## The Battle for a Home

it was two hundred paces. It stopped at the bank just behind my hall. There was no need to build it up there. Then we used my ponies to fetch the stones which lay to the south of the hall and we began to build the wall. It was slow going for we had to use the biggest and flattest stones on the bottom. Each night I felt my backache with the exertion but I knew that it was making us both stronger.

When Laugardagr arrived we were up early and led our ponies down to the beach. We had made sleds to carry the stones. Skutal and Sigurd's boys had already begun, with their fathers, to collect the stones which littered the beach. It would help them for they would have fewer stones to damage their fishing boats. We had six ponies and, after a little coaching, four of the children were able to lead the ponies up the hill. We spent the morning hauling. I then allowed the boys to take the ponies to the sea. Both had worked hard enough and my ponies enjoyed the sea. We ate fresh bread and newly made goat's cheese while we looked at the task ahead of us.

The two brothers looked at our efforts, "How high will the wall have to be, lord?"

"Do not worry Skutal we will not be hauling stones for long. I wish the stones to be as high as a man's chest and then we will use wood to make a palisade." I pointed to the timber we had collected when we had rescued Gille. Sven the Helmsman had taken all the longer pieces of timber for repairs on the drekar and to make masts. They had left the branches which were the height of a man. They had been seasoning for two years. Gille and I had already split some of them. We would have enough.

Skutal nodded and wandered over to the ditch. He stood at the bottom and the bank we had made was higher than him with his arms raised. "This will deter an enemy."

"It is a start. A hersir must care for his people."

By the end of that first Laugardagr, we had laid one course of stones around the perimeter. Gille and I found that with two men and their children helping us we could work much faster and so we just left that work for Laugardagr. One day in seven was all that I asked from my bondi. It meant I could continue to work with Copper, my new colt. Gille worked with the foal, Dawn's Light. She would be a fine filly in time. She and Copper were half brother and sister. I would not wish to breed them and so I knew I would need another stallion and a mare. I wondered how Dream Strider would take to that.

## The Battle for a Home

By the time Ein-mánuðr came, we had the stone wall finished and a gateway made. I was confident that by the end we would have a wooden wall around us. With just one way in and out we would be as secure as it was possible to be. We had prepared the timber we would use for the palisade. With one end already sharpened, we just had to hammer them in and then sharpen the top.

The appearance of the Frankish ship one late afternoon, sailing across the bay, gave us added impetus to our work. Skutal raced up to warn us. "See lord, a Frank."

"Are there warriors on board?"

"We saw shields, lord, and they wore helmets."

I did not bother with a saddle; I threw myself onto Dream Strider's back and galloped hard to the headland by the haunted farmhouse. There I would have a better view. It was not a large ship. The Franks built tubbier boats than we did. They were slower but they could carry a large crew. I saw that this one had hove to just outside the bay. The skeletons of their ships in the bay were a hazard to them. They were marked by the masts which still stood out of the water at low tide. Eventually, they would rot and disappear but, for now, they marked their grave. Skutal and Sigurd were familiar with them and used them for the fish seemed to congregate around them. I watched the ship. The sunlight glinted off metal. There were warriors on board. I wondered if our new wall and palisade attracted their attention. Then I realised that this was a scouting expedition. They were looking at our defences. The last time they had charged in recklessly. They had learned their lesson. They would be coming back. After a short time, they raised their sail and set off north. I watched them leave and then returned to my hall and Skutal.

"They have gone but they may return. If another Frank enters the bay then bring your families up here. I have weapons within and we can defend our home."

"Do you think they will return, lord?"

"I know not but I will go to visit with the Jarl on the morrow and seek his advice."

That night I knew that Mary was unhappy. She snapped at Gille for little things he did wrong and her brow was both knitted and furrowed. I stood, "Gille, go and see to the horses. Tomorrow you shall come with me." When he had gone I said, "Do not take your anger out on Gille. He does not deserve it. If you are unhappy about something then tell me. Do not brood. This is how you were when you lived in the village. I thought

# The Battle for a Home

we had gone beyond that. Do not keep your dark thoughts to yourself. Therein lies madness. Tell me what bothers you."

She nodded, "You are right. I should speak more. I was happy here. I had begun to feel safe and then you build a wall and ships appear. You freed me and I am grateful but if aught happened to you and I was taken again then...."

I smiled, "I will not let anything happen to you and you are a Christian. You will not take your own life and for that I am grateful. I would not be happy if you were not here. We have a pleasant life and I would not change it."

For some reason that made her smile, "But how do you know we will be safe here?"

"That is why I go tomorrow. If you are afraid to be left alone then come with me but I thought you did not like the stad of the clan."

"I do not but I would not be here alone. I will come with you." She reached over to touch my hand. Her hand was soft and her touch gentle. I liked the feeling. "Thank you for what you said."

"What did I say?"

"That you would not be happy if I was not here."

Just then Gille re-entered and she let go of my hand. The moment was gone. Mary was a good rider and she and Gille rode my two mares. I noticed that she had dressed in her best and she had made sure that Gille did too. It made me smile and so I put on a better kyrtle and combed my hair and beard.

As we approached the walls of the stad of the clan I could hear a great noise. It sounded like wailing. They had no one at the gate and that was unusual. As I rode through I saw that the warriors were all in the middle, where we normally held our Thing, and there was a heated debate going on. Our appearance briefly silenced them.

I dismounted and walked toward them. Siggi White Hair looked distraught. I had never seen him upset. No matter what disasters had befallen us he had always been calm. "What is it Siggi?"

"We have had news today to chill the blood of even the bravest of warriors. The Jarl and his wife, along with his hearth weru, were attacked by the men of Wessex as they sailed home from Dyflin. The new drekar was sunk and they all perished. The Jarl is dead. The last of the sons of Thorfinn Blue Scar has gone to the Otherworld. The whole family has been taken." He shook his head, "I was not there to protect him! I have let down the Jarl."

## The Battle for a Home

Before I could take that in Arne Four Toes said, "Aye and Windar's Mere is no more. Eggle Skulltaker destroyed it. Jarl Dragonheart has gone to war. The world changes, Hrolf the Horseman. We are a backwater here and know nothing of the outside world. While we enjoyed life the Norns were spinning and their webs have spread far indeed."

I nodded, "Aye. The Weird Sisters have not finished with us, it seems."

Siggi White Hair suddenly seemed to notice that I had brought Mary and Gille, "And this is strange too. What brings you here?"

"I also bring dire news. Yesterday a Frank came into my bay. I think he was a scout. I fear there may be danger from the north. I came to seek the advice of the Jarl. It seems my journey is wasted."

## Chapter 2

It was as though a storm erupted as everyone tried to speak at once. Mary had dismounted and gripped my arm. I understood her fear. The Jarl's wife had been someone who liked Mary and offered her some protection. Now she had no one. I saw the looks she received from the women who had made her life a misery. They were venomous.

Siggi suddenly grabbed the horn we used in battle and sounded it. All went silent. Still gripping the horn he glared at all the men around him. I realised that we now had less than a boat's crew. The Jarl had taken his hearth-weru and all the young men. We had less than thirty warriors now.

"Are we women that we must rend our clothes and cry out? We are men. We are Raven Wing Clan! The Norns have done this. It is *wyrd*! We do not bemoan it, we do something about it!"

Ketil Eriksson said, "But what can we do?"

"We hold a Thing! We offer our opinions and then the men of the clan will make a decision."

I handed the reins of my horse to Gille, "You watch Mary. I am part of this."

I stepped forward to join the circle. The last time we had done this we had been three deep. Now we were almost a single circle. Siggi said, "Hrolf, tell us what you think the presence of the Frank portends."

"We had begun to build a wall. I did not want a repeat of their last attack. I wanted somewhere we could defend. Perhaps they just spied it out. I do not know. I am no galdramenn and I cannot see into the future. It was but one ship little bigger than a knarr. I believe they are just watching. If we wish to know more, then Ulf Big Nose and I must go to the mainland." I waved a hand around the circle. "However, I do not think we have enough men to risk sending two abroad."

Arne Four Toes said, "Aye we need Ulf. He too is wise."

## The Battle for a Home

I nodded and turned, "Gille and Mary, take Dream Strider and ride to Ulf. Ask him to return here."

Mary, in particular, appeared pleased to be able to do something. They mounted and galloped off.

Siggi nodded his thanks. "Then if there is no immediate threat from the Franks we look at the other two problems. The destruction of Windar's Mere is tragic for we knew their warriors but we chose to leave the Dragonheart. Had we men enough then we could have gone to his aid and fought this Skulltaker. That is not to be which leaves us with the problem of the Jarl. We need a leader. A Clan without a leader is like a drekar without a steering board."

Silence fell and I felt you could have cut it with a knife. All of us had been oathsworn. We had followed Jarl Gunnar Thorfinnson. Now he was gone there was a void. Our oaths ended with his death. None had contemplated another leader and now it had been forced upon us.

Erik Long Hair said, "The Jarl made Hrolf the Horseman and Ulf Big Nose Hersir. Perhaps he wished one of them to be Jarl after he went to the Otherworld. They are both mighty warriors and have brought honour to the clan."

It was a ridiculous idea and I spoke immediately, "I know not about Ulf Big Nose but speaking for myself I do not think Jarl Gunnar wished me to replace him. He wished me to watch the north of the island and his decision was wise for I have brought news of danger. I am young and there are other, older, wiser heads head who could lead the clan successfully. I am flattered that I should even be considered but I am not yet ready to be the Jarl."

Bagsecg Beornsson said, shrewdly, "But one day you will eh, Hrolf?"

I smiled, "Perhaps but I will need a better beard and a few grey hairs first."

Erik Long Hair was like a dog with a bone, "Then what about Ulf Big Nose? He has age and he is wise."

Arne Four Toes shook his head, "And he is not here."

Harold Fast Sailing said, "Perhaps Sven the Helmsman might be Jarl. If we are to raid again then we need someone who knows the sea."

Sven shook his head, "Like Hrolf I am flattered but that is all I know, the sea. Like you, Harold Fast Sailing, I am happier with a drekar beneath my feet and a Jarl must lead the shield wall. He needs to be a renowned warrior. I believe that Ulf Big Nose would be the wisest choice."

# The Battle for a Home

Siggi said, "And he is not yet here. We will eat while we wait for him. It is fortunate that we have Hrolf the Horseman, his horses and his people. If we had not then Ulf would not be until the morrow."

Brigid, the alewife brought out a barrel of ale and most of the men headed there for beer. Siggi and Rurik came to me, "You could be Jarl, Hrolf. I would follow you and I know that Rurik and others would."

I shook my head, "The Eriksson brothers would not and they would challenge me. I think I could defeat them but now is not the time to be losing warriors. We need every man regardless of how reckless he is."

"And that is why you would be a good jarl. You think of the clan."

Siggi shook his head. "Ulf and I thought that when we followed a young jarl and swore to protect him that he would be our last lord. I served his father and he is dead. Now the last of his sons is gone." He shook himself as though to clear thoughts and memories from inside his white head. "At least we have a crew who are well-armed. Thanks to the Hibernians we are both well protected and provided with weapons to defend ourselves."

"How did we discover what happened to the Jarl?"

"The King of Wessex sent his head back to Dyflin along with that of Jarl Gunnstein Berserk Killer's daughter. The Jarl of Dyflin is not happy!"

"The new drekar was not lucky then?"

"No, and I fear that the Jarl may have offended the Norns for he named her *'Queen of the Seas'*. It does not do to risk the wrath of the Weird Sisters."

Arne Four Toes returned with horns of ale for us. "Those Eriksson brothers are blowhards! They are talking of having a younger Jarl who will take the clan on raids to make them rich."

Siggi snorted as he took the horn, "With barely a crew for the drekar where would we raid? They need to think about how we survive. If the Dragonheart can have his home threatened then we are in even more danger."

"Who is this Eggle Skulltaker?"

"A Dane. From what I heard he destroyed not just Windar's Mere but the settlement at Ulla's Water too. Jarl Dragonheart will be angry, especially after the death of his son."

I began to feel guilty about leaving the Dragonheart's crew. Had I brought bad luck? As I looked around the settlement I realised how many

## The Battle for a Home

men had died both in our recent battles and in this latest tragedy. I should have sent for Skutal and Sigurd. This concerned them too.

We all turned when the horses galloped in. Ulf was a better rider now than when I had first met him but, even so, he was still pleased to be off my stallion. He strode over and Siggi shouted, "We hold the Thing again!"

Erik One Hand rushed over with a horn of ale. Ulf nodded and said to Siggi, "Is this true? The Jarl is dead?"

Siggi nodded, "Aye he is."

He and Ulf clasped arms. He and Ulf looked as though someone had torn their heart out before them. I had never seen Ulf upset before. They spoke quietly together for a while and then nodded. They touched their Thor's hammer. Both had served the Jarl a long time. I saw the Eriksson brothers looking impatient. It annoyed me. Ulf and Siggi had had a lifetime with Jarl Gunnar. That was not to be dismissed lightly.

Rurik waited until they had both joined us and then said, "Erik Long Hair suggested that you be Jarl."

Ulf looked around at everyone and then burst out laughing, "Me? I do not like people and I enjoy being on my own. That alone would prevent me from being jarl. Have you no one better in mind?"

Erik Long Hair said, "We suggested Hrolf but he said he was too young."

"Aye he is but I would follow him." They all looked at me again. "What say you, horseman? Is this your dream?"

"It is my dream but this is not the time." I touched my horse token around my neck. "I have visited with the witch at the edge of the world and she told me that I would lead men but in the dream, I had a full beard and I had a son. This is not meant to be."

I saw nods. They could accept that.

Knut One Eye shouted, "Then I suggest my brother Ketil! It is time we had someone young. He will lead us to glory!"

Ulf snorted, "He will lead us to doom. I would sooner follow a donkey than one of the Eriksson brothers."

Knut One Eye's hand went to his sword. Siggi White Hair shouted, "Touch your sword Knut One Eye and you die! You know the rules!"

Ulf Big Nose said, "But come to me after, Knut One Eye, and bad leg or not I will make your brother the last of his family!"

Before another row could begin I said, "We are missing the most obvious candidate. It seems to me that Siggi White Hair, who advised the

# The Battle for a Home

Jarl, should be our new Jarl. His hearth-weru protected the Jarl but it was Siggi to whom he went for advice. I would follow him."

Ulf Big Nose smiled and put his arm around Siggi, "This was meant to be, my cuz. You should have been jarl years ago and we both know it. You should lead the clan for the alternative is those two mindless lumps, the Erikssons. Accept and I will follow you again."

All but the Eriksson brothers and their two friends shouted the same. I turned to Siggi. "Do you accept or should we go through every warrior and dismiss them? You are Raven Wing Clan. You are the heart of the warriors. When we fight in the shield wall it is your voice we hear. What say you?"

My eyes pleaded with him and eventually, he nodded, "I accept." There was a cheer from all save the four dissenters. He held his hands up, "With a condition. When I am weary of the task and too old to fight in the shield wall we will hold a Thing and see if there is another who could lead the clan."

We all nodded. Ulf Big Nose asked, "And this news of the Franks. What do we do about that?"

"I have thought about that. They need a warning that we are still dangerous to cross. We take the drekar and we sail along their coast. If they think we are raiding then they will stay close to home. The ship needs a voyage does she, not Sven?"

"Aye she does and we need to rearrange the oars. We have lost the hearth-weru. I do not think we have enough men to raid do you?"

"Then we will rearrange the oars and we do not need to land. We just need to scout and threaten. If they are planning an attack then their preparations should be obvious. We sail in three days' time."

I nodded, "Then I had better get back to my home. It is the closest part of the island to the Franks and needs protection."

"I would you stayed here. We need to talk."

"I am sorry Jarl. Ulf here pointed out that I had a responsibility to my people. They need me. I will sail with you for I am part of the clan but I will leave my home and people so that they can be defended."

Ulf nodded, "That is at it should be. I will stay here until we sail." He lowered his voice and his words were just intended for Siggi and me, "I think, old friend, that we need Hrolf and myself to scout. He speaks the words of the Franks. If we can discover their plans it will save a fruitless voyage."

# The Battle for a Home

"You may be right. I will send the knarr captain back to Dyflin and tell him of our news. I will inform Jarl Gunnstein Berserk Killer that if he wishes to raid Wessex to collect weregeld we will join him."

Rurik and Arne Fur Toes wandered over, "Aye the honour of the clan demands it and it might quieten the Eriksson boys."

"Arne, I will happily quieten those two down permanently!"

Siggi shook his head, "No Ulf Big Nose. They spoke in haste. We know that is their way." He was already the jarl. I could hear the authority in his voice. He turned to me, "We will see you in three days, Hrolf."

Mary was quiet as we headed back to my hall. "Must you go? Why do you have to seek trouble?"

"We do not seek trouble but we need to know why the Frank was sniffing around our bay. We will not be away for long and I will make sure that you, Gille and our people are safe."

"I am more worried about you. The others will be on the drekar and it will be you who is with Ulf Big Nose surrounded by enemies."

"That is enough!"

She remained silent.

As we dismounted I said, "Gille and I will work on the wall. I want you to tell Skutal and Sigurd what we do."

Sulkily she stormed off down the hill. Gille shook his head, "Why do women take on so, lord?"

"They are different to us, that is all. I would not change them. She cares for us."

He laughed, "She cares for you, lord!"

I put his words from my mind. They were an unwanted distraction. I needed to make my home as safe as it could be. "We will put up the palisade. I had planned on embedding it in the stone wall but we do not have time. We will put it outside the wall and above the ditch."

We began to work. It meant we did not have to build a fighting platform and we could complete the work in a faster time. It was a two-man job. Gille held the post while I stood on the stones and hammered it down deep into the soil. I wanted the length of a man's arm buried beneath the newly built bank. We had finished three when Mary returned. From her red eyes, she had shed tears. "I have told their wives. They are out at the nets."

"Thank you."

"Can I help?"

# The Battle for a Home

I smiled. It was her way of building bridges. "Some food would be welcome. This will take until after dark."

Sigurd and Skutal came a short while before the sun set. I told them our news and they threw themselves into the work. "If we had been there, lord, we would have supported Siggi White Hair. Our father said he was the wisest man in the clan."

Skutal asked, "Will you need us on the drekar, lord?"

"I would prefer you here. We do not go to fight and I would be happier knowing my home was safer."

They seemed pleased about that and worked even harder. By the time they left, we were exhausted but we had a wooden wall along the north side of our hall. We trudged into the hall and were greeted by an aromatic smell. Mary had made a stew. I was so hungry that my stomach ached.

"That smells good."

"The first of the herbs were ready. When they are young they have a better flavour. I am pleased you are happy."

We ate in silence for Gille was as hungry as I was and Mary watched us devour the stew, the fresh bread and the cheese. Her beer was the equal to Brigid's and I smiled in satisfaction.

"Will the walls be finished before you go?"

"They will. Then I will show you and Gille how to fetch in the bridge over the ditch to add protection to the gate. If Skutal and Sigurd are here then they can do that but you two need to be able to do this."

"It would be hard for us to defend the walls especially if there are just the two of us."

"I would say almost impossible so I hope that you have company. We have plenty of arrows and spears. An enemy can be deterred from climbing a wall. We have made the ditch wide and before I leave we will fill it with water."

"But the water will soak away."

"It will but it will leave the bottom muddy. If they have ladders then they will sink. We will have sharpened the stakes to make it hard to climb over. These will be Franks and not Vikings. If they do come then keep fighting even though they may outnumber you."

"I am a woman!"

"Use a spear. If they get close use a hand axe. A man cannot climb a wall, hold a shield and wield a weapon."

# The Battle for a Home

They considered that and then Gille said, "Lord, how do you and the clan manage it then?"

I laughed, "We are Vikings and the rules which apply to ordinary men do not apply to us!" For some reason that made them both laugh and the evening ended in good humour.

Thanks to Skutal and Sigurd, as well as their families, the wall was complete at the end of the second day. Skutal's eldest proved quite adept at sharpening the palisade with the adze and hand axe. I showed them how to lift the bridge and make it into a second gate and I showed them all the spare weapons. I had collected them since I had first joined the clan. There was even the curved sword of the blackamoor who had been the first warrior I had killed. There were bows, arrows, spears, two axes, a hand axe, four seaxes and three swords. None of them was of the best but Gille put an edge on to them and they would do. You can kill a man with a branch of a tree.

"How will we know when to come and join your family, lord?"

"If you see the Franks then you come. If you fear for your lives then you come. We will be away for a couple of days only."

I left before dawn on the day I had said I would return to the clan. I did not take my mail. I would be scouting. I took Heart of Ice, my shield and my Saami bow.

I would be riding to the village. "I will leave Dream Strider with Erik One Hand. He is a kind man and Dream Strider does not mind him. It may make the mares pine for him. When he returns, who knows, they may make more foals!"

I was about to mount when Mary ran to me and, throwing her arms around me, kissed me. It was a kiss of passion and not farewell. "Return, Hrolf the Horseman. I do not wish to be alone!"

Gille turned away and I mounted. I know I should have said something but nothing came to mind. I had been taken aback and yet Ulf had said something already about this. Was this the Norns weaving their threads again?

# Chapter 3

Siggi White Hair would not be rowing, he was Jarl Siggi now. He took it upon himself to allocate our benches. With fewer rowers, we had just two to an oar. I was with Rurik One Ear by the steering board. Opposite were Ulf Big Nose and Arne Four Toes. We had the place of honour. It was not that we were the strongest but we were the most dependable and Siggi had sat with us. As we headed out to sea he began a chant to help us row and to make us one clan, again.

> *Through the waves the oathsworn come*
> *Riding through white tipped foam*
> *Feared by all raven's wing*
> *Like a lark it does sing*
> *A song of death to all its foes*
> *The power of the raven grows and grows.*
> *Through the waves the oathsworn come*
> *Riding through white tipped foam*
> *Feared by all raven's wing*
> *Like a lark it does sing*
> *A song of death to all its foes*
> *The power of the raven grows and grows.*
> *The power of the raven grows and grows.*
> *The power of the raven grows and grows.*

As we turned around the headland the wind came from our steerboard quarter but we still rowed. It would make us whole again. The divisions of the land would be eradicated by our drekar. We headed to the Frankish shore. We would sail to An Oriant. There Ulf and I would slip ashore to discover what we could. The drekar would then sail along the coast to keep an eye on our island before returning, a day later, to pick us up. Sven said that if the winds proved unfavourable he would anchor in my bay. For that I was grateful.

# The Battle for a Home

All the work I had done on my wall had prepared me well for the voyage and while some of the others looked to be weary I was ready to row for longer. Ulf too, a hard man, looked to be comfortable. I noticed Siggi as he identified those who had a problem. Jarl Gunnar had never bothered overmuch about how we rowed. Siggi knew that it was as important as the shield wall. We headed in to shore. We had most of the day to get close to An Orient. We would land some five miles west of the stronghold. We would have to last for most of two days and a night but I was confident that we could do so.

We headed in to the small river to the west of An Orient. We saw fishing boats which fled when they saw the dragon ship approach. We pulled in to the eastern shore. Ulf and I had done this before and we slipped ashore without any fuss. We did not look back. There was no need. The drekar would head west and we would head east. They would return for us and wait. If we died and did not return then others would scout. That was the way of the clan. We waded through the shallows to the shore and clambered up the bank. We headed to the woods which lay ahead of us. We had seen no one as we had headed west but we would take no chances. Once in the eaves of the wood I unslung my bow and readied an arrow. Ulf sniffed. When I had first seen him do this I wondered why. Now I knew. He nodded and pointed east. There was no danger close by.

I followed Ulf as he loped along the hunters' trails. My job was to watch his back. Despite his age, Ulf could run as long as any man I ever knew, even with a bad leg. I was indebted for the work I had put in with my wall. I was able to keep up with him. He had lost his speed but not the ability to run all day. His bad leg gave him a strange gait. I saw that I could see the difference in the mud when we ran through wet sections. I was becoming a better scout. With his keen sense of smell and the senses of a hunting dog, he kept us out of trouble. Even I could avoid places that smelled of wood smoke but I had no idea that there were Franks on the greenway until he led me into the undergrowth and we waited with bows ready.

I thought he had heard things for we waited for a long time and then I felt the movements of horses walking along the path. Their hooves sent vibrations through the ground. Then I heard their voices. I could make out most of their words. We did not move as they came down the path past us. There were six of them. Two looked to be nobles and I saw they carried hunting bows. Ulf let them move some way down the path before

# The Battle for a Home

he led us out. I was desperate to tell him what I had heard but he would speak when it was safe. Until then I would remain silent.

He held his hand up when I could smell wood smoke again and the sound of animals. He took me from the greenway and we went into the woods. He sniffed and then said, quietly, "Speak. What did the Franks say?"

"They were hunting. The lord of An Orient, Ambhoc, is gathering his men for a feast."

"They attack our island?"

"They did not say so but it would make sense."

"Then we need to see what ships they have. That will tell us the number of men they bring. We will approach from the sea. Take off your helmet. Put your cloak over your shield. If we are seen then our bows might mark us as hunters returning from an unsuccessful hunt."

When we were ready we ran towards the sea. This was empty land. The trees in which we ran had little game. The Franks had so much timber that they did not need to cut them down. We were alone. We smelled the sea long before we saw it. As we cautiously edged out I saw our island to the south of us. It was a grey smudge. The beach lay before us and we kept it to our right as we ran the last couple of miles to the entrance of the harbour.

An Orient was the largest harbour I had ever seen. We knew from our voyages up and down the coast that it was sheltered from the storms which battered this coast in winter. They had, on the east bank, a citadel. It was a stone tower from which they could watch the sea and the entrance to their harbour. I suspected that they lit a fire there when it was foggy to guide ships in. I had sometimes seen a glow in the distance when I watched from my headland. We sheltered on the opposite bank so that we could observe it and look up into the harbour. It was just four hundred paces from us across the wide entrance to An Oriant harbour. It was high with one entrance and we could see the sentries at the top. Glancing upriver I saw the island which lay in the middle of the harbour. It was uninhabited but looked to give shelter. It was there I saw their ships. They had eight of them. Beyond the eight I saw the masts of others but there only looked to be four or five of them. This was the fleet that they would use to attack us. On the other bank, they had their homes, their halls and their walls. They had a stone and wooden fortress.

Ulf led us inland a short way, using the trees for cover to have a closer look at their fortress. We spied their hall and its stockade. It was made of

## The Battle for a Home

stone and wood. The walls were twice as high as a man. It was a substantial fortification. It made my wall look like an animal pen. We did not have enough men to take it. It was almost a mile away but we could still hear the hubbub from within. It was busy. There looked to be many people there. We had seen enough and Ulf led us back through the trees. It was gone noon. It had taken many hours to reach here. We would have to avoid the greenway on our return. There may have been more than one party of hunters.

We reached the river well after dark. We had food and water with us. We ate dried cod and drank from our water skins. We took it in turns to sleep. Ulf was naturally taciturn and silent. I was alone with my thoughts. Should I have accepted the offer to be jarl? I dismissed the idea as soon as it crawled into my head. I was not ready. It may have been that the Norns were testing me. Perhaps, in spurning it, I would never lead my own band. I knew, however, that had I taken it I would have had to battle those like the Eriksson brothers and others to hold on to it. That might have destroyed the clan. I did not regret my decision.

As dawn broke I woke Ulf and we headed to the shore to await the drekar. She came from the dark of the west and she was a welcome sight. With her raven prow, she cut through the water like a powerful sea monster. We waded into the shallows and were hauled on board. We did not leave immediately. Our news was too important. "Well?"

Ulf pointed east. "They are coming. Warriors are gathering and we have seen their fleet. They have at least ten ships."

Beorn Beornsson said, "That could be five hundred warriors. We could not defeat that number."

Ulf flashed him an irritated look. There was little point in stating the obvious. Siggi nodded, "Then we have a number of choices. One is to wait for them and make the end of the Raven Wing Clan a tale to be told throughout the ages."

Ulf Big Nose said, "Save that we will all be dead and no one will live to tell the tale!"

Siggi White Hair sighed. They were old friends and knew each other well. Ulf's outburst could be tolerated. "A second choice is to leave the island and find a new home." He nodded to me, "That would suit Hrolf the Horseman."

This time it was Ketil Eriksson who spoke, "But we have only one drekar and we have families. Where would we go?"

## The Battle for a Home

Siggi nodded, "And we have a third choice. We go to the Franks and make a peace with them."

There were rumblings then for that was not our way.

"There is a fourth choice."

Every eye switched to me. Siggi asked, "A fourth?"

"If they have no ships then they cannot attack us. We attack their ships at anchor. They are yet to be loaded. They will have a watch onboard and the sentries will not be mailed. If we attack at night then we can set them on fire. We might even block their harbour."

I had surprised all of them. Sven the Helmsman asked, "And what of their watchtower on the headland?"

"It will be night and they will not see us but if you wished we could land men and eliminate them."

Ulf Big Nose shook his head, "It matters not. If they do see us they can signal the citadel and the ships but by then it will be too late. I like the plan."

We all looked to Jarl Siggi White Hair. He nodded. "Let us do as Hrolf the Horseman suggests. We will wait here until dark. We can gather kindling from the forest and use pots to allow us to use fire."

We had spare pots on board. They were used to store the cheese and pickled foods we brought on board. We could now use them to make fires on the shore and then carry them safely on the drekar. It was a more reliable method of starting a fire than using a flint.

Leaving just the ship's boys on board we returned to the land to collect that which we needed. We gathered kindling and pine resin. Once back on board half the crew rested while the other half watched. When I watched I took the opportunity of sharpening my seax. I would not take Heart of Ice with me but a seax was a better weapon for slitting throats. I wandered to the stern.

Sven the Helmsman asked, "Where are the ships anchored, Hrolf?"

"They are between the island and the mainland."

"Within the range of a bow?"

"Perhaps but the Franks do not have good bows. I think it is too far. Besides, you could tie up to the boat at the east. We would be protected."

I had thought Siggi was sleeping but he was not. Without opening his eyes he said, "We must board all of them at once. If not then they will cut their anchors and run."

"Then there will be a problem, Jarl."

He opened his eyes and sat up. "Why? What have you not told us?"

"We have told you all but eight are anchored in a line and the others further upstream."

Sven looked up at the pennant. "Then the gods may favour us. The wind is coming from the south. If you fire the eight and cut their cables then, with the tide and the wind they have a good chance of fouling the others. It will be easier than trying to block the channel. You will need to lower the sails."

"And how do we get off the ships?"

"You swim and we will pick you up."

Siggi nodded, "It is a risk but the risk to the clan is even greater if we do not destroy their ships. We can only use three men to a boat. That will leave the barest number to sail our drekar." He smiled, "This will be a challenge. If we succeed then I truly am meant to be jarl."

Sven the Helmsman smiled, "And if not then it will not matter for we will all be dead."

We rowed in silence. We did not have the sail lowered. We wanted to be as small a target as we could. I would be with Rurik One Ear and Arne Four Toes. We had been given the ship which was closest to the citadel. We would have the greatest chance of surprise but, equally, the furthest to swim if we did succeed. That was why we were chosen. We were the best swimmers. We took off our boots and clothes save for a pair of short breeks. We could swim back naked if necessary.

As we headed into the dark of the east Sven nodded and pointed to the cloudy sky, "The Gods favour our venture."

We rowed slowly, without a chant. It was hard until we turned to enter the harbour. There was no shout of alarm from the watchtower but by the time we swept into the bay then it was too late. With the wind behind we barely had to row. Sven took us directly towards the citadel. We would be the first to board and so we stood and collected our burning pot. Rurik carried it by a rope which ran around its rim. Arne had the grappling hook and I had the seax. Until we boarded that would be the only weapon. I would have to be swift. I could see now that there were three larger ships moored upstream of us.

We could not avoid being seen when we loomed out of the dark just thirty paces from the end two ships but they hesitated for they could not see the dragon prow. We looked like any other long low ship. Suddenly the alarm was given and we heard shouts. Sven put the steerboard over as he shouted, "Steerboard oars in!"

## The Battle for a Home

We swung around the end two ships. The wind was against and our turn stopped us as though we had run into a stone wall. I held the shroud with my left hand and stood on the topmost strake. Arne, holding the kindling, threw the grappling hook but I had already leapt into the dark even as he threw it. I landed lightly on my feet and ran towards the two men of the watch who had woken. They raced to me with swords drawn. I saw that they were the curved swords they liked further south. Pausing only to grab a looped rope I did the unexpected and ran towards them. I hurled the coiled rope as I did what the Hibernian champion had tried with Ulf Big Nose. I rolled beneath their flailing swords. The rope hit one and I drove the seax deep into the inside of the thigh of the second. Blood gushed from the fatal wound. I stood and, as the second man tried to throw the coils of rope from him, slashed my seax across his stomach. It was razor-sharp and he watched his entrails race from his body like a sack of worms.

Leaving Arne to deal with any other crew I picked up one of the swords and ran to the anchor. I hacked through it in one blow and then ran to the steering board. I pushed it hard over. Rurik had placed the pot at the foot of the mast and he scurried up to lower the sail. I heard a cry as Arne despatched one of the sentries. I turned and saw a fourth, a young ship's boy. He looked at me and then leapt into the harbour. An uncertain watery future was better than three fierce Vikings. Arne laid the kindling around the base of the mast. He then grabbed as much wood as he could and piled it on top. As I watched I saw that two other ships were under our control and **'Raven's Wing'** was now facing the sea and waiting for the fire starters to join her.

Arne shouted, "Come on Rurik before those three ships upstream escape!"

"I am doing my best!"

I shouted, "Don't bother untying the ropes! Cut them!"

As soon as Rurik slashed the ties holding the sail it dropped and the wind caught it. Already moving in the right direction we now moved with the wind coming from our steerboard quarter. Rurik slid down the shrouds and joined Arne. Arne looked over, "Ready whenever you are, Hrolf."

"The ships are beginning to move. You light the fire and I will take us closer. There is little point in coming this far and letting them escape."

They nodded and waited. I could see that seven of the ships were in our hands and the second and third were already on fire and heading

## The Battle for a Home

upstream after us. The watches on the three ships further upstream had seen our intention and were cutting their cables in an attempt to escape. They were heading upstream to safety and I knew that they would escape the fires of the last couple of ships. I had to stay on longer.

"Hrolf!"

"You just jump! I can swim to the shore. Tell Sven to pick me up below the watchtower."

They set the fire going and then ran to me, "And what if he cannot pick you up?"

I shrugged, "Then it is *wyrd*. You will watch over my family?"

They nodded but Rurik said, "You were not destined to drown, Hrolf the Horseman! We will see you on the drekar!"

They stood on the stern rail and then leapt into the water. They had, perhaps, four hundred paces to swim. They would make it. As the flames leapt up the mast they seemed to make us travel even faster. When the fire burned through the sheets and the shrouds I knew that the mast would not last long. It was hard to see the three ships ahead and I had to trust that I was going in the right direction. I saw one heading for the far bank. When its mast suddenly shivered I knew what had happened; it had run aground. That one could not escape. The smoke and the flames were making life uncomfortable for me. The dried wood of the deck around the mast was already on fire. I would have to time this so that I did not perish. Looking aft I saw that the other ships were echeloned behind me. Without helmsmen, however, their course was in the lap of the gods. Only my ship would strike where I chose and for that reason, I had to get it right.

Suddenly the flaming mast, weakened by the fire at the base and with the weight of the sails unsupported, crashed forward. The stern bounced up a little and we were now bow heavy. It did, however, afford me a view of the river ahead. The two ships which had not run aground had fouled each other. They were just forty paces from me. The burning mast had now set fire to the bow and the raised stern acted as a sail. The wind raced us along. As the fire spread towards me I realised that I had used up all of my luck. Putting my seax in my teeth I jumped into the water.

As I came up I looked around to make sure I was swimming in the right direction. Already two of the burning ships had struck the grounded one and it was afire but the rest had begun to settle in the water. If my fire ship did not strike then the Franks would still have two ships to use. I doubted that would be enough. I swam on my back to enable me to watch

## The Battle for a Home

the voyage of my doomed ship. There was no hurry and I had further to swim than the other fire starters. I saw the two ships spring apart as the ropes which had fouled were severed. Someone had been careless for the mast of one fell astern. It may have been the work of the Norns for my fire ship settled over the fallen mast and flames ran like rats towards one of the Frankish ships. When I saw men hurling themselves overboard I knew that we had succeeded. They had but one ship left. I turned on my front and began to stroke towards the shore

My way was lighted by the three burning ships which were on the bank. They would be lifted at high tide but for now, they were a beacon. The water grew colder as I swam. The tide which had begun to turn when we attacked now rushed and I had to fight it to reach the other shore. It took me longer than I thought. The fires from the ships began to die. I could still see, in the harbour mouth, **'Raven's Wing'**. As I crawled ashore I realised that I had landed in a swampy part of the coast. It explained why there were neither houses nor fishing boats. I lay there like a beached whale trying to get my breath back. Taking the seax from my mouth helped.

The Norns were watching over me. I heard the two Franks as they approached. They were not heading towards me but the burned-out boats. I turned my head as slowly as I could. They were two hundred paces from me and would pass me by at least sixty paces. The muddy, swampy land could not be crossed easily. I saw that they had come from the watchtower. I had to get to the headland below it. I began to back slowly towards the water. I kept my eye on the two men but they were busy looking at the burning ships. I caught occasional words but nothing which made sense. When my foot touched the water I pushed with my hands and the rising water lifted my legs and I floated. I pushed myself backwards and then used my hands to walk myself against the tide and down towards the tower. I needed somewhere on land I could walk. I kept my seax in my right hand. I had a feeling that I might need it. I saw that there was a beach inland from the tower. I headed for it. Once on the sand, I risked rising.

When I looked in the harbour there was no sign of the drekar. Either she waited beyond the harbour entrance or I had been abandoned. I put that chilling thought from my mind and headed along the beach. I began shivering as I did so. I suppose it was inevitable but it did not help me. I was convinced that my chattering teeth would be heard by the men in the tower. The closer I came to the tower the more I realised that it was an

# The Battle for a Home

imposing structure. It was at least ten paces high and looked to be as big as my hall. I wondered how many men it could hold. It had been built perilously close to the rocks which marked the edge of the beach and the headland. I had to step onto the rocks to negotiate it.

I was halfway along when the spear was hurled at me. Ulf Big Nose had begun to train my senses and when I felt something from my left I instinctively pulled back. The spear scored a line across my chest as it passed before me. Had I not moved back then it would have struck me in my neck! I picked it up and held my seax in my left hand. I heard the shouts from inside the tower. I moved as quickly as I dared along the slippery, seaweed-covered rocks. I was just happy that the Franks did not use a bow. Had they done so then I would have been dead by now! I saw a light as they opened a door in the tower and three warriors came toward me. One had a spear while the other two had swords. None had mail. The worst thing I could do would be to panic and I kept moving steadily. They made the mistake of rushing and one of them slipped. I heard a sickening crunch as his leg jammed between two rocks and was broken.

The two who were left were coming at me obliquely and would reach me before I could reach the headland. There was a large rock ahead of me and it obscured my view of the sea. I turned to face my two opponents. One had a spear and one a sword. I braced myself to wait for them. They split up and that decided me. I bounded across the rocks and pulled back my right arm. I hurled the spear at the swordsman and hit him in the middle. The force of it knocked him over but it was a mortal wound. Changing my seax to my right hand I grabbed the spear of the last Frank just behind the head. As he tried to move his feet he slipped and pulled me down on top of him. I plunged the dagger up under his ribcage and into his heart.

More men came from the tower and I turned. I hurried towards the rock. The rising tide meant that I could no longer walk around the headland and so I threw myself into the sea and began to swim. If the drekar had gone then I would swim back to my home. There were bigger waves here beyond the protection of the land and I could not see too far ahead as waves and rollers crashed down on me. I thought, briefly, of turning around but that way led to death. At least this way I had a chance. I turned on my back and crabbed. It was easier that way although I could not see where I was going. I felt my breeks, now sodden, begin to pull me down and so I shed them. I found the going much easier. I caught sight of a lightening sky to the east. It would not be dawn for some time but that gave me hope. I would be able to see where I was going.

Then I heard a voice. It was Ulf Big Nose. "Unless you intend to swim all the way home do you want to grab this rope?"

I turned on my front and reached for the rope. The drekar was just ten paces from me. I was hauled aboard. I had survived. As I flopped like a fish on the deck they began to sing as they rowed me back across the bay to my home.

*The horseman came through darkest night*
*He rode towards the dawning light*
*With fiery steed and thrusting spear*
*Hrolf the Horseman brought great fear*

*Slaughtering all he breached their line*
*Of warriors slain there were nine*
*Hrolf the Horseman with gleaming blade*
*Hrolf the Horseman all enemies slayed*

*With mighty axe Black Teeth stood*
*Angry and filled with hot blood*
*Hrolf the Horseman with gleaming blade*
*Hrolf the Horseman all enemies slayed*
*Ice cold Hrolf with Heart of Ice*
*Swung his arm and made it slice*
*Hrolf the Horseman with gleaming blade*
*Hrolf the Horseman all enemies slayed*

*In two strokes the Jarl was felled*
*Hrolf's sword nobly held*
*Hrolf the Horseman with gleaming blade*
*Hrolf the Horseman all enemies slayed*

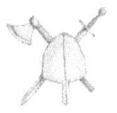

# Chapter 4

It took some days for me to totally recover. The rocks had badly cut my feet. I used the excuse to ride Dream Strider as much as possible. Although Mary was pleased to see me return and still alive she had heard of my exploits thanks to Rurik One Ear and Arne Four Toes. She did not see it as heroic but foolhardy and reckless. I tried to tell her that was who I was. She did not understand for she had not been brought up like a Norse woman. As my feet began to heal I supervised the completion of my defences. I had not had time to fill the ditch with water and I did so now. Skutal and Sigurd's sons fetched seawater in barrels on the backs of my ponies. They thought it was a great game. I knew that the ground would dry but we had enough rain on the island for it to fill up again soon. The ditch also had the advantage of making the hall and the land around it drier when it did rain.

On the way back Siggi White Hair had asked me if I would visit the clan's home more. I had promised him I would try to do so. When I felt ready I broached the subject with Mary. Since my return, things had been a little awkward between us. Neither of us had mentioned the kiss. On reflection that was a mistake. Ulf Big Nose had always told me to face problems and not to hide away from them. I was hiding. The subject of a visit to the clan seemed an easier and more predictable choice.

"I will be travelling to the village of the clan tomorrow. Would you like to come?"

She nodded, "I would. You have faced your enemies and I must face mine. They cannot hurt me."

"And you should not have to suffer their tongues either. You have a place here. Since Seara went to the Otherworld you are the one who sews the finest garments. They will soon learn your value."

And so we rode, the three of us, to the village. The story of my exploits had been told in the village for as we entered I was surrounded. The warriors had always held me in esteem and since the younger ones

## The Battle for a Home

who wished to fight me had gone I was, once more accorded a position of honour. The exceptions were the ones who supported the Eriksson brothers. I noticed, sadly, that now included Karl Swift Foot and Gunnar Gunnarson. Brigid and the other women also crowded around me too. I think that was one reason they resented Mary. They were jealous.

"Go! Back to your work! I would have words with the hersir!" Siggi White Hair had assumed the mantle of Jarl well. The women were all shooed away by their menfolk and Siggi took me into the hall. It was a fine hall. Jarl Gunnar had tried to make it a palace for his wife. Siggi almost rattled around in it but he seemed happy enough.

He still had the Jarl's servants and slaves, "Beer, cheese and bread!" They scurried off. "We have not had time to talk since the raid."

I shook my head. "It seems like a long time ago now."

"You had no need to take such a risk. It was brave and we appreciate it but it was unnecessary."

"If I had not done so then there would have been two ships left to our enemies. They still might have come."

He shook his head, "No they would not. We had damaged enough of their ships to stop them. They still might come but it will take some time to rebuild. Do not have the death wish upon you, Hrolf."

His servants brought in the food and beer. "I do not. I have much to live for and, in truth, I never think I am close to death."

"Ashore, alone, half-naked with a knife and fighting armed men is close to death, my young friend. Believe me."

"Then I will be more cautious next time."

He laughed, "No you will not but so long as you think a little more this old man will be happier. You and Ulf Big Nose are the only two who can advise me. You are young but you have a head on your shoulders. Ulf is wise and my oldest brother in arms but he is like a bear now and prefers his own company. If I am to be Jarl I need your help."

"And you shall have it." I toasted him with my horn of ale. "And what would you have of me?"

"Soon Jarl Gunnstein Berserk Killer will call upon us to raid Wessex. We are honour bound to help him. However, we cannot afford to lose warriors. I need you and Ulf to ensure that they do not lose their heads when we go into battle. The two of you are listened to. When we fought the Hibernians it was your wild charge which won the battle for us but it almost cost us too many men. Six warriors died in that charge who need not have died. Use your skills but use your mind more, Hrolf. I am a

## The Battle for a Home

gruff old warrior. You are the one who can come up with solutions that are new. You did so with the fire ships. Jarl Gunnstein Berserk Killer owes you favours. Do not be afraid to call in that debt."

"I do not like to do that."

"I know. You have more honour than is good for you. "He stood, "Now the other thing is this woman, Mary. What are you going to do about her?"

"What do you mean?"

"You know that the women of the village will continue to make her life a misery until she is your wife. Once she is your wife then they will have to respect her." My mouth opened and closed. "You like her do you not?"

"Yes but."

"What is wrong? Is she cold to you?"

"Cold to me?"

"In bed."

I found myself blushing, "I have not lain with her! She has her own quarters."

He burst out laughing. "Too much honour! Take her as your wife. She will bear you fine children. This is not an order but advice from an old man who wishes he was your age. For many reasons, I chose never to take a wife. Now I am old I regret it more. Do not make the same mistakes I did."

Was this the Norns at work?

"I will think on your words for you are wise and as a father to me."

We spoke of Siggi's plans for the future for a while and then he said, "I have not asked you to be my oathsworn. I know that your thread has a different course. When you are ready to leave and to fly from here I will understand."

"But Jarl I thought it was understood. I have fought with you in the shield wall! I will not desert you now."

He smiled, "That is different. The bond of warriors who have fought together never loosens. That is there unto death but it does not mean we follow the same path. I fought with the Dragonheart as did you and I would fight with him again but when Jarl Gunnar brought us here then we followed a different thread." He stood. "This is not something which is likely to happen soon, Hrolf the Horseman, for we barely have enough warriors for one drekar. I wanted you to know that when the time comes

## The Battle for a Home

for you to leave it will not cause a rift. We will still have friendship and, I hope, an alliance."

As we left I asked, "Where will we get more men? The Jarl brought many from Dyflin. Here we are far from our folk. Do we wait for the children to become men?"

"In truth, I know not but I cannot believe that we were gifted this land for us to have it taken from us or for us to wither and die. For the present, we make ourselves as strong as we can. We wait for the summons of Jarl Gunnar Berserk Killer."

Mary and Gille were talking with Erik One Hand and Brigid. We went over to them. Jarl Siggi walked directly to Mary and embraced her. It took her by surprise. "It is good to see you. We are not graced by your presence often enough. Your skills with a needle are legendary."

She soon recovered and said the right thing, "I am honoured that you say so."

"I would have a kyrtle made. I have nothing which is fine. Now that I am Jarl I would have a kyrtle with a raven upon the chest. Can you make me one? I will pay."

She smiled, "I would make one for nothing and of course, I could. I will need to measure you."

He laughed, "And you will need plenty of cloth for I am not the twig which is Hrolf the Horseman! I am like a stout old oak! Come the day is passing and I need ale. Brigid, broach another barrel."

The day turned into a celebration. Jarl Gunnar had been many things but he was never generous. Siggi had always had treasure. With no wife and children on which to lavish gifts, he had acquired a substantial hoard. Now he was spending it. He knew we would gain more soon and, as Jarl, he would have the dragon's share. We were seeing a different jarl.

The commission from the jarl was the event which made the women, or most of them, accept Mary. Others came to ask for clothes. As we rode home in the early evening she seemed happy. "I may need others to help me."

Gille said, "Do not look at me! I have fingers like spades!"

"I was thinking of girls or women."

"Until we get slaves there are always the wives of Skutal and Sigurd."

"Are they skilled?"

Gille laughed, "They can gut a fish faster than any I have ever seen but I fear the cloth they sewed would not smell pleasant."

She shook her head, "That would not do."

## The Battle for a Home

"The two girls do not help with the fish yet and they have small nimble fingers."

"It takes time to teach even basic skills."

"Then I shall go raiding and find you slaves."

"No! I will work with them if their mothers are willing. I need you close to home."

We were approaching the hall. "That may be out of our hands. We are promised to help Jarl Gunnstein Berserk Killer. He raids Wessex in a revenge raid. I will have to go."

Her good humour evaporated like an early morning mist. When we reached home I said, "Gille see to the horses and feed the animals eh? I need to speak with Mary."

I put more wood on the fire and wafted it with my cloak to make the flames rise. Mary went to go to her chamber. "Wait, we need to speak." She turned. The fire suddenly brightened and bathed her face in a warm glow. I smiled, "The firelight makes you look a little happier. I am glad. I took her hands. "I have not spoken of the kiss you gave before I last left to raid and that was wrong. I believe it means you care for me and fear being alone here. Now you worry that I will leave you again and may not return."

In answer, she threw her arms around my neck and buried her face in my chest. She began to sob.

I spoke softly in her ear, "I too would miss you if you were not in my life. Today I saw you accorded more honour than at any time since you first came. What say we become man and wife? As the wife of a hersir you, too, would be respected and I would like you as my wife."

It sounded awkward when I said it and I wondered if I had said too much. She raised her head. I saw that her cheeks were wet. "That is my hope! I would be your wife!"

"Then we shall be married."

"But there is no priest."

"And I am no Christian. There is a ceremony but it is pagan and may offend you. We will marry ourselves this night when Gille returns." She hesitated. "If you wish me to take a priest from the mainland and make him our slave I will do so. That is the only way you can be married by a priest."

She shook her head, "No, we will do it your way."

Just then Gille came in. He stopped for he knew something was amiss, "I will...."

# The Battle for a Home

"Come, Gille, we need you. Mary and I are to be married. You are witness that this was in accordance with both our wishes." Mary nodded.

Gille grinned. "Aye, lord! Rurik One Ear said it would not be long before you did this. It is *wyrd*!" He picked up his sleeping cloak. "I will sleep with the horses this night."

I shook my head, "You need not. A warrior does not need privacy. The Viking way is not to hide away."

"I know, lord, but this is your wedding night and Mary is the daughter of a noble. I do not mind. Gerðr is warm and her filly too."

With that, the wise young warrior left us. I did not know what to do. Mary did and she pulled me to my sleeping place. That night we became as one. I had a beard and I was a man but that night I became a real man and my life changed forever.

# The Battle for a Home

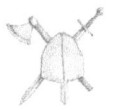

# Chapter 5

We had but a week of bliss before Rurik came to fetch me. It was seven days I had never experienced before. I had thought that when I had slain other warriors I was a man. I now knew that was but part of it. "Hrolf, Jarl Gunnstein is here. He and three drekar are approaching the island. Jarl Siggi says we sail on the morning tide."

"Tell him I will be there."

"I will go down to Skutal and Sigurd. As I am here I will see what they have caught."

Gille joined him. Since we had returned he made the journey each morning. I had taken to eating oysters each day and Gille went down to pick them for me. I looked at Mary. "We knew this day would come."

"Aye, we did. Do not worry, husband. There will be no weeping and storming to my chamber. If you say you will return then I will believe you. Besides, it will give me the chance to improve the skills of Anya and Ambroch." The two daughters of my fishermen had proved to be more skilful than Mary had expected and they were able to help my wife. Not yet good enough for fine work, they were able to tack material together which saved Mary time. She had told me, as we had nestled together, that she believed they had potential. She was certainly happier. I knew not if that was because she had help or because we were married.

When Rurik and Gille returned Rurik One Ear had a grin on his face. I guessed that Gille had told him my news. He said nothing but I knew that when we sailed he would. I prepared myself for lewd comments. It was the warrior way and I would have to endure it.

I went to war with a new kyrtle beneath my mail. Mary had teased some sheep wool and then sewn it onto a kyrtle. She had even managed to sew the head of Dream Strider on the front. She wanted to make sure that I had as much protection as possible when I went to fight the Saxons of Wessex. It replaced the one I had worn in Hibernia. The fight with the champion and the subsequent battles with the wild warriors of that island

# The Battle for a Home

had meant it either needed repair or replacing. Mary replaced it. She had learned from her earlier effort and this one was even better than the first.

Gille asked if he ought to come with me. He was now of an age when young men took to the oars. I would have wanted him to be with us but I wanted him to watch my family more. Similarly, Sigurd and Skutal came to speak with me. "It is not right that the rest of the clan goes to avenge our honour. One of us, at least, should come with you."

I nodded, "You do not need to but if one chooses to take an oar then that is good."

It was Sigurd who came. He had a helmet, a shield and a spear. I gave him one of my old swords. He would not take the Frankish one given to me by the merchant from Andecavis. He said, "It is too good for me. I am not a swordsman, lord. I would be as skilful with an iron bar but I have courage and I will stand in the shield wall."

Gille came with us and we rode to the stad. He would return with our horses. The embrace and the kiss from Mary kept me silent all the way there. The last week had shown me that I had been foolish in delaying the decision I had finally made.

When the Jarl had arrived the night before, Jarl Siggi had held a feast for Jarl Gunnstein. I saw bleary-eyed warriors heading down to their drekar. I handed my reins to Gille, "I look to you and Skutal to watch my family and my people while I am away. I know that you will care for my horses."

"I will lord. I know now what is needed and I will not let you down."

I watched him lead my stallion north to my home. I wished I was with them. I turned and headed towards Jarl Siggi's hall. The Jarl from Dyflin saw me approach and he smiled broadly, "Here is the hero come to join us. Now I know that the gods will favour this raid. We have the two mighty warriors who drove the Hibernians back to their caves!" He embraced me. "And I hear you have taken a filly too! Hrolf the Horseman will prove that he is a stallion eh?" Rurik had wasted no time in spreading the word! He was a gossip.

Any response I might have made was drowned out by the shouts and cries from the clan. The banter and the ribbing had begun. We headed down to the drekar. As we clambered aboard I said to Sven the Helmsman, "Sigurd Einarsson comes to war with us. He is skilled with boats."

"Aye, I know. Until we have more men you will need to take an oar but I would teach you how to sail a drekar."

Sigurd looked happy, "Aye, I would like that!"

I took my oar and waited for the Jarl to board. All I knew was that we were going to raid Wessex. That was a large place. Rurik One Ear joined me and while we waited he gave me the news that the Jarl from Dyflin had brought. "The Dragonheart slew Eggle Skulltaker. Windar's Mere was avenged."

"I am pleased. That is how it should be."

"Jarl Gunnstein thought it was a good omen for this raid."

"I hope so. Where do we raid?"

"Hamwic."

"We have raided there before. Is not that close to Wintan-ceastre? We have but six drekar and King Egbert has a large army."

"They were the ones who slew the Jarl and his bride. They have the heads of the dead above their gate. King Egbert is to the north. He fights Mercia. It is said that he is close to victory." Leaning in he added, "The Jarl Gunnstein says that King Louis the Pious backs Egbert with coin and that King Egbert hopes to be Bretwalda."

"Bretwalda?"

"High king of the land of the Saxons. It is said that with Mercia defeated he can then conquer Northumbria and the land of the East Angles. Jarl Gunnstein has planned this well. If we are successful at Hamwic then he would raid Wintan-ceastre too. We hope for many slaves and much treasure. It is said that the men who killed the Jarl came from Hamwic. The heads of our brothers were placed outside its walls."

"Then this is *wyrd*."

With the Jarl aboard, we headed out to sea. We were smaller than the other five drekar. Jarl Gunnstein had not only his own warriors but others from Orkneyjar and the northern isles. Some were kin to Jarl Gunnar Thorfinnson. They recognised jarl Siggi and Ulf and waved to them. They were the last of the warriors from Jarl Gunnar's northern home.

Siggi began the chant and we sang lustily.

> ***The night was black no moon was there***
> ***Death and danger hung in the air***
> ***As Raven Wing closed with the shore***
> ***The scouts crept closer as before***
> ***Dressed like death with sharpened blades***
> ***They moved like spirits through the glades***
> ***The power of the raven grows and grows***

## The Battle for a Home

*The power of the raven grows and grows*
*With sentries slain they sought new foes*
*A cry in the night fetched them woes*
*The alarm was given the warriors ready*
*Four scouts therewith hearts so steady*
*Ulf and Arne thought their end was nigh*
*When Hrolf the wild leapt from the sky*
*Flying like the raven through the air*
*He felled the Cymri, a raven slayer*
*The power of the raven grows and grows*
*The power of the raven grows and grows*
*His courage clear he still fought on*
*Until the clan had battled and won*
*The power of the raven grows and grows*
*The power of the raven grows and grows*
*Raven Wing goes to war*
*Hear our voices hear them roar*
*A song of death to all its foes*
*The power of the raven grows and grows*
*The power of the raven grows and grows*
*The power of the raven grows and grows*
*The power of the raven grows and grows.*

It was the first time that Sigurd had rowed and I could hear his voice as he joined in. It made him one of the crew. It made us all as one. We were ready for war.

We rowed until we had left the shelter of the land and then the winds from the south and west took us north. It was at that moment, when we laid down our oars, that Siggi addressed us. "Today is the first time we go to war without Jarl Gunnar Thorfinnson at the fore. When he led us it was the hearth-weru who protected him. I have no hearth-weru and I need no one to protect me!" He shouted the last part and we all banged the deck with our hands. "But we need leaders and the hearth-weru were leaders. I have decided that the two hersirs, Hrolf the Horseman and Ulf Big Nose will be leaders. Hrolf is on the steerboard side and he will lead those rowers. Ulf Big Nose will lead the rest."

Ketil Eriksson asked, "But why? We did not need them before."

## The Battle for a Home

He laughed, "We did. We lost warriors because of reckless acts which brought neither victory nor honour. We are too few to waste warriors' lives. We will not shirk battle but we fight to win and to survive. If we do not then the clan will die and I am not willing to let that happen. You will follow Ulf Big Nose's commands in battle Ketil! You are one who needs a strong hand to control you. You are a fine warrior but a wild one!" Everyone cheered at that. We knew what he was like. "Today we are one of six clans. Today we share the spoils with others but today is also the day that we begin to grow. This time next year we will have two drekar and crew to man them!"

Arne Four Toes said, "I would not risk another ship from Bolli. Perhaps his drekar only sail for the Dragonheart. We lost the Jarl!"

"You may be right but we have Sven the Helmsman. He knows ships. We have a bay by the haunted farmhouse and we have trees across the water. Why can we not build our own drekar?" No one had thought of that and even dour Ulf Big Nose nodded. It was a beginning.

As we neared the coast of Wessex the afternoon light was fading. Those who did so donned their war faces. I did not. I donned my mail. I gave Heart of Ice one last sharpen and I touched my horse token around my neck. That had brought me luck before and a warrior knew how important luck was.

We rounded the island which lay close to the estuary just after dark. We were not leading. Our drekar was behind that of Jarl Gunnstein. His plan was simple. We would sail up the estuary and begin to attack immediately. He did not need any scouts for we had raided this burgh before and knew how the land lay. We had no doubt that they had improved the walls but we had over two hundred warriors. With King Egbert to the north fighting the Mercians with his best warriors we would be able to punish those who had slain our kin. As we passed along the coast we heard church bells tolling. They were warning of our approach. Dragonships were to be feared.

As we rowed up the coast towards Hamwic, Rurik said, "They will be ready for us."

Behind us, Erik Green Eye said, "Aye and they will be filling their breeks!"

"Rurik is right. They may try to take their treasure and holy books to Wintan-ceastre. We do not want that."

The tide was against us as we rowed up the Hamble. It delayed our arrival until the dark of night. Had I commanded I would have laid up to

## The Battle for a Home

the west of the island and avoided detection and tiredness. We had rowed for hours before we landed. We were tough warriors but I feared it would come back to haunt us. We poured ashore from our drekar. We were the second to land and Jarl Gunnstein had already organized his men ready to attack. "Jarl Siggi, have your men form the second rank."

"Aye."

I took my place to his left while Ulf went to his right. I held my spear. When attacking a wall that was often the best weapon to use, especially when men were standing above you. I stood behind Thorgeir Sigurdsson. He was the leader of the jarl's hearth-weru and a mighty warrior. Over his shoulder, I saw the defences. They had a ditch and wooden walls with a tower at each corner. Jarl Gunnstein had some archers and I hoped that they were good. If they were then we stood a chance of reaching the walls with few losses.

I did not know the warriors who stood behind us. Most came from the north. There Thorfinn Blue Scar had been the most powerful Jarl. Now he and all of his sons were dead. The ones who were with us were seeking treasure. I had no doubt that although they fought together with us and Jarl Gunnstein, they would turn on each other quickly once they returned home. I noticed that fewer than one in five had mail. They were poor warriors and would seek to enrich themselves at the Saxon's expense. A Saxon sword was a prized weapon. I needed none for mine had been made by the father of Bagsecg in Cyninges-tūn. There was no finer weapon which could be made for he had created the sword which was then touched by the gods!

Jarl Gunnstein Berserk Killer turned and said to Jarl Harald Fine Hair from Orkneyjar. "Hold your men here as a reserve. This does not seem to be as well defended as I expected."

"We will be ready but we shall still share in the treasure?"

"Of course!" He held up his sword and shouted, "Today we avenge those who were slain by these Saxons." He pointed at the remains of the ten heads which adorned the wooden wall. "They will rue the day that they risked our wrath!"

We began to bang our shields rhythmically. It was intended to intimidate. It sounded terrifying, especially to those within the walls who sheltered and listened. The ones on the wall knew what was coming. That is always easier.

"Forward!"

# The Battle for a Home

I would have scouted the ditch which surrounded the burgh but Jarl Gunnstein was eager to close with the Saxons. His archers were behind the rear rank and the thirty arrows fell along the wall. Most were stopped by shields but so long as it kept them occupied then we were happy.

"Shields!" As we neared the ditch we raised our shields. I put mine over the head of Thorgeir Sigurdsson. I put my spear over his right shoulder. The dark night became darker as a warrior from the northern isles covered me with his shield. I felt his spear rest on my shoulder.

"Stop!" We were blind now and dependent on those at the front who could look down below our shields. "Ditch!"

The men of Dyflin descended and we followed carefully. The better warriors were in the centre and we negotiated the slope down well but we heard cries from the far left and right of our line as others slipped and, in slipping, allowed the Saxons to hurl spears at them. I looked at the bottom of the ditch.

"Halt!"

There appeared to be no traps and it was not muddy. The harder part was to get out of the ditch for the bank was steep. I heard the crack of stones on our shields as the defenders hurled them down from the ramparts. They were annoying more than anything. The angle of our shields deflected them as they threw them on us. Ironically the stones aided us. Thorgeir Sigurdsson shouted, "Pull the stones down. They will make steps!"

It was little enough but when the stones were pulled from the bank where they had fallen they made steps. Men were still being struck on the flanks but in the centre, close to the gate, we were unharmed... at the moment.

Thorgeir said, "Hrolf, push with your shield as I rise and then follow!"

"Aye!"

I had to move my shield from over his head to do so. It was a risk and as a lead ball clanged off his helmet I wondered at its wisdom. Thorgeir Sigurdsson stepped onto the stones and, using his spear as an aid stepped up as I pushed. He rose to the top of the bank and immediately put his shield over his head. Keeping my shield up I stepped forward and held my spear up. As the mighty Thorgeir pulled I sprang up to join him on the bank below the wall. Others had emulated us. I turned and was pulling up a warrior from the north when a spear was hurled down and it hit him in the shoulder. He landed heavily but another held his spear up and I pulled.

# The Battle for a Home

We now had a toehold on the bank. The Saxons above us were using their spears in an attempt to shift us from our precarious perch. I saw Jarl Gunnstein and his hearth-weru as they began to hack at the door. Thorgeir Sigurdsson turned his back to the wooden wall and made a cup for my foot with his hands. "You are lighter than me. Up and clear the ramparts! We will follow!"

"Aye!" I slipped my shield around to my back and stepped onto the hands. Even as I was boosted up I saw the Saxon with his spear pull his arm back to end my life when I reached the top. As I was lifted I hurled the spear before he could stab at me. It hit him in the middle and he plummeted from the fighting platform. I landed heavily and a second warrior stabbed at me with his spear. I knocked the head to the side with the back of my left hand and then punched him on the side of the head as hard as I could with my fist. He fell screaming to the floor four paces below us. I felt something strike my back but my shield took the blow.

In one motion I drew my sword and swung it around in a wide arc. The man whose axe was embedded in my shield had no weapon and my sword bit into his unprotected neck. Blood spurted. I backhanded my sword again and it found the flesh of an arm. I had cleared a space. There was no one within three paces of me. I hefted my shield around and shouted. "Come! I have space to kill! Who will join me?"

Thorgeir leapt up whirling his sword as he did so. He stood with his back to me and said, over his shoulder. "We will clear a space for those coming up! On!" I stepped forward. I knew I had the easier task for my shield was on my left and that was the opposite side of the wall. A Saxon screamed at me and ran towards me with a whirling axe. He brought it around in a wide arc to smash against my shield. I had taken the advice of Dragonheart and used hammered nails to outline my horse's head. The axe struck the boss and then was stopped by the metal heads of my nails. However, it was a mighty blow and I had to step to the right. The wooden wall behind me stopped me from falling. I brought Heart of Ice over my shoulder. The Saxon blocked it with his shield. He, however, had no wall to stop himself and as he began to overbalance I pushed harder against the shield. He too fell to the ground.

I felt a shield against my back and I heard Rurik One Ear say, "I have your back. Let Raven Wing Clan clear this wall!"

Reassured by my clan brother I roared a challenge and ran towards the three Saxons who stood before me. I was wearing mail. I had on my head my helmet with mask. Even though there were three of them they

# The Battle for a Home

hesitated. That is always a mistake. With my shield before my face, I hurtled into them. If you cannot find flesh with your weapon you are in trouble. As I rammed into them one tumbled from the fighting platform while my own sword swept before the heads of the other two. One turned and fled. Rurik's spear jabbed over my shoulder and into the face of the third. It was as simple as that. There was one left before us.

Below I heard the axes as Jarl Gunnstein's men hacked at the gate. I saw Saxons piling wood against it. "Raven Wing Clan!" I jumped from the wall landing on one of the bodies of the men I had slain. It broke my fall and I sprang to my feet. Rurik and Arne Four Toes joined me and with those on either side of me we marched towards the gate. We were outnumbered but we were outnumbered by men with inferior arms and armour. I suspected the better warriors were with King Egbert.

Some of those piling the wood against the gate turned to give us battle. We turned our shields as one and our sword poked over the top. Wearing mail and being large warriors gave us an advantage over these men who faced us. When they ran at us their spears found wood and metal. Their open helmets found our swords. They did not move the three of us.

I shouted, "Now!" We all stepped forward as one. We did not even need to think about it. I thrust my sword hard at the helmet of the warrior before me. He flinched and was rewarded by the boss of my shield catching him on the jaw. As he tumbled backwards Arne's sword pierced his thigh. Rurik brought his sword over his head. The warrior he struck was stabbing his spear at me. As I turned my head slightly his helmet and skull were split asunder.

There was now a gap for three were down and I punched again with my shield to clear some space. I had quick hands and my sword darted out to find the unprotected middle of a greybeard. I tore my sword sideways. He fell writhing at my feet trying to hold in the red and black snakes which erupted from his flesh. There were two men with their backs to us and they were piling timbers behind the gate. They did not see me and my sword ended their lives quickly.

Thorgeir Sigurdsson, his cheek bleeding, joined me with three of his warriors. "You have done well. Sigtrygg, open the gate and we will finish these."

The six of us fell upon the remnants of the Saxons at the gate. They did not last long. I turned to Thorgeir, "None of these had mail. There must be better warriors somewhere else."

## The Battle for a Home

Thorgeir pointed. Dawn was breaking in the east and its first light showed a stone tower. There were men at its top. "They are there. The Jarl will burn them alive!"

With the gate open the men waiting outside flooded in. Jarl Gunnstein snarled, "Where are these Saxon dogs?"

Thorgeir pointed, "They have withdrawn to the tower."

Arne Four Toes said, "And they have put barricades between the houses, Jarl."

"That will not help them. Come let us end this." He turned to Siggi, "Jarl, take your clan around to the north gate in case these rats try to flee."

Ketil Eriksson said, "But what of the treasure?"

Siggi snapped, "Obey orders or find another clan." He turned back to the Jarl, "We will do as you ask."

We trudged out of the gate. I sensed that some of the men were unhappy that we would not be there when the tower fell and we found the treasure. I knew that we had gained entry and showed our courage. The other clans had yet to have the chance. I did not mind.

As we marched around the perimeter Ulf Big Nose said, "These walls smell strange. I think they have treated them with seal oil."

Karl Green Eye said, "I have heard of such things before. I believe it preserves the wood but I would not like the smell."

Sometimes a thought nags at you but no matter how much you pick at it you cannot bring it to mind. So it was with me. Something did not sit right. We had met the weakest of opposition. The last time we had raided it had been much sterner. What was different?

As we neared the northern gate we heard the sound of animals and people. With the light now flooding from the east it became obvious. They were evacuating the burgh.

"Stop them!"

There were only thirty of us but we were well armed and we were warriors. We ran to the men and those with arms. Falling upon them we showed no mercy. The only treasure would be their weapons and their women. We would take them. The gate was still open and suddenly riders burst forth. These were mailed. These were the elite warriors. I saw a priest with them too. They rode through their own people. I ran to get at them. I managed, by pushing aside some women, to reach the last three. I blindly swung my sword and felt it bite into the leg of the penultimate rider. It sliced through to the side of the horse which reared and threw him from it. He fell writhing to the ground but the rest escaped.

"Hold the prisoners. Let us make sure no one else leaves."

Even as Arne and Rurik led our men to obey their orders there was a whoosh of flame from the gate. Suddenly the flames began to race around the wooden walls. Even as I realised the significance of the seal oil the last four riders burst from the gate. Arne and Rurik slew one but the other three rode down our men. Ulf swung his sword, not at the rider but at the pony. He hacked through it and the dead horse tumbled over, killing the rider as it fell. A second rider had a lance and he lunged at me. I did not flinch but grabbed the haft and pulled. He was not using stiraps and he fell from its back. He lay stunned on the floor and I put my sword to his throat. I said, in Saxon, "Move and you die!" Then I turned, "Sigurd."

"Yes, lord?"

"Put your spear to his throat and if he moves end his life."

"Aye lord."

I ran to Siggi, "It is a trap! They were not barricades but bonfires. They are trying to kill the men inside."

"Pull down the gate and the walls next to it! Fetch water from the river!"

Ulf Big Nose pointed to Ketil and Knut Eriksson, "And you two make sure none of these slaves moves."

"Jarl Siggi, I have a prisoner."

"Hold him until we have halted the fire."

Just then Thorgeir, Jarl Gunnstein and twenty of his men rushed through the burning gate. Some of them had their clothes on fire.

"Use your cloaks to put out the flames!"

We were lucky, only one of the warriors was badly burned. Arne and Rurik managed to pull down the gate and one side of the wall. More warriors came out coughing and spluttering. By the time the sun was getting high in the sky, the fire had died and Hamwic was a smouldering ruin. Warriors who had survived the inferno made their way out of the death trap to join us. They were led by Jarl Harald Fine Hair. His clan, like ours, was largely untouched.

Jarl Gunnstein Berserk Killer's armour was covered in soot. His face was blackened too but his eyes burned with anger. "Jarl Harald, are any left alive inside?"

## The Battle for a Home

The Jarl from Orkneyjar shook his head. "I have brought with me the only survivors."

Jarl Gunnstein took out his sword. He said to me, "Is this the only warrior who survived?"

"Aye Jarl. A couple escaped us on their horses but we slew the rest. The warriors who fled rode up the road. They will have gone to Wintan-Ceastre."

"And that is where we will go when I have spoken to this nithing!" He turned to Jarl Siggi. "You speak Saxon do you not, Jarl?"

"I speak enough to question him."

"I want to know who ruled here and who devised the plan."

We went to Sigurd. I nodded and he removed his sword. Siggi hauled the man to his feet. He was dressed in mail and looked to be a housecarl. They were tough men and I doubted that he would reveal much. I understood enough of Saxon to make out most of what he said.

"Who commanded here?"

The man remained silent.

"Who started the fire?"

He continued to stare at Siggi.

I noticed that although he had a cross around his neck he still wore warrior bands and there was another token hanging next to the cross.

Siggi turned to Jarl Gunnstein, "He refuses to speak, Jarl. Shall I hurt him? Perhaps the threat of the blood eagle might loosen his tongue."

The Jarl from Dyflin shook his head, "Look, he wears warrior bands. This man is hearth-weru. He will die before he tells us anything."

"Let me try." I walked over to him and put my hand towards his face. He did not flinch. I reached under his mail and pulled out the cross and the crudely made symbol of the wild boar. This man purported to be a Christian but he was a pagan. I had the measure of him and I said, "You are oathsworn and your master lives." His mouth said nothing but his eyes flickered and answered me. He had done his duty and was willing to die for the man who had abandoned him.

I tore the two tokens from his neck. Holding them apart I said, "Which one would upset you to lose I wonder?" I took the silver cross and threw it to Sigurd who gratefully caught it. The Saxon said nothing. I put the wild boar token on the ground, spat on it and ground my heel upon it. The Saxon lurched towards me. I had been expecting it and I punched him hard on the nose before he could get close to me. His face erupted in blood and cartilage Arne and Rurik ran to hold his arms.

# The Battle for a Home

I nodded, "So you still believe in the old ways. Your master did not. He followed Egbert and he converted. Your master is not worthy of your death. He fled and left you. Our leaders do not leave their clan to die. Your Eorl is a coward."

I saw him strain against my two friends. Jarl Gunnstein asked, "What did you say to him, Hrolf the Horseman?"

"I called his leader a coward. This man plays at being a follower of the White Christ. He follows the old ways. He believes in dying with a sword in his hand." I turned back to him and said, in Saxon, "Tell me the name of your Eorledman and we will put a sword in your hand and send you to the Otherworld as a warrior."

He said nothing at first but I saw the debate he was having with himself.

"I will give you a warrior's death."

His eyes brightened, "You swear?"

I heard a murmur from behind as he spoke.

"I swear."

"I will only tell you his name."

"And that is all I want." I saw him wrestling with the decision. He would still have kept his word if he just told us the name of his leader. What could be gained?

"What does he say?"

"I offered him a warrior's death if he told me the name of his master."

"Good." I heard a sword being drawn.

The Saxon said, "Eorledman Ecgfrith of Hamwic. He is my master."

I picked up his sword and, gesturing to Arne and Rurik to release him I handed it to him. If he chose he could have used it on me but I watched him nod his thanks and hold it in two hands as Jarl Gunnstein Berserk Killer's sword took his head.

"Eorledman Ecgfrith of Hamwic."

"Thank you, Hrolf the Horseman. Once again I am in your debt. Thorgeir Sigurdsson, have the slaves and the mail taken to the ships. Divide it evenly and have those who have suffered wounds and burns guard them. We eat and then march on Wintan-Ceastre. We will teach this Eorledman Ecgfrith of Hamwic the price of angering Vikings."

# Chapter 6

Jarl Siggi smiled, "And you did not think you were ready to be jarl." He shook his head. "You are still too reckless!" he turned, "Find food and see if there is any ale." Although we were outside the walls there were many huts which lined the river.

I waved Sigurd over. "Take the warrior's mail and weapons. You can have the helmet and the sword. Wear the mail until we return to my home and I will let Gille have that."

"And the cross?"

"You keep that. Sell it for there are many who would pay coin for it."

He shook his head, "I will melt it down and make myself a token. My wife has second sight. She can put a spell on it. I wear one made of copper. Silver will give me more protection when we face the wrath of Ran."

I nodded. I did not realise that his wife had powers. It showed me that I had not paid enough attention to my people. Jarl Dragonheart knew everything about all those who lived within his lands. I looked at myself too much. I would never achieve my dream of a home on the mainland if I did not understand those that I led. "Then find the spare horses. We will take them with us." Three horses grazed by the side of the greenway. If I had the chance I would take them home with us. They were smaller than my horses but they were horses and they were what I needed.

Arne Four Toes said, "You are too generous, Hrolf. Why did you not keep the mail and sword for yourself?"

I cocked my head to one side, "I have a sword made by Beorn Bagsecgson. I have a full mail byrnie and a helmet which is superior to that of the Saxon. Why should I keep it?"

"You would be richer."

"And I am richer now. Sigurd is bondi. He protects my land. If I find more weapons and helmets then I will give them to Skutal. There is more to being rich, Arne Four Toes, than having pots of coins buried in a hall."

# The Battle for a Home

Rurik One Ear laughed, "And that is why you are Hersir and we are not!"

Fed and watered we headed north at noon. It was not far to Wintan-Ceastre. We had raided here once before. They had rebuilt Hamwic but the churches which lay between the two settlements were still empty shells. The animals had been taken from the fields and it was like walking through an empty land. It was not good for our war band as Jarl Gunnstein and his men became angrier as we marched. They needed to vent their anger as did the others who had lost warriors.

Jarl Harald Fine Hair and his men led for they were eager to gain the glory we had. They kept a fast pace. Even so, it was late afternoon when we saw the wooden walls of Wintan-Ceastre rising ahead of us. This was a bigger nut to crack. The last time we had come we threatened only and they had paid us gold to leave. Then we had had hostages and now we had none for they had learned their lesson and the land around was empty. Jarl Gunnstein sent the surviving men from Orkneyjar to the north gate. Jarl Harald Fine Hair had a full crew but the other drekar now barely mustered one crew. The dead and the wounded had come from that drekar and Jarl Gunnstein's.

Thorgeir waved Siggi, Harald Fine Hair, Ulf Big Nose and me over. He said, "Jarl Gunnstein is wondering how we take this place. The three of you raided here with Jarl Gunnar. What can you tell us?"

Ulf pointed to the walls, "They are made of wood but they are built on stone. They are higher than the ones at Hamwic and we would need ladders. The ditch has traps and water. It is twelve paces wide and has two bridges across it. It is as deep as a man sitting on another's shoulders. If you tried to descend you would be slaughtered. They have wells within the burgh for water." He waved a hand around the warriors who remained, "Is this enough to assault the walls? I do not think so."

Thorgeir smiled, "Is the champion of the Raven Wing Clan afraid?"

"Am I afraid of losing my life for no good reason? Aye. We could lose half of our men climbing across the ditch and up the walls."

Jarl Gunnstein said, "What would you suggest?"

Siggi White Hair asked, "What is it that you wish? We have had vengeance on the men of Hamwic."

"Not the man who planned this; not the Eorledman."

"Then you need to have more men. We have the crews of just under four drekar. There are just over one hundred who could fight. We would lose perhaps thirty or forty getting over the walls. We might well win but we would have barely enough men to sail home."

"They must pay!"

Thorgeir said, "Why not do what they did the last time and pay with their gold for the lives of our men?"

"We have no hostages!"

I said, "But, Jarl, if you make them fear for their lives then they might be willing. Egbert is far from here and cannot come to their aid. If they believed we could destroy them then they might be more willing to pay."

Jarl Gunnstein nodded, "But I cannot see how we would be able to manage that."

"There is a way. We use their own weapon against them."

"Own weapon?"

"Fire! We have seal oil on the drekar and there will be pots. We fill the pots with the seal oil and, after dark, we throw them at the gate. If our archers send fire arrows then the gate will burn."

"But they have water and they will douse the flames."

"They may but if our archers continue to loose arrows at them then they might not. If their gate is gone it still leaves the ditch but they would be more willing to talk." I shrugged, "It is worth the delay. Besides if the gate was burned we might be able to make a bridge and we could attack as you would like."

"Then try." He pointed to the horses. "Take those."

I grinned, "I intended to, Jarl Gunnstein. I am Hrolf the Horseman! Sigurd, Rurik, come with me." I mounted the one I had identified as the stallion. He would be the hardest to ride. There were no stiraps; however, I had ridden for years without them. We galloped back down the road. It did not take long. The captives had been gathered together and were looking fearful. The warriors who looked after them had been injured in the attack and would not be kind to them.

"I need pots from the settlement and seal oil to fill them."

Sven the Helmsman and Harald Fast Sailing were more organised than the others. They found what I needed. They found pots with stoppers in them and they tied ropes around their necks. We had enough oil and pots for ten of them.

Sven asked, "What do you need them for?"

"We are going to burn Wintan-Ceastre."

"Good for some of the warriors who have been burned need a healer such as Dragonheart's! They are keen for vengeance!"

# The Battle for a Home

"Have one of your ship's boys fetch my bow!"

"Erik, you heard the hersir! Run!"

A sudden thought struck me. "Are there any captives who behave as Mary did?"

"What?"

"Mary was the daughter of a noble. She was dressed better and kept apart from the others. Are there any girls or women like that?"

"No, but there are a pair of boys. They are almost youths. They have leather boots. Their cloaks are rough though."

I wandered over to the captives and saw the two he meant. They had hair which had been combed and their boots were well made. I lifted the rough cloaks they wore and saw, beneath, tunics which fitted and had delicate needlework. These were the children of nobles. I went to a woman and asked, "How many children does Ecgfrith have?" She was gripping her daughter close to her and I half drew my sword. It was a threat only; I would not harm a woman and child.

Gripping her child tighter she said, "Two! Sons!" Although she tried not to she could not help her eyes flicking towards the two boys with the boots.

I slid my sword back and walked over to them. I yanked them both to their feet by the back of their tunics. "You two are coming with me." I pushed one towards Rurik. "Put him on the horse before you. Sigurd, you do the same. Keep them safe. They may bring us great wealth."

The boys struggled until my two men gripped them so tightly that they could hardly breathe. They were persuasive warriors. Erik ran up to me with my Saami bow and quiver of arrows. I had a feeling that I might need it.

It was the middle of the night when we arrived back at the siege. It was exactly halfway between dusk and dawn. Jarl Gunnstein looked at the two boys. "Who are these?"

"I think that they are Ecgfrith's sons. We will find out after we have burned their gates, Jarl. Then it will be daylight and he will be able to see them."

"If this works then I will give you a share of my treasure too!"

All the archers gathered together and Thorgeir selected the men who would throw the pots. We needed the gate and the wall on either side soaking. Half of the archers would use fire arrows. They were not as accurate but as the Saxons did not have many archers we could afford to approach them closely. I was with the archers who would clear the walls.

# The Battle for a Home

When all was ready a line of warriors with shields walked before us. They stopped five paces from the ditch. I joined the other archers behind them. I pulled back the bow. I saw a helmet glinting in the moonlight. I loosed. The warrior disappeared as he pitched backwards. The other archers joined me and soon there were no heads to be seen. The Saxons took cover. The archers with the fire loosed theirs as Thorgeir shouted, "Now!"

The shields parted and the men ran to the edge of the ditch where they whirled around before releasing their pots. I saw a warrior with a spear rise and my arrow hit his arm. The spear clattered down and he took shelter. The fire arrows were burning on the wall. As the seal oil hit the wall and spattered the flames suddenly took hold and began to lick up the walls. As more arrows hit the oil the fire spread. We heard the alarm in the town.

Now was the time of the archer. When the archers with the fire arrows had finished with their arrows they used ordinary ones. The Saxons had two choices, open the door and try to quench the flames from outside or pour water from above. They chose the latter. Those that tried died. There were a limited number of places they could use and we archers had every part of the gate covered. We stopped when it was obvious that they would let the fire burn. I guessed that they were using their water to damp the walls which were not on fire in the hope that it would not spread. They were, largely, successful. It spread, perhaps a man's body on either side of the wall we had fired. As dawn began to break the fire began to die.

The town was surrounded. Had we been those under siege then we would have sortied for we were fewer in number than they were. The difference was that we were Vikings and they were Saxons. They were the sheep and we were the wolf.

As the light grew we could see that they were prepared for our attack. The Saxons formed a shield wall behind the ruins of their gate. We now saw their strength for there was a line of twenty warriors who faced us and all wore a byrnie made of iron. Their shields prevented us from seeing those behind. None of us was worried by their numbers. We had never met a Saxon warband we had not been able to defeat.

Jarl Gunnstein said, "Jarl Siggi go and tell them we will speak with them. Jarl Erik Haraldsson, bring the two captives but keep them hidden from view. I would surprise this Ecgfrith."

Siggi said, "Come, Hrolf in case my Saxon is not up to it."

## The Battle for a Home

I took my bow with an arrow ready in case of treachery. We both removed our helmets. They distorted sound and we needed to know exactly what was said and, perhaps, offered. Our shields were around our back. It was a sign we came to talk.

Siggi shouted, "We come to speak with Eorledman Ecgfrith."

The ones in the front rank turned and passed the message on. I recognised the Eorledman as he stepped forward. He had been one of those who had fled on horses the other night. I wondered how he had come to leave his sons. Perhaps they had been on horses with men who had been slain. The Eorledman had fine mail. His helmet also had a boar on the top. He was older than I was. I had expected that from the age of his sons.

He stood and shouted, "I am Eorledman Ecgfrith and I am charged with protecting this burgh in the absence of the king. Why should I speak with barbarians?"

Jarl Gunnstein had come behind us and Siggi translated for him. "Tell him because I have destroyed his gate and can walk in any time I like."

The Eorledman laughed, "You have not enough men and the ones you send would bleed as they tried to scale the ditch. We can rebuild a new gate. Can you make the dead come to life?"

Jarl Gunnstein smiled, "Tell him, perhaps." As Siggi translated he shouted, "Jarl, fetch the boys."

As soon as he saw them the Eorledman's face fell. He recognised them. Then his mask was replaced. All pride and arrogance had gone and I saw him pale with fear. "And what do you think I will do now?"

Siggi looked at Jarl Gunnstein who said, "Say this very clearly. If he wishes to have these two returned alive then he will give me five chests of coins to pay for the drekar's crew he has destroyed."

As Siggi translated I saw the Saxon lose his temper. He shook his fist and spittle flew from his mouth as he answered. "You will get nothing from me! You are pagans and you will burn in hell! We will join with King Louis to wipe you from the face of the earth."

"Is that your final answer?"

"It is!"

Jarl Gunnstein took his seax and, grabbing the youngest of the two boys, slit his throat. The Eorledman and his son both shouted, "No!" at the same time. The Saxon shield wall began shouting. They were angry and ready to fight us now.

## The Battle for a Home

"Tell him if they wish to come and fight us, we are going nowhere. We will happily wait for them."

When the Eorledman heard the words he turned and looked at his men. They were eager and they were ready. His face was filled with resignation when he turned back to us. He did not have the confidence in his own men to trust in a victory.

"If I agree how do I know that my son will be returned to me?"

"You have my word. I am Jarl Gunnstein Berserk Killer and I am never foresworn."

When Siggi translated his words the Eorledman nodded. "I agree. I will fetch the chests now."

I felt sad that the young Saxon had been slain. We lived in a cruel world. The Jarl had made an enemy of his son as well as Ecgfrith. I thought it sad that the Eorledman did not have the confidence in his men to fight us. His son would be alive and, who knows, he might have won. We would have taken the offer in a heartbeat. Now that I had a wife I knew that I would have children. I would ensure that nothing like this could ever happen to my son.

The other Saxon boy was shaking. I went to him. "You will not be harmed. Your father has paid the ransom."

He looked up at me. He was visibly shaken. "Why did the barbarian chief kill my brother?"

"He told your father what he would if your father did not agree to our terms. A man must keep his word. If he does not then the world loses meaning."

"Would he have killed me too?"

I looked him in the eyes and nodded, "He would not even have thought about it."

"But then he would have nothing."

"He would. He would have had vengeance for his daughter whom your father slew and his grandson who now lies in the sea. Remember this. Everything a man does in this life has consequences. It is like a stone thrown into a pond. The ripples keep going long after the stone has sunk to the bottom."

He seemed to see me for the first time. "Would you have killed my brother?"

I shook my head, "No for I would not have made the threat. I would have found another way to relieve your father of his gold." He nodded as though he could understand that. "What is your name?"

## The Battle for a Home

"Oslac."

"Oslac, son of Ecgfrith, today you have had your life spared. Now begins your life for you were dead and the Jarl chose to end the life of your brother. Do not waste that life for you now live the life you have and that your brother will never have."

"You are wise."

"No, I am just practical. I was a slave once and my life was saved by another Viking. One day Hrolf, son of Gerloc, will do something with his life. You, young Oslac, should do the same."

We stayed in Wessex for three more days after we had secured the treasure. Each day we raided small churches and isolated farms. We collected many animals. On one raid the rest had left the church we had found laden with candlesticks, candles, fine cloth and well-made goblets. I was walking around the church to see if anything had been missed. I was about to leave when a voice from somewhere, I think deep inside me reminded me of Aiden, Jarl Dragonheart's galdramenn. He always searched beneath their altars. Sometimes there were precious objects there. I kicked away the wooden altar and dropped to my knees. Sweeping away the dust I saw that there was a wider gap between the stones. I ran my seax around it. I levered up one end and found that I could lift it for it was only as wide as my two hands. I lifted the stone and saw that, beneath it, was a small chest. It was the size of one of my hands and I was disappointed. It could not hold much. It took it out although it was hard to do so. The box was well made. I opened it and saw that what lay within was the largest golden cross I had ever seen. It was as long as the box and as wide. The box looked to have been made for it. All the work had gone into the size for it was plain. Beneath it lay some bones. They would be the relics of a saint or one of their holy men. It would be worth money.

I stood and was about to leave when the voice came to my head again. I would give the cross to Mary. She was the only follower of the White Christ on our island. She would appreciate it. I took it out of the box and slipped it into my leather pouch. I felt guilty but Aiden had told me, as had Jarl Dragonheart, that the voices we hear in our heads are the spirits and we should obey them. I did not know it but the Norns were spinning once more. The taking of the golden cross was *wyrd*.

As a reward for my service, I was given a small chest of coins and Jarl Gunnstein allowed me to take the three horses back with me. Sven was not happy but I promised that I would make sure they were calm on the

## The Battle for a Home

journey back. We were overloaded. We had our share of the treasure as well as slaves and some of Jarl Gunnstein's crew. They were keen to join our clan and as they were not oathsworn there was no bad blood. We had lost no warriors and gained four. Our numbers were growing. Jarl Harald Fine Hair also promised to tell others who sought a home away from the far north of Raven Wing Island.

As we left the blackened shell that was Hamwic I hoped that this raid would not come back to haunt us. I suspected that Jar Gunnstein would feel the wrath of our enemies but I hoped that our small island would be ignored... I was wrong.

# The Battle for a Home

## Chapter 7

We barely made it home afloat. Someone had to be watching over us for the water was almost lapping over the sheerstrake. We made for my bay. The jetty there would ensure that we lost no slaves when they were landed. They were taken off first and Ulf Big Nose, with six warriors, escorted them home. I was given two small girls. Their mother had fallen between our drekar and the Dyflin drekar when we were loading in the river by Hamwic. She never surfaced. The rest of the crew thought that the two girls were bad luck. After the death of the Saxon boy, I felt that the Norns had given them to me to make a better life. I landed my chest with my share of the treasure. Jarl Gunnstein Berserk Killer had kept his word and given me a large part of his treasure too.

Sigurd went to fetch Gille and I took the horses from the ship. The stallion, jet black with a white blaze on his forehead, seemed reluctant to leave the ship. I was forced to sing to persuade him to leave. Gille was waiting by the time he was landed and he held him for me. The two mares were easier to manage and the three of us led the two girls, horses, treasure and mail, up the slope to my home. I turned as the drekar backed out of the bay. I saw the relief on Sven's face as she rode higher in the water. Our life on the island would go on. Sigurd chatted to Gille as we walked up the hill. The two slaves held hands and followed.

Mary came down to meet us, "Who are these?"

"They are slaves. Their mother died and the clan did not want them. I said we would give them a home. You could do with help around the hall could you not?"

She flashed a look of disbelief at me. "How callous! They have lost their mother and you think of them as goods to be used!"

I shook my head, "Did your father not have slaves too?"

"That is not the point! What are their names?"

I shrugged, "I know not. Ask them!"

"Men!" She put her arms around them and took them inside the hall. I looked at Sigurd, "Is your wife like this?"

## The Battle for a Home

He grinned, "All women are like this lord! I have had days of peace and now I will return to all the problems which happened while I was away. I will be blamed because the wind blew or did not blow. I will be blamed when the children misbehave. Such is life!" he held up his sword, "Thank you for the sword, helmet and coins, lord. My brother will be keen to join you next time! Enjoy the mail, Gille. It served me well."

After he had gone Gille said, "There is mail?"

"Aye. It may be too big but you will grow into it. One day you will go to war with me and you will need to be dressed properly!"

The new stallion began to become agitated. I looked at Gille. "I think that for tonight we will hobble him and put him in the enclosure. I do not think that he and Dream Strider will get on. Tomorrow we build him a separate stable."

Gille nodded, "The mares should be fine with him. Have you named them yet, lord?"

"Not yet. I think we will let Mary name the mares. It may make her less angry. Would you like to name the stallion?"

He nodded, eagerly, "I knew his name as soon as I saw him. He is Night Star. See how he is as black as night and yet he has a star on his head."

The stallion seemed to nod in agreement, "It is *wyrd*. Come let us feed and water them. The voyage was a hard one. Perhaps a night on the island may make him calmer."

It took some time to see to them and then I went in to speak with Dream Strider, "You are still my horse. Do not be jealous of Night Star. We need his blood to make your offspring stronger. Tomorrow I will ride you and Gille will ride Night Star. Then you will see he is no threat to you."

By the time I entered my hall, having washed, it was dark. The two captives were sitting in the corner, by the fire, eating. We only had three chairs. Gille and Mary were waiting for me at the table. Mary said, coldly, "You and Gille will need to make two more chairs tomorrow. They cannot squat like animals."

"They seem happy enough and when Gille and I were slaves we had to make do with the floor." I began to ladle food into my pot bowl. I was hungry. There had been so many people on the drekar that I had not eaten. I did not say that to Mary she would think I was ingratiating myself with her. "This is good."

She nodded, "I discovered their names." I looked up. "The younger is Eda and the elder Cwen."

I smiled, "Why do you smile? They are pretty names."

"They are but I think their mother named them in hope of a better future for she was a poor woman. Their clothes are ragged. They are thin and have not eaten well."

She looked at me quizzically, "What do you mean?"

"Their names; Eda means wealthy and Cwen means queen."

"I suppose the mother thought a fine name would make up for their poor background."

"I still think that they are fine names and they will have better clothes and more food here!"

I poured myself some ale, "They are slaves!"

"And just because they are slaves does not mean that they cannot be cared for. You care for your horses. Would you not lavish the same attention on human property too?"

She had a point and I nodded, "They may be trained to use the needle perhaps?"

"Perhaps but I will need to speak their language better."

"No, teach them ours that will be easier. We have few enough Saxons here. Better they forget their past and become Norse. They are both young and will soon pick it up."

Mary was showing just how maternal she could be. I left her and Gille to see to the slaves and went out to walk around my hall. I did not think there was danger but it was a good habit to get into. I stroked my new horses and stood with them for a while. I wanted them to get used to me. Nipper sniffed them suspiciously but he did not bark. I decided not to give Mary the golden cross yet. She would think I was trying to bribe her. I would keep it for a more appropriate time.

When I entered the hall it was in darkness. I made my way to my bed and Mary waited there for me. I could hear the heavy breathing from the other three which showed they were asleep. Mary kissed me and hugged me, "What was that for? I thought I was an evil man."

"Gille told me that Sigurd said no one else wanted the girls. They were unlucky. The others wanted them to be thrown overboard."

"They would not have done that."

"And yet Jarl Gunnstein Berserk Killer slit a young boy's throat. Vikings are cruel."

"Am I cruel?"

## The Battle for a Home

She nestled closer to me, "No you are not but then you are not a true Viking. You wear the mail and wield the sword but I know your heart and it is not a Viking. You are different. I am glad that I married you."

"Good for there was no one else likely to marry me."

We made up for the time spent apart.

The next day I was up early. "Come Gille we will ride the two stallions to the clan. There are still goods for us to bring back. Jarl Siggi was going to share out the rest this morning." We had taken a great deal from Hamwic. Those who had fled had known that the burgh was to be burned. They carried their goods with them. The rich had fled earlier but we still did well out of it.

It was when we mounted the horses that we could see the real difference. Dream Strider was a good three hands taller than Night Star. They appeared to behave themselves as we set off but I knew that would change when the mares came into season. We would have to be careful when that happened. Nipper raced ahead of us and I enjoyed being back in the saddle. We would have to add stiraps to the saddles we had brought back, but that was not a major task.

When we reached the settlement we arrived at the perfect moment. Jarl Siggi had begun to share out the goods we had brought. Only warriors who had been on the raid would benefit. There was a share for Sigurd which we would take back. Rurik came over to me as I dismounted, "Siggi did not share weapons with you, Hrolf. He said you had enough."

I nodded, "I do."

"He gave you more of the pots instead."

"And that will please Mary."

Rurik looked uncomfortable, "He was going to give you more slaves but the Eriksson brothers said you had two already. Everyone pointed out that no one wanted those two. But they were noisy about it."

I shrugged, "I care not. The two will be fine but I fear the two brothers are getting a little above themselves."

"That is what Ulf said. He hit Ketil and then left with his share."

I laughed, "Ulf is his own man. The brothers must be glad he refused to be Jarl. If he had done so then I think they would have been outlawed. He does not suffer fools gladly." I noticed that Rurik had a smile on his face. "You look happy. Did you get that which you wished for?"

He nodded and pointed to his hut. He had left the warrior hall the previous winter. I saw a young female slave there. She was seated at the door. "Jarl Siggi gave me the first choice of the females as I have no woman. I picked her. She has good hips and will bear me many children."

I laughed, "I am pleased. I did not like you being alone!"

The division was complete. Jarl Siggi came to me. "There is your share and Sigurd's. I am sorry there is not more. You deserved it."

"I have more than enough. Jarl Gunnstein gave me some of his share and besides I have the three horses and the mail."

Rurik said, "Ketil Eriksson complained about that too."

Siggi shook his head, "I told the young cockerel that they were given by Jarl Gunnstein and it was his raid."

"They are both good warriors. They are reckless but they are no cowards. I only have to see them on these visits. I will lose no sleep if they do not like me."

"Good. I plan to raid again in Skerpla. The new men who said they wished to join us might be here and the Franks will have gathered in their early harvest."

"Which Franks?"

"I thought to sail to the land south of the Issicauna. We have not raided there before. It is on the border which may mean they have good defences but there are many small villages. We could raid a number of smaller places. Our lack of warriors would not hurt us there."

"Good, for we would not need to be away for longer than seven nights and we would be close enough to our island. I like it. That gives me time to work on my land. We have new quarters to build for slaves and horses. We are growing."

He nodded, "And there is another family who wish to farm the north side of the island. They would live close to Hrolf the Horseman."

"Who is it?"

"Erik Green Eye. His wife is with child." Siggi looked troubled. I do not think it was just the Eriksson brothers. There was something else but I could not tell what it was.

Rurik said, "The Eriksson boys have caused trouble again. Knut One Eye's wife does not like Erik Green Eye's wife, Acca. Erik would have fought with Knut but he always has his brother to back him up. He thought this for the best."

"I am happy. I like Erik and he is a doughty warrior. It is *wyrd*."

I stayed just long enough to speak with Erik One Hand and Brigid and collect my goods. As I was leaving Erik Green Eye came over to me. "Jarl Siggi says you are happy for me to farm by you?"

## The Battle for a Home

"I do not farm and the Einarsson brothers both fish. I have no farmers close to me. It will be good. I hope your wife does not mind horses. I now have a herd."

"No, she is happy. And your wife, Mary, she will be happy?"

"She will be happy. I will have my men help you build your hall when you come."

He looked almost embarrassed, "We would come on the morrow unless you think that is too soon."

"No, I will send Gille with my two mares and they can pull the carts with your goods."

He looked relieved, "Thank you for this, hersir."

"We are all one clan! It is a pity that not everyone realises that."

When we arrived back Mary was delighted with the pots. They would mean we had spares. When I told her the news of Erik and his wife she was remarkably happy about it. "I liked Acca. It will be good to have a baby around here. Where will they build their hall?"

I swept my hand around. "They can have anywhere. If more come there may be a problem but we need someone to grow crops. This is *wyrd*."

She shook her head, "Just when I think I understand you then you come out with the word! Superstition!"

I smiled, "Like your White Christ who died and then walked again amongst men!"

Shaking her head she went off to organise her new goods. I laughed, "Come Gille. We have work to do."

We had the timber already and the new stable would be adjacent to Dream Strider's. By putting the mares between the two stallions we hoped that it would make for a calmer stable. By the end of the day, we had almost finished it, including the turf walls. All that we were left with was the task of adding a roof. We left that for the next day. Of course, I received scowls from Mary as I had not made the chairs for the slaves.

I had to work alone the next morning as Gille went to bring Erik and his wife. By the time they had arrived, I had finished the roof and one of the chairs. I just used a round from a large tree and four legs. There was no back but it would enable one of them to sit at the table. The second would not take long. Mary made a fuss of Acca as Gille and I walked with Erik to choose the site for his new home. He chose the place I would have chosen. It was in a dell with high ground to the east and west but to the north, he had the sea. Gille and I had already cleared most of the trees and the ones which remained would be used to build his home. We began immediately. By dark, we had eight timbers buried in the ground and two crosspieces over the ends.

We would have even more company that night as Acca and Erik shared our hall. Fortunately, I had managed to make the second chair in the afternoon while Gille and Erik were hewing logs. The two slaves had to sit on the floor again but I was, mercifully, not in trouble. After three days the house was finished. The turf walls were sturdy as was the turf roof. They had the goods they had brought from their home in the stad. Their new hall was bigger than the hut they had had. I saw Acca looking enviously at Mary's cooking pots, dishes, knives, and spoons.

The month passed quickly. This was always a busy time of year for us. There were many tasks which claimed our attention but it was healthy to be so busy. We were building a village. Erik seemed to complete us. We now had seven men to defend the bay as well as the four young boys. I had the animals to provide milk while the Einarsson brothers provided the fish. Until his first crops were harvested Erik hunted. Those were the good times. And then we readied ourselves for war. Skerpla was upon us.

By the time I left the two slaves could speak our language and they had begun to speak with me. They had seemed happy enough to chatter like magpies with Gille but had always been wary of me. Mary was happier too. When I said that Skutal and Gille would be coming to war there were no tears. I think the fact that there were others around her helped. She had changed from the frightened young hind who had fled to the cave.

The four of us walked to the ship. I used Rowan and Hazel to carry our gear. It had been Mary who had named my two mares after her favourite trees. Everyone who was Christian had a little of the pagan in them. Mary showed it by her love of nature and trees. I was happy for the names suited my two placid mares. Smaller than Gerðr and Freya they were sturdy animals and would serve my herd well.

When we reached the ship I saw that there were more warriors. A knarr had come from Dyflin with ten warriors who wished to join our clan. Four had families with them while the other six had slaves with them. They had all been on the Hamwic raid. They had told Jarl Siggi that there seemed more opportunity to live a better life close to the land of the Franks and to Wessex. The Hibernians were fierce fighters and had little in the way of treasure. I could see why they came. It meant we had three men on some of the oars. Skutal and Gille, as new rowers, joined

## The Battle for a Home

the new men at the bow. Siggi would move rowers around while we were at sea. As we stepped aboard I saw the pained look on his face. Something troubled him.

We set off just after noon. We did not have far to go. We would sail west around the headland and pass the two islands which lay off the finger of land the Franks called Cotelin. When we had sailed to the Issicauna we had seen that there were many villages along the coast and, more importantly, churches. As we had not raided there before Siggi hoped for complete surprise.

We had to row, as we headed north along the western coast of Cotelin. Siggi used a chant to help the new rowers and to make them part of our clan.

> ***Raven Wing Clan goes to war,***
> ***A song of death to all its foes***
> ***Through the waves the oathsworn come***
> ***Riding through white tipped foam***
> ***Feared by all, the raven's wing***
> ***Like a lark it does sing***
> ***A song of death to all its foes***
> ***The power of the raven grows and grows.***
> ***Through the waves the oathsworn come***
> ***Riding through white tipped foam***
> ***Feared by all, the raven's wing***
> ***Like a lark it does sing***
> ***A song of death to all its foes***
> ***The power of the raven grows and grows***
> ***The power of the raven grows and grows***
> ***The power of the raven grows and grows***

We had yet to honour Jarl Gunnar but when winter came and men sat around fires repairing mail and thinking of past battles then a song would be composed and when we raided again we would sing it and honour him and his hearth-weru. Until then we sang the old songs. When we turned to the steerboard, to head east along its northern coast, we were able to stop rowing and prepare for war. The wind came from the northwest and sped us along our way.

As we prepared some of the new men asked why we did not raid the places we had passed. There were many to be seen and they looked to have small palisades. Siggi was patient with them for they were new. "We may raid them on the way back if we find nothing where we are going but we listen for the bells which tell us of places of the White Christ. They bring riches. Where there are churches there are richer men. If there is no church then oft times they have nothing worth taking. We have slaves. What else do the poor have to offer warriors of the Raven Wing Clan?"

I did not know if we would be scouting and so I delayed putting on my armour. As this was Gille's first raid he was a little nervous. I saw that his hands were red raw from the oars and I smeared some of Aiden Galdramenn's salve upon them.

"Where do I fight, lord?"

He looked different in his mail. Slightly too big it made him look even younger than he actually was. His spear, sword and shield were well made but did he have the skill to use them? I had taught him but he had not fought before.

I adjusted the mail about his shoulders to make it sit better and I said, "There is no shame staying at the back. Position yourself at the rear behind me for I command one wing of the clan. If a Frank comes before you then keep your shield high and use your spear to keep him at bay. Look for weakness. Keep your feet well apart so that you do not fall. The first time you fight is the hardest. Watch others. See how Rurik One Ear and Arne Four Toes fight. They will be before you."

Skutal appeared. He had on his brother's helmet and carried his shield and the sword I had given him.

"You two stay together in the fighting. Protect each other."

"Aye lord."

I turned to Erik Green Eye, "Watch these two, Erik. They are from our home."

"I will hersir."

As we turned to head south we passed along the eastern coast of the Cotelin and the sun dipped below the horizon. The result was that night fell faster than normal. The winds which had taken us swiftly east now slowed as the land took away some of their force. We would not have to row again but we would be sedate as we headed south. We had ship's boys at the bows and at the masthead. Ulf Big Nose was there too. He would tell us both of danger and of churches.

# The Battle for a Home

One of the ship's boys, Siggi Far-Sighted, ran down the centre of the drekar, "Ulf says there are rocks off to the steerboard. He says to slow down and head away from them."

Sven signalled for the sails to be reefed. We needed to slow even more. Harald Fast Sailing hurried to the bow to speak with Ulf.

They were away some time and I began to wonder where we were heading. They came back and Ulf pointed to steerboard. "There is a church bell and I can smell wood smoke and incense."

Siggi smiled, "A church! Where away?"

Harald pointed due south. "There looks to be land to the south of us."

Sven put the steering board over a touch and we headed towards the church. Ulf was at the bows with the ship's boys and, by using hand signals we avoided the rocks. Soon we could all hear the bell. As Ulf had warned me of the smell I, too, detected the distinctive smell of burning incense. The priests of the White Christ used it in their ceremonies. It was a good sign for it was expensive. If they had coin to spend on such luxuries then it would be a rich church.

Rurik pointed to steerboard, "Look, the land is there. This must be an island."

Ulf Big Nose nodded, "They like to build the churches that contain their monks in such places. They think it makes them safe." He turned to me. "I do not think that the jarl will need us to scout."

I nodded. However, the fact that these were monks also meant I would not need my mail. I decided to leave it aboard the drekar. I could move faster without it. Sven steered to the east of the island so that we would be hidden from the land by the island itself. We found a small landing area just big enough for the drekar. Had we not had Ulf we might have ended up tearing the keel from beneath us. The island did not look to be large. From east to west it appeared to be no more than a thousand paces long. We could see the church. It was on a slightly higher piece of ground. Our sail had been reefed so that we were just making way. It meant we were as small a target as we could be and against the pitch black of an eastern sky, we would be invisible.

I went to the steerboard bow. I could see that it was low tide and there were rocks exposed to the right of us. Ulf was with me and he held up his hand. Sven turned the steering board so that we turned into the wind and we stopped. Ulf and I leapt into the water. There were flat rocks beneath our feet. We made our way carefully over the weed-covered rocks. When the tide came in the drekar could come closer. This suited us for the land proper was still more than two hundred paces from us. Ulf waved the rest of the clan forward and we found the safest route towards the land. I heard a splash as someone fell into the water. They would not hear such a noise on the island. The bells had ceased but I could hear the chants which drifted over on the breeze.

Ulf snorted when he heard the splash but to be fair to the unfortunate warrior we had no mail to worry about. Once we reached the sand we stopped and Ulf let his nose detect danger. If there were men watching then he would smell them. It was unlikely but Ulf was always careful. I peered ahead. The church and the buildings around it were just four hundred paces from us. There appeared to be neither ditch nor wall. They used the sea as their defence. It was a mistake. As the rest of our men reached us they split into the two halves.

Siggi said, "Ulf Big Nose, take your men and cut off an escape to the land. There may be a causeway and it is low tide."

He nodded and waving to his men, loped off.

Jarl Siggi turned to me, "Come Hrolf, let us see if our first raid alone can be successful." I saw him clutch at his Thor's hammer. I nodded and, gripping the horse around my neck, invoked the help of the gods. I hoped the Norn's prediction was true. I prayed that I would have a home on the mainland and I would lead Vikings who rode horses.

"I will lead Jarl."

He nodded and I saw the pain etched on his face again.

We spread out in a wide line and headed towards the unprotected monastery. It was obvious to me that was what it was. We had raided enough of them. It was a large one for there were many outbuildings. The fact that we had heard the tolling of the bell meant that they were at prayers. The smell of incense and the chanting confirmed that. It would make it easier for us. They would all be together in the church.

A dog barked as we passed through the small gate. It was to keep animals in rather than raiders out. I put my hand out and the dog came to sniff me. Satisfied it followed us. It was not a guard dog. Nipper would have had an intruder's fingers! We could now hear their chanting. The church was a large one. It looked like one of our halls save that it had a small tower and a bell. There was one door before us and I guessed that there would be a second at the far end. We did not hurry for Ulf Big Nose had further to go to get around the far side of the buildings.

I waited by the door. Pressing my ear to it I could hear the chants from within. It was a service. The Jarl drew his sword as we approached the door. He nodded to me and I opened it. It opened inwards. He walked in and I followed. The interior was lit by many candles. It looked beautiful with a soft glow which cast interesting shadows on the walls. The priest at the front had his head bowed and we walked a few steps into the church before he raised his head, saw us and shouted, "Norsemen!"

It was as though a stone had been lifted for the priests ran like disturbed woodlice. It was pointless. Our men stood in the doors and, as they ran behind their altar towards the far door Ulf Big Nose and his men appeared. One of the priests made the mistake of swinging an incense carrier at Ketil Eriksson. He was slain for his trouble. The ones with him fled back to their altar where they all cowered.

"Hrolf, you speak their words. Tell them they will not die if they behave."

I addressed the priest who had been at the front. I guessed he was a leader. "Jarl Siggi White Hair promises that if you do not try to run then you will live. If you try to escape then you will die."

"What do you want pagan? We are men of God and not violence."

I spread an arm and said, "Your riches of course and your Holy Books for they are worth money and, perhaps, some of your priests to sell as slaves. Men pay money for priests who can read. Others like men with soft hands!"

"You will all rot in hell for this!"

I shrugged, "We do not believe in your hell. Now tell your priests to sit on the floor!"

He turned and said, "Do as the barbarian says. God will punish him and the Count will come with his men and slay them."

I turned to Siggi. "He says there is a noble nearby. He might be on the mainland."

"Then you and Ulf can scout it out. Go now while it is still night." Raising his voice he shouted, "Search the church and the buildings. Take whatever we find back to the ship."

I turned to Gille, "The Jarl may need you to translate. Stay close by him."

"Aye, Lord."

I found Ulf. He was searching the dead monk. "He is a piss poor monk, He only has a wooden cross."

"The Jarl wants us to scout out the mainland. There may be warriors there."

## The Battle for a Home

"The tide is rising. We may get wet." We hurried out towards the far end of the island. I could see that there was a causeway. In the middle, it was already underwater. "Come, let us see how far we can get before we have to swim."

"But if we get across how will we get back?"

"I have no idea. One problem at a time eh?"

Once again we had slippery, weed-covered rocks to negotiate. Fortunately, this was a causeway and was not as bad for there were flat stones underfoot. We had six hundred paces to go but after a hundred paces the water rose first to our knees and then to our waists. I wondered if we would have to swim but then the land shelved. The level of the water dropped. We had time to spy out the land. There were fishing boats drawn up on the sandy beach and fishermen's huts close by. They did not present a danger. We scrambled up the beach and sheltered behind a boat.

Ulf was the expert but I had done this before. I scanned the land slowly allowing my eyes to become adjusted to the shadows and the shapes. I saw a large hump rising above the village. It looked man-made. I stopped scanning and peered at it. I could just make out a dark finger rising from it; a tower. This was a Frankish burgh. They did not name them thus but that was what they were. Ulf waved me forward and we slipped through the huts. I saw the sky becoming lighter in the east. Soon it would be dawn. By then we would either have to be back on the island or hidden from view.

Ulf used every piece of cover he could as we approached the high ground. Closer to it did not look man-made. It looked to be a rocky hill they had adapted as a citadel. They had built a tower and a wall on top of the natural contours of the land. There was no ditch. This was a refuge. Ulf nodded. He had seen enough and we hurried back to the causeway. The tide was racing in and we waded through the water. When we reached the deepest part we could no longer wade but had to swim. It was not far and we only had swords and helmets to worry us. When my feet found the stones I began to walk again. I saw the sky lighten to our right and we hurried to be hidden before we were seen. As soon as the fishermen woke then we would be seen for they would pass our drekar. The longer we remained hidden the better.

When we reached the church we saw the drekar being loaded. Jarl Siggi was readying himself for a rapid departure if our news was bad. He looked up from the chest he had just opened. "These are rich monks. This

# The Battle for a Home

is the third chest of coins we have found and there are six holy books. What did you find?"

"There is a causeway. Fishing boats are on the beach and there are huts further inland. This is a haugr with walls and a tower. I think that is what the priest meant. There is no ditch. The tide is coming in and we will be cut off soon. If the drekar were to land on the beach we would be within sight of the burgh."

Jarl Siggi nodded, "Get something to eat. The monks had food prepared. We will load the drekar and see what daylight brings. We may go across the causeway at low tide."

As Ulf and I went to the place the monks ate, drawn by the smell of food, I said, "It is a risk, Ulf. We may be cut off."

"The drekar can come to the beach. It all depends upon the force we face. We have more men now."

"But not all are mailed."

"These are Franks. They are like weak Saxons. I fear them not."

We joined the other men who were still eating. We finished off the food which the monks intended for themselves. It was filling and we washed it down with the wine we found close to their altar. There was not enough to get drunk but just enough to make me feel warm again after my dunking.

The Jarl came over to us as we ate, "Ulf Big Nose, your men can rest now while Hrolf and his men watch." He pointed to the candles and put a seax mark halfway down. "Change when the flame is there. I will be on the drekar."

I gave a wry smile, "Our rest will be all the more pleasant for we will anticipate it."

Ulf shrugged, "So long as I sleep, I care not!"

I gathered my men and divided them up. A third watched the priests. The rest were spread out and hidden to the west of the island. We would watch the land. I sat with Gille, Skutal and Erik. We sat near the edge of the causeway. The priests had planted fruit bushes there for it was sheltered from the north by the monastery and faced south. Beneath the fruit-laden branches, we were invisible.

Gille reached up and took a plum. He pulled it off and popped it in his mouth. He spat it out. Erik laughed, "You can tell it is not ripe yet. They begin to soften when they are ready to be plucked. Another moon and they will juicy."

"I know horses and not plums!"

## The Battle for a Home

"When we have tilled the land I will plant fruit trees. In our homes to the north, it was hard to grow such plants. Here it is easy. We are windswept and by the sea yet these plants prosper. It is just a shame that our island is so rocky. This would be a good land to farm."

Skutal nodded, "Aye and to fish. When I loaded the drekar I saw hundreds of them in the bay. It is sheltered here and slightly warmer. This too would be a good place for a fisherman."

"You could sail here."

"Aye, Gille, but the catch would not be as fresh when we landed it. Our fish is so fresh that it needs no cooking. We preserve it as soon as we land because want nothing to go to waste."

It was pleasant just sitting and talking. I determined to do more of this when we returned home. I would invite my men to join me for some beer and cheese. We would watch the sunset and make our world a better place in which to live.

"Lord, there is movement. The fishing boats are going to put to sea."

"I see them, Gille."

"They will see the drekar!"

"We are safe enough. The tide is in and they cannot cross the causeway yet. Jarl Siggi wishes to know the strength of the opposition. He is not afraid to fight but there is little point in fighting an army. There are other places to raid. We passed many villages on the way here. We can always go back at our leisure and raid as we go. We have already had much success. There were three chests of coins as well as the animals and holy books."

The ships disappeared behind the island. I knew that they would see the drekar and guessed that they would return. After a short time, they almost flew back to the beach and raced from their boats.

"See where they go. I am guessing the citadel but there may be another place close by."

They did, however, run to the citadel. I saw them wend their way up to it. There was no ditch but there was a path which would expose them to missiles from above. It reminded me a little of Bebbanburgh.

"Gille, go and find the Jarl and tell him that we are discovered. I think he might know already but it is our duty to keep him informed."

Without exposing himself Gille disappeared and ran towards the drekar. I saw five riders descend and make their way, with the fishermen, towards the beach. They were well mounted but only two wore mail. They both had simple helmets with no nasal and they both wore mail

## The Battle for a Home

byrnies. It looked to me as though they were split down the side. They had round shields which were smaller than ours. One rode before the others and I guessed he was the lord. The other mailed warrior carried a banner with green and yellow stripes. The other three had helmets but no mail. Their horses were more like Dream Strider than Night Star.

The noble pointed and one of his men rode north. He pointed again and a second went south. He was trying to find out the true threat of a solitary drekar. Jarl Siggi ghosted behind me. I pointed, "He has sent scouts to see if we have landed north or south of here."

"He is cautious and not reckless. That tells me much."

"It is almost time for your rest. Go, take your men and get some sleep. Wake Ulf. The tide will not turn for another couple of hours. We will wake you."

The men who had been in the monastery asked what we had seen. Arne Four Toes said, when we told him, "Then why do we sleep?"

"Because when the tide is right we can walk ashore and fight these Franks. The Jarl thinks that we are strong enough to defeat them and we can use the causeway and the beach to our advantage. Jarl Siggi White Hair is not a reckless warrior. He has fought in many battles and knows there is more to winning a battle than just having more men!"

Arne grinned, "Good! I did not want to miss out by sleeping through a battle!"

# Chapter 8

"Lord, it is time."

Gille's hand shook me from a deep sleep. I had been riding Dream Strider. It had been a good dream. I had also dreamed of something which I did not as yet understand. I saw a golden helmet. It was not mine for there was no face mask but it shone and there was gold upon it. I did not know what it meant. "Come, Gille, it is time for me to don my armour."

It did not take long to put on my mail byrnie. Like the Franks, it was split down the side to enable me to use it on a horse. So far I had only done that once. He handed me my sword belt and shield. I slipped the shield around my back and hung my helmet from my sword hilt. Gille gave me a spear.

"You and Skutal will be at the rear. I know you have a mail byrnie but you are not yet ready to trade blows with a Frank on a horse."

As we walked through the church I saw that the priests were no longer there. "Where are the monks?"

"Jarl Siggi put them on the *'Raven's Wing'*. He said we could not afford to have men watching them."

I nodded. It made sense. It was now just past noon. The sun was high in the sky. It would be hot work if we fought. As I approached our men I saw the enemy. They were drawn up on the beach. They had twenty horsemen and the rest were what the Saxons called, the fyrd. There looked to be a hundred or so of them. We would be outnumbered by three to one. I saw that the causeway still had water in the middle but it looked to be just waist deep and the tide was on its way out.

I walked to the front rank and joined Jarl Siggi White Hair and Ulf Big Nose. Siggi laughed, "They hope that we will be foolish enough to march over and fight them and then be cut off by the tide."

Ulf snorted, "And that is precisely what we will do is it not?"

## The Battle for a Home

Siggi nodded, "We will. I see nothing there to make me afraid. Sadly, Hrolf, we will not have enough room for the horses! We will have to eat them instead."

"I prefer eating them to riding them!" Ulf did not mean that. He was a fair rider and liked horses.

"Shall we go then? It seems a shame to keep them waiting."

Ulf said, "I can lead if you like or Hrolf. I know you are not well." This was unusual for Ulf Big Nose rarely made allowances for anyone.

Siggi shook his head, "The day I let someone else lead is the day I cease to be a warrior. Thank you, Ulf but I will lead." He turned and raised his sword, "Raven Wing Clan, we go to war. Keep your lines and listen for our words. No one gives orders but myself or my hersir! Knut One Eye that means you restrict your shouts to abuse to the enemy!"

"Aye Jarl!"

We began banging our shields and singing.

> ***A song of death to all its foes***
> ***The power of the raven grows and grows***
> ***The power of the raven grows and grows***
> ***The power of the raven grows and grows***
> ***A song of death to all its foes***
> ***The power of the raven grows and grows***
> ***The power of the raven grows and grows***
> ***The power of the raven grows and grows***

We kept a steady pace as we walked across the slippery, weed-covered rocks. We had to slow when we passed through the water which came up to our knees. The ones on the sides found themselves up to their waists but we kept our line.

As we left the water Siggi raised his sword, "Halt!"

There were still fifty paces before we reached the beach and another fifty before we would reach the horsemen. The causeway before us was slippery with uneven rocks covered in barnacles, limpets and weed.

Siggi shouted, "Archers, see how many you can hit!"

The ten men at the rear had no mail but they had, in addition to their swords, bows. A mere ten arrows does not sound much but if it was repeated then it was enough. In the first fall of arrows, two of the men without mail fell. A wall of shields came up. Of course, a shield can protect a man but it cannot protect a rider and a horse. When the arrows fell amongst the horses I saw that it caused agitation and riders pointed at us. A horse was struck by three arrows and it reared before galloping off. It dragged the rider by the stirap. It did not get far for it was mortally struck. The rider lay still. A rock on a beach can be as deadly as a sword or an axe.

That proved too much for some of the horsemen. They charged. When they did so it seemed to incense the rest and all of them charged. The noble was reluctant but he had to lead. They came, not in a straight line, or with any kind of order but in an angry mass. The sand slowed them but when they reached the rocks they found that the hooves of their horses had no purchase. They slid. Even some of the fyrd slipped and fell. The noble stopped and shouted something. A horn sounded.

"Now, Raven Wing! Now!"

We did not run but we marched purposefully towards the disorganized rabble before us. I saw Gunnstein Gunnarson finish off a Frank trapped beneath his flailing horse. The Franks hurried back to the beach. As soon as we reached the sand we began to move more quickly. The Franks tried to turn to give their horses the advantage. If they could jab and stab with the spears they might be able to organize a line behind them. We gave them no chance to do so. The centre of our line was composed of the most experienced warriors. I was next to the Jarl and Rurik was next to me. We had twenty mailed warriors who had fought together so many times we could tell with whom we fought by smell. We kept marching and, as the horses turned, as one we locked shields and jabbed forward with our spears. The leader's horse was speared by Jarl Siggi. My spear took him under his right arm and Ulf's pinioned his leg to his horse. We pushed and horse and rider crashed to the sand.

All down our line it was the same story. The eight horses and riders who faced us were slain. I saw the survivors trying to rally the foot. There were still far more of them than us. We also had to clamber over the dead horses and riders.

"Forward!"

We stepped together again. That would have been the moment to charge us but they were too busy trying to organize and we managed to step over the bodies and reform.

"Archers!"

The ten archers had moved forward with us and their arrows found flesh for the Franks were slow to raise their shields. Raising his sword, for his spear was still embedded in the dead horse, Jarl Siggi led us forward. The Franks had courage. They met us beard to beard but it was

# The Battle for a Home

boys against men. I punched my spear forward. The Frank I fought blocked it with his own shield but my strike was so hard that the edge of his shield rammed against his head and he stepped back. Before he could recover I punched with my shield and knocked him to the ground. As I stepped over him I skewered him to the beach.

A warrior hurled his spear at me as I stepped forward. I took the blow on my shield and he ran at me waving his sword. I lunged at his middle and he impaled himself upon my spear. The surviving horsemen had reformed and they charged. The six of us in the middle had cleared our lines. There were no warriors before us and the horsemen rode towards us.

"Lock shields and brace!"

The warriors behind us pushed their shields into our backs and we put our right legs behind us. With my shoulder leaning into the shield I held my spear above my shield. With a good helmet, I was safe from the Frankish thrusts. At worst I could lose an eye. Knut One Eye had proved you could be a good warrior with one eye. It was worth the risk. The Franks advancing walked into the points of our swords and spears. The warrior before me killed himself. He tried to move out of the way of my spear but the press of men behind was too great. I helped by pushing hard to make his end swift. I pulled back and thrust again. My second strike was blind for I could not see an enemy. When I felt something hard I pushed even more. I heard a cry and then there was no resistance.

Sometimes a battle turns on a single moment at other times the enemy simply loses the will to fight. This was one such battle. The mailed men in our centre had destroyed their best. Two horsemen remained and they galloped north for help. When they fled the ones who were left decided they had had enough and they ran for their citadel. We were victorious!

"Raven Wing! Raven Wing! Raven Wing!" We banged our shields and we chanted. We had not had enough and were ready to fight more but none were left.

"Ulf Big Nose, signal the drekar to close with the shore. Strip the dead and load it onto the drekar. Hrolf the Horseman, bring your men and we will ascend to the haugr!"

I looked around. Two of the new men had wounds but they did not look to be life-threatening. Erik Green Eye had a scar along his face. "Warriors of the horse! Come with me and let us see what glory we can achieve!"

They roared. Siggi looked at me, "Warriors of the horse?"

I shrugged, "It just came out!"

We moved in an informal wedge up the slope. I remembered the warriors wending their way up, "Keep your shields above you. We know not who awaits us!"

In truth, I was not worried. I could not see the Franks leaving men inside their citadel. They had thought that their horses would frighten and move us. They were wrong. Jarl Siggi walked ahead of us. He did not bother to raise his shield but he glared at the earth ramparts as though daring a Frank to try to hit him. We climbed and found the gate to the citadel open. Siggi paused and I took the opportunity to race ahead with Rurik and Arne beside me. The citadel had a large flat area. There was a tower and a warrior hall. There was nothing else. This was not a place where men lived. It was a refuge.

Suddenly four horsemen galloped towards us from behind the warrior hall. "Shields!"

I hurled my spear at the leading rider and then I drew my sword. Arne and Rurik had their spears on either side of me. My spear hit the leading horse in the chest. It gamely galloped for three strides and then it died. With its head tucked under it fell forward. The rider was thrown towards us. I had my sword held out and he fell onto Heart of Ice. He was dead in an instant. The other horses split and made their riders easy targets for Arne and Rurik whose spears plunged into the sides of the two riders. The last horseman was forced to rein in. There were dead horses and riders before him. A spear was hurled from behind me and hit him in the chest. The rider looked down at the spear which had pierced him. Then he looked up and fell sideways from his saddle. I looked around and saw my men congratulating Gille on his fine throw.

"Beorn Fast Feet and Karl Swift Foot, take four men and make sure there are no surprises ahead!"

"Aye hersir."

I turned, "Gille, Skutal and Erik, take the mail from these warriors and their weapons." I nodded to Giles, "Today you became a man, Gille! Well done!"

The Jarl and I headed towards the warrior hall while Karl and Beorn took their men up the tower. The warrior hall was more luxurious than ours. They had chambers leading off from the main hall. There were weapons lying around. Obviously, our sudden attack had taken them by surprise.

"Search beneath the floors for chests. Warriors like to hide their gold."

## The Battle for a Home

It was Erik Green Eye who found the hidden chest. It looked as though the warriors had all used the same chest to keep their treasure. It was not a huge chest but there was gold and silver as well as copper. We heard a cry and ran out. Karl Swift Foot stood on the top of the tower and was wiping his sword on a kyrtle. "There were men hiding here. They hide no longer." There were two bodies close by. Neither had a sword.

Jarl Siggi said, "I will leave you to clear this citadel. Bring the treasure to the beach and we will load it. We sleep on the island this night and feast on roast horse! When it is cleared then burn it."

It was easy to set fire to it. The wood was bone dry and they had a cooking fire. We used the brands and the straw from the stables to make an inferno.

We were all laden as we headed down to the beach. We had one horse which had not bolted and we used that to carry the mail and the weapons. Sadly it had hurt its leg and we would not be able to take it home. Rolf Arneson and Harald Haraldsson butchered the dead horses and we carried the meat to the beach as well.

When I arrived Jarl Siggi had one prisoner, a young boy of twelve summers. The rest of the fishermen and villagers had fled north with the horsemen and the fyrd. Ulf organized the food and Jarl Siggi said, "Question him. I would know what lies close by."

The boy was terrified and I smiled and put my hand on his shoulder, "If you answer my questions you will live. If I am happy with your answers then I will let you go. Do you understand?"

He nodded.

"What is your name?"

"Bertrand, son of Guillaume."

"Bertrand, where will the men on horses and the warriors go?"

He was terrified and I know he thought he was going to die. He was a Christian and without a priest to hear his last words he would go to hell. He talked. "They will go to Ćiriċeburh."

"Ćiriċeburh?"

"It is to the north of here and is on the coast. It has a wall." He dropped to his knees and grabbed my hand, "Do not kill me."

"I promised you that I will not. Are there any other fortified places?"

He shook his head. "We are safe here. No one bothers us."

I stroked his hair. The terror in his eyes showed he thought this was a precursor to his death. I smiled. "Go now. Find your people. We will not hurt you." I pointed to the lamed horse. "Take this horse. It will make the

## The Battle for a Home

journey easier. The horse will die anyway. Tell your people that we are coming. They can fight and die or accept us as their masters and live. Do you understand?"

"I do and thank you for my life, master."

He leapt onto the horse and kicked it in the flanks. It lumbered forward. I did not know how far this Ciriceburh was but I doubted the horse would reach it.

I turned to Siggi. "North of here, on the coast is Ciriceburh. It has a citadel. There is nothing else between here and there."

"What did you tell the boy? He looked almost happy."

"I said that if they fought us they died but if they accepted us as their rulers they would live. Did I do wrong?"

"No Hrolf and you have shown sense that a greybeard would envy." He put his arm around my shoulder. "I told you that you are a jarl. It is just that you do not know it."

"Did we lose many men?"

"Four, although one of them clings on to life. I know not why. He has been gutted. Valhalla is a better prospect."

I did not enjoy the feast. I have never been a fan of horsemeat. Skutal went along the shore and collected thirty or so oysters which we ate. "I do not know why they do not collect these, lord. There are hundreds. I have heard that you can farm them."

Erik Green Eye was intrigued, "Farm them? How?"

"You suspend a rope from something which floats and they cling on to them. When you pull them up you take the ones that are ready and leave the rest."

I was intrigued by the idea of farming the sea. "Could you do that in our bay?"

"I could try but the waters there move too quickly. Here. They are perfect. The causeway stops the water moving too quickly."

We loaded the drekar the next morning and set sail. The priests had begun to become a little loud and angry during the night watch. They made the mistake of annoying Ketil Eriksson and he slew two. It quietened the rest but Jarl Siggi was less than happy. He put his face in Ketil's, "That is coin you have killed. Next time cuff them and keep them quiet!"

I saw the resentment on the face of Ketil and his brother Knut. This would be remembered.

# The Battle for a Home

We rowed north and my part in the victory was noted by the chant. Gille and Skutal had not sung it before and I think that they were even more impressed than any.

*The horseman came through darkest night*
*He rode towards the dawning light*
*With fiery steed and thrusting spear*
*Hrolf the Horseman brought great fear*

*Slaughtering all he breached their line*
*Of warriors slain there were nine*
*Hrolf the Horseman with gleaming blade*
*Hrolf the Horseman all enemies slayed*

*With mighty axe Black Teeth stood*
*Angry and filled with hot blood*
*Hrolf the Horseman with gleaming blade*
*Hrolf the Horseman all enemies slayed*
*Ice cold Hrolf with Heart of Ice*
*Swung his arm and made it slice*
*Hrolf the Horseman with gleaming blade*
*Hrolf the Horseman all enemies slayed*

*In two strokes the Jarl was felled*
*Hrolf's sword nobly held*
*Hrolf the Horseman with gleaming blade*
*Hrolf the Horseman all enemies slayed*

We had to row until we caught a westerly and then we used the sail. The boy we had freed would not be close to this citadel. We would be arriving after dark and Siggi White Hair wanted them to wake with a drekar standing offshore. When the boy arrived with his news we hoped it would terrify them. As night fell we sailed silently along the coast. Ulf Big Nose was at the prow. Sven kept us as close to the coast as he could without risking the rocks.

Ulf joined us and said. "Anywhere along here you can anchor Sven. I smell wood smoke and I smell pigs. There is a large settlement nearby."

That was good enough for Sven and Siggi. We raised the sail and lowered the anchor. With the ship's boys to keep watch we all slept!

# The Battle for a Home

When I awoke it was still dark. I joined Ulf Big Nose and Sven the Helmsman at the steering board. They pointed to the land where we could see the Frankish citadel as an unnatural shadow. We were, perhaps, three quarters of a Roman mile too far east.

Ulf said, "We should wake the crew and row until we are closer. The effect will be greater."

I could see that Sven the Helmsman was vacillating. He did not want to take the decision and he said, "I will wake Siggi."

Siggi agreed with Ulf and we woke the crew even as the first grey appeared in the east. We kept the sail furled and rowed silently. The grey light meant that Sven could take us closer and we stopped rowing and lowered the anchor half a mile from the shore. Most of the crew ate or drank but I stood with Siggi and Ulf to examine the place. I could not see a river and there were no boats in the shallow bay. There was, however, a small hill fort. At least, in the grey light, there was something on a hill about a thousand paces inland.

"It does not look much bigger than that which we destroyed the day before yesterday."

Ulf shrugged, "It may be that a lord lives here. I do not think the Franks are lovers of the seas. Their boats are little more than knarr and they do not make ports where they can make berths and trade."

Siggi stroked his beard, "If we lived here I would make this a fine port. See there are stones there to the east and they could be used to make a breakwater. It is a larger version of your bay, Hrolf."

"It is and what do you intend Jarl?"

He waved a hand at the drekar. It was filled with monks. There were too many to sell. "We will see if we can use these monks for profit. We can sell them back to their own people. We can sail towards our island and raid other places along the way." He winced as pain raced through his body. He was not well. When it passed he said, "Your idea was a good one Hrolf. I think we come back here. This could become our cow that we milk when we need gold." He looked down the drekar. "They have eaten. My mind is made up. Sven, take us in."

"Aye Jarl."

We headed in to shore.

# The Battle for a Home

# Chapter 9

"Put on your war faces! We land!"

The men all cheered and donned their armour. By the time that was done and we were ready to row it was daylight. The burgh was awake. We could see the walls manned. There were huts and homes by the water and their occupants had fled to the safety of the walls.

As we rowed in Rurik asked, "We have warned them. Perhaps we should have gone in when it was dark."

"We can see now that the bay is benign but we did not know in the night. Besides, this is more terrifying for those within the walls. They see a dragon ship coming. The people who fled here from the haugr will have told them how we slew three times our numbers. Our measured, slow approach, will add to their fear. They will imagine us as more terrifying than we are. When we land they will see us as bigger and more powerful. It will put fear in the hearts of their warriors."

"Yet it is a hill fort. They cost men to take them."

I nodded, "But if this is like the one we burned there will be no ditch. They do not use archers and their shields are smaller. I think the Jarl is right. Why raid the burghs of Wessex when there is easier prey here?"

The Franks did not contest our landing. While the majority of our men formed up Jarl Siggi sent Skutal and the others without armour to search the huts. They found little enough although Sigtrygg Rolfsson found a small pot, buried in the earth inside a hut containing coins. The land below the low mound had been cleared. They had made a path but the fields on both sides had been tilled. We were able to approach the mound in three lines. At the front, we had the better warriors. We were the older ones and there were twelve of us led by Siggi. Behind us were the Eriksson brothers and the new warriors from Dyflin. The third rank was made up of the warriors who were new or had no mail. We were a flattened wedge.

We halted below the walls and Siggi looked up to assess the potential for an attack. The one on the haugr had had but one way in and one way

## The Battle for a Home

out. Did this one have the same? We could not see a ditch but the entrance was high up and the path to it twisted and turned so that the defenders could harass anyone attacking the gate. There was no space to use a ram. Siggi turned to me and said, "Send your man, Skutal, around the back to ascertain if it has another way out."

I did not turn but shouted, "Skutal Einarsson, run around the burgh and return to me! Tell me what you see!"

"Aye hersir!"

He appeared to my right and ran. He ran so that his shield was facing the burgh. They had a couple of archers for arrows were loosed at him. None got close. Most fell short and those that had the range fell well behind him.

Ulf Big Nose said, "Their archers are poor. Looking at the fall of arrows I think they are short hunting bows. Ours have a greater range." He jammed his spear into the ground and said, "I will be back!"

He left us. Anyone else might have been questioned, but not Ulf.

We studied the walls. They were lined with men. Not all were warriors. I counted just twenty helmets on the front wall. There was a banner flying from the gate. It had yellow and green stripes like that borne by the noble at the haugr. The sun was higher now and it shone on the spearheads of those on the walls. I noticed that they were like the ones the other Franks had used. They were broad-headed with a bar below the head. They were more like a boar spear and would be hard to throw. All of this was stored in my mind for, to a warrior, knowing your enemy's strengths and weaknesses was more than half the battle.

Skutal appeared and stood before the Jarl. He was panting. "They have a few men on the walls to the east, south and west, but most are here on this wall. There is no ditch and this is the only gate."

"You have done well. Return to your place."

Ulf returned and he handed me my bow. He had his too. I had given it to him as a gift. He looked at Jarl Siggi who pointed to the burgh. "There is but one entrance. What have you in mind, old friend?"

Ulf gestured to the walls with his bow. "The walls are two hundred paces from us and the fighting platform is thirty paces higher than we are. Their bows were used from a height and yet they reached barely one hundred paces. If Hrolf and I can loose a few arrows from here it might make them even warier. When we close with the walls we can use our own archers. I think we can hurt their leaders. They will be over the gate. What say you, Hrolf?"

# The Battle for a Home

I nodded, "It is worth wasting a few arrows and it will warm up my sword arm!"

I rammed my spear into the ground and took off my shield and helmet. I carefully selected an arrow. This was well within range but I wanted it to fly straight and true. There were two figures who stood out on the walls. One had a helmet with a plume and next to him was a standard-bearer. Ulf said, "You take the banner."

"Aye, whenever you are ready!"

We knew each other well and we pulled back as one. Our arrows soared high. Those on the wall expected them to fall short as their arrows had. The one with the plume had a shield. At the last moment, he tried to pull it before him. The arrow plunged into his right arm. The standard-bearer had no shield and a sudden gust of wind took his banner before his face. My arrow hit him in the chest and flung him and his standard from the walls. There was a cheer from our men. It was a symbolic moment for their banner had fallen. That could take the heart from the bravest of warriors. Ulf and I sent another arrow towards the walls but they had seen our skill and they sheltered under their shields. We wasted another four arrows and then laid down our bows and quivers.

Jarl Siggi said, "Now we will see how they stand! March!"

We stepped forward and Ulf roared, "If any step on our bows I will tear them a second mouth!"

We headed towards the walls. From their attempts on Skutal, we knew the range of their weapons and we did not need to raise our shields. When we were close enough for them to think about releasing Jarl Siggi shouted, "Shields!"

We brought our shields up to overlap. The rim of mine was just below my nose. An arrow could strike me and I was confident that it would find no flesh. The same could not be said for those within the walls.

"Archers! Loose!"

As a few Frankish arrows struck our shields our ten archers halted behind us and released. Our bows had a better range and our archers were quite safe where they were. As we stepped closer I saw at least four of our arrows find their mark. Two archers fell over the wooden walls. When we reached the entrance the Jarl shouted, "Halt!"

It was only wide enough for five warriors. We had to change our formation. "Front rank, move with me. The rest wait here until you are ordered forward."

# The Battle for a Home

The twelve of us moved, with our shields over our heads, onto the gravel path which rose to the gate. We had a roof over us and we began to walk. The only danger came from stones and spears from above. I knew, from the spears they used, that they would be useless if they threw them and so we endured a barrage of stones. Our locked shields meant that they could bear the weight but that was sorely tested when we turned the corner and a body, struck by an arrow landed on the top. It made us stop. Jarl Siggi said, "Tilt!" We lifted up one side and the body fell. The stones grew in intensity as we made our way up the incline towards the gate.

We had one short turn and then we were before the gate. Gunnar Stone Face and Harold Haroldsson stepped forward. We held a wall of shields above a space before the gate and the two of them slipped their shields over their backs. They began to hack at the gate with their axes. Siggi nodded to Ulf who roared, "Knut One Eye, bring the second rank!"

Suddenly we were showered as they poured boiling water from the walls. Our shields bore the brunt and the odd drop which struck flesh annoyed rather than hurt. The two men continued to hew at the wood. Rowing for many hours gave us all strength that those who lived on the land could only imagine. The two men would not tire. The Eriksson brothers brought their eighteen men to join us. We now had a force of thirty warriors. No matter who faced us I was confident in my brothers. Our clan was as one.

When a spear darted out from a gap in the gate we knew we were almost through. Ulf pulled the spear as it came through and was rewarded with a grunt as the warrior's head struck the gate.

Siggi said, "Ready! How goes it Gunnar?"

"One more blow each, Jarl and the bar will be almost through." He and Harold gave one last mighty blow and then stepped back. The five of us from the front rank brought our shields down and locked them together.

As stones were thrown down at us Siggi shouted, "Now!" The five of us hurled ourselves at the weakened gate. It creaked, cracked and then burst open. We cascaded into Frankish warriors who were surprised by our sudden entrance.

I jabbed my spear at a face. It struck the warrior's eye and, as he screamed his hands came up to grip my haft. When he fell backwards my spear was torn from my hands. I moved my shield up to block the blow from a spear as I drew Heart of Ice. I could not see the warrior for it was

# The Battle for a Home

from the side. I was slow and it hit the side of my helmet. My helmet had let me down. I had not seen his approach. I saw stars. Instinctively I swept my sword to the right and when it hit something I half-turned and saw the Frank. A spear keeps an enemy at bay but his thrust and my step had taken me inside his spear and it was now a piece of wood with a metal end. We were so close that I could not stab and so I used the guard to punch him in the face. I hit his nose so hard that it broke. I heard the crack. A broken nose makes your eyes stream. I shifted to the side and back and, pulling my sword behind me, rammed it up into his chin and skull. His helmet flew into the air. I used my shield to push the corpse from my blade.

"Push them away from the gate to allow our men in!"

Ulf Big Nose had something of the berserker in him. He roared and using his sword and shield at the same time, he hacked and punched his way into the Franks who stood before us. Arne Four Toes followed him. The warrior I had killed had left a gap and I stepped into it knowing that Rurik One Ear would be right behind me. The Franks were using spears. Four of them presented them like a hedgehog. I shouted, "Rurik, throw your spear!"

He hurled it from a range of fewer than three paces. The leading Frank had no time to react and the spear buried itself in his chest. Even as he fell I leapt into the gap between the other three spears. I sliced sideways at one throat as I punched with my shield at a warrior to my left. The fourth tried to punch me with his shield. It was of typical Frankish design; it was pointed and intended to be used offensively. The point stuck in my shield. I moved my left arm away exposing his side and I rammed my sword so hard that it came out of the other side. Rurik took a mighty swing and the head of the last warrior before us, fell. We now had a gap.

"Stand to one side!" The Jarl's voice was one we obeyed. Fresh warriors led by the Eriksson brothers burst into the fray. They were not tired and were armed with sharp weapons. They would bear the brunt of the next advance. As our archers rushed in I looked for Gille and Skutal. They both lived still and they followed on behind our reserve warriors. If the Norns had spun the right thread then they would live. If not I would see them in Valhalla for they had swords in their hands.

I saw that Erik Green Eye had a cut leg which Karl Swift Foot was binding. I knew that my face bled and most of the others who had assaulted the gate bore badges of honour. My mask had stopped me from

# The Battle for a Home

seeing my enemy and yet I had still been wounded. It was a sign. Gunnar had had his cheek sliced open by the spear which had jabbed through. His stone face was now carved like a rock.

Ulf pointed to the hall which lay on the far side of the citadel. A line of warriors stood before it. Our fresh warriors were slaying those who still stood between us. The skills of our men and our arms made us superior in every way. These were warriors who were used to fighting from the backs of horses. They could always ride away, rearm and return to the fight. You could not do that when you fought within walls.

I shouted, "They have their people in the hall. Those warriors are the only ones who stand between us and them. If we defeat these warriors then we will have won."

"Then we fight in a wedge."Jarl Siggi White Hair turned, "Archers form up behind our wedge."

We formed the smallest wedge we ever used. Siggi was the point and I was behind to his left next to Ulf. Rurik and Arne were behind me and Erik Green Eye behind Ulf. With four warriors behind them, we had Beorn Fast Feet and Karl Swift Foot as the two who would fill the gaps for any who fell. I picked up a Frankish spear. It was not as good as my own but it would do. I sheathed my sword but slipped my seax into my left hand.

Siggi shouted, "Clear a space! Raven Wing Clan!"

The twelve of us and the ten archers began our chant. It helped to keep us in step and gave each of us extra courage. I know not why this was but it worked every time. Perhaps it was like the priests of the White Christ singing their paeans.

***Raven Wing goes to war***
***Hear our voices hear them roar***
***A song of death to all its foes***
***The power of the raven grows and grows***
***The power of the raven grows and grows***
***The power of the raven grows and grows***
***Raven Wing goes to war***
***Hear our voices hear them roar***
***A song of death to all its foes***
***The power of the raven grows and grows***
***The power of the raven grows and grows***
***The power of the raven grows and grows***

# The Battle for a Home

### *The power of the raven grows and grows*

Our last line took us close to the Franks. They were in a single line. They had yet to feel the power of a Viking wedge. The small number of us must have looked pitifully few. Then the arrows fell and, as we closed to five paces, Jarl Siggi shouted, "Charge!"

The arrows made the Franks lift their shields and the three of us at the front of the wedge rammed our spears into the unprotected middles of the three Franks who faced us. We punched their bodies out of the way and stepped forward allowing the ones behind to do the same. When our last line was through Beorn and Karl used their spears to make a hole which was twelve men wide.

"Circle!" We turned our backs on each other to form a defensive circle and the Franks attacked. Our archers had an easier time now for there were backs facing them. Knut and Ketil led the rest of our warriors to fall on the backs of those who tried to get at us. As Ulf slew, the plumed leader the battle ended. Men threw down their weapons, dropped to their knees and shouted. I guessed it was for mercy. We usually ignored such pleas but we looked to Siggi when he shouted, "Let them, live. Take their weapons from them! Raven Wing Clan!"

We all banged our shields and took up the cry! We had won!

Jarl Siggi, bleeding from a wound to his arm said, "Hrolf, ask who is the headman."

The surviving warriors all stood when they realized they were not to be slaughtered. They were amazed, I had no doubt, to be alive yet. I went up to the one whose eyes met my gaze. He was not afraid of us. He had been the last to throw down his weapon. "Who is the leader here?" I already knew but needed confirmation. I spoke to the bloodied warrior with the dented helmet and plume.

"Brego there and you slew him."

"Then who speaks for your people?"

He looked around and said, "That would be me I am Baldred, the brother of Brego."

"Tell your people to come out of the hall. We will not harm them nor enslave them."

He laughed, "You think me a fool?"

I smiled, "There is no other way out of the hall. We broke down the gate to your citadel. Do you think that a small door would stop us? We have spared you but if you annoy us then you will die."

## The Battle for a Home

He nodded realising that we had the advantage. "This is Baldred! Open the door and come out. The Vikings have said that they will not harm you." He looked at me. "If this man is foresworn then he will not go to Valhalla."

I smiled, "You know our ways."

"I have sailed the oceans and spoken to such as you. What is your name, Viking? You fight well."

"I am Hrolf the Horseman."

He looked surprised, "A Viking horseman? I have never heard of such a thing."

"Perhaps I am the first." The door opened and an older woman flanked by three other women with grey hair stepped out. Their jaws jutted as though they dared us to harm them. These were the matriarchs of the Franks. "Come, you will not be harmed, I have given my word." As they came out I recognised the boy we had spared. I smiled at him. "Did the horse survive?"

"No, it died on the road."

"A shame but he saved you did he not? He will be in Valhalla."

Jarl Siggi said, "Tell them that we have spared them but they owe us. We will take tribute now and when we return at harvest time we will take more."

I nodded and told them. They looked surprised. Baldred said, "You keep your word? We will neither be slain nor enslaved?"

I shook my head. "This and your settlement by the island now serve us. We have priests with us. If the Bishop who lives close by wishes them returned then we would like a chest of coins. If we have not heard by midsummer's day then we will sell them in Dyflin."

"You are strange raiders."

"We are Raven Wing Clan and we live on the island by An Oriant."

While we had been talking Ulf had led some of our men into the hall. They came out with chests. There were three of them. Siggi said, "Take two and leave them one."

Ketil Eriksson asked, "Why leave them any?"

Siggi shook his head, "When you have a cow you do not milk her dry. We will return at harvest time and collect food. If it is not enough then we will take all of their treasure. This is a test. Hrolf, will they tell followers of the White Christ that we have their monks?"

I asked, "Who built the monastery?"

"King Louis."

## The Battle for a Home

"Then he will be keen to have his monks returned safely and their holy books." He nodded. "They will not be mistreated but he has until Midsummer Day to send the treasure to our island. There is a bay on the north of the island. He is to send it there."

"You have my word that we will do so." He smiled, "When you broke through our gate I thought my days were ending. The air smells sweeter now."

"Aye, it does, does it not?"

We loaded the drekar. I saw the disappointment on the faces of the monks when I told them the news. I believe they thought we would have died attacking their citadel. We had planned on another raid but with what we had taken from the two Frankish settlements there was no need. We headed for my bay. Unpredictable winds meant it took a night and half a day to do so. I spent long hours looking at my helmet. It was battered in two places. It still fitted but it would need repair. There had been a warning and I had to heed it. I needed a new helmet. Suddenly as the sun began to emerge from a low cloud and bathed the sea in a golden light I knew what I wanted. The sun was a sign and the Norns threads became clear to me.

We arrived home in the late afternoon. It was safer to unload the priests at the quay and march them south than try to land them in the sea. Skutal, Erik, Gille and I were pleased for it meant we were home sooner.

Rurik said, wryly, "Perhaps I should move here too!"

I laughed, "There is room aplenty but would your wife enjoy it here?"

Rurik's wife was a gossip and she enjoyed the company of lots of people. Our bay was quiet. "You are probably right!"

Jarl Siggi said he would send our share over to us and so the four of us left the drekar. Skutal's wife was relieved to see him. He had brought her treasures he had found himself on the battlefield. Some of the women had left fine kyrtles and dresses. He had taken one for his wife as had Erik Green Eye. I had not for I knew Mary. She was the daughter of a noble and something taken in a raid would not do.

"You did well, Gille."

"I did not take my sword out of my scabbard and I am not certain I hit anyone with my spear."

Erik Green Eye said, "You were there supporting the warriors in the front. Your spear might have prevented the Frank from wounding a warrior in the rank before you. It takes time to know how to fight on a battlefield. It is not like practice."

"Erik is right and when you were growing up you were not learning how to be a warrior. Erik and the others were."

"You were not."

"No, I was not but I was lucky. Jarl Dragonheart and his crew trained me. You can blame my lack of skill."

Shaking his head he said, "I will work as hard at being a warrior as being a horseman. You have but five of us who are your warriors. We are part of the raven Wing Clan but our horses mark us as different, lord. We have been drawn here for a purpose. We are chosen. Perhaps we will become your hearth-weru. If we do then we will need to fight as one. We should be the best that we can be."

Erik smiled and said, "He is right, lord. This is *wyrd*."

And so that day we became as one. Not yet a clan we were becoming a band of brothers much as Jarl Dragonheart had gathered around him. My dream was closer to becoming a reality.

# Chapter 10

The smell of baking bread greeted Gille and me as we entered my hall. The two slaves Eda and Cwen ran to us each carrying a horn of ale. Eda said, "Here is an ale for the warrior who is come home safe. Welcome master."

She beamed. I saw Mary smiling. She had obviously drilled them. "Thank you, Eda, that was beautifully said! I thank you and it is good to be home and see such beautiful ladies waiting on us eh Gille?"

"It was worth the journey, lord. Thank you Cwen!"

Mary came and kissed me as the two slaves hurried to the fire and the pot which was bubbling away. "That was well done. They practised for a whole day to get it right."

"It is good to be home." I held her tightly to me. I missed you."

"As you were sleeping on a drekar with the likes of Rurik One Ear and Ulf Big Nose I do not take that as a compliment!"

"Then tonight I shall show you just how much I did miss you."

She giggled, "My lord!" I emptied the horn. It was good ale. "Was it a good raid?"

"It was. You will be pleased to hear we neither enslaved nor slaughtered everyone. The Jarl has decided to be a sort of lord to the two villages. We slew Brego who ruled them before. His brother Baldred rules now."

She looked up, "I never knew Baldred but I knew Brego. He was the cousin of my father, Lothair."

"I am sorry. I did not know."

She shook her head, "I did not like him. He was a little too familiar when he came to visit."

"Familiar?"

She shivered and said, "It does not matter. Needless to say, I am not upset. This seems like a new turn of events. Are you changing your nature?"

# The Battle for a Home

"We are still Vikings but our numbers mean we cannot do what comes naturally to us. We have not the warriors yet. But I am happy with the Jarl's decision. We now have a possibility of a home on the mainland and that is my dream."

She hugged me, "And mine too! Come let us eat!"

"First I will wash. Come, Gille let us smell a little more like men and less like fish!"

I took a cloak and headed down to the sea. After I had bathed I dried myself with my cloak and, carrying my clothes, headed back to the hall. Gille followed. In the hall, Mary helped me to dress and Eda combed and oiled my hair. When the food was ladled out I was ready for it. Life was good.

Our share of treasure was sent the next day. It was brought by one of the new warriors. Einar Asbjornson. He was young, no more than twenty summers old. After he had delivered my share he hesitated, "Hersir, I am here to ask a favour."

"Ask for you have done me one already."

"I have a young wife, Morag. She is but thirteen summers old and she is fey. She finds the stad too busy and noisy." He hesitated, "Some of the women there, well they are not pleasant towards her. I would like to build a home here."

"You are welcome but it is quiet here."

"She would like that. She was a slave from the land of the Cymri. She does not have many of our words yet." He shrugged, "She was a slave and I bought her. She pleases me."

"Then you are more than welcome. Fetch her."

He almost ran off. I went to tell Mary. She seemed remarkably happy about it. "This is good, my husband. These new people are choosing to live here. That says much about you."

Shaking my head I said, "No it says much about those in the stad who like to gossip. I am pleased that we are small. I would not like us to grow too big."

"Husband if you wish to live on the mainland and have a horse herd then you will need many people. Think on that," she added, shrewdly.

Once again we were thrown into the maelstrom of building a home. It was however much easier for we now had more backs to share the load. The two slaves seemed almost happy to be helping and threw themselves into everything that was asked of them. Mary took to Morag

# The Battle for a Home

immediately. The girl was shy and clung to Einar like a limpet. Mary and Acca took an arm each and led her into my hall. I smiled. It was *wyrd*.

It took but two days to finish the house. It was further inland than Erik's and even more sheltered. I was not certain about the suitability of the land for farming; it seemed to have more rocks than soil but Einar wished to raise sheep and goats. The grazing was good. More importantly, they were happy with its position.

That night as I sat with Gille and Mary enjoying a fish stew I commented on that. "If he relies on just sheep and goats he will have to live off cheese and what they can forage."

"They are young and they will learn. I learned."

"Besides, lord, he can buy. I have coins already from one raid! Soon I will be rich!"

"Do not spend your coins yet. Sometimes we just bring back cereal or animals. Sometimes it is slaves. The treasure we found on the last two raids was exceptional!"

"But the holy men will be ransomed? There will be coins coming for them."

I nodded, "But do not spend that which we do not have. The ransom will be shared. The Jarl will take the largest portion for he led."

"You took the priests."

"We all did and they will be cared for. None were harmed nor will be. Jarl Siggi will set them to work while we wait for their ship. It is said the King of the Franks paid for the monastery."

"He is a pious man. I hope this does not bring down the wrath of God upon us all." Mary made the sign of the cross almost surreptitiously.

"We have been raiding monks and monasteries for years. I think we would have felt it already!"

Gille and I returned to the horses and their schooling. The two stallions did not seem to mind each other and that was a good thing. If there had been rivalry it would have surfaced before now. We worked from dawn until dusk with all of my horses. It was a joy to be with them. Not long before Midsummer Day Gille and I rode them to the stad. We had not been there since before the last raid and I had some business to conduct. I also wished to see my friends.

We were about to leave when Mary came out. "Here it is the tunic for the jarl it is finished." She held it up for me to see. The needlework was exquisite."

"He will love it!"

## The Battle for a Home

When I spied Rurik he was seated outside his hut with his wife and they were enjoying the sun. We reined up next to him. "It is good that you are here, Hrolf. You can hear my news. I am to be a father. My wife is with child."

His wife beamed, "I will fetch some ale."

"Do not stir yourself. This is cause for celebration. I will fetch a barrel from the alewife. Gille, take the horses and water them."

"I will come with you Hrolf." As we walked towards Brigid's ale house Rurik said. "I am seriously considering moving to your hall. The Eriksson boys are doing what they do best. They are causing trouble. I am certain that Hildegard is behind it. The Jarl does not see the way that Hildegard and Emma make the other women do what they wish. Beorn Fast Feet is no longer the warrior he once was. His wife has changed him too. Besides the Jarl is not in the best of health."

"You are more than welcome to come. There is room but Erik Green Eye has the best farmland. It would have to be pasture."

He nodded, "I will wait until the gold comes for the priests. If there is enough I will move. The land I farm is little enough but it does bring in a crop which keeps us through the winter."

We reached Brigid's and I noticed that two priests were working for her. Erik One Hand, her husband, said, "I will be sorry to see these priests go. They know their ale."

Rurik nodded, "He is right Hrolf. The beer was always good but they have made it even better."

"And I get no credit for that?"

Erik soothed his wife with honeyed words, "My love, we all know that it is your ale which is the nectar of the gods, but you must admit that they have been a help."

She nodded, "You are right. What can I do for you hersir?"

"I wish a small barrel of ale to celebrate Rurik's news."

"Aye, it is good. There are many women carrying young warriors now. The Gods are making up for the treachery of the Saxons of Hamwic."

Erik asked, "How is your stad now? It must be growing. Do you not resent having to share it with others?"

"No, for they are good people. We can live our own lives but we know there are others to help when we need them."

Erik swept his good hand around the village. "This is not the peaceful place it once was. Many blame Jarl Siggi but it is not his fault. He always lived alone and he still does. He rarely sees any save his slaves and

## The Battle for a Home

servants. It was Ulf Big Nose and yourself with whom he liked to talk. Since we returned from the raid he has spoken more with the chief priest. They spend their days talking to each other."

I paid for the ale, "Rurik I will join you shortly. I need to speak with Bagsecg."

"More mail?"

"No, I need a new helmet."

I strode over to the far corner of the settlement where I could hear the clanging of hammer on iron. Sparks flew as he beat out a sheet of metal. His wife Anya looked to be pregnant again. They had four children already. It seemed to me that as soon as one was born our blacksmith began work on his next one! He stopped work when he saw me. I had known him in Cyninges-tūn and we were old friends. When we spoke it was as though we had never left the Land of the Wolf.

"Hrolf the Horseman, it is good to see you! What is life like as a hersir?"

I smiled as I clasped his arm. It was like trying to grip an oak, "Remarkably easy. I just raise my horses and life is good!"

"See, I said we should move north!"

I looked at Bagsecg, "You too?"

"My wife does not like the gossip and intrigue here but this is where my work lies. I have many orders for weapons and mail. The raids have brought wealth and they spend it here."

"There is more to life than money!" She picked up their youngest and stormed back into the hut.

"I would move but..."

I understand. You would be more than welcome if you came."

"Thank you. I will think about that. Certainly, the water by the bay would make my life easier. My slaves spend half of the day fetching water. It is a steep path to the sea from here. Now, what did you want of me? I cannot think you came here to hear us complain!"

"I would have you make me a helmet."

"What is wrong with the one you have? Many warriors ask me to make them one just like it. The mask makes it an expensive one but they are still willing to pay."

"It is a good helmet but my vision is restricted." I handed it to him. "See here and here are where I was struck. I am not such a poor warrior that I cannot fend off a Frank or a Saxon but these blows were struck from outside my view."

# The Battle for a Home

"But it protects your head."

I nodded, "I have thought of that. If you make a conical helmet which is strong then you could put a band around the bottom and attach a piece of strong metal to cover my nose. I would still be able to see and my helmet would have the strength to protect my head."

He nodded. "And you would have the mail hanging down as you do now?"

I shook my head, "No for that makes the helmet sometimes slip. I would have a hood of mail which I can wear beneath. It would protect my neck and my throat. My byrnie is strong but it does not protect my neck."

Bagsecg took a piece of charcoal and went to a cut log. He sketched out the helmet upon it. "Like this?"

"Aye but here, on the piece of metal which goes down to protect my nose I would like it to go up and across."

"Like the crosses the priests of the White Christ wear?"

"Just so." I reached into my leather pouch and took out the large one I had taken in Wessex. I would have you use this. Gold is strong, is it not?"

"Aye it is but this would make your helmet valuable. This is a fine piece of gold. This would pay for a whole mail byrnie."

"It is already valuable for it might save my life!"

He laughed, "I will begin work now. It should be ready when the Jarl next raids."

"Thank you, Bagsecg Beornsson, and if you ever wish to come to my bay then you would be more than welcome."

When I reached Rurik he and Gille had broached the barrel and had a horn waiting for me. "Here's to a Viking son!"

"Aye! I hope he has two ears! It makes a helmet fit better!"

It was good to be with Rurik. He was an old and valued friend. We laughed and we joked as warriors do. Arne Four Toes wandered over and we offered him a horn of ale. After the second horn, he said, "I miss this. We just talk and enjoy life. The younger warriors drink too much and end up fighting. Perhaps I am getting old."

Rurik shook his head, "We were never belligerent when we drank. It is not our way. It is a sign of the times. Jarl Gunnar's hearth-weru would stop fights."

"Then, perhaps, as Jarl Siggi's oldest comrades we should do as they did."

# The Battle for a Home

Rurik said sadly, "There are but two of us. You, Hrolf, make fleeting visits and Ulf Big Nose is never here."

"You know it seems to me that our most peaceful time is when we raid. At least then we are all on the same side!"

It sounded so strange that we all laughed. Our laughter fetched Jarl Siggi from his hall. He was with Sven the Helmsman and Harold Fast Sailing. I noticed that he looked a little drawn and I remembered Rurik's words. "Good to see you, Hrolf."

"And you Jarl Siggi White Hair. Take a horn of ale. We celebrate Rurik becoming a father at last!"

They sat and toasted the mother to be. "This is *wyrd* Hrolf for we were going to visit with you."

"You are always welcome."

"Sven has been to see me. The drekar is getting old. We either need to replace her or repair her."

Sven said, "I would say replace her but I have only helped to build one drekar as has Harold. The Jarl is loath to use Bolli because of the disaster which befell Jarl Gunnar."

Jarl Siggi said, "We have spoken and think the best solution would be to build a shipyard in your bay. It is perfect. We can get the timber from Neustria. The bay is sheltered and we can reach the yard easier."

"If you seek my permission then you need not. I am happy."

"Good. We thought to build a knarr first. The techniques are the same but it will take less time. '**Raven's Wing**' will not need to be replaced until next year and the yard will enable Sven to make the necessary repairs."

"That is a good idea."

"Sven, Harold and the slaves would need a hall by the water."

"There is room. Skutal and Sigurd do not take up much space. So long as your work did not interfere with their fish traps then I do not think there would be a problem. They live on one side of the bay and the other side, beneath the farmhouse, is both flat and without buildings."

"Good." He smiled. "Your stad is growing, hersir."

Arne Four Toes nodded vigorously, "Aye, Rurik and I may join you soon."

Jarl Siggi frowned, "You would both leave here?"

Arne Four Toes looked at Jarl Siggi. "It is the young warriors and their wives Jarl. You do not see it but they cause disharmony in the stad. I would stay but my family..."

# The Battle for a Home

I nodded, eager to support my friend, "It is true, Jarl. Even the smith, Bagsecg Beornsson, is unhappy."

"Then I must leave my hall more often and begin to exercise my authority!"

Arne said, "If you need our help, Jarl..."

"If I need your help then we need a new Jarl. I should be able to control a few reckless warriors and the tongues of their wives."

"It is not the warriors we worry about but their wives!"

Gille collected the orders for Mary. She now had the monopoly on fine garments and the two slaves were becoming more skilled each day. Morag and Acca were also taking on some of the less demanding work. It allowed Mary to concentrate on the more difficult work which made her clothes special.

We gave the Jarl his tunic. His face lit up and he beamed, "Your wife has a skill which is a gift from the gods." He reached into his pouch for coins.

I shook my head, "No, old friend. This is a gift. You have already given much to me and it is time to repay that."

He nodded, "Thank you Hrolf." His voice was a little thick and he coughed. As he did so a speck of blood came out. He shook his head, "Too much ale last night!" It worried me.

As we headed back, in the late afternoon, Gille said, "We will soon be a little crowded on our side of the island hersir. What about the horses? They need room. When they foal they need quiet."

The thought had crossed my mind too, "I know but there is nothing we can do about it."

"We could build an enclosure further away from the huts. Perhaps we could build it behind the house of Einar Asbjornson. The grazing is good there and will not affect his animals." Gille was now able to think things through. He was no longer a slave. He was his own man.

"Good. We will do that."

Mary was remarkably philosophical about the new neighbours at the shipyard. The ones who were coming were not the ones she had fled. Sven's wife was a quiet mouse of a woman. The Gods had determined that she could not have children and so she just kept home for Sven. Her sister, Harold Fast Sailing's wife, was the opposite and she had four small children. She was too busy to be a gossip.

With all the men we now had it took just three days to help them build their hall. We were lucky we had slaves to help us but it was far bigger

## The Battle for a Home

than the ones we had built before. I realised that the store of timber would soon be gone and we would need to replace it from the mainland.

When I mentioned this Sven nodded, "Aye, I know. As soon as the ship from Frankia has brought the ransom I will ask the Jarl to let us take wood from the mainland."

Harold said, gloomily, "If they come."

"I think they will. Mary said that King Louis himself founded the monastery."

"Then I hope you are right."

After we had finished and I walked back to my hall I realised that we would have more people to protect if danger came. As I crossed the bridge I saw that if we deepened and widened the ditch as the Saxons had then we would be safer. That would require slaves. We had just the two girls. That had been enough. Now it was not. Before winter came I would need slaves and we would have to make my hall a haven.

When Sven and Harold sailed the drekar into our bay then our world changed forever. Now we would use my bay as the main point of departure. When the clan went to raid we would have many people waving goodbye. I knew that Mary had not thought of that. I would not mention it. She had been happy of late and I did not wish to spoil the mood.

Sven had enough wood to begin the keel. It would not have been enough for a drekar but a knarr was much shorter. He and Harold would take their time. So long as it was ready for the harvest time it did not matter. We would sail her to Ċiriċeburh and collect the tribute. Already Sigurd and Skutal had shown an interest in being her crew. As soon as their sons were old enough they would take over as fishermen.

# Chapter 11

Sigurd and Skutal had been at sea and it was they who raced into the bay with the news that a Frankish ship approached. "Gille, ride to the stad and take a mare with you. Bring back the Jarl."

"Aye lord," I noticed, as he rode away on Night Star that Gille was almost fully grown. His exercises and sword practice with Einar and Erik had made him broader. He would soon be able to fight in the shield wall. Mary disappeared along with the two slaves. Before she left she flashed me a look of irritation. I wondered what I had done wrong this time. Sometimes I thought I needed a galdramenn to understand my wife. At least that way I might know her thoughts!

I strapped on my sword. It was just one ship and I did not think it brought danger but it did not do to be careless. I walked down to the jetty. Skutal and Sigurd shooed their families up to the headland. "Go and see if you can see the ship better from yonder!"

"But father..."

"Just do it!"

They went, reluctantly. I noticed that Sigurd and Skutal had strapped on their swords too. I watched the ship as it tacked back and forth against the prevailing wind. I wondered if they would anchor or tie up to the quay. Their captain decided on the latter. I suspect it was the fact that there were just two of us although I saw Einar and Erik making their way to join me along with Harold Fast Sailing and Sven the Helmsman who had both left their yard. We had a reception committee of sorts.

I noticed that the ship had a healthy complement of warriors. All wore mail. Along the side were shields with red and white stripes. They were obviously the bodyguard of a lord. Sven and Harold were seamen and they caught the lines that were thrown and tied the tubby vessel to our quay.

I waited and eventually, four warriors stepped from the vessel. They had shields but their swords were not drawn. They formed a guard of honour for the noble who stepped from the ship. He was not a big warrior

## The Battle for a Home

but he had fine mail and a red and white plume on his helmet. It would mark him out in battle.

I stepped forward, "I am Hrolf the Horseman, hersir of this place."

I did not bow. I was a Viking and we bowed to no man, not even a king. I did not think this was the king. By his reputation Louis the Fat was a bigger man.

I saw him considering if he ought to speak with me. Then he said, "I am Hugh, Count of Tours and the representative of King Louis, the Holy Roman Emperor."

If he thought to impress me he was wrong. "I am the one who speaks your language. I will be the one with whom you will negotiate."

"Negotiate? We were told to bring a chest of coins."

"And that chest will determine how many of your priests you take back with you. If it is enough you have them all. I hope your king was generous. We have grown used to the monks. They make good slaves."

"Slaves? You have been working them?"

"Of course. We had to feed them and nothing is free."

I was deliberately provoking him. If I was to have a home on the mainland then I needed lords such as Hugh of Tours to fear me. Aquitaine was to the south of where I wished to live but the fact that he had been sent showed that he had influence in this land.

We turned as we heard hooves slithering down the shingle slope. It was Gille. He leapt from his horse. "Lord, the Jarl comes."

"How long?"

"They are walking."

I turned to the Frank, "Your priests are on their way. We can wait by my home if you wish. We have beer."

"Beer? Do I look like a peasant?"

I did not say what he looked like. I shrugged, "There is shade from the sun there but it is your choice. You can wait here if you wish. We are thirsty and we will ascend. Your monks are walking and it is five Roman miles. They may be some time."

I led my men as we walked back up the hill. Mary had put on her finest clothes. She looked at me with surprise when we reached her. "Why have you left the Franks at the shore?"

"I invited them up but they declined. Apparently, Hugo of Tours does not drink beer."

"Oh, Hrolf! You are so pig-headed."

# The Battle for a Home

"I was not going to force him to come. When it gets hot enough he will come, or not. I am not concerned either way." I waved my men to me, "Come we will have some ale at any rate!"

I had just poured a horn when Gille said, "Lord, the Franks are coming. They are bringing the chest." I saw that there were ten men with Hugo of Tours and they were walking up the shingle slope.

I avoided giving a smug smile to Mary. There was little point in pushing my luck. I said, "Gille, get Eda and Cwen to fetch eleven beakers for our guests. I suspect they will not use horns."

"Aye lord."

The chest looked large enough but I suppose it depended upon the coinage within. Mary curtsied when Hugo of Tours approached. "My lord, welcome to my home. I am sorry we only have beer but it is made of the finest ingredients."

He looked surprised, "You are of our people!"

"I am called Mary. I was the daughter of Lothair of Rheims. We lived in St. Nazarius. The Vikings took me."

"You are a slave?"

"I was but now I am the wife of the hersir."

He spoke quietly although it must have been obvious that I could overhear all that they said, "I can buy you back from this barbarian."

She flushed and said, "Thank you lord but I am happy with him. Perhaps I can make him more civilised."

They both looked at me. I saw that Hugo of Tours did not agree with my wife. When they tasted the beer I saw that the warriors quaffed it without a second thought. Hugo of Tours sniffed it and sipped it. His face became as sour as the taste in his mouth.

I was about to say something when Mary said, "My lord you sip wine but you drink deeply from beer. It tastes better."

He handed her back the half-drunk beer. "I am not thirsty." Turning to me he said, "How long will they be?"

"I told you they have five miles to walk. They will get here soon enough. I think they tire of working with their hands!"

Nipper began to bark. It was a sure sign of visitors.

"They come. Soon we will see how many of your priests you take home."

Jarl Siggi, looking as dignified as he could, sat astride Gerðr. She was a placid horse and not as big as Dream Strider. The monks marched behind and then our warriors, all armed, followed. When the white-

# The Battle for a Home

haired leader of the monks saw Hugo of Tours he dropped to his knees to give thanks. Ketil hit him on the side of the head and, picking him up unceremoniously, pushed him towards us.

"I thought you said you had treated them well."

"If you want them to sail before the tide turns then they have no time for prayers!" I was, however, annoyed with Ketil. It had been an unnecessary act. I would speak with him later.

Gille held Gerðr's reins as Jarl Siggi dismounted. He approached us, "This is Jarl Siggi White Hair of the Raven Wing Clan." I changed to Norse, "This is Hugo Count of Tours."

Siggi said, "Have you seen the coin yet?"

"I waited for you."

"Ask him to open it."

"The Jarl would like to see how much you value the monks."

Nodding to one of his men the Count stood back. The warrior opened the chest and it was filled with coins. Siggi went to it and put his hand deep within it. He pulled up a handful. The ones on the top were gold and silver coins. The ones at the bottom were copper. Siggi deliberately let the copper coins slip through his fingers. They landed on the shingle path and some rolled down the hill.

"Tell him this buys half of the monks."

I spoke loud enough for the monks to hear, "The Jarl says this is not enough. There is copper here. We can get more coins by selling them in Dyflin. You can have half of them. The rest will be sold." We had no intention of selling them. It was a long and unnecessary voyage but they would not have them cheaply.

The monks dropped to their knees and all began to pray once more.

"No! This is a great deal of money." The Count obviously took us for fools who did not know the value of a priest.

I shook my head, "It is not. You have seeded the copper coins with a few gold and silver. You think we are barbarians and that we are stupid. We are not. If you wish me to count out the money before you then I will do so and I will then tell you the value of a Frankish priest in the markets of Dyflin, or the kingdom of Cordoba!"

The last barb struck home. The Caliphate of Cordoba had made forays into Aquitaine. The Count shook his head, "No! That will not be necessary. Philippe, fetch the second chest."

The warrior ran down the slope. It was a mistake for it was slippery underfoot and he fell. Our men cheered and jeered. The Count coloured.

## The Battle for a Home

Mary said, to ease the tension. "Would you like some bread and cheese? Both are fresh?"

I think he agreed just to regain dignity. However, when he ate I saw his eyes widen. We made good bread and our cheese was the best I had ever eaten. It brought a smile to his face. "You should come back to civilisation with us. We can offer you a better life than this."

I turned. I had had enough of this, "Mary, daughter of Lothair, if you wish to return to the mainland with this man then do so. I give you permission." I spoke in Frankish. Gille understood and he looked ashen. I did not want the others to hear it they might be offended.

She took a breath and then held my hand, "No I will stay here with this man. He is a good man and I believe there is hope for him."

I smiled my thanks. The Count rolled his eyes and shook his head in disbelief. The warrior returned, huffing and puffing. He had a much smaller chest. The first one had been the length of a sword and the width of an arrow. This one was as long as a seax and half the width. The Count opened it and poured the golden contents onto the other chest. "Enough?"

I looked at Siggi and cocked my head to one side. Siggi nodded, "He can have all of the priests."

I turned and smiled, "They are yours to take!"

We escorted the Franks to their ship which they loaded quickly for the tide was receding. The Count said before he left, "I have learned much in this visit. I will remember your name, Hrolf the Horseman."

"Good for I will not hide from you, Frank! I am a Viking and I fear no man!"

We walked back up the hill. All of the men from the clan were there save for Ulf Big Nose and so the Jarl began to divide the coins. We brought out my table to enable us to do so. The Jarl's share was the largest and he filled the small chest with his share. The next largest were mine, Ulf's Sven's and Harold Fast Sailing. The rest was divided equally. Gille's eyes widened when he saw his share. Our warriors all had leather pouches and satchels and they filled them.

They were about to leave when I said, "Ketil Einarsson, there was no need to hurt the priest. His prayers could not hurt us and it almost meant we had no trade."

He squared up to me. "Who are you to tell me what I can and cannot do?"

I spoke quietly, "I am hersir and I decide what happens on my land."

# The Battle for a Home

"Your land? It is the clan's land!"

"I will not argue with you. You are in the wrong. You know it as does every warrior here."

Knut One Eye leapt forward, "I am a warrior! I am here and I say my brother is not wrong."

"I am sorry, I meant every warrior who has more sense than a flea!"

"You insult me. I will have satisfaction."

Jarl Siggi stepped between us. "The hersir is right and your brother was wrong."

Knut ignored the Jarl's words, "I have been insulted. Go get your helmet and we will fight here!"

I saw Mary start but Rurik restrained her. "Gille fetch my helmet and shield."

"Do not forget his mail."

"No, Arne Four Toes, I do not need mail to defeat a one-eyed wild man who has yet to grow up!"

I had insulted him. He wore mail and carried his war axe. He was flushed and I knew that he and his brother had been drinking.

Jarl Siggi said, "This is a serious thing, Knut One Eye. Are you certain you wish to do this?"

"I am certain! This cockerel has been getting above himself ever since Jarl Gunnar gave him the title. He and his high and mighty Frankish bitch think they are better than we are. He will learn the error of his ways."

Until then I was just going to teach him a lesson but he had insulted Mary. I donned my helmet. Soon I would have a new one. This one would do. I hefted my shield as the warriors formed a circle around us. The rules were clear. If you stepped from the circle then you forfeited. There was little room for manoeuvre. After touching my horse amulet and asking for the help of the gods I took out Heart of Ice.

Knut swung his axe easily from side to side. He was bigger than I was. I looked into his eyes and saw his plan. He intended to kill me. Honour only demanded disarmament or first blood but I could see in his eye that he would kill me or maim me. This was more than avenging an insult. The two of them had been looking for the opportunity and I had given it to them.

I saw that Acca and Morag were on either side of Mary. Our two young slaves were looking intrigued by what was about to happen. It would come as a surprise to them.

# The Battle for a Home

Knit made his intention clear as he lurched at me swinging his axe in a figure of eight. It stopped any attack I might make. I moved my feet quickly and sidestepped out of the way. His brother took it as a sign of weakness and he cheered. I would weaken Knut. I had no mail and I was fast. I twirled my sword in my hand. I did it to annoy him. It did. He suddenly swung sideways as he tried to catch me unawares.

I stepped out of the way and he cried out, "You are a girl! Stand and fight! Horse lover!"

I laughed for it was intended to insult me, "Do you have a problem seeing me Knut One Eye? Then keep your good eye on me for I will be as quicksilver!"

As he swung an overhand blow to my head I whipped my body around in a full circle and brought the flat of my sword into the middle of his back. I did not want to blunt my blade. I saw links sheared. It was a powerful blow and I heard his grunt of pain. Before he could react I swung in the opposite direction. His guard was down and my sword sliced across his middle. His baldric was sliced in two and I saw that I had torn some of his mail links.

He roared like some wild beast and raised his axe again. He held his shield before him I sliced my sword across his thigh as I spun away from the misdirected blow which embedded itself in the earth. I saw blood on my sword. He was wounded. The drink had dulled his senses and he felt it not. I stepped back. Ketil Eriksson was just behind me and he stuck out a foot. I tumbled to the ground. Knut saw his chance and roared in joy. I heard Mary scream. I watched the axe come towards me. Had I worn mail I am not sure I would have survived but I managed to roll out of the way. Instead of my flesh, Knut's axe hacked into his brother's foot. I saw bright blood spurt.

I stood and said, "Your brother is hurt. End this now!"

He shouted, "This ends when you die!"

He was furious now. He saw the blood on his axe and knew that it was his brother's. As he roared into me I used the trick I had seen the Hibernian champion do to Ulf Big Nose. I tucked myself into a ball as I rolled beneath his wide swing. Unencumbered by mail I sprang to my feet and slashed backwards with my sword. Heart of Ice bit into the back of his leg and severed the tendons behind his knee. His leg would not support him and he dropped to his knee. I stepped behind him and smashed my shield into the back of his head. He tumbled to the ground, unconscious.

# The Battle for a Home

There was a brief moment of silence and then Rurik and the majority of the clan all cheered. I had won. I said, "They need healers, "They are both fools but they have courage!"

Mary burst free from Acca and Morag and threw her arms around me. "I thought you were dead!" She said huskily into my ear.

"It will take more than a half-drunk reckless fool to kill me. Thank you for caring and thank you for rejecting the Count's offer."

She kissed me, "I will tell you more when they have all gone. I will go and prepare our meal. You will be hungry."

Jarl Siggi shouted for silence, "Let all men of the clan know that this was fair save for Ketil Eriksson's intervention. Hrolf the Horseman, do you wish Ketil Eriksson to be punished?"

I shook my head, "He was helping his brother and I forgive him. I am unhurt. Let us forget this."

The warriors, like Karl Swift Foot, who were in the Eriksson band, went to help their friends with bandages. Neither would be a complete warrior again. I saw pure hate from Hildegard and Seara, their wives. I had not made any friends there.

Jarl Siggi said, "We will return home now. Thank you for your hospitality, Hrolf the Horseman. This has been an unexpected result." He lowered his voice as he clasped my arm, "Perhaps this may curb the two cubs."

I shook my head, "I think not. I fear I have just created a division in the clan. I am sorry."

He shook his head. "You had to respond to the challenge and you handled yourself well. I would have killed him."

Rurik, Arne, and Beorn, all of them clasped my arm as they left and all said something to show that they supported me. I did not enjoy the moment and I should have.

When all had gone those who were my warriors surrounded me, "Hrolf! Hrolf! Hrolf!"

"Thank you for your good wishes but I take no pleasure in this victory."

Einar said, "I am new to this clan but that is why I will follow you, Hrolf the Horsemen. The gods have touched you. I can see that and it is an honour to be one of your warriors."

Mary insisted that all stay to eat with us. It was a fine feast. I saw the young boys of Skutal and Sigurd admiring my sword. They would be warriors. I could see that. Eda and Cwen served the food. They both

## The Battle for a Home

stopped on either side of me and kissed my cheek at the same time. Eda said, "We would have been sad if you had died."

Cwen said, "And our mistress did not tell us to say that, lord!"

It made me smile.

Later that night, as we cuddled together, Mary nestled into my neck. "Is that what you do when you fight?"

"Aye but I wear armour."

She sighed, "Then I am happy for you were never in any danger. You danced around that fool as though he was pinned to the ground. It is no wonder that you are so successful."

"One day I may meet someone who is better."

"Perhaps," I remembered her words after I had fought. "Before I fought you said you had news. What did you wish to tell me?"

She kissed me, "I am with child. You are to be a father!"

# Chapter 12

My life changed in that instant. I had grown up without a father. Gille had had his father taken from him too. We both knew how hard it was growing up like that. I now had a family to provide for. As I went about the business of the farm I found myself looking, increasingly critically, at our home. On the surface, we wanted for nothing but I saw that our good life was a veneer. The island was small and land for farming was limited. We needed space to grow. I looked at the wives and children of my men. Skutal and Sigurd's wives were always bearing children and even Morag showed signs of being with child. I looked north, to the mainland. We had seen somewhere that we could make our own. The rude, crude huts by the haugr could be developed into a good home. The Franks had already done the hard work of making a citadel. It would not take much to make it defensible.

For all my ideas and plans, however, we would be restricted until we had a knarr. I needed my own drekar too. I would not be making a new home any time soon but that did not stop me from planning. Jarl Siggi had planted the idea by giving me his blessing to leave. I had not done so. Now I might leave the clan. I had now made enemies at home. I kept my thoughts to myself. If I shared my dream it might evaporate like morning mist.

Ten days after the fight Sven and Harold brought the drekar into our bay. We had almost exhausted our supply of wood. We needed to hew timber and to let it season so that we could finish the knarr by harvest time. The Eriksson brothers were missing. I said nothing as we boarded the drekar. Jarl Siggi did not look like his normal happy self. He was even paler than he had been when last he had visited. The plan was to row directly north. We had tried to avoid taking from our neighbours, the men of Vannes, but that had not stopped them from assembling a fleet to attack us. Jarl Siggi decided that we would sail due north and land just ten miles from An Orient. There were huge forests there and we would be able to hew trees and have a short journey home.

# The Battle for a Home

As we rowed I saw that our crew was smaller than normal. Rurik explained, "The Eriksson brothers cannot walk yet. When you hamstrung Knut you stopped him from being a warrior. The two of them are now brewing ale in competition with Brigid. The ale is not as good but their supporters shun Brigid."

"Supporters?"

"A knarr, on the way to Olissipo called in and six warriors landed. They asked the Jarl if they could join the clan. They had weapons and were young. He allowed it. Those and some of the older crew, like Karl Swift Foot, welcomed them and they are a clan within a clan. They are the ones who are not here. They said that they did not hew trees. They were warriors. Words were said and they asked that Jarl Siggi either lead a raid or let another become jarl."

"So I have destroyed the clan."

Arne Four Toes had been listening, as had Ulf Big Nose. Arne said, "No, Hrolf, for Ketil and Knut were determined to try to defeat either you or Ulf. You were champions and by defeating you they could have a claim to be jarl."

"If they had tried me they would have more to worry about than a hamstrung leg and missing toes!" Ulf spat over the side.

Rurik said, "You were not there and Hrolf was."

"The Jarl is keen to build a knarr and then we can trade. He wants another drekar too."

"We barely have enough crew for this one!"

"He sees the rise of opposition. Siggi is a kind man. He is no Harald Black Teeth. He would be more like Jarl Dragonheart. He should make the Eriksson brothers outlaws. We should take them and their families to the mainland and abandon them there."

"But he will not."

"No, and each day they infect more and more. The stad is divided down the middle. I thank the Allfather that Bagsecg Beornsson is there. They will not take him on."

"No wonder the jarl looks older. We have more treasure than any jarl, save the Dragonheart and yet he looks unhappy."

"He needs a healer too. His slaves say he coughs much in the night. We have heard him."

Ulf shook his head, "We all grow old. My wound aches now when rain is coming and I cannot run as far as I did. You younger warriors will soon have to bear the burden we have carried."

# The Battle for a Home

"Burden?"

"Aye, Rurik, wisdom and experience. We pass it on to you. Neither Siggi nor I have children else we would have passed it on to them. It was our choice and no matter how much we might regret it there is little we can do about it now. You are our children."

It was a chilling thought. Not many years earlier I had been a lowly follower being cuffed by Ulf for doing things badly and now he was telling us that the clan's safety lay in our hands.

Sven took us into the small beach. Although we wore no mail we all had our weapons. While men hewed trees some of us would watch for enemies. Gille knew the land for he had been a slave here and it was Ulf, Gille, myself and Erik Long Hair who would scout out the land. As the others landed and prepared to chop down the tallest trees we headed into the forest. Ulf and I had our bows. If we saw game then we would hunt.

We had not travelled far, perhaps two thousand paces may be more when we heard noises. It was the sound of axes on trees. Ulf and I had done this before we waved Erik and Gille behind us as we readied an arrow and then made our way through the forest. The dark and gloomy tree-filled vista became a little lighter and we hunkered down in the undergrowth to peer into the lightness. Ulf and I bellied forward. We stopped just at the edge of the clearing. There were men from An Orient. They were also cutting down trees. I saw that they had a huge pile of timber ready. I worked out that this was to rebuild the ships we had burned. There were six guards and six hewers of timber. They had four horses that they were using to haul the timber to a pile which was covered by an old sail.

Ulf and I had scouted together so many times that we knew each other's thoughts. If we went back for the rest of the clan then we could save ourselves some work. We looked at each other and backed out. We were able to do so silently but Erik Long Hair was not as silent and he broke a branch. The guards heard the noise and ran towards us.

Ulf stood, "We fight! Draw your weapons!"

He and I loosed an arrow each. The two Franks who were just twenty paces from us fell each with an arrow embedded in his chest. I had a second arrow ready in my hand and I struck the third Frank. Two had run to the side and I heard the clash of steel as they tried to get at Gille and Erik. Gille had improved but he was fighting a veteran. I drew back my arm and sent an arrow into the side of the warrior's head. Leaving Erik to finish off his man I said, "Gille, get to the horses."

## The Battle for a Home

The tree fellers had their axes ready as we burst from the trees. I sent an arrow into the chest of the largest man. A second arrow whipped over my shoulder to take a second and the four who remained fled towards An Orient. Erik came over to us, "Sorry!"

"No matter. It was *wyrd*. Get to the Jarl and bring the men back here. We can take this timber and be gone before they are back from An Orient. Go!"

I turned to Gille, "Attach the traces of the horses to the largest logs and when our men come have them take them to our drekar."

"Aye, lord." The men took one of the horses. "Three are better than none."

Ulf said, "We should get down the trail and make some traps to give us early warning. Pick up an axe. Come." Taking two of the axes the tree fellers had been using we ran down the greenway which led to An Orient. It was as wide as a cart but it was not Roman. There was no ditch at the side. A thousand paces from the clearing there were some saplings. With trunks as thick as my leg, they were perfect. We began to chop them down. We felled them so that they lay across the greenway. The axes were sharp and we hewed six each. The greenway was blocked. They would be able to move them but it would take time. We then went into the forest on either side and hacked down the very thin trees the thickness of my arm. When they could not use the greenway they would try the forest. This would slow them down. Finally, we used our seaxes to cut thorny brambles and wild roses. We laid them in the gaps we could find.

Satisfied Ulf nodded and said, "Come let us see how the Jarl fares."

Siggi had seized our opportunity. By the time we had returned the pile of logs was much smaller. He was there with Rurik and Arne Four Toes. "Two more trips will see this back at the drekar. It has been cut and split. The Franks have saved us much work."

"They will be here soon Jarl Siggi. You two come with us and we will wait deeper in the forest. The Franks will have but eight miles to cover and they will be on horses. The men who fled had one horse. I am guessing that they will be back here before we have taken all of the wood."

"So long as it is in the water, ready to be towed then it matters not. You will need to give us warning Ulf and Hrolf."

"We can do Jarl Siggi. We need to use surprise." Ulf nodded his agreement. "Arne you guard Ulf's back and Rurik mine. We will use

## The Battle for a Home

these bows. I have twenty arrows. We should be able to discourage them."

Ulf growled, "And when I say fall back then move! I do not want your wife to be a widow Hrolf the Horseman!"

We settled down by the barricade of logs. We took opposite sides of the greenway and we waited. Gradually the silence that had been there when we arrived ended as birds and animals resumed their activity. We stayed as still as possible. Ulf and I found it easier than the other two. We had done this before. We were patient. I heard the sound of horses. They were in the distance. I glanced over to Ulf, thirty paces from me and he nodded. The four of us took shelter in the bushes and waited.

I had my bow half drawn and ready. Four arrows were in the earth by my feet. Rurik's sword and seax were drawn. I saw a flash of yellow and green as the Frank's horses pounded up to the barricade. One of them did not see it in time and as he pulled up his horse crashed into the branches throwing the rider into the middle of the tangle of trees. He screamed in pain.

"Find a way around!" The mailed leader with the green plume pointed his spear to the sides. I saw a pair of riders heading in our direction. I was forty paces from them and had a clear line of sight. They had no shields up and they were not mailed. My arrow hit one in the shoulder and knocked him to the ground. His companion turned to look for me and my second arrow hit him in the face.

There were shouts from the other side as Ulf did the same and the leader shouted, "Ambush!" I sent an arrow at the leader. He had just pulled up his shield and my arrow thudded into it. Ulf's arrow hit his horse which reared and threw him. There were shouts and cries from confused and wounded men as they sought their invisible foe. I peered into the forest. They had gone to ground and dismounted. They would now be creeping along to get us. That suited us for it bought more time for the Jarl to finish his work.

I saw a hand ahead of me as it tried to clear a path through the thorny bushes. It was a left hand and so I aimed a hand span to the left of it and loosed an arrow. I was rewarded with a cry and the hand disappeared. I watched as the plume rose and Ulf's arrow clanged into it. The helmet disappeared.

I heard the Frank shout, "Spread out. There are only two of them."

In spreading out and moving they exposed themselves. I loosed at any flesh I spied. I was not killing but I was wounding and that would slow them down. Suddenly there was a clash of steel to my left and Ulf shouted, "Run!"

I said, "Go Rurik and I will follow."

He nodded and ran. I was not being heroic by staying. They would hear us and know we were running. They would expose themselves. I had three arrows left. I used them well. Four men burst from cover thirty paces from me. I sent the three rapid arrows in their direction. Two fell and the other two took cover. I slipped my bow over my shoulders, turned and, drawing my sword, ran after Rurik. Our path was clear and we soon made the greenway. I saw the other three ahead of me. Ulf glanced behind him, "Go I am unhurt!"

I saw the forest lighten as we approached the clearing and then heard the sound of hooves behind me. Three of them had negotiated the barricade and were thundering towards me with lances eager for vengeance. I stepped from the greenway so that I had a tree behind me. I held my sword in two hands. An arrow flew down the greenway and stuck the leading warrior in the chest. One went left while the other came for me. I saw him raise his arm to stab down at me with his spear. Even at that moment, I was able to judge it to be a mistake. An underarm blow would have been better. I jinked to my right and, as he adjusted his strike, I stepped to my left and swung my sword two handed. The spear caught the side of my helmet as my sword hacked into his leg. It was stopped only by the saddle but the blow was so hard that the horse jerked around. With just one leg in the stirap, the rider was thrown from the saddle and his head crashed sickeningly into the tree.

"Run, Hrolf, run!"

I needed no further urging and I ran after my comrades. The clearing was empty and devoid of timber. We kept running. I could hear hooves behind us as more Franks negotiated the barricade. There was no greenway on this side of the forest. We were on hunters' trails. Horses could not move as fast. When I smelled the sea I knew we were close to safety. Jarl Siggi had half of the men fashioning a crude raft which Harold Fast Sailing had attached to the stern of the drekar. The other half of the clan had a shield wall ready. Gille stood with the three horses.

As we panted to a stop Ulf said, "They will be on us soon!"

"Then we face them here! Stand in the wall."

I shouted, "Gille, bring the horses to me."

I went to the gorse bush which was close by and hacked off three branches. When Gille arrived I took the traces of one and held them

# The Battle for a Home

while I lifted the leather harness over its hindquarters. I put the gorse underneath it and then released the traces and the harness. When I slapped the gorse it took off and galloped towards the advancing Franks. I handed some gorse to Gille. He did the same as I had. The two horses took off together. I quickly joined the shield wall. I heard a cry from the forest. The Franks had run into the wild horses.

"Jarl!"

"Back towards the sea. Do not show your backs to the Franks."

Eight horsemen burst out of the forest. They had spears and I saw that the plumed leader was with them. They charged toward us. Rolf Arneson had one of the woodmen's axes and he hurled it through the air. It spun end over end. Even as the Frank tried to move out of the way it embedded itself in his horse's neck. It fell into the path of a second. Erik Long Hair also had a woodman's axe and he stepped from the line and swung it two handed to smash into the skull of a second horse. I felt water beneath my feet. "Erik!" He nodded and ran back to join us.

Arrows were loosed from the drekar as the ship's boys threw ropes to help us clamber up the side.

"Lower the sail! Take to the oars!"

We watched as the Franks waved their impotent fists at us. It would not be a swift voyage home but it would be short and we would not be pursued. The Franks had done the work for us and we were joyful. We had had to spend less than half a day in the land of the Franks. We sang! Once again it was my song. I was proud to be in Raven Wing Clan among my brothers in arms.

> *The horseman came through darkest night*
> *He rode towards the dawning light*
> *With fiery steed and thrusting spear*
> *Hrolf the Horseman brought great fear*
>
> *Slaughtering all he breached their line*
> *Of warriors slain there were nine*
> *Hrolf the Horseman with gleaming blade*
> *Hrolf the Horseman all enemies slayed*
>
> *With mighty axe Black Teeth stood*
> *Angry and filled with hot blood*
> *Hrolf the Horseman with gleaming blade*

# The Battle for a Home

> *Hrolf the Horseman all enemies slayed*
> *Ice cold Hrolf with Heart of Ice*
> *Swung his arm and made it slice*
> *Hrolf the Horseman with gleaming blade*
> *Hrolf the Horseman all enemies slayed*
>
> *In two strokes the Jarl was felled*
> *Hrolf's sword nobly held*
> *Hrolf the Horseman with gleaming blade*
> *Hrolf the Horseman all enemies slayed*

The wind took us the last thousand paces into the bay. Sven swung us around so that we would have an easy job moving the timber we had towed. We used the oars to back us in a little closer to the beach. As we hauled it ashore I saw that we had more than enough to build the keel of a drekar as well as enough to finish off the knarr. Sven was pleased, "Much of it is seasoned and they have even split some for us. This, though, is the most beautiful sight." He tapped a mighty oak which was longer than the hull of *'Raven's Wing'*. "When this is seasoned we shall use it to make our new drekar."

Harold said, "We will need more men here to help us finish the knarr and then we can begin work on the drekar."

Arne said, "We will move here. I am eager to learn the art of shipbuilding. Besides, my wife might prefer it here."

"I will come too, Arne."

"Aye and me too."

"And me!"

Before we knew it half of the crew had decided to treble the size of my stad. Jarl Siggi asked, "Is this good, Hrolf? Will your wife object to so many people?"

"It is not the number of those around us it is the quality and these are good people. She will be happy and this is *wyrd*."

It took until early evening to haul all the logs up to the storage area above the high water line. The horses made it easier. The men who would return to live in the bay until the knarr was built left first. Jarl Siggi had to rest in my hall. His coughing was worse than it had been. I noticed that he coughed up blood.

"Jarl Siggi that is not good. You should see Brigid. She is a fair healer." This was one of the many times I wish we had Aiden or Kara from Cyninges-tūn. They were not only healers, they were witches and had great powers.

"I am old. This is nothing. When he spoke with me the priest of the White Christ told me that there is no cure for my illness. It is a punishment from the gods." He beckoned me to sit by him on the log. "You know that you are the son I never had do you not? I have watched you grow over the years and seen how men follow you. I would have been proud if I had a son who was half the warrior that you are. But I warn you to beware of the Erikssons. Neither is whole and you are being blamed. I do what I can but I am an old man. Beware."

"I will and I thank you. You are more than welcome to share my hall. Mary would enjoy it."

He laughed, "I am an old and cantankerous man. I do not need to worry about the feelings of slaves. I like my own company. I enjoy thinking of those with whom we sailed. Jarl Blue Scar asked me to sail with his son and to guide him. I fear I failed there. You are my second chance and the fact that so many wish to live here with you is a good thing. I am happy."

That night I told Mary all. She looked sad, "I feat that the Jarl has the coughing sickness for which there is no cure. My mother's father had it. He coughed more each day and we found him one morning, dead."

"Perhaps we should send for Aiden the galdramenn."

"There is no cure! The priests tried all that they could for he was a great lord and had fought alongside Emperor Charlemagne."

I was not convinced but I did not wish to argue with her. We spent the next day building huts for the clan who chose to live with us. When Brigid and Erik One Hand turned up, pulling a cart, I was surprised.

Brigid shook her head, "Since Hildegard began brewing beer it has become a war and I am with child again. It is not worth it. You do not mind if we live here?"

"Of course not. The men need their beer and Mary likes you." That would be the crucial factor. If Mary did not like them then I would not allow them to live here. I liked Karl Swift Foot but if he asked to live here I would say no. His wife had been one of Mary's tormentors.

Sven and Harold spent the first two days choosing the wood that they would use to finish the knarr. They were particularly pleased with the pine they had for the mast. It was more than long enough and would allow Sven to make a strong mast. We had a second which made a perfect yard. I spent some time with them because I was interested in the building of a vessel. When I saw them with furrowed brows I became worried myself.

"Is there a problem?"

"Not yet but there will be. We can make do with a stone anchor but they are not very strong. We need a metal one and Bagsecg is running out of iron."

The Land of the Wolf had abundant iron but here there was none. "When the knarr is finished we could sail it to the Sabrina. There are many iron mines there and they always need coin."

"We will need much for we will need two anchors for the drekar."

It was a relief to actually have the men working on the knarr. We swarmed over her like ants. We were strong men and most of the work required strength. Anything which needed skill was the province of Sven and Harold. They took a whole three days to make the steering board. While they did that we made it watertight with tarred wool. We had a spare sail we had taken from the Franks but we would need more. Time passed quickly and soon it was almost harvest time. The tar had had four days to set but Sven and Harold were still nervous as they launched it in the bay. We had yet to step the mast and this was merely to see if she floated and if there were weaknesses. Unlike a drekar, once the mast was up and in position it would not be taken down. A knarr was too small to carry spares. If she lost her mast... she was lost. Skutal and Sigurd acted as crew. They knew the waters of the bay better than any. Using two of the drekar's oars they sculled around the bay until they were all satisfied.

Rurik and the rest of the crew went with Sven to bring around our drekar while Harold, Sigurd and Skutal erected the mast and yard along with the sail. She was ready. Her first voyage would not be a long one and she would have a consort. Harold, Skutal and Sigurd would crew her with Einar Skutalsson and Einar Sigurdsson as ship's boys.

When **'Raven's Wing'** arrived she was crewed by fewer men than I had expected. Jarl Siggi was on board but he did not look healthy. Ulf Big Nose stormed ashore. Rurik and Arne helped the jarl onto the jetty.

"What ails him?"

"It is the coughing sickness. Only his slaves and Bagsecg and his wife had attended him. The rest kept clear. The majority of the clan said that they did not wish to travel. It was bad luck with the Jarl ill. When he died they would elect another jarl to take his place."

# The Battle for a Home

I could not believe it. They were willing to let the Jarl just die. "Take him to my hall. Mary will care for him. We should go back and teach those ingrates a lesson."

The Jarl stirred and shook his head, "No Hrolf. This is *wyrd*. My slaves are with me. I will not be a burden."

"Jarl Siggi this is not right."

He passed out again. His slaves carried his chest ashore. "Take it to my hall and take orders from my wife. She commands in my absence."

After they had gone I said, "Have we enough men to go to Ċiriċeburh?"

Ulf Big Nose said, "We have nothing to lose. Jarl Siggi gambled that by allowing them to keep some of their treasure we would benefit with a harvest. That gamble has not failed. If it does then we decide what we do." He turned to Sven, "You need to test the knarr do you not?"

He nodded, "Of course."

"Then this is as good a voyage as any. If we leave before dawn we can be back after dark. What say you? Shall we go on the morrow?"

I stood straighter, "We will and we will do this for the jarl."

I left the others to load the knarr and the drekar. I headed back to my hall. Mary came out and she looked pale, "He is close to death, husband. If he were of our faith I would have sent for the priest."

"Then keep his sword by him at all times. That is our priest!"

For once she did not argue. "And what shall I do about the slaves?"

I pointed to the abandoned farmhouse. Its roof and walls still stood. "Let them sleep there."

"But it is said to be haunted."

"They do not know that and besides there is nowhere else. We will have to build another hut."

She shook her head and laughed, "Once there were but three of us and now we are a village."

"I am sorry."

"No, this is meant to be and they are good people. Christ told us to share what we had. You may be pagans but I am a Christian still."

Just then Siggi Bagsecgson ran up, "Hersir, my father said could you bring your horses. He wishes to leave the stad but they will not let him. Ketil and Knut have him. He is a prisoner."

"Gille go and fetch Rurik, Arne and Ulf. Tell them there is trouble and we are needed. Young Siggi, go and ask my wife for some small beer for you. You have run hard."

"I would come back with you."

"No, your father sent you so that you would be safe. Did the other men know he sent you?"

Shaking his head he said, "I crept out. They did not see me. They were arguing when I left."

I went to the stables and began to saddle Dream Strider. When I had finished I saddled Night Star. The other three arrived with Gille. "Has Gille told you?"

"Aye, he has." Ulf had his shield and his sword. "Let us finish this."

"Do we not need more men?"

"We do not go to war. We go to make things right."

"Gille, stay here and look after my wife. Tell her we will have more guests before dark."

"I can come with you. I am a warrior and I can fight."

"I hope that the five of us can prevent a fight."

Ulf rode Night Star. Arne and Rurik rode bareback. I led the two new mares and Ulf the two ponies. It did not take long to reach the palisade. They had not left a watch and I could hear raised voices. Einar Bloodmark and Sven Guthrumsson were holding Bagsecg while Vermund Squint Eye hit him. His face was already a bloody mess. Anya, Bagsecg's wife, held her children about her. I saw their eldest son, Beorn Bagsecgson being restrained by Karl Swift Foot.

As soon as we entered they stopped and stared at us. Knut had a crutch as did Ketil. They both stood, "What brings you here to our stad?"

Ulf threw his leg over the front of Night Star's neck and landed easily on his feet. He strode over to Ketil and without warning brought his fist back to smash him in the middle of his face. He flew backwards and lay in a heap. "I should have done that years ago! This is not your village it is our village."

I had walked over to Karl Swift Foot. I did not need to say anything. He looked shamefaced, let go of the boy and backed away. I turned and led the youth towards the three who held his father.

Ulf said, "Who gave you pair the right to give orders?"

"The Jarl is gone! He will soon be dead. The clan have elected me Jarl."

Ulf burst out laughing, "A one-eyed hamstrung runt as a jarl? Have you lost leave of your senses?"

I had reached Vermund Squint Eye. His hand began to move towards his belt. "Draw that sword and I draw mine. When I draw Heart of Ice

# The Battle for a Home

there is always blood. Ask Knut One Eye. Do you wish it to be yours?" He backed away; I looked at the two who held Bagsecg. They released him and he fell. "Beorn, go to your father."

Ulf said, "Our blacksmith wishes to come to our hall. We will escort him there. Does anyone object?"

With Ketil still unconscious and four of them cowed by me, there was no support for Knut who tried to make the best of it. "Take him. We have more warriors coming from Dorestad. When their drekar gets here we will see who rules this island. Their leader, Guthrum the Skull, will destroy you and your lickspittles!"

Ulf laughed again, "If they are runts like you one good fart will blow them back to Frisia!"

"Rurik and Arne fetch the cart. The mares can pull it. Anya, you and your children ride the ponies. Beorn, put your father on Dream Strider."

"I can walk." His words came out slurred through his bloody mouth.

"I know but I say you shall ride." Ulf and I went to the smithy. The only things which Bagsecg would need would be his anvil and his tools. When the cart was brought the four of us managed to get it in the cart. We laid the tools around it. I saw my half-finished helmet. I knew it to be mine as it had a golden cross. I put that and the other half-finished items in the cart. We could not take the metal. We would have to get some more.

I could see that Knut was becoming increasingly angry at his impotence. I watched him as the horses began to pull the cart away. I walked over to him, "As far as I am concerned you are a nithing. Stay away from my stad. You are not welcome."

He laughed at me, "When my new men get here we will see who rules this island."

Ulf and I walked at the back of the family. He gave his horse to Anya. "We cannot take all the men to Frankia."

"I know. They will be up to mischief if we do. You will need to go for we must have someone who speaks Frank."

"Then let me just take the knarr. We do not go to fight anyway."

He nodded, "That makes sense. Take the best men."

"I will."

"And I pray that Sven and Harold have made a sound ship else it will be a short voyage."

# The Battle for a Home

When we reached my hall the women came to Anya and her children. They gave them comfort. The men looked at Bagsecg and his injuries. He was a tough man but they had given him a severe beating.

"One on one I would have had them! They are cowards. They hit my son and it distracted me. When I am well I will show them how I can fight!"

"Get well and decide where you want your smith. We have all the time in the world."

He suddenly saw his cart. "My iron! Where is my iron?"

"We will get you more. It seemed better to get you away from them first."

"What do you know of these Frisians?"

He told me and my heart chilled. We had more enemies now than we had before and fewer warriors to fight them.

# Chapter 13

We left Sigurd and Skutal at my home. I took Rurik, Erik, Arne and Gunnar Stone Face. For what we had to do this was more than enough. Surprisingly Sven and Harold were also both happy. It would give them the chance to tease the faults out of the drekar and we would have a large crew in case there were problems. The previous night I had sat, for most of it, with Mary at Siggi White Hair's bedside. He was awake, most of the time, and in pain. We talked. When we spoke it seemed to ease his pain. Mary showed a side I had not seen before. She was caring and she was patient. As we headed north I reflected that I had made some good decisions in my life but Mary was the best.

It felt strange to be on a knarr and not a drekar. We had named her after Jarl Dragonheart's daughter, '***Kara***'. She was a volva and we thought it would bring us good luck. I stood, at the bows of the tubby ship which seemed dangerously close to the waterline. We had two ship's boys and they were perched precariously on the yard. It was an easy motion and we sat on either side of the bows. There was no figurehead and we had a fine view of the coast ahead. Sven was testing our new ship and he put her over gradually to run parallel with the coast. The knarr could sail, almost into the wind but her speed was half that of the drekar.

"What did Bagsecg tell you of the Frisians?" Arne Four Toes was at the steering board with Sven and I stood with them.

"It was the day we were hewing wood. A strange drekar pulled into the bay and Vikings disembarked. They were old shipmates of Vermund Squint Eye. Knut and Ketil took them into the Jarl's hall as though it was theirs. They stayed until noon and then left. That was all that Bagsecg knew."

"But you have worked out the whole story?"

I nodded, "Aye Arne. They have made a bargain with them. They give them the island and they acknowledge Knut as Jarl."

"He has one eye and is hamstrung!"

## The Battle for a Home

"And he is a fool. They will take the island and then take over the stad. It is why I left most of the men with Ulf. I feared that if they left they might do harm to our families."

"Then the sooner we return home the better."

Sven and Harold had us shift the ballast about in the bottom and seemed happier with the trim of the vessel. She appeared sound and we had no need to bail. There were no leaks. She appeared responsive to the steering board and our shipwrights were happy.

"I am confident we can build a drekar now."

"Do we need to? We can barely crew the one we have."

Sven shook his head. He knew *'Raven's Wing'* better than any man. "She has suffered too much damage over the years. She is a fine vessel but she is old. Jarl Thorfinn Blue Scar sailed her before he gave her to his son. I would not take her through the dangerous waters off On Walum again."

I nodded, "And Bagsecg needs iron. We will have to sail to the Sabrina."

"Then we must take this vessel."

We sailed in silence for a while. It was not truly silent. There was the creak of the sail and the snap of the sheets. There was the splash of the waves on the bow but those noises seemed to be natural and faded out of hearing. A master sailor like Sven could feel the wind and adjust the steering board without even thinking about it.

It was Rurik who stated what was obvious to us all, "We cannot stay on our island with the Eriksson brothers and a shipload of Frisians. We have families. We are too few to sail and leave men to guard our homes."

"I agree but wherever we choose our home there will be danger."

"I fear Vikings. I do not fear Saxons or Franks."

"We could return to the Land of the Wolf."

I nodded, "We would be welcome and it is a land that I love. We would be safe. However, Bagsecg left there to make a name away from his father and I wish to have land where I can raise horses." I shrugged, "When we return I will ask the Jarl to hold a Thing. This is a decision for the clan."

"I fear we are a clan no longer. That which bound us is gone. When the Saxons slew the Jarl they tore the heart from our people."

We were in a sombre mood as we headed east towards Ciriceburh. Sven took in a reef or two for we were travelling quickly. As we neared the stronghold I smell burning. Ulf Big Nose would have smelled it many

# The Battle for a Home

miles since. I sprang to the steerboard side. I peered to the coast and saw a thin haze of buildings which had been burned and were now ash. I pointed, "It is Ćiriċeburh! It has been sacked!"

For us, this was a disaster. We had counted on the grain from their harvest. Now it looked as though no one was left alive. I saw dead warriors littered before the citadel. We had not brought mail but we had brought our shields, helmets and swords.

"Let us arm ourselves and go ashore. Sven, be ready to take us out quickly."

The knarr drew more water than a drekar and we landed chest-deep in the sea. Luckily we had no armour and we waded ashore. With swords drawn the five of us approached the beach. Who could have raided? The bodies we passed were the Franks. I saw that the citadel had been burned. There was little left of it. "Rurik and Arne, check the woods. Erik and Gunnar come with me and we will see if any live."

We ascended up the ramp to the burned gate. I found more bodies of dead Franks. As we made our way to the hall I saw that they had been outnumbered but fought to the end. I found Baldred by the warrior hall. He had been gutted like a fish. I could see they had done it after he had died. From the blood around him, he had taken many enemies with him. I felt sad. I could have worked with Baldred and now he was gone. There was no one left alive.

We headed back to the others. I saw that they had found people. There were not many. Rurik and Arne did not speak their language and the women and children who survived looked terrified. I smiled, "Erik go and fetch food from the knarr. These will need it."

"Aye hersir."

"What happened?"

It was an older woman who spoke. I remembered her from our first visit when her steely glare defied us. "The men of Vannes came! They pretended to come as friends with warnings of Viking raiders. Baldred did not believe them but the priests said these were Christians and were to be trusted. They killed our warriors and took our women and children as slaves. We few are all that remain. We fled to the woods. They took our crops and they took our animals. There will be no food to see us through the winter. We will starve."

I shook my head. "My men will bring you food now. If I can then I will return and bring you more food. Stay here. I am certain a lord will come to your aid. If not ... I may return."

## The Battle for a Home

The woman, who looked old enough to be my mother, gripped my and kissed it, "I know you are a pagan and a barbarian but you are our only hope. If you do not return then I fear you will find bones."

I nodded, "You follow the White Christ. Do not give up hope."

As we left I saw Bertrand, the boy I had spared. He had hidden in the woods when we had approached. He had learned to be wary of strangers; even those who had been kind to him. He waved as we left.

We boarded the knarr. I had offered hope to the Franks but there was an air of defeat on the knarr. We had counted on the wheat we would have taken as tribute. Even as we sailed east I began to plan how to feed my family and the other families. We needed bread and the few crops of oats we grew would not keep us through the winter. We needed a Thing.

The fact that we returned so quickly and sailed so high in the water told any who watched that we had failed. Sven the Helmsman smiled, "At least we know we made a good knarr."

"She is sound. Will you begin work on the drekar?"

"I will." Sven stared south. "Perhaps we could trade for wheat."

"That looks to be the only solution."

I left Sven and Harold to fend off questions from Skutal and Sigurd as I went with Rurik and Arne up to the hall. I saw, by the water, the rest of the men as they laboured to build Bagsecg's new home and smith by the water. There was just Gille and Einar by the hall. I waved to them and then went alone to speak with Jarl Siggi. The two slave girls were by his bed as was Mary. His eyes were closed.

"How is he?"

He opened his eyes and gave me a wan smile, "Ask me yourself. Your wife and these two little ones have the hands of a healer. I have not coughed for some time and I feel no pain."

Mary who was on the other side of him gave a slight shake of her head. I forced a smile, "Good then you shall soon be up and about and ready to lead us once more."

"Did they have the tribute ready?"

You did not lie to a dying man nor did you lie to an old friend. "The men were all dead. They were raided by the men of Vannes. The harvest was taken."

He closed his eyes, "I am a failure then. I had thought to leave a legacy for my people. I have never had children but I thought to be as a kind father who leaves his children hope when he has gone."

# The Battle for a Home

"You are not a failure." I took a deep breath. "Jarl Siggi, the Franks who are left in Ċiriċeburh look to us for help. That is your legacy. I would hold a Thing. I have it in my mind to move the clan to the haugr where first we raided."

He opened his eyes. "There is a monastery on the island. Would their King allow it?"

"We are Vikings still. I think we could hold the haugr even if assailed but I also think we could live in peace with our neighbours. It was what Jarl Gunnar and you tried here with the men of Vannes. Perhaps this time it will hold. Do I have your permission to speak with the men this night?"

"Aye, you have." He closed his eyes.

Mary said, "But you will need to send Gille for Ulf. He left for his home again. He was an angry man when he left."

"We thought to buy grain."

He nodded, although his eyes remained closed, "That is good. I cannot fight and I cannot even rise but I can use my gold. I give my gold to the clan. Use it to buy grain. I fear I shall never spend it more."

"I thank you for the clan. I will leave you now Jarl. Know that I will do all in my power to hold the clan together until you are well again."

"I know. It is *wyrd*."

Mary followed me out. "He is still dying. Morag knew of a distillation which stops pain. It does not cure. She used the nightshade."

"But that is a poison!"

"She gave a very mild dose but it appears to work. Beneath the furs he is bones. The slaves told me he has not been eating of late but he drank a great deal. That is another sign of the coughing sickness. The Jarl may not last more than three days."

I suddenly remembered the baby. "Will this harm our child?"

She smiled, "It is a good thing for Christ will bless us for our kindness. Our child is fine. This will pass and he will grow."

"He?"

"I know not for certain but in my dreams of late I only see a boy."

"But you are a Christian."

"And a Christian can dream too. Our priest told us a story from the Bible where a holy man dreamed for the King of Egypt. If it is in the Bible then it is good."

I nodded. There was still a little of the pagan in my wife. Once outside I shouted, "Gille, go and fetch Ulf. We must hold a Thing. Take a horse with you. And be careful. Watch out for the others. I fear they are our

## The Battle for a Home

enemies. Tell Ulf the Franks were destroyed by the men of Vannes. There is no grain."

Our men laboured until after dark and then made their weary way up the hill. I used the horn to summon those who were not at my hall. The space we used was the one before the old farmhouse, now the quarters for the slaves. Mary had used the Jarl's slaves to help her make bread. It used up more of our precious store of wheat and oats but the people needed feeding. Seara and Anya brought dried fish and the families ate while we spoke.

Gille and Ulf had not arrived. I felt that we had to begin. With the jarl unable to leave his bed it was my duty as Hersir to begin.

"Jarl Siggi is still too ill to leave his bed but he has given me permission to hold this Thing. The men of Vannes have destroyed the Frankish burgh. We have no grain." Murmurings began and so I stepped from the middle inviting someone else to speak.

Beorn Beornsson stepped forward, "We have granaries at the old stad. Why do we not go and fetch them?"

Bagsecg shook his head as he stepped forward, "We would have to fight for them and men would die. I am happy to die for the clan but who would feed my family if I died?"

Harold Fast Sailing looked at me and I nodded, "We could buy grain. We have gold and what good is gold if you are starving?"

"Jarl Siggi told me to spend his gold on grain."

That brought nods and smiles. The women looked relieved. They could not speak at a Thing but they could use their ears. Just then we heard the sound of hooves and we looked up to see Ulf and Gille. They dismounted and, dropping the reins came to join us.

I told them what we had just decided. Ulf nodded and stepped forward, "I have spent the night and the day thinking of our problem. There are not many of us left from the crew that first left Ljoðhús all those years ago. Jarl Siggi and I are the oldest of them. We were younger men when we left. We travelled to the Land of the Wolf and it was good. Jarl Gunnar sought greener grass and we found Raven Wing Island and this has been good. I thought to end my days here. I like my hall and my solitude and I like the company of the people here." He gave a rare smile, "When I choose to have company."

Men laughed for we all knew his ways. He was like the hedgehog. His prickles kept people away.

## The Battle for a Home

"However if I think of the clan and not myself then I know that the clan must leave this island. We have enemies whose hearts have become black. I do not trust those who live to the south of us and if Frisians come... well we all know how treacherous they can be." He turned to me, "Hrolf the Horseman here has had a dream. He dreams of a home in Frankia. He dreams of a home where Viking warriors ride horses. I thought it was foolish until we went to the haugr and then Ciriceburh. If the Norns have, as I believe they have, been spinning once more then the destruction of Ciriceburh by the men of Vannes is a sign. I believe that the clan should go there and begin a new life."

He stepped back.

Bagsecg stepped forward, "We have just moved here! We have fled from danger and you say we fly to an unknown danger."

Ulf said nothing and I said nothing.

Skutal Einarsson stepped forward, "You may be right, Bagsecg. My brother and I brought our families here from the other bay and we have been happy here. We have our fish traps. We can live alone and yet Hrolf the Horseman and others are here to protect us should we need it. But even though I say this and I am happy here I would go to the haugr. I have told my brother that it is a better place for us to fish. We could farm the sea there and there would be a greater bounty from Ran. I would go with the hersir."

Rurik stepped forward, "And I!"

Others joined him and then Sven the Helmsman said, "We have used his name overmuch but Hrolf the Horseman has been silent when men have spoken his thoughts. I would like to hear them."

I was aware of Mary watching me carefully as I stepped forward. Everyone was listening and time seemed to have stood still. I knew that this was a propitious moment. I thought back to that cave and the witch. I heard her words to Jarl Dragonheart as though I was back in the cave. *'You have saved this child and he has a line which stretches into the future. His family will be remembered long after you are dead, Jarl Dragonheart, but they will not know that they would have been nothing without the Viking slave who changed the world. Your time with him is coming to an end.'* I remembered my dream. None of this was my doing. I was following the thread the Norns had spun for me. It is said that if you break a Norn's thread then you end your life. I had no choice.

"When I served the Dragonheart I dreamed in a witch's cave. The dream showed me living not on an island but in a land where horses could run. I believe I have seen that land. Franks live there now. When Dragonheart went to the land of the Wolf there were Saxons there and the old people. Jarl Dragonheart lives amongst them. I would live in the land by the haugr. I would live in the land of the horse."

Silence followed my words and then, one by one the men nodded. The last to do so was Ulf Big Nose. "Then until Jarl Siggi is well Hrolf and I will lead the clan."

"Aye. And we will use Jarl Siggi's coin to buy wheat but we must also help Sven make the new drekar."

Bagsecg, who was no sailor, asked, "Why? What is wrong with *'Raven's Wing'*?"

"She is old and she is frail. I fear she had the worm. Hrolf is right we need a new drekar."

Bagsecg nodded, "Then I see that this is *wyrd*. We are meant to begin anew. I thought I had ceased changing but I see that is not so."

The Thing over men stood and spoke. I turned to Ulf. "Jarl Siggi has not got long to spend in this world."

"I know. I could smell death when last I spoke with him. It is why I left. I did not want to see my brother in arms rot away. He should have died in battle."

"We need you, Ulf Big Nose!"

"For a while, perhaps, but I am here for a purpose and that purpose is to see you lead this clan to a new life. When that is done I will return to my home on the island and end my days hunting."

"But the Frisians!"

He shook his head, "We have scouted together and you know my skill. When I can no longer hide from Frisians or the likes of the Erikssons then I deserve to die. Do not fear for me."

But I did fear for him. Siggi and Ulf were like two fathers who had shown me how to grow into a man. If Siggi died and Ulf stayed on the island I would be without a guide.

I did not go to trade. I gave that task to Gille. He could speak with the Franks and those who lived south of the Liger. Skutal and Sigurd crewed for Harold Fast Sailing and we gave them a small chest of coins. "Buy whatever grain you can. Buy as much as you can. Return quickly."

Gille had grown and he clasped my arm as warriors do, "I will not let the clan down, lord. I would live in the land of the Franks and ride behind your banner."

# The Battle for a Home

Ulf also stayed to help us build the drekar. The days of Haustmánuður were filled with the hammering and chopping of a whole clan trying to build its future on the water. *'Raven's Wing'* watched us from our mooring in the middle of the bay. I found it sad for we were replacing her. Siggi had begun to deteriorate even more and was now barely breathing. Ulf Big Nose kept looking at the drekar and one day he said. "When my old friend dies we should give him a funeral on the drekar. Send him to sea and burn the dragon ship with him. It would be fitting."

"Until we finish the new one that would be foolish."

"This is out of our hands, Hrolf the Horseman. The Norns have spun their threads."

Siggi did not die within the three days Mary had prophesied. He seemed to fight the sickness as hard as he had fought our enemies. He clung to life. By the time the knarr returned we had the keel finished and we were working on the strakes. It was a crucial time. All the hard work could be undone if we made a mistake. We stopped work as we unloaded the knarr. We would start the strakes the next day. The arrival of the wheat, oats and barley was a cause for celebration.

Harold told us that they had sailed to Olissipo rather than the Liger. "The Moors there made us welcome. We saw ships of war on the Liger and I thought it safer to sail further south. Our Frankish gold was well received there!"

"Then perhaps you could sail soon with Bagsecg to the land of the Cymri. We need iron."

"But the drekar!"

Sven said, "It needs labour that is all. We begin to fit the strakes on the morrow and tar the wool. It is a laborious part of the building. I will begin to carve the prow."

That interested us all. None of us had yet decided what the prow would be. "What will you carve, Sven?"

"I know not Harold. I have never carved one before but I was told, when I first went to sea, that the gods used your hands to make the prow which was right. I have a fine piece of oak and I have seven days. It will take that length of time for the hull to be finished."

"Then we will sail on the morning tide."

Sven worked away from us. Siggi woke that first morning as Sven carved and called for my wife. The slaves brought him down, on his bed, to the shelter we used by the beach. She said, "He woke bright-eyed. I have not seen him so before. He drank some honeyed ale. He says he will not die without seeing the new drekar and the prow."

None of us would argue with him and his slaves made him a bed beneath the shelter where he spent most of the day with his eyes closed but he would occasionally open them and watch Sven work. Mary was concerned and she stayed with us for a while. "He should be dead. He has had no food for seven days and it is only his skin which holds in the bones yet he lives and I saw life in his eyes."

"His spirit is strong. He was always a warrior who never flagged in battle. Perhaps the drekar will cure the coughing sickness."

She shook her head, "I have never heard of such a thing but so long as he lives then I am happy." She smiled and put my hand on the small bump. "I felt our son move this morning."

"I feel nothing."

She laughed, "That is because so long as he shares my body I am the one he pleases and not his father!"

She was happy and that was my only care too.

I joined in with the others as we applied the tarred wool. It was a messy job but not a job to be rushed for it kept the drekar watertight. The work on the masts and yards had to wait until Harold returned. The figurehead could not be rushed.

Two days after Siggi had joined us I noticed that the carving now had a sort of shape. It looked half-human. Sven saw me looking and smiled, "I worked without knowing what I carved. At first, I thought the dragon was Fáfnir. It looked human and then the more I carved the more I realised that my hands were carving Siggi. It is *wyrd*."

"And do we have a name for the drekar yet?" The name was as important as the prow.

"I thought Fáfnir for that was what I carved but I am not certain."

"We will wait until the drekar is ready. Siggi and Ulf need to be consulted too."

"Will Siggi still be with us?"

I looked over at him. He looked at peace. "He seems to be waiting for something. His sword never leaves his side. Perhaps it is the birth of the new drekar."

"Perhaps, it may be a birth or a death at any rate."

Our days were so long that we were almost too weary to eat. It meant we slept well. That night it proved too well. We were woken, in the

## The Battle for a Home

middle of the night, by Jarl Siggi White Hair's voice shouting, "The drekar! The drekar!"

I grabbed my sword and donned a kyrtle. I ran, barefoot down the shingle. I thought he meant our new drekar but he did not. He stood in the shallows waving his sword and continuing to shout his warning. I looked to the bay and there was not just one drekar, there were two. Men had boarded *'Raven's Wing'* and were taking her.

"Awake! Enemies! Raven Wing Clan, awake!"

Warriors poured from their huts. Skutal and Sigurd were the closest and I saw the two of them sending arrows at those on *'Raven's Wing'*. It was just a hundred paces from shore and tantalisingly close. When I reached the quay I could just make out Karl Swift Foot raising the sail. They were taking our drekar. I did not recognise the one steering but from his garb, he was a Frisian. Skutal sent an arrow very close to him and he ducked. The tide was high but on its way out. At high tide, the skeletons of the Frankish ships, sunk a year earlier, could not be seen but their masts were ready, like deadly daggers, to strike the unwary. As the helmsman ducked he took the drekar across the masts and we all heard the sound of timbers being torn. As the sail dropped the wind caught it and there was a crack and what sounded like a wail as the yard fell onto the bow. Those trying to steal it leapt into the water and began to swim to the Frisian drekar. Those on the shore all cheered. I did not. Our ship had died. Already she was settling.

Then I remembered Jarl Siggi. I turned and ran back to the place I had seen him shouting the warning. When I reached the place he was not there. I ran up the beach to his shelter and he lay there with his hands folded about his sword. Mary, Brigid, Ulf and Sven were with him.

"He is dead, husband. When the ship sank he fell back and life has left him. Jarl Siggi White Hair is no more."

I dropped to my knees and plunged my sword into the sand. I am a warrior and I have killed more men than I care to remember but that day I wept. I wept for a noble man and the true father of our clan. He had been waiting but it was for death. He died when his drekar did. *Wyrd.*

# Chapter 14

When the tide went out it left our drekar half submerged. The wrecks beneath stopped it from sinking to the bottom. When the next storm came it would break up the drekar but, until then, it remained a skeleton half out of the water. Ulf was the most upset I had ever seen. He sat by his friend and stared at the wrecked drekar. We dressed Siggi in his armour and his finest clothes. He only had one set.

Sven said, "You know we said that Siggi deserved a good burial. I think the Norns have given us one."

Ulf heard us, "What?"

I said, "You said he and the *'Raven's Wing'* should burn them together. The Norns have given us the chance to do this. That way his grave cannot be despoiled and we will mark his grave for all time."

Ulf stood. "He would like that! I will light the fire. It is the least I can do for my brother in arms. We will do this at high tide. The clan should say goodbye to him properly."

We dressed in our finest armour and clothes. I did not know it but that would be the last time I would wear my old helmet. It seemed fitting. I had fought at Siggi's side in that helmet and I should wear it when I bade farewell. Six of us carried his body down the slope to the waiting fishing boat. Ulf, Arne, Rurik, Erik One Hand, Beorn Beornsson and I carried our friend. He was no weight. The coughing sickness had taken his flesh leaving bones with transparent skin. Mary and Brigid had wept as they had dressed his emaciated body. The warriors of the clan followed and their families lined the path. We walked in silence. When we reached the fishing boat we laid the bier on one while we boarded a second. Erik Green Eye and Erik Long Hair would sail us to the wreck in fishing boats.

The dead Frankish ships had given *'Raven's Wing'* support along her length so that it was almost level. We climbed aboard and then lifted our friend and laid him beneath the mainmast. The only damage which was visible was the broken yard. A pool of blood showed where arrows had

# The Battle for a Home

hurt those who stole her. We laid kindling about the bier and then soaked the Jarl's body and the mast in seal oil.

Then Ulf sang Siggi's death song. We used it thereafter as a chant when we rowed. It inspired us.

> ***Siggi was the son of a warrior brave***
> ***Mothered by a Hibernian slave***
> ***In the Northern sun where life is short***
> ***His back was strong and his arm was taut***
> ***Siggi White Hair warrior true***
> ***Siggi White Hair warrior true***
> ***When the Danes they came to take his home***
> ***He bit the shield and spat white foam***
> ***With berserk fury he killed them dead***
> ***When their captain fell the others fled***
> ***Siggi White Hair warrior true***
> ***Siggi White Hair warrior true***
> ***After they had gone and he stood alone***
> ***He was a rock, a mighty stone***
> ***Alone and bloodied after the fight***
> ***His hair had changed from black to white***
> ***His name was made and his courage sung***
> ***Hair of white and a body young***
> ***Siggi White Hair warrior true***
> ***Siggi White Hair warrior true***
> ***Siggi White Hair warrior true***
> ***Siggi White Hair warrior true***

Then we bowed our heads and I used my flint to make a flame. It sparked and lit the brand which Ulf carried. We all lit from his and plunged them into the pyre. The flames leapt. All of us had our hair singed but we stood and each of us said farewell to our old comrade.

Ulf turned, "Let us go lest our old ship takes us too."

We boarded the fishing boats and we rowed back to shore. The flames completely covered the drekar. It was a fitting end for a ship of war. It was right that Siggi was alone with her. The last part to burn was the raven at the prow. The black smoke spiralled up to the skies like a bird ascending on the air currents and Ulf said, "Good. He has gone to the Otherworld. He is in Valhalla; see the raven takes his spirit there."

# The Battle for a Home

When the blackened skeleton sank beneath the waves, to lie beneath the waters of my bay, we headed back to my hall. Mary and the other women had left as soon as we had boarded the drekar. It was warriors who watched the drekar burn. The women had ale and food ready for us so that we could say goodbye to our old friend. We would drink! With horns filled we drank without stopping to send him on his way. Then we told stories of Siggi and how we would remember him. Unusually for a warrior, the women all had stories about him. Although unmarried he had always been a kind and gentle man around women and children. It explained the tears for they would miss him.

Ulf said, "I knew his father, Ragnvald. He was a powerful warrior and a great leader. He would have been jarl had his brother not murdered him."

"That must have angered Siggi."

Ulf nodded, "That was when he went berserk. It was his uncle he killed. Men said his hair went white because he went berserk but it was the death of his father and the killing of his uncle which did it. I think that was why he had no children. He told me if he had had a child he would have called him Ragnvald. I liked that name."

"You knew his father well then?"

He gave me a sad look, "I was Siggi's cousin. It was my father that he killed." He shrugged, "It was *wyrd*."

I was shocked at this revelation but it explained much. "But you fought alongside Siggi!"

"We had all sworn an oath to Ragnvald, even my father. Had Siggi not killed him then I would have done so. My father had no honour."

None of us had heard the story before. We sat there just taking in the bond that existed between the two cousins. "Who became Jarl then?"

"Thorfinn Blue Scar. He was the youngest brother. He was our uncle. That was when we swore an oath to protect his eldest son, Jarl Gunnar. Jarl Thorfinn Blue Scar gave Siggi and me the treasures of our fathers. He was a good man. He did not need to do that. He could have kept it all but he said it was blood money."

I looked at Ulf with new eyes. The older members of the crew did too. We had shared oars with these two men and yet not known any of this.

Erik Long Hair, who had known Siggi for a shorter time than the rest of us, asked, "What of his weapons, treasure and slaves? If he had no family then who gets them?"

## The Battle for a Home

Ulf and Sven pointed to me as Ulf said, "The weapons go to whoever needs them but the remainder of his treasure and his slaves go to Hrolf. He made that quite clear to both of us."

Brigid concurred, "Aye he told me, when I gave him his draught, that Hrolf the Horseman was the closest he had to a son."

Rurik said, "You are rich!"

I said, "I would rather be destitute so long as I could have my friend back. I shall miss him. I shared an oar with him for a long time."

Rurik nodded, "And I am no consolation am I? I tell you what, my friend; I will give you my good ear in which to speak. How say you?"

Everyone laughed and the mood changed to one of celebration. When it became too noisy Ulf took me to the headland. Neither of us was drunk. We knew how to control our drinking. Others did not. "We will need to do something about this new threat."

I nodded, "I had already thought on that but I would wait until the new drekar is in the water. I would like us to move to our new home before winter bites but we need to discourage Knut and his Frisians."

"You know that I will not be coming with you?"

"Aye."

"It will be for you to lead our people. I am grown too solitary. You are one of the few I enjoy speaking with. Siggi was the other."

I understood him but I did not agree with him. You could never win an argument with Ulf and I would not try. "We will miss you."

He waved a hand to the side, "Just remember all that Siggi and I taught you. You are a fair scout and a good warrior. It remains to be seen if you can become a good leader. Siggi thought so that was why he left you his treasure. A leader needs coin."

"I will and this night I will keep watch in case they come for more mischief."

"I will leave now. I will slip away. I do not like fuss. I will scout out their walls in case they are up to something. I will return tomorrow with my weapons and we can plan our attack."

"Be careful!"

He laughed, "You sound like Siggi. I will."

When the men had drunk too much they passed out. Erik Green Eye joined me as I sat in the tower we had built in my stockade. I peered south. "I can watch Erik."

"I know, hersir, but I did not drink too much and my family lives here. Do you think they will come?"

"I know not their minds for they are not as we are. They are devious and they are lazy. I would come but I know not if they will. Ulf is watching out there. I take comfort from the fact that I have heard nothing. As soon as the drekar is seaworthy and our knarr is back I intend to attack our foes. They outnumber us but this is our island and we know it. And we have a secret weapon."

"Secret weapon?"

"Aye, horses. The Frisians will not expect that."

No one came and dawn brought bleary eyes and thick heads. Sven soon had everyone working on the drekar. It was the best cure for too much ale. I told them all, as we worked, that when she was afloat we would begin to move to the haugr.

Sven was still carving the prow and it was looking more like Siggi as a dragon every day. "We cannot take everyone on one journey."

"I know. We take Bagsecg, the women and children and half of the warriors on the first trip. They can begin to make the haugr defensible. Then we take the horses and the rest on the second voyage."

"And if Knut One Eye tries to stop us?"

"Then I will deal with him." It was my closest friends who were working with me that day. "Ulf is staying here."

"He will not come?"

"No Rurik. Siggi's death took the heart from him. We will visit him but I could not persuade him to join us. His mind is made up."

"Our world is changing."

"It is."

Ulf arrived in the late afternoon. He seemed surprised that anyone had been worried about him. "They were busy getting drunk last night. I could have slit the throats of both crews and none would have been the wiser!"

Now that we were moving home Bagsecg did not bother to set up his smithy. He used his prodigious strength to help build the ship. One job he did finish, however, was to complete my helmet. Two nights after we had resumed work on the new drekar he came to me with a sheepskin. He opened it and said, "There is your new helmet and mail."

I was eager to try it on. I slipped the mail hood on. It fitted tightly to my head. He had made it so that it covered my chin and came to just below my mouth and above my eyes. I had good vision. The new helmet fitted perfectly. He had made it in four pieces and there were iron strengtheners joining the four pieces. It came to a slight point. Swords

## The Battle for a Home

would slide down it. The golden cross in the centre made it look different. It looked like the helmet of a lord. I found that I could see much easier to left and to right but the helmet was much lighter than my older one.

"It is perfect."

I reached into my leather pouch but he waved it away. "I do this for a friend."

I pressed the golden coin into his hand." And I give you this as a friend too. Your skill is what I reward. Thank you."

Each night we mounted a guard in my wooden tower. The view it afforded meant that we could see almost a mile away although that was less in the dark. Nipper and the horses were our best warning of danger. The dog barked and the horses whinnied when any stranger came close.

The day we launched the ship was an important one. Did she float? We had ropes on her in case we had to pull her ashore quickly. We had rolled her down to a cradle we made at low tide and we waited for high tide. There were just Sven and myself at the steering board. Sven had built her and I would captain her. I had hoped that Ulf Big Nose would have done that but he had made his views quite clear. The tide rushed in, it always rushed. Gradually we began to rise. The deck had yet to be fitted and we had no ballast yet. The wood made for natural buoyancy. While Sven stayed at the steering board I went along the keel on my hands and knees looking for the telltale spurt of water. I found none. I rose at the bow and waved. Sven gave a cheer and shouted, "You can pull us in now! She floats!"

We celebrated on the beach. "What now, Sven? The mast or the prow?"

"It is time she was named and her prow was fitted. We will do that now and tomorrow we fit the mast and yard."

I already knew that she could take eighteen oars down each side. At the moment we did not have that number of rowers but we hoped to increase our number.

"And the name?"

"I have thought on this." He looked at Ulf. "I had thought to name her after Siggi but I know that it is unlucky to use a warrior's name for a drekar. There were no women in Siggi's life but, to me, I saw him as a dragon. The figurehead I have made is of Siggi as a dragon. I would name her **'Dragon's Breath'**."

# The Battle for a Home

Naming a ship was a critical moment in a drekar's life. The name had to sing. I thought it did. Ulf nodded. Just then a gust of wind came from nowhere and, although the ship was held to the shore by ropes the bow rose and fell as though it nodded.

Ulf Big Nose said, "That is clear then. Siggi approved the name. We have our drekar."

We worked long into the early evening. I was too excited to eat and I had not ridden for some days. I saddled Dream Strider and went for a dusk ride. The nights were getting cooler and I kicked Dream Strider on. I rode towards Ulf's house and when I reached it reined in and walked him while he cooled a little. Nipper had kept up with us well. As we headed through the wood to the clearing Nipper growled. Ulf Big Nose was eating in my hall. It had to be an enemy. I drew my sword and edged Dream Strider forward. It was then I heard them. They were Frisians and there were two of them. I knew that from their voices for they were inside. I pointed to Nipper, "Stay!" I hissed. He sat. I went closer to listen to them.

"If he was a friend of the jarl he should have money!"

"There was nothing beneath the floor. He must have it with him. We'll get it when we take the village!"

"But then we will have to share it!"

"There will be plenty to go around. That one-eyed runt told us that."

I had walked Dream Strider to the side of Ulf's hut and waited. The two of them came out. They must have smelled my horse for they suddenly turned. It was too late. I brought my sword down on the head of one of them. The second tried to draw his sword and flee at the same time. I swung my sword in an arc and ripped him open from his crotch to his neck.

Dismounting I searched them. They had swords, seaxes and two spears. I took one of the swords and hacked off the two heads. I rammed them on the butts of the spears and headed towards the stad where the others were holed up. I knew I was near from the noises they made. I headed towards the greenway to my home and I planted the two spears on either side. It was a warning.

When I arrived back at my hall I saw anxious faces. As I stepped into the light Mary gasped when she saw blood on my kyrtle. "It is not mine. I discovered two Frisians going through your hut Ulf. They were searching for your treasure. They paid for that with their lives. But I learned that they plan an attack. It was as we suspected."

# The Battle for a Home

"They would find nothing there. I brought all with me and it lies in your hall."

"Then we should attack them now!"

"No Arne, we need the crew of '***Kara***'. There may be only four of them but we need every warrior we can get."

"Hrolf is right. I have scouted their settlement. There are forty Frisians. We are not strong enough. We watch and we wait."

It brought the celebrations to a sudden and sober end. "I thought that we would just be able to leave this island and find a new home. Why will they not leave us in peace?"

"Because they want what we have. They know that Jarl Siggi had treasure. They know that I have much gold. The men who were searching Ulf's hut were looking for his treasure. And they hate me. I am the flame which draws the moths." I put my arm around her. Bagsecg had told me that when a woman bore her first child she was fragile. Mary was a Frank and not as robust as a Viking woman. "Fear not. When the knarr returns, we can begin to send our people to our new home."

"Will that be without danger?"

"Of course, there will be danger but the men of Vannes have emptied the land. They think they had taken all that is to be had and will not return. At least they will not return this year. We have grain. Siggi bought that. It is part of his legacy. We will have a short time over winter to build our new home. We will use that time well."

"But you will fight these enemies who are your kin first."

"We will if only to deter them from doing so in the future."

As we curled up to sleep my worry was that Knut and Ketil would remember the pleasant land around the haugr and they would seek us there. We had to end this decisively.

Fitting out a drekar took time. There were sheets and shrouds which had to be fitted perfectly. Ballast had to be loaded so that the drekar had balance. The prow and the mast changed the way the ship moved. I gave Sven the more inexperienced warriors while I took the rest to keep watch on the enemy. I took my bow as did Ulf. We were not there to battle them but to spy on them.

I took Nipper and led four of our men. Ulf led the other four. We were not mailed and we wore no helmets. If we had to battle then we had lost. I stopped a mile from the village. It was on a high part of ground with scrubby bushes and spindly trees. It was scant cover but it would conceal a few men. Ulf had led his men to the trail which approached our home

## The Battle for a Home

from the north. It was close to his home and he knew every blade of grass.

I spread my men out and settled down with my dog next to me. It was noon as the weak sun climbed to its zenith that his ears pricked and he stood. I gave a low whistle as I stood and readied an arrow. My dog gave a low growl and I patted his head. He lay down in his hunting position. He would wait there for my next command. I knew that Rurik, Arne, Erik and Einar would all have their bows ready. I could not see them but they were ready. I heard the warriors as they came down the greenway from the village.

I peered through the bushes which lay before me. They were about two hundred paces from me. Gunnstein Gunnarson led eight Frisians. As they drew near I heard them. "I will tear out their lungs and make myself a drinking vessel from their skull! Olaf was like a brother to me."

"Aye, but what was he doing so far from the village? The jarl thinks he was working for himself and Karl."

"We are Vikings! It is what we do!"

I pulled back on my bow. I aimed at the Frisian who was next to Gunnstein. He sounded like a leader. The others would wait until my arrow struck. I had a longer range and I waited until they were closer so that the other four could hit their targets. I released when they were a hundred and fifty paces from me. I had good arrows and my first struck him in the neck above his byrnie. The spurt of blood which erupted told me that it was a mortal wound. Gunnstein fell with two arrows. Rurik and Arne hated a traitor. One Frisian was hit in the arm while a second in the leg. I loosed my next arrow but the Frisian managed to bring up his shield. The two wounded men were despatched and four arrows showered the rest. Two more were wounded and their three comrades grabbed them to help them back down the greenway. They were not cowards but how do you fight an enemy you cannot see?

I managed to hit another warrior in the leg as they disappeared back to the village. "Quick! Search them!"

When we reached them Gunnstein was still alive although he was dying. As the others stripped the mail from the Frisian leader and the weapons from the others I knelt over Gunnstein. "My sword!"

I handed him his sword.

He nodded, "I am sorry we became enemies Hrolf but family." He had married Ketil and Knut's sister. I nodded. "I will soon see Jarl Gunnar. I will beg forgiveness from..." His eyes closed and he died. I took the

## The Battle for a Home

sword from his dead hand as Rurik and Arne came to strip the mail from his body.

"You are too kind. I would not have given him his sword!"

"Arne, we fought with Gunnstein in a shield wall. He changed. Loki stole his heart. I gave him his sword for the warrior he was not the one he had become. Let us go. They may return."

When we reached my home Ulf had not returned but the knarr had. I hurried down to the quay where the iron was being unloaded. Sven was already there speaking with Harold. Harold Fast Sailing shook his head, "I knew that something was amiss. I felt a weight upon me as we headed through the islands. I thought it was the witch now I know that it was my old friend passing to the Otherworld. If we had not gone for the metal...."

"Jarl Siggi would still be dead and we would not be able to make the weapons we need." I saw six warriors standing by the knarr. None had mail but all had a sword and shield. They had helmets but they did not look like Vikings. They were round skull caps. "Who are these, Harold Fast Sailing?"

"These warriors were stranded in the land of the Cymri. The king of that land paid them as warriors."

One stepped forward, "I am Gudrun Witch Killer and I lead these men, hersir. The King did not pay us much and when we saw brother Vikings we asked leave to serve you."

"Have you heard of us?"

"We came from Orkneyjar and we called in at the land of the wolf. There they told us of Raven Wing Island."

"And where is your jarl?"

"Our ship was wrecked by the rocks close to the Sabrina. All those with mail perished. We five were the only survivors. We carried our shields and swords. We lost everything else."

"Would you serve under me for I am young?"

"Harold Fast Sailing and Gille have told us of you and your deeds. You are young but you are skilful. You have defeated the Hibernian champions. We will take our chances if you will have us."

I took out my sword, "This is Heart of Ice. It has had a spell cast upon it, Witch Killer. Will you each swear an oath on the blade?"

"Aye, hersir."

One by one they swore an oath. Gudrun was the oldest and the other five were all my age. "Then I take you as my oathsworn until I release you from your pledge, welcome Gudrun Witch Killer, Karl Anyasson,

# The Battle for a Home

Beorn Tryggsson, Olaf Head Breaker, Ulf Strong Swimmer and Kolbjorn Olvirson. Welcome to the Raven Wing Clan."

They headed up to the hall and Harold said, "They seem honest warriors fallen on hard times."

"I hope they do not bring us bad luck." Sailors were very superstitious.

"Perhaps they have had all the bad luck they are due, Sigurd. Now we can begin to move our people. How goes the drekar?"

"With Harold to help me, by tomorrow."

"Then when Ulf returns we can see about buying time for us to load the two vessels with the first of our people. Come I need to see Bagsecg."

My blacksmith was still toiling at the drekar. His prodigious strength was like that of two men. He stopped as we approached. "Bagsecg, we can leave for the haugr tomorrow but I must lead the warriors here to stop the enemy from making our task impossible. I need you to lead those I send and to defend them until we can be picked up from our island." He nodded, "You will only have the boys, the old men and the wounded like Erik One Hand."

"It will be enough."

His wife Anya chided me, "Hersir we are Viking women! We do not blow over in a breeze. We can work and we can fight. You bring our men to us when these nithings have been taught a lesson."

When Ulf returned, late in the afternoon, they had not spied any enemies. While half of the women prepared food and the other half helped Bagsecg, Sven and Harold to load the ships I held a council of war with our men.

I had already spoken with Ulf and we were in agreement. "Tomorrow we begin to leave this island. It will take our ships a day and a night to reach our new home and unload. It will take a day and a half to return. We need to buy three days for them. We cannot abandon our home for there are still things we need to take. Ulf and I intend to meet the Frisians before they reach here."

Karl the Tall said, "Is this our army, Hersir? I count only twenty-five warriors."

"And that is six more than we had yesterday. Besides we will not fight as we normally do. All of those without mail will use bows. I intend to mount four of you to join Gille and me on our horses. Ulf will command the archers and those with mail."

"Vikings on horses?"

## The Battle for a Home

"Yes, Gudrun Witch Killer. You did not think they named me Horseman for nought, did you? I can ride and I can fight on a horse. If the Frisians wish to defeat horsemen they make a solid wall. This might give us an advantage."

Rurik nodded, "And the archers can then hurt them while they stand."

"If they break then we will have them on our horses. What we will not do is to charge them! We break them down. We annoy them. We make them become frustrated and make them charge us. That is where Ulf and our mail will halt him when he is weakened and he is wild."

"But do you know that he will come?"

"He will come. We have bloodied him twice and the Frisian cannot afford to lose men without avenging them. He may even try to come tonight. We will watch." They nodded. "Remember we do this so our families can have a safe home. We fear no Frank living or dead. We will battle for our new home but that battle begins here. If we die then we have died for the clan and that is no bad thing. Jarl Siggi White Hair died for us. Let his sacrifice not be in vain!"

# The Battle for a Home

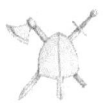

# Chapter 15

I did not sleep in my hall. I dozed in the tower with Rurik and Gille. It was Nipper's growl which awoke us. I had an arrow ready in an instant. The attackers were noisy and they were clumsy. We had laid logs and branches across the path leading to the hall before dark and they stumbled on them. I loosed three arrows blindly at the noise and was rewarded by a cry.

"To arms!"

My men had slept in mail and with arms close by. They raced to the path. Ulf was with them and I heard a scream as he slew the first Frisian. This was a battle in the dark and I had done all that I could in my tower.

"Come! This is blade to blade." We clambered down the ladder.

I left my bow and drew my sword and seax. Leading Rurik and Gille I followed Arne and Erik as they ran to the sounds of combat in the dark. A figure I did not recognise loomed up out of the dark. He reacted quickly by raising his sword but I reacted quicker. I blocked his sword with mine and rammed my seax under his raised arm, deep into his body. I pushed it from me. A battle in the dark can be frightening. What saved us was our familiarity. We knew where the ditch was. We had laid the logs. As the enemy tumbled into our stake filled ditch others tripped on logs. There was no honour in killing them but we sought no honour. We just wanted them dead!

The sound of them fleeing brought us to a halt. Ulf shouted, "Stay here, Hrolf! I will make sure that they are gone."

"Hold! Is anyone hurt?" My men all answered me. "Take their weapons and we will deal with their bodies in the morning."

Ulf came back sometime later. He wiped his seax on the kyrtle of a dead Frisian. "They fled back to the village. They were not happy." He then came closer and spoke quietly, "Another Frisian has joined them. They have more men recently arrived. I made one speak before I sent him to the Otherworld."

"Then we have tomorrow to end this."

# The Battle for a Home

He nodded, "I will go to the village and scout out their true numbers. I will pick up any weapons from their dead."

"Be careful. We have twice the number of enemies now."

He laughed as he went. "Not quite. I think you will find there are eight of them who died here and two more on the way back to their hall. We are whittling them down!"

There was little point in going to sleep. "Gille, let us take the ponies and foals down to the knarr. I would send them to our new home."

"They will not like the voyage and the foals will miss their mothers."

I nodded as we went down to the stable, "I know, that is why you will be going with them."

"But I thought I was going to ride with you and defeat the enemy."

"So did I but I need our animals to be safe. The foals are our future and they will need the ponies. You can return with the knarr. We will still be here."

"But there are two crews of Frisians."

"It does not change my plan. If there are more of them then we will have a bigger target."

By the time dawn broke Sven and Harold had already begun loading our drekar. The old men would have to row the drekar. It would not be a true test of her as a ship of war but she would be a knarr for one voyage. The women would also have to row. It was now even more urgent that they left as soon as possible. Brigid was the driving force. She chivvied and she scolded. When women became tearful at their parting she chastised them. Both vessels were heavily laden and I hoped that my captains would cope. Sigurd and Skutal were there to assist Sven and Harold. When they returned they would sail their two fishing boats to our new home.

Mary's face was red and wet with tears, "Our son will not like this upset, wife. Be happy for we go back to the land of your birth."

"Come back to me, husband. I need you. Your people need you. With Siggi gone there are just you and Ulf who can lead us. They all know that."

"I will take care, now board for the sooner you get there the sooner they can return."

I felt a lump in my throat as the two vessels headed north to catch the wind from the east. It was a cold wind and would bring snow to the high ground. It brought a chill to the bones to us but, more importantly, it

## The Battle for a Home

would mean they would not need to row until the haugr was in sight. The gods were with us and the Norns' webs were working.

Ulf arrived after they had left. He looked disappointed. "I had a gift for your wife. I left this in your hall with my weapons. I thought I would return before she left." He handed me a small chest. "Give it to her when you reach your new home."

"What is it?"

I went to open it but Ulf snapped, "It is a gift for your wife! She will be the one to open it." He began to lay out his weapons. "I was not certain what we might need so I brought them all." He shouted, "If any of you have a poor weapon then take one of mine. They have served me well over the years."

"What did you spy at the village?"

"They are preparing for war. I was close enough to hear this Frisian. He was not happy with Knut and Ketil. They had said that your home could be taken easily. We proved them wrong. Next time they come in force."

Once we were armed we saddled my horses. Arne, Rurik, Beorn, Erik and Einar were all familiar with horses and I mounted them and gave them each a spear. "You need to use the spear to thrust at the enemy. Your stiraps mean that you can stand and thrust down." I pointed to the mail that Rurik wore. "See, there is a gap between the byrnie and the helmet. Strike there. Do not charge and pull the horses away if the enemy threatens."

I turned to Gudrun and his men of Orkneyjar. I handed Gudrun my old helmet. I wore my new one. "Use this one. It is better than the one you were given in Cymru. The rest of you men take the ones we took from the Frisians last night. Take two spears too. I would have us kill them at distance."

Ulf said, "Follow me and I will lead you to the killing ground. When we fall back we make for here and Hrolf's walls. They are sturdy and the ditch is filled with traps." We had embedded new ones and sharpened them. Ulf grinned, "I have another present for the Frisians too." He dropped his breeks and emptied his bowels onto the stakes in the ditch. Others laughed and emulated him. If any warrior fell on stakes covered in excrement they would be poisoned. I stayed on my horse. I had eaten little in the last day and I had nothing to leave the Frisians.

When they had finished we marched off. There was no one left at the hall or the stockade. It was just the ghosts from the haunted farmhouse

# The Battle for a Home

and Siggi White Hair's spirit who remained. I wondered how many of us would return. I felt as though I was saying goodbye to my home.

I had two spears with me. I had a heavier one in my left hand behind my shield and a throwing one in my right hand. I had told the others not to throw but I had practised. I would have one extra chance to kill an enemy before we closed with them. As we rode I realised that I needed a smaller shield on my horse and one that had a better shape. This one would have to do. I found the new helmet much better. It felt as though I had a clearer sight of any enemy.

Ulf's killing ground surprised me. It was at the bottom of a dell with a wood behind it. The greenway passed through it on the way to my home. I looked up at the rise which led to the village. The path was well worn. "Why here?"

"It is dead ground, Hrolf. If you annoy them they will charge after you because there are so few of you. They will not see us. When you flee, go left and right. The archers will have a clear sight of the enemy. You can then ride around their flanks."

"This was not my plan."

"No it is mine and it is a better one. Remember we delay them today and then disappear. We fight them again tomorrow and vanish. Then, when the drekar and knarr return, you can escape and leave me to my island. Now go for we need to make this killing ground even deadlier for our foes. We need an hour!"

"You heard the general! Let us ride." We rode to the top of the rise. I looked behind as we crested the rise. We had only gone ten paces when Ulf and the others disappeared from sight. He was right. If we could make them pursue us then we could give them a surprise. I hoped Ulf knew what he was doing. We could ride away but he and his men might be trapped. Of course, Ulf knew what he was doing. He and Siggi had been fighting when Jarl Dragonheart was still living on the Dunum. Perhaps I could persuade him to come with us to the haugr. We needed an old wise head like his.

When we had travelled a mile or so I turned in the saddle, "We are here to make them charge us. I want no heroics from any of you. "

"It is all I can do to stay in the saddle!" Beorn was not a comfortable rider yet. I would have to teach him and the rest of the clan how to become better when we reached Frankia.

As we neared the village I slowed. I could hear the noise inside the wooden walls I had helped to build. I knew its strengths and I knew we would never be able to take it with so few warriors. Yet there were no men on the walls. They were all within. I led the five of them to within forty paces of the gate then I said, "Stay here."

The bridge was still in place across the ditch and I rode towards it. I could see the backs of the warriors. They were listening to someone standing in the doorway of the jarl's hall, out of sight to the right. When I was ten paces from it I spurred Dream Strider. As we clattered over the bridge I saw men at the back turn and look in surprise. I chose the largest warrior I could and, galloping to within ten paces of them, hurled my spear as hard as I could. It went through his mail and into his stomach. I wheeled Dream Strider around and was across the bridge again before anyone could move. I turned around in a line with my men ready to face the enemy.

They had seen me ride in but not the result."What did you do hersir?"

"I let them know we were here and gave them a warning that they needed to keep guards on their walls."

The mob of men ran out towards us. As I had expected it was the ones without armour who ran towards us first. They were faster. "Follow me. We turn to our left and stab as many of them as we can. I will lead and Rurik, bring up the rear. You have Night Star. He is the fastest. Do not get caught by them. Now ride."

We cantered towards them. I held my spear overarm so that they would think I intended to throw it again. They kept running. Why did they need to fear but six men? I saw that one warrior was outrunning the rest. I timed my turn so that he was ten paces in front of me. I jerked Dream Strider's head around and raised my arm. I feinted a throw and kept riding. He raised his shield quickly. When nothing hit his shield he lowered it to see where I was. I was next to him and I plunged my spear deep into his neck. I pulled it out again and shifted it to an underarm grip. The second warrior held his shield close to his head and chest. My spear tore into his thigh. I pulled Dream Strider's reins and headed back the way I had come. I glanced over my shoulder. My men had only managed to hit three warriors but they had made them stop. When I reached the spot where we had charged I reined in and waited. I wanted Dream Strider to catch his breath.

Erik Green Eye was grinning when he reined in. "I can see you are a true horseman. Two strikes with your spear and two dead men. We barely wounded three of them."

I shook my head, "One was just struck in the leg."

# The Battle for a Home

"Look hersir. He lies dead in a pool of blood. You struck something vital."

They had become wary. I saw Knut One Eye limp over to a warrior with a huge black beard and a skull rammed on a spike on his helmet. I guessed it was Guthrum the Skull. He pointed at me. The warrior nodded and shouted something. The Frisians began to form ranks. I wished I had brought my bow. I could have hit Knut One Eye and ended his treacherous life. The Frisian jarl put a line of warriors without mail in his front rank but then put a row of his better warriors behind them. He was inviting us to charge again but when we did so a second time the lightly armed men would have shelter behind the others. He would not catch us that way.

"We wait. It will give the horses the chance to rest and we are in no hurry. Talk to your horses and get to know them."

The Frisians began taunting us. My men were too clever to respond and it did not hurt us. I saw Knut and Ketil join the Frisian and speak with him. He nodded and spoke again. Suddenly ten men on each side detached themselves and ran to try to outflank us. I noticed none of them had armour.

"Hersir?"

"Wait. When I ride follow me. We will go left." The enemy warriors were using a good plan but there were not enough men for it to succeed. We were mounted and it would take more than ten men to make me worry. The Frisian line moved forward as the two flanking warriors began to pass us. They thought they had us trapped.

"Now, Dream Strider!" I galloped directly at the third man in the line to my left. He was fifty paces from me. They had a gap between them and could not form a shield wall. He made the mistake of running. I stabbed him in the back with my spear and then wheeled to my left to bring my spear into the neck of the second Frisian. The one who was leading threw himself to the floor. He must have been told that a horse will not step on a man. Normally that is true but when a horse is moving quickly it cannot help itself. Dream Strider's hoof crushed his skull and I led my men towards the dead ground a mile away.

Glancing over my shoulder I saw that they had done better this time. Four others had been hit and the last three had run back towards the shelter of the main band. The ones on the far side had formed a shield wall in case we charged them. We did not.

# The Battle for a Home

"Keep going!" I rode for half a mile and stopped again half a mile from the ambush. I could not see Ulf and knew that we would be invisible too. The enemy had to run hard to keep after us. That suited me for they would be tired. They had seen what happened to individuals and were presenting a solid wall of shields. I let them get to within a hundred paces before I put the next part into operation.

I shouted, "Guthrum the Skull, you have been deceived by Knut One Eye and his half-witted brother. This island has nothing for you. There are many places to raid and yet you choose to take on a small clan. Are you afraid to fight someone stronger?"

He shook his head like a dog trying to dry itself, "I am not afraid of you. I have never met a horseman I could not beat." He held his two handed war axe above his head. "Come close enough to Thor's Maiden and you will find that a horse is no protection."

"Then step forward and we will see!"

"Hersir!"

"Do not worry, Arne Four Toes, I do not have the death wish and I will see my son born."

Guthrum the Skull pushed his way forward and stepped clear of his men. He kept walking toward me. As I had expected he had his shield around his back because he needed both hands for his axe. I had fought men with such an axe before. They were deadly but if you had quick hands and reactions then you could defeat them. The difference was, that I was now doing this on horseback. My mount needed to be as quick as I was. "Be ready my Dream Strider. Today we show the world how a Viking can ride a gift of the gods!"

I kicked him in the ribs and he leapt forward. I wanted him to move as fast as possible. I wanted to be a blur. I wanted this Guthrum the Skull to strike at thin air. He began to swing his axe in a double loop. He was not yet ready to strike but he needed to build up the speed of his axe. He expected me to go to his left so that I could use my spear. When I was five paces from him I jerked to the left and then to the right. He swung at where I should have been. Standing in my stirraps I stabbed down across the left-hand side of my horse's head as I passed the Frisian chief. He had mail but it was a boar spear I used and I was strong. It came away red and I saw that I had hit him in the shoulder. I wheeled around him as his men raced to get the man who had wounded their leader.

"Ride!"

# The Battle for a Home

Their leader now wounded, they were like a pack of wild dogs and all order was gone. They ran as a mob. There were no lines and no shield wall. They wanted to get to grips with us as soon as they could and end this. Erik was the fourth in the line. "Erik, go left!" We peeled left and right as I saw the small band of warriors waiting behind a line of embedded stakes. Ulf had built himself a citadel! We rode away from the ground before the shield wall. I knew it would be laden with traps. We reined in behind the archers. Rather than deterring the Frisians the small shield wall seemed to spur them on. The archers began to rain death on them as soon as they crested the brow. Those without armour fell quickly.

The ones with mail and better shields managed to escape death and they lumbered and barged past their less armoured brothers. They built up speed and, as they reached the steeper ground began to run even quicker. It was hard to keep their feet and suddenly those at the front slipped on wet grass. Unable to keep their balance three fell, bringing down others. Our archers found flesh then. The ones following slowed down and approached a little more cautiously. They just gave our archers more time to hit them. Once they reached the flatter ground they formed a shield wall. They had twenty mailed men in a solid double line and they stepped forward. The ground was a muddy morass which had been soaked by Ulf and the others. Stepping forward from the protection of the stakes Ulf and six warriors stabbed with their spears at men struggling to keep their feet. Then they retreated back to the protection of the stakes.

"Forward!" I led my horsemen towards the Frisians. They thought we were going to attack at the same time as Ulf. They hurriedly echeloned their line to face us.

Just then I saw Guthrum the Skull, supported by Ketil Eriksson, stand at the top of the brow of the hill. He shouted, "Back!" as his standard-bearer blew his horn. The survivors tried to extricate themselves from the mud but my archers continued to hit them.

I raised my spear and said, "Viking horsemen, forward!"

We followed the retreating Vikings. We speared as many as we could. The more we killed today the fewer would be there to fight us the next day. None of the Frisians asked for mercy. They gripped their swords and tried to defend themselves as the six of us worked our way up the hill. Halfway up I shouted, "Stop!" The last thing we needed was for us to walk into a trap. We returned down the hill to join Ulf and the others.

# The Battle for a Home

We had slain over twenty men. We were still outnumbered but it was a victory. Raven Wing Clan had reason to celebrate.

We sang as we headed home to my stockade.

*The horseman came through darkest night*
*He rode towards the dawning light*
*With fiery steed and thrusting spear*
*Hrolf the Horseman brought great fear*

*Slaughtering all he breached their line*
*Of warriors slain there were nine*
*Hrolf the Horseman with gleaming blade*
*Hrolf the Horseman all enemies slayed*

*With mighty axe Black Teeth stood*
*Angry and filled with hot blood*
*Hrolf the Horseman with gleaming blade*
*Hrolf the Horseman all enemies slayed*
*Ice cold Hrolf with Heart of Ice*
*Swung his arm and made it slice*
*Hrolf the Horseman with gleaming blade*
*Hrolf the Horseman all enemies slayed*

*In two strokes the Jarl was felled*
*Hrolf's sword nobly held*
*Hrolf the Horseman with gleaming blade*
*Hrolf the Horseman all enemies slayed*

# The Battle for a Home

# Chapter 16

It was cold fare we ate. Mary and Brigid had left us two barrels of ale, cured ham, pickled fish and cheese. We ate. Ulf laughed as my riders complained of their wounds- the saddles had chafed them!

"If that is the only wound you have after such a battle then think yourselves well off. I remember when Siggi and I were young, sometimes there were but five men left after the battles we fought."

Erik Green Eye said, "Yet you must have been good for you have no wounds which show."

"We were lucky I think and Siggi and I fought as a pair when we were young. He guarded my back and I guarded his."

I washed down the salty ham with the dark beer, "And then you became scout and Siggi watched the jarl. Why were you not hearth-weru?"

"We wished to be but Jarl Gunnar wanted to choose men who were not family. He said that he knew his family would watch out for him so why did they need to be hearth-weru? If we had been hearth-weru then we would have perished with him and his family. We had a part to play here. It is *wyrd*. The Norns make nothing simple. Siggi had to be here to warn us of the attack by the Frisians and me...? I can still wield a sword and use my mind."

"And now what?"

"And now we watch. Each man pairs up with another. One sleeps while the other watches. They will try to get the horses. I will watch with Hrolf." He stretched, "And I will exercise the authority of age and sleep first. Wake me when you tire, Hrolf the Horseman."

"Aye Ulf."

The men paired up and I saw those on watch look at me. "Two in the tower; the rest on the walls. I will watch the horses. Do not doubt yourself. If you hear or see anything then call out. There are too few of us for doubts."

# The Battle for a Home

I had taken my helmet off and I left it by the fire. It rested on my shield. This was the time for Heart of Ice. I walked to Dream Strider. Nipper raised his head and, seeing that it was me, went back to sleep. I stroked Dream Strider's mane. "Today you were as the steed of a god. I was proud of you. Tomorrow, or the day after, we leave this home and I will be sad. I enjoyed those days when you and I lived alone and we rode where we chose. Things change. You are a father and I am to be a father soon. With that change come responsibilities. You will sire a herd of horses which are ridden to war by Vikings. We will be the first to do so. The witch, on Syllingar, told me it would happen. We have to leave but I know not what the land of the Franks holds for me. We will face it together."

He nuzzled my head and his huge, rough tongue, licked my hair. We were like Siggi and Ulf. We watched each other's backs. I stepped away from the stable to allow him to sleep and I stood just down from the walls of my palisade where I could watch the stables. I rested my back on the single copper beech we had left. Its twisted trunk rendered it useless for timber but its branches and leaves gave shade in summer. Mary liked the colour of the leaves in winter. With my sword in my hand, I leaned against it and I listened.

I smelled them before I saw them. I smelled the ale soaked clothes and the sweat. I picked up a stone and tossed it at Rurik's head thirty paces away on the walls. It hit his good ear and he turned. I pointed into the dark and he nodded. He disappeared. He would rouse the others.

I held my sword slightly behind me as I peered into the dark. If I did not move then I would be invisible. The convoluted branches and trunk of the beech hid me. I heard a curse. It sounded close. I looked closer and saw four figures creeping forward. They were forty paces from me and were shadows. Ulf had been right. They were coming for the horses. Ulf appeared next to me. He was the only one of those in the stockade who could move so silently. I pointed and he nodded. I drew my seax.

They would have to pass us to get to the stables and so we waited. It seemed impossible that they would miss us but, as the four approached I saw that they were watching the walls. I recognised three of them. It was Karl Swift Foot, Knut and Ketil Eriksson. Ulf was to my right. Ketil led. His maimed foot gave him a distinctive limp. The fourth warrior was slightly behind Karl Swift Foot. I would have to kill him first.

Ulf did not wait for me. We knew each other well. He swung his sword into the middle of Ketil's stomach. I slashed at the throat of the

# The Battle for a Home

fourth man as I stabbed at Karl Swift Foot. Karl had always been a good warrior with fast hands and he deflected the blade down. It bit into flesh but it was his leg and not his neck. Ketil's cry shattered the silence of the night. If there were others then they would be behind these four. We had to kill them quickly. We were close together and Karl punched at me with the hilt of his sword. Even though my seax came up he sent me backwards. I had no helmet to protect me. He turned and ran. I followed.

He was Karl Swift Foot and he could run faster than me but he was hampered by his leg and his shield. I heard no more noise and I guessed these four were the only ones who would be coming. I brought my sword over as I neared him. We were on the greenway and it was open. My sword caught him on his back. The mail held but the blow hurt him. He whipped his sword around in a wide arc. Had I not had quick reactions he might have gutted me. My seax sparked against the sword. The flash briefly lit us. I swung my sword at neck height and his shield blocked it. My seax darted in beneath his sword. The oblique tip was perfect for finding a way through mail. It tore the links and cut through the kyrtle beneath. He grunted. I twisted and pushed even harder. He brought his sword over to punch me again but I was ready and my sword met his. We were face to face.

"You turned against your own people!" I pushed even harder and my left hand came up against his mail. I twisted and turned the blade inside him.

"I married Ketil's people. You were my enemy."

I could feel his sword arm weakening. "We fought in a shield wall. You forgot your oath." I pulled my sword hand back and punched at his hand. His sword flew from it and I turned my seax inside his body and tore it out. He screamed. It was like the cry of a vixen in the night. I heard birds take flight. He fell backwards.

I kicked away his shield. He was not yet dead but he was close. "Sword! Give me my sword!"

Sheathing my own I picked his up. I held it by the blade. "First, what did you intend?"

"Kill your horses. Gudrun Skull Taker said that Knut and Ketil had not fought. They should destroy the animals."

"I thought Knut was Jarl."

Karl laughed and blood trickled from the corner of his mouth. "So did he."

"And what do the Frisians intend?"

# The Battle for a Home

"Today they come for you. You will not get to use your horses. They have long spears and another drekar arrived. They have replaced the ones you slew. Sword!"

I handed him his sword.

"I am sorry we parted as enemies. You were a good ..." He died.

I turned and ran. His cry might have brought Frisians. When I neared the stables I was met by the grisly sight of three skulls sitting on spears. Ulf was there. I nodded, "He is dead. They come this morning. We will move the horses down to Sigurd's hut before dawn. They have more men. We will need to hold them at the walls until the ships return."

Ulf nodded, "*Wyrd*."

We were all awake and having had the enemy so close none would go back to sleep. We led my horses down to the wooden quay. Laying their saddles there we tied them to the roof of Sigurd and Skutal's huts. I would try to save them before the end but if not...

When I returned to my hall I saw that Ulf had found the last of my seal oil and he and my men were soaking the walls of my stockade and hall with it. He poured it on the outbuildings which had housed my pigs, fowl and even the stables. They were all full of hay and dung. They would burn. He said, "We fight until we can hold them no longer. You built a good wall here, Hrolf the Horseman. I am impressed. You built just one gate. We leave by the gate and fire the walls. We fight our way to the beach. There are two fishing boats there. If any survive then they will hold six each. Twelve of us might survive."

Rurik nodded, "Who wants to live forever? We will have a great tale to tell in Valhalla and Siggi White Hair will approve."

Ulf nodded, "I feel him close by."

We placed our bows on the fighting platform along with the throwing spears. Erik and Einar took the rest halfway down the slope to use when we fell back. When all was ready we stood our watch on the walls.

Sigtrygg Rolfsson asked, "When will the ships get here?"

"It will be a long day dying, Sigtrygg. The drekar cannot move swiftly. She will have but a handful of men on the oars. The knarr? That is in the lap of the gods. If they give us a wind then they will reach us by noon."

Ulf did not honey his words. The enemy would be here by dawn and in such overwhelming numbers that they would force the walls and then take a terrible revenge on us. The hope was that some of us would survive. I did not know about the others but I believed that I would

# The Battle for a Home

survive. Aiden and Kara would have understood the voice I heard in my head which told me that I would live and see my son born.

Nipper warned us. He was by the stables below us and he growled. I pointed to the beach, "Find Dream Strider." He ran off. Perhaps he would live. I hoped so.

I did not think that they would come while it was dark. They knew of our traps and the fact that four warriors had not returned was another warning. I hoped that they would have stayed up all night drinking themselves into a warrior fury. Wild warriors made more mistakes. Ulf and I were in my small tower. It was only big enough for two. Our Saami bows had a longer range than the others. We could hit them from a greater distance. We had a pot of burning coal with us and some fire arrows.

When the sun first began to appear Ulf said, "Today we fight until there is no hope left and then we fight some more. If this is our day to die then it is to help the Raven Wing Clan live. We will not throw our lives away but we will die hard!"

I looked at the new men: Gudrun Witch Killer and his comrades. "You owe the clan nothing, Gudrun. You have already served us by fighting as you have done. There is neither shame nor dishonour if you choose to leave. There are fishing boats for you to use."

He shook his head. "We came to you poor and without hope. You have given us mail, weapons and something to believe in. We took an oath and we will honour it!"

We saw the shadow that was a column of our enemies when the sun was well risen. They came down the greenway for it was safer that way. They came as a column eight men wide and six men deep. Their leader was not at the front. He and his hearth-weru walked at the rear. This was not two crews. He had reserves. I saw Gunnstein Gunnarson in the front rank.

From our lofty perch, we could send an arrow over two hundred paces. We had plenty of arrows and I raised my bow. I released an arrow high and shouted, "Gunnstein Gunnarson! You are a traitor! Die!"

My voice carried across to them and he stared at me and then realised I had a bow in my hand. As he looked up my arrow plunged into his head. The column was disrupted and Ulf sent an arrow into a warrior who wore no mail in the third rank. They quickly reformed. Ulf and I began to send arrow after arrow towards those in the third and fourth ranks. Those warriors had no mail. They held up their shields for protection. We

## The Battle for a Home

loosed twenty arrows in the hundred paces they took before they came within range of our other men on our walls. We only hit three but we made them slow up. Then the others began to rain their arrows at the same place. A gap began to appear between those with mail who were more reckless about our arrows and those with no mail. The number of arrows began to cause casualties. Few were mortal but they were effective. We would not be facing fifty men. If Guthrum the Skull wanted us dead he would need his reserves.

The men on the walls who had no bows now readied their spears. They would be used when the enemy tried to cross the ditch. The Frisians had brought no ladders. I wondered what they would do to bridge it. I hoped they might try to cross the stinking faeces covered pit. When they neared the outbuildings ten of them left the line and raced with their axes. They intended to use the buildings as a bridge. They would tear them down and use their timbers.

Ulf grinned as he lit a fire arrow. "I must have the mind of a Frisian! I thought they might try this." He sent an arrow into the roof of the stable. We had placed kindling there and on the tops of the other outbuildings. He sent another arrow into the wall. When a warrior tried to reach up and remove it I pinned his arm to the wall. As the flames caught they set fire to the warrior's beard. He tore his arm from the wall leaving flesh which began to burn. They ran to the next building but Ulf's arrows had already set them alight and there was now a wall of flames behind the Frisians. Guthrum the Skull was trapped on the other side. His men were leaderless.

The smoke and the flames panicked them and the men with spears found targets. As their bodies fell into the ditch some of the braver warriors risked stepping on their dead comrades to reach the wooden wall. I loosed the last of my arrows.

"I will go and help them on the walls."

Ulf turned and gave me a rare smile, "It has been an honour to see you grow into such a warrior. Make your son a good Viking, Hrolf the Horseman." He was saying farewell.

"And I will remember you and Siggi until the end of time. My son will hear of Ulf Big Nose and Siggi White Hair."

He turned and sent another fire arrow into a mailed warrior who had just stepped onto a body in the ditch. He began to burn. "Now go! We have talked enough. Now is the time to kill. Leave when you can or you must. I stay here!"

# The Battle for a Home

I slung my bow over my shoulders and descended the ladder. My shield was at the bottom. I picked up a spear. Turning to my men I said, "We are winning! They will need their reserves."

The dead and wounded bodies in the ditch were mounting up and the pressure from the warriors behind grew. I pulled back my arm and jabbed it at the head of a warrior trying to climb up the wall. The spearhead scored a line along his arm and then gouged a lump out of his cheek. He tried to grab my spear with his wounded arm and pull me from the wall but I had been expecting the move. As he pulled I went with it and he began to lose his balance. I pulled the spear back and he lost his grip. He screamed as he impaled himself on a stake.

We were not having it all our own way and warriors had reached the fighting platform. I hurled my spear at a warrior who was just about to clamber over. It drove into his thigh and hip. He lost his grip and fell. Drawing Heart of Ice I ran towards the two Frisians who had just slain one of the new men, Kolbjorn Olvirson and was about to strike Gudrun Witch Killer from behind. I brought my sword down on the back of his head. He had a good helmet but the force of it must have shattered his skull for he tumbled to the side and into the ditch.

Gudrun slew the man he had been fighting and turned, "Thank you, hersir. Kolbjorn has had vengeance!"

"They fall back!"

The flames had died a little and there was less smoke. The Frisians ran back from the walls. They had lost half of their number. Not all had died but enough to weaken their resolve. "See to the wounded. Who have we lost?"

"Karl the Tall and Kolbjorn Olvirson are in the Otherworld. I have a bloody arm and Arne Four Toes now has four fingers too!" Rurik did not sound downhearted by his wound. It was a badge of honour.

Arne shouted, "I can still fight Rurik One Ear."

"See to the wounds. Get some ale and some food. This is not over."

Suddenly Ulf shouted, "To the north, I see the knarr! They are coming!"

Suddenly we had hope. "Rurik, go down to the quay and wait for them. Load the horses as soon as they arrive."

"I can still fight."

"Then you can load the horses too. Go." I turned to Erik Green Eye. "I want you by the gate. When we leave you will need to open it and clear any Frisians who are on the other side. Erik Long Hair can help you."

# The Battle for a Home

So far they had not reached the gate but I was under no illusions. When they attacked next they would. I ascended to the fighting platform. "Can you see them, Ulf?"

"Aye, and they have been busy. The other men were not the reserve they were cutting down logs. They intend to breach the wall."

"They are in for a shock then. There is earth behind the wood."

He shook his head. "They can bridge the ditch. Be ready to leave with the men. I will fire the walls."

"No! I will stay with you. It is a two-man job at least!"

"No, Hrolf, I can do this. Once you followed my orders. Do so again. Get the men to the quay. Prepare a shield wall for when they pursue you." He pointed to my hall. "You can fire your hall! It is your right to do so."

I nodded and raised my arm, "I salute you."

"And I will have this whole island to myself when you are gone! I will enjoy the peace!"

"Rurik, get the men down to the quay as soon as you have placed kindling around the walls. I will follow."

"And Ulf?"

"When he has fired the walls he will join us."

"Come on, you heard the hersir!"

I grabbed a brand. I saw Ulf sending arrow after arrow towards the advancing Frisians and I heard them cheer. They could see it was but one man. We did not have long. As I stepped out of the gate I saw the knarr. She was still over a thousand paces from the shore and with the wind against her, the progress was painfully slow. I went into the hall. Everything that could have been taken was gone but what it held was irreplaceable. There were memories in every part of it. There was the room Mary had used. The corner she had sewed. There was the sleeping place where my child had been conceived. Soon they would all be gone save inside my head. I took the brand and went to the end room and lit the kindling which lay there. Then I did the same in the main hall. The turf had dried out, as had the wood, and the flames leapt up as I opened the door to step out. I headed back to the stockade and the gate. I heard the sound of logs ramming the walls. They would soon realise it was pointless and would use them like bridges. Even as I stepped inside I saw a Frisian climb the wall. I took a spear and hurled it at him. It caught him a glancing blow and he disappeared but others took his place. Then I saw Ulf turn and aim an arrow at me. It was a fire arrow. It smacked into the

## The Battle for a Home

kindling by my feet and the flames leapt. He waved to me as he sent another five arrows towards the other walls. Finally, as Frisians poured over the walls he threw down the pot with the coals. It erupted at the bottom of the tower and I saw flames leap up towards Ulf.

"Ulf!"

He climbed onto the top of the tower and taking out his sword shouted, "I am Ulf Big Nose of the Raven Wing Clan! I have lived long enough. Allfather take me!" He dived down towards the mass of Frisians who had just poured over the walls. He landed amongst them and was on his feet in an instant. His whirling sword took heads and hands. Even as the flames and smoke stopped my view I saw that he was being hacked to death but I heard his cry at the end. "Raven Wing Clan!"

I turned and ran. The smoke made my eyes water. At least that was what I told myself. Halfway down the slope, my men waited in a shield wall. I saw, behind them, *'Kara'* as she made the last tack. Soon she would land. When I reached my men I saw that the top of the slope was on fire. The flames had finally spread to the haunted farmhouse. The ghosts would have a home no more.

"Quickly Rurik, load the knarr. Erik Green Eye, Erik Long Hair, Gudrun. You stay with me. We will buy time."

I could hear cries and shouts from the burning stockade. As the smoke began to thin they would realise that they could get around the stables. I had one spear left. I pulled my shield around. The other three flanked me. We did not stand with locked shields. We just had to slow them and give the others time to get my horses on the knarr. They were my most valuable cargo. They were my family's future.

A handful of warriors burst through and I saw them shout to others. "Here they come. Remember we are just slowing them down. We back down the slope slowly."

The first eight men ran at us recklessly. I jabbed my spear, not at the warrior's head which he protected with his shield, but the knee he exposed. I jabbed and twisted. As the spear came out and his knee buckled I slashed my spear sideways at the next Frisian who was busy trying to spear Erik Green Eye. The head tore across his right arm and Erik stabbed him.

"Back!" We took two steps back while jabbing at the Frisians who were now more cautious. I saw more men emerging from the smoke. We had forty paces to go. I could hear my horses whinnying and Gille singing to them. I shouted, "When they are loaded leave! We will use the fishing boats!"

A mailed Frisian charged at me swinging his axe. I thrust between strokes and my spear went into his middle. He was a big man and he grabbed the spear from my grasp. I drew Heart of Ice. Stepping forward I swung it at head height. It took the Frisian by surprise but he still managed to ram me in the side with his spear. Bagsecg's mail was good but the blow tore links and I was only saved by Mary's padded kyrtle.

"We are loaded! Run!"

There seemed to be too many of them for us to disengage without losses and then half a dozen arrows flew over our heads. As shields came up I stabbed forward as did my three companions. We all found flesh and there was a gap. We turned and ran. I held my shield above my back. I felt something heavy crash into it and I nearly fell. I saw that the knarr was forty paces from the shore. Sigurd sat in one fishing boat and Skutal in the other. We threw ourselves into them. The arrows from the overcrowded knarr kept the Frisians at bay.

Skutal lowered the sail and his nippy fishing boat leapt like a dolphin across the water. "That was as close as we could make it hersir. Another stride or two and they would have had us."

"Where is the drekar?"

"We did not have enough crew for her. The wind was against us. Sven sent the knarr." He shrugged. "He did not want to lose his new ship."

"I understand. I would have done the same in his position but will the knarr make it? She looks overcrowded."

"She is a sturdy vessel. She will make it." He nodded to the bow. "Hersir you had better see to Erik Long Hair. He has a wound."

I saw that Erik Long hair had taken a thrust to his thigh. It was bleeding heavily. I tore a piece of cloth from his kyrtle and cut a length of rope from the anchor. I wrapped the cloth around the wound and then tied the rope tightly. "You must release it regularly or you will lose the leg."

"Aye. That was a battle to remember. Less than twenty men held off two boatloads of Frisians!"

"Ulf's last stand will long be remembered."

"Did he go berserk?"

"No, but he had little left to live for. He sacrificed his life so that we could live. He gave his life for me. He is happy now because he is in Valhalla. There will be heroes there who are jealous of his end."

## The Battle for a Home

I turned and watch my island home disappear in the east. There were few left, now, of the crew of our original drekar. We were starting afresh with a new longship in a new land. It would not be easy but we had learned from our mistakes. My small stockade had been well built but I could improve on that. We needed to make a citadel which could withstand attacks from large numbers of men. I had ideas. I knew that the next battle would be a battle for a home, our home. I would lead the clan and I would do so in memory of Siggi and Ulf.

# The Battle for a Home

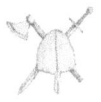

## Chapter 17

I was more worried about the horses than the knarr as we headed out beyond the headland to sail along the coast. The waters became choppier. I knew that Gille would be watching my horses but I would have been happier if I was with them. Sigurd and Skutal kept us as close as they could to the knarr but we had to bail so much that the knarr gradually left us behind. The bailing helped us to forget our predicament. We were too busy working to think about drowning. It was almost dark when we turned east. I knew that the haugr was not far away but in the dark, we had no way of knowing exactly where it was and there was the danger of running into the rocks or the causeway. We had had Ulf's nose the last time we had come here. He was now in Valhalla. In the end, we almost ran into *'Kara'* which had anchored.

Harold leaned over. "I would not risk running onto the rocks. Sven would tear me a new mouth if I did so."

I turned to Skutal, "Are we in any danger?"

"No hersir. We are shallow and if you keep watch from the prow then we should be safe enough.

"We will land and I will get the others to light torches and guide you in. My horses have spent long enough afloat."

"Aye, and we have spent long enough with their dung too!"

"How are they, Gille?"

"They miss you lord but they will last a little while longer."

With Sigurd close by, we headed towards the beach. I saw the telltale bubbles of white water. "To the left! Rocks!" Skutal eased us more to steerboard. I noticed that the water became calmer. Soon I saw the beach and we ground on to the sand. I jumped into the water which came up to my knees. The bottom was sandy."Sail back to Harold and have him follow you."

"He will ground her here, lord."

"It will not hurt the knarr for this is sand." The two fishing boats pushed off again. Erik Green Eye joined me. "Have you a flint?"

## The Battle for a Home

"Aye."

"Find something to fire and I will find driftwood." I was taking a risk. I was gambling that the nearest folk to us would be our people. A fire would attract them and we would find our new home. I hurried along the beach. As I had expected there was dried wood above the waterline. I retraced my steps and found Erik. He had some dried grass from the dunes. He managed to get a flame and by blowing on the dried grass and kindling we managed to get a fire going. The knarr now had a beacon.

I peered down the beach. When we had raided we had not needed to travel north of the haugr. I remembered some dunes and they looked to be a mile north of the haugr. Was that where we were? I heard the flap of the sail as it was furled behind me. The knarr loomed up out of the dark. Its bow ground on the sand. It lurched and the horses whinnied. I ran down, "Get the gangplank out. Gille, lead Night Star and I will lead Dream Strider. The others will follow."

I pulled myself aboard and untied my stallion. "Come, boy. You have done well. We have a new home." He trusted me and followed me across the gangplank and onto the sand. I handed the reins to Erik. Soon we had all six horses ashore. Saddle them and I will ride to the haugr with Gille. We will light beacons for you."

Rurik said, "What of us?"

"Stay aboard. You warriors are now the treasure of the clan. You must be protected as carefully as gold. Give me the chest Ulf gave for my wife."

He clambered back aboard and brought it to me. Gille and I mounted our horses and, each leading two mares, we rode down the sand. In the dark nothing was familiar but when I smelled wood smoke I knew that there were houses close by. Then I saw a darkened lump to my left. It was the island and we were close to the haugr. I headed slightly right and saw another mound rising and the pinprick of a watchfire. When Bagsecg said, in very poor Frank, "Who goes there?" Then I knew we had found our new home.

"It is Hrolf the horseman and Gille. The knarr is north of the island but needs a beacon."

"We did not light one for fear of enemies."

"The warriors who survived are aboard the knarr. We will risk a fire." I dismounted and walked into the camp. They had been busy and there was a shelter up already. As we approached people awoke. Mary heard my voice and ran to me, "You are safe!"

# The Battle for a Home

"I am and we have much to do." I kissed her. "When my warriors have landed then we can speak." I saw wives and mothers waiting for news. The men are on the knarr. We will light a fire to guide them ashore."

With many hands working we soon had a large fire burning on the beach to the south of the island. I saw, by its light, the drekar anchored in the deeper water. Sven waved. He would have questions. The knarr and fishing boats eventually appeared and headed towards our guiding light. When all the men were ashore it was a joyful scene. Only one mother had lost a son. She was comforted by Brigid and Mary. The rest had been given a new chance at life. Most had expected a son or husband to die. As we stood around the beach fire Bagsecg asked, "And Ulf?"

"Ulf Big Nose chose to take many Frisians with him. They will rue the day that they attacked Ulf's clan. He did not want to begin a new life again. When Siggi died his heart died too. This was *wyrd*." I handed the small chest to Mary. "He gave this to you. He tried to see you before you left. He was sorry to have missed you."

Mary nodded, "I knew he would not be coming."

"Are you becoming pagan?"

"No husband. It is just a feeling that this would not be Ulf's home."

Mary walked over to the fire and opened the chest. She smiled and then closed it. As she walked back I saw that she was crying.

"The present he gave me was his treasure. He did not want to leave it on the island." She shook her head, "For such a gruff man he had a heart which was kind. I will miss him and Jarl Siggi too."

I nodded, "He gave away his weapons too. The only weapon he valued which he kept was my gift of a Saami bow."

Bagsecg said, "Siggi thought of you as his son as did Ulf. I know he was proud of your achievements. We will remember him."

"We will, for this new home would not be possible without him. Come let us go to the camp and get a little sleep before dawn. We have much work to do."

It was good to cuddle, beneath a fur with my wife. We were surrounded by the clan and there was no privacy but sometimes words are not needed and we held each other tightly. I had been close to death and Mary had not known if her child would be born an orphan. We shared those thoughts and we were content. I knew that the spirits of the dead watched over us.

When dawn broke I saw that they had just managed to make one large shelter. Winter was almost upon us and we needed to work hard. Even

## The Battle for a Home

the wounded would have to shoulder their share of work. Sven and Harold used the ships' boys to begin to make a jetty. That way we could unload and load the ships easier. I took the rest of the men to the haugr.

As we approached Arne said, "It is a pity Jarl Siggi White Hair chose to burn it."

"It is, Arne Four Toes, but we did not know that we would need it did we? Besides this gives us the chance to build it the way we want."

Bagsecg asked, "You know what you wish it to look like then?"

"I do. There are three parts to this. We make three halls at the top of the haugr. Winter is coming and we need shelter. I think we can just fit in three halls. Then we build the wooden walls around for we need defence. There will be enemies. Thirdly we make a ditch. The Franks did not have one and it cost them. When that is done we build another wall and ditch to enclose our workshops, ovens and forges. I have learned from the past."

I turned and looked towards the island. I could see no smoke.

"Where are the monks?"

"Their homes are empty. We found none. It is like the day you raided. The priests have not returned."

I suddenly say Siggi's hand in all of this. "Then we save ourselves some work. We take apart the monastery and use that to build our homes. There are stones and there are timbers. They even have tiles upon the roof of the church. We begin now."

"What if this French king objects?"

"Then he will see a different side to his new neighbours. I will not make war on him but if he provokes then we will show him that we are Vikings."

I left Bagsecg to organize the men while I took the women who were not preparing food or caring for babies to begin the work of clearing away the burned buildings. It had been some time since our raid and the weather had helped us. By the time the first materials arrived, we had cleared half of it. The one disadvantage we had was that our new homes would be more like those of a Frank than a Viking for we used the old materials to build our new one. That was a good thing. We were a new people. We could adapt. I had a vision in my mind of what this would look like when we had finished.

At noon Mary trudged up the slope to bring me a horn of ale. "You should not have climbed this hill."

## The Battle for a Home

"I will have to do this when we live here besides you look tired. Erik Long Hair told me of the battle. You were close to death."

"Yet I survived because I was meant to come here. This is *wyrd*." I laughed, "I know you do not believe in this, *wyrd*, but you do believe that this is meant to be."

"I do. So, tell me what we will see when we have finished for it is in your head and I cannot see it."

"This is a natural hill. The Franks just adapted it for a home. We will do more. We will have three halls here, at the top and we will have a palisade which runs around the top. There will be, as at our home on Raven Wing Island, but one way in and out. We will have a gate with two towers. The towers will take time to build. Then we will have a ditch which will encircle the workshops, stables and animal pens. That too will have but one gate. The ditch will be deep and we will have a channel to the sea so that we can flood it when we choose."

"We would be an island?"

"When we choose to be, aye. The one way in and out will be close to the jetty which Sven and Harold are building so that we can be supplied if we are besieged. The only danger we had was the island but the monks have abandoned it."

"If we had used the island we could save work."

"We could but it is too small for our people. This will be the beginning. Others will come to join us and there are those, such as the people who live at Ċiriċeburh who will come to live here."

" Ċiriċeburh?"

"When we came for the tribute the survivors said they would not survive the winter. I gave my word that we would help them."

"Even though they are Franks?"

"Jarl Siggi had the idea. He said we would not take all from them but use them as a farmer uses a cow to take milk when we needed it. I gave my word and I believe that this, too, is *wyrd*. I may be wrong but I lead now."

"You will be Jarl?"

"No, for that was Siggi. I will lead the people. What they call me is irrelevant."

And so our new life began. It took seven days for us to build two of our halls and the weather changed just when the last roof went up. I gathered my men around me. "We have one more hall to build."

"One more? There is enough room here for us all."

## The Battle for a Home

"Aye Arne Four Toes. But I intend to bring back more people. When we have made a start on the last hall we have other tasks to complete. We have grain but it must last us the winter. I need half of the men to build the first wall around the halls and the other half to hunt and gather wood. I will go with Gille to Ċiriċeburh. There are people there who may need our help. I will return with them if they wish to come."

"You would take Franks into our homes?" It was an honest question from Beorn Beornsson.

"It is what Jarl Siggi would have done. Besides we have lost warriors. We need to build up the clan. There are women there without husbands and there are young men who can become warriors." I paused, "If you wish to hold a Thing and choose a new leader..."

"No, we are happy with your decisions, Hrolf the Horseman, for you have saved the clan. It is just that this is a new way for us."

"It is, but I feel in my heart that it is the right one."

That night, as we cuddled together, she said, "You remember that room you built for me at the end of your hall?"

"Aye."

"Could we not have one built here too?"

I had thought of that already. "We have built our halls on the only land which is not rocky beneath the surface. It would take a god to crush them and allow us to make foundations."

"Oh." She sounded disappointed.

Then I had an idea. I know not where it came from save that I had seen a building like this in Andecavis when I had stayed as a spy. "We could build another floor on the last hall; the one we have yet to build. Then we would have as much room as we liked and it could be somewhere we could defend. Tomorrow we will look into this."

My men were quite happy to build a second storey. It was not any more difficult. It just took longer. Once we had used rocks to buttress the walls and found a way to lock the floor of the first storey into the walls the work flew by. The work also allowed me to talk to all of my warriors about my plans. I was no Jarl Gunnar who would decide to do something and expect the clan to follow. I was more like Jarl Siggi. I wanted them all on my side.

When I was certain that all knew my plans I left with Gille and two of the mares. The two new ones were in foal and it was a good portent that they would be born in our new home. We rode mailed and I took my bow. This was not Raven Wing Island when we had first arrived. Here there were enemies for we were the invader. Each time I took my bow in my hands I was reminded of Ulf. It was not a sad memory. He had died when he had chosen. Few warriors are given that chance.

When we had visited Ćiriċeburh we had done so by sea. This time we headed across country. I was able to spy out the land and see potential danger. The land was flat and heavily wooded. We saw few farms as we headed northwest. Nipper was with us. Gille told me that he had spent the whole voyage staring from the stern of the knarr and watching for me. Now that he was reunited with Dream Strider and me he was happy and raced ahead of us acting like a smaller version of Ulf Big Nose. He would smell out danger.

We found the first villagers just half a mile from the settlement. There were four emaciated women and a child. When Nipper barked they fled into the forest. They had been collecting the last of the berries that the birds had not eaten. I called to them, "We mean you no harm." But they fled. I took off my helmet and hung it from my saddle. I pushed back the mail from my head. Gille did the same. We were frightening them.

We passed freshly dug mounds close by the charred remains of the church. They were newly dead. There were more women and children to be seen when we neared the village. They fled to the charred remains of the citadel. Only two remained to face us: one was the older woman who had said they would all be dead when I returned and the other looked to be a younger version of her.

The older woman smiled. I saw that many of her teeth had fallen out. That was a sign of a poor diet. "So Viking you came back. Did you want us as slaves?"

I dismounted, "No, mother. I promised that I would return. My people have landed just twenty miles from here. I can offer you food, shelter and protection."

"And what would you have in return? Our bodies?" She laughed but her lack of teeth made it come out as a cackle. "You would not enjoy them. Not even my daughter's here. We are all skin, bone and rotting teeth."

"When my jarl came here he made a bargain with Baldred. He said we would come back and collect tribute and in return, we would protect you. We did not protect you. I am here to make good on that promise. We are few in numbers and you would have to work for your food. "

Her daughter tugged at her ragged dress, "Mother we will die. Better slavery than death by hunger."

## The Battle for a Home

"Twenty miles is a long way and we are hungry already."

"Have you a cart? We brought two horses. We could carry those who are too weak to walk and there will be food at the end of the journey."

The woman took my hands in her claw-like grip and stared intently into my eyes. She nodded, "I see no deceit in your eyes but Bertha, my daughter, is right. We have little choice. We buried six in the last month. Soon there will be no one left to bury the dead."

"Good. What is your name, mother?"

"Matildhe."

"Then Matildhe gather your people. Gille, find a cart or a wagon."

The matriarch shouted, "Come he means no harm." At first, no one moved." I order you to come."

The women and children appeared from where they had been hiding. "They obey you."

She nodded, "Baldred and Brego were my sons. I carry on for them." She examined the women and children as they approached and then shouted, "Bertrand! Stop hiding and come!"

The boy I had saved stepped from behind the ruins of the church. He had a short sword in his hand and a leather helmet. He approached cautiously never letting his guard drop. "I let you live when we came. Why are you afraid now?"

"The men of Vannes said they would let the men live if they let them take their grain and then they slew the men."

"I see. I never break my word and you are safe. We have taken over your old home. Would you return there with us and make a home amongst us? We can use warriors who are not afraid of their enemies."

"I am a boy and not a warrior."

Gille spoke, having found a wagon, "And until the hersir took me I was a boy who knew horses and nothing more. Now I have killed our enemies. You can do the same."

"I would like that."

"Hersir, the wagon is yonder it is old but the wheels turn and it will carry at least fifteen of these women and children. We will have to use ropes as traces."

"Bertrand, go and help Gille." They went off with the two mares. "Matildhe, have the women who are weak and the babies climb into the wagon. If we leave now we can be at the haugr by dark."

She frowned at the unfamiliar word, "The haugr?"

"It is what we call the place where the monastery was. It is our home."

# The Battle for a Home

Gille, Bertrand and I walked. I mounted Matildhe on Dream Strider and Bertha on Night Star. As we walked we discovered more about these new members of our clan. We also learned about the monastery. Bertrand had been back to the monastery to see if they could help. When he had reached the island the warriors of King Louis were taking the altar and other things we had left. Bertrand had asked for help and they had laughed at him. Their leader had said that as they had no men to defend them they would have to rely on God's generosity. He also found out that they were moving the monastery to the Issicauna. It was then that Bertrand learned to trust no one.

Matildhe chuckled, "It is strange, Viking, is it not, that God uses a barbarian and a pagan to save us?"

"We have a word for such things amongst my people. We say that it is *wyrd*. Perhaps you would say it is God's will."

"You are a strange pagan."

"Perhaps that is because my wife is a follower of the White Christ, a Christian."

"And she is happy to live with you?"

I laughed, "We do not eat babies and we do wash! Live with us for a while and then judge us."

She looked at Gille, "Will we be safe from your lusty young men such as this one?"

"As you said, Matildhe, at the moment you are not in any danger save from falling and breaking your limbs but when you and your people are fit and healthy it may well be that some of my young men may wish to take a bride. But they will ask and they will not take. If they tried they would answer to me and be outlawed."

"You are young to be a leader."

"Like you, we have lost our wiser heads so the clan is now my responsibility."

Even though we were talking Nipper kept his guard up and Gille, Bertrand and I listened for danger. There was none. We were a mile or so from the coast when we began to smell not just wood smoke but the smell of cooking meat. When you are hungry your senses become keener. I saw Bertha's eyes widen, "Is that your camp we can smell?"

"It must be for we passed no people on our way to your home."

She smiled, "I have not touched meat since..."

# The Battle for a Home

Matildhe put her hand on her daughter's. "Not since the men of Vannes came. Well, it is time we broke that fast if this Viking lord will allow it."

"I invited you and you shall share the bounty. It is our way."

Nights were getting longer and we arrived at the settlement after dark. Part of the outside wall was up but that mattered not for there were large pieces of meat being cooked and it was food that they needed. Nipper's barking had alerted both my sentries and Mary. She approached us with a smile on her face. The unborn child gave her a natural glow and I saw the relief on the faces of Matildhe and Bertha.

"Welcome to our home. You must be hungry and cold. Come by the fire. We have made space for you in the small hall. I am sorry that it is so rude and bare but we have just arrived recently."

Matildhe climbed down and knelt. She recognised the nobility in Mary instantly. It was in the way she spoke and carried herself, "My lady thank you for your hospitality."

"Come," She waved her arm for the others, "Come to the fire."

As they passed her Mary came to me and kissed me on the cheek. "This was a Christian thing to do!"

I shook my head, "Vikings are hospitable too. We have more in common than you can know."

I ate with my men for the women crowded around the women keen to see to their needs. "The wall goes well."

Bagsecg nodded proudly. "We did as you suggested and made the mound level. It took longer but we put the timber in front of the ditch."

"Good. As the men who fought the Frisians will tell you a solid fighting platform, which is wider than a couple of planks, is better for fighting."

Einar Asbjornson asked, "Did you see any enemies on your journey, lord?"

"There was nothing. It was like a wasteland. I saw little farmland save that around the destroyed citadel. I fear we will not be growing our own grain next year."

"We have plenty. But we need a granary."

"Then we build that on the high mound. I want this area to be for workshops, stables and slave quarters."

"We only have the six slaves of Jarl Siggi's left."

## The Battle for a Home

"We will be getting more. We spend the time before midwinter making our home stronger and then we can plan our raids and make our trades." I nodded to Harold, "You will need to choose a crew."

"But what have we to trade?"

"I know not yet but we are a resourceful people, are we not? Mary and her women can make fine clothes. We have carvers of bone. Bagsecg you now have iron. Can you make goods for trade?"

"Aye, and it will be easier here. I have water closer to hand and will not need to have my boys fetching pails." He smiled, "It is like my father's forge in Cyninges-tūn!"

"Then after Samhain, we will trade with Dyflin. It will be good to get news and perhaps there may be more men like Gudrun who seek an oar."

Rurik smiled, "So we still raid then?"

"We are Vikings. It is what we do."

Bertrand had been sitting by Gille and listening. "I am a Frank. Do I get to kill my enemies?"

"What enemies are there for you?"

"Any whom I do not know! The Bretons took my family and the Franks washed their hands of us. If Vikings are the only ones who will help me then I will be a Viking."

I nodded, "You do not have to be Norse to be a Viking. The greatest Viking has no Norse blood in him at all. Jarl Dragonheart of the land of the wolf was born of a Saxon and a Celt. Gille will help you become a warrior but one piece of advice, do not hate all Franks. You are a Frank. Your family were Franks and the people who took you in were Franks. Choose your enemies and choose your battles."

We worked from dawn until dusk and often beyond. We worked with a will. Winter was coming and soon we would have to battle rains, winds and possibly snow. We knew that, until we had our outer wall up then we were vulnerable. I was convinced that with our outer wall erected then no enemy could breach our walls. The hardest part, and the one which took the longest, was digging the ditch which ran around our outer wall. It had to be deep and lined or else the sand and the soil would fill it. In a perfect world, we would have used stones alone but we had not enough and so we used the smaller branches from the trees we used to make the palisade. We used shingle and rocks from the beach to pack behind the wood. We even began to use open baskets filled with small stones. They proved the fastest means of building our outer defence. As we cleared the trees we let our animals take all the foliage and undergrowth and then

## The Battle for a Home

burned the stumps. Once the stumps were burned our strongest men dug out the roots and the women worked the soil. We had beans and we would plant those for our first crop.

Sigurd and Skutal did not work on the walls for their task was to fish. They put in place their ropes to farm the mussels and oysters. At first, we had scant pickings but the two were confident that in time we would have a good harvest. My two sea captains were keen to put to sea but they understood the need for our defences to be in place. When they were not helping us they were making the jetty stronger by dropping rocks to make a breakwater to the north.

We spent a whole two days building a dam and a sluice gate to the sea. Then we would be ready to flood the ditch. The whole of Haugr, as we now called our home, came to watch as we waited for the high tide. As it was my idea I was the one who was chosen to break the dam and lift the gate. If I did this wrong then all our work would have been wasted. I lifted the gate and was relieved that it worked. It was sturdy and, made of oak, would last as long as a drekar. Then Rurik, Arne, Erik and I began to remove the dam. The first stones were hard to shift but once they had gone then it became easier as the incoming tide rushed around our outer defences. We had a veritable river running around the lower stockade. At first, I worried that it might burst the banks but we had built well and the water subsided to form a salty foamy barrier as deep as a man and five paces wide. The bridge and gatehouse were still a little bare; we had work to do there. They would need a pair of small guard towers but we could gain access to the land easily by crossing it. As the water whooshed around the people cheered. We still had towers to build and stakes to sharpen but we now had security and we celebrated.

# Chapter 18

The knarr left with six men on board. We did not have a large cargo to trade but we had gold. I told Harold Fast Sailing to buy whatever he thought we needed.

"Such as?"

"We have no seal oil. It will be cheaper in Dyflin than here."

"It would be even cheaper further north."

"And you would be away longer. We need neither pots, for we can trade for those with the Franks, nor do we need slaves but if you can buy animals for breeding then that would be a useful cargo for you to bring. Any grain would be welcome. We are short of rope but we have enough timber. Ask Sven if he needs more canvas. We will need to trade for iron later in the year but for now, that will suffice."

"I am afraid to waste your gold."

I smiled, "This is some of the gold that Siggi and Ulf gave to me. If it serves the clan then it is not wasted. They would want it to make us more secure here."

Happy that he knew my wishes he left.

Mary was becoming larger by the day. The women of Haugr, even the new ones, seemed to regard this new baby to be momentous. Perhaps it was because I now led the clan. We had many new babies. I was one of the few, save for the five new men, who had yet to toast the birth of a child. There were eight boys and six girls born already. My new men had been envious but, with the Franks we had rescued becoming healthier day by day, soon they were casting glances in their direction. Mary and I were delighted with this new direction. For the first time we had some privacy where we could talk. With our huge room in the largest hall, we could talk at night. During the day it was the place where Mary would work with her women on the garments they made. They left each night but that meant, when we cuddled beneath our furs, we could talk.

"Your son was busy today. He kept moving."

"You know it is a boy?"

# The Battle for a Home

"I believe it is. The older women from Ċiriċeburh say that when its heart sounds like your horse galloping across the turf then it will be a boy. Matildhe listened yesterday and said it sounded just so. He will be a boy."

"When will he arrive?"

"He will come when he is ready. He is not ready yet. The women who know such things tell me this. I am pleased that you brought Matildhe and the others. They have helped me. The women from our island mean well but they are Norse. I know we all give birth the same way but..."

"I understand."

"When is he likely to be ready? What I want to know is how much longer do I need to worry?"

"He should be here after the midwinter feast. His head is up near my breasts."

I cuddled her. "Then our son has good taste for that is where I like to be!"

Now that we had our defences in place I took to riding abroad with my men. Bertrand was a good rider and I let him ride Gerðr. With two mares in foal and the young horses not yet ready to ride I only had one horse left and Einar Asbjornson had shown the most affinity with horses. That was more important than anything else. We did not take shields. Gille and I were still working on a smaller version of my larger shield. Bertrand had no mail yet but we had a spare helmet and he wore that. We gave him one of Ulf's swords and a spear. He was smaller than Gille but I could see that, if we fed him up then he would be a strong warrior.

We rode south. Bertrand only knew the land to the north and west. I needed to know what lay beyond. We were ten miles from our home when I spied a farmhouse. We had our helmets slung from our saddles and our heads and mail covered by cloaks. The farmer who came from his barn took us for Franks. Only Einar did not speak their words and he remained silent.

"I do not know you. Where are you from?"

" Ċiriċeburh."

"Ah, the place destroyed by those Norsemen. I hope you have better luck than they did."

I said nothing.

"What brings you out on this bone-chilling day?"

"I thought to visit with the noble who rules this area."

## The Battle for a Home

He shook his head, "Since King Louis took the monks away and the Leudes, Baldred, was killed there is no one."

"Then who takes your taxes?"

He gave me a cunning smile, "If there is no lord to collect taxes then we pay none."

"But you have no protection."

"What protection did they have when the heathens from the north came? We are far enough from the sea that we would have a warning. If the dragon ships are seen then those on the coast flee inland. The road passes through here."

"Then where is there a stronghold?"

"Valognes. They have a wall and there is a lord there. It is only six miles down the road."

"And he does not collect taxes?"

"His land stops there." He pointed to a hedgerow at the end of his field. My land was owned by the church." He suddenly frowned, "And who gave you the lands? If you are a neighbour of mine I should know where you live."

"We are not close. We have occupied Ciriċeburh. There was no one living there."

He laughed, "Good luck then for the Vikings will come again."

"Perhaps. Farewell."

We turned and headed back up the road. I had discovered enough. We were safe from an incursion for a while but the most interesting information was that the locals thought that we had destroyed Ciriċeburh. That told me that someone was spreading lies and warned me that men of Vannes, the Bretons, were an enemy to be feared.

Bertrand was a bright boy and it was he who brought up the lie. "You did not destroy Ciriċeburh."

"No, but we did attack it. As you are aware, the Bretons took advantage of that. We will keep a good watch to the west."

He nodded and stroked Gerðr's mane. "This is a good horse."

"I am happy with all of them but we will be using her for breeding. I intend for all my warriors to be mounted."

"All?"

"We can control a large part of this land with horses."

"Then you intend to stay."

"That is why we left our island home to come here."

# The Battle for a Home

Of course, what I did not say was that there would come a time when King Louis or the lord of Valognes would want us off their land. I wanted that to be as far in the future as possible. When that day came we would fight for this scrap of land I had claimed.

Even though the walls were finished we did not stop working. Sven had the drekar to complete. She had sailed from our island hurriedly. During the winter we would need to give her serious trials to make sure she flew as Sven assured me she would. We worked on our two gates, adding towers. I had learned much from the tower I had built at my hall. It only needed protection on three sides and that made it much easier to ascend and descend. We built a walkway over the gate to link the two towers. The gates themselves were solidly made but the bridge in front of them had two ropes so that it could be hauled up and added an extra strength to the main gate.

The ditch around the haugr was deepened and the spoil added to the outside of the ramparts so that it would be harder for an enemy to mine beneath them. The work kept the warriors occupied and helped us to bond with the new men. As the days grew shorter so the weather grew colder. We had no snow but there were icy fogs and rainstorms filled with sleet. And all the time my wife grew larger and I began to worry about her. I had brought her to a place where we could be in danger. Was I ready to make the sorts of decisions I had been making?

The knarr arrived the day after we had finished the gates. The drekar still rode at anchor and this was the first time we had tested the new jetty. The knarr rode higher in the water than I would have expected and I wondered if Harold had managed to trade. Six warriors stepped from the knarr. One had mail while the rest looked as though they knew how to fight. They strode towards the stockade. I saw that it had surprised them. I met them on the grassy area close to the bridge.

"I am Hrolf the Horseman. I am hersir."

"I am Finni Jarlson. These are my men and we are from Ljoðhús."

"Jarl Thorfinn Blue Scar?"

"He was my father."

"Then why did you not take the name Thorfinnson."

He smiled but it was a sad smile, "My mother had another husband. I only discovered my true father after he was dead and my mother close to death. She told me before she died. I took the name Jarlson. I like it."

I nodded, "As do I. And why have you come here?"

# The Battle for a Home

"We had a long journey from Ljoðhús after the men of Alt Clut conquered it. We had more men and we took our knarr to find new lands to the west but all we found was death in the stormy seas close to the edge of the world. Six died and we were washed up on the west coast of Hibernia. Another four died when we fought our way to Dyflin. I had intended to join Jarl Gunnar Thorfinnson for he would have been my half brother but Jarl Gunnstein told me that he had died. We have been waiting for your knarr to trade. The Jarl told us that Siggi White Hair and Ulf Big Nose were on your island. They are kin or so my mother said. But Harold Fast Sailing told me that they had died too. It seems we are here but I know not the reason."

"I do. It is the Norns who have directed you. We need warriors who can fight. We have women but warriors are few."

"We have only what you see. If Jarl Gunnstein Berserk Killer in Dyflin had not been generous to us then we would have starved."

"It is what is in your heart and minds and not what you wear. We will take more armour and we will make sure you do not go hungry. Now, who are your men?"

"I am Knut the Quiet."

"Asbjorn Sorenson."

"Sigismund of Ljoðhús."

"Karl the Singer."

"Audun Einarsson. Finni Jarlson is my big brother."

"Well, you are welcome. Come to the warrior hall. We have three. I live above the one for the unmarried warriors."

As we walked Finni said, "I have never seen such a fort. I have heard of the ones the Dragonheart has on his land but they are nothing like this."

"The haugr was here before and was a fort but we took it easily. I made it this way for I thought it would be harder to take."

"If this is from your head then I am impressed. It looks almost impregnable. From what I have heard you are not a normal Viking. Harold Fast Sailing tells me that you ride horses."

"That is true but we still raid by sea. It is just that the Franks ride horses to war and if we are to defeat them then we must meet them beard to beard."

He laughed, "I like you already and yet you are so young that you barely have a beard."

## The Battle for a Home

I nodded, "I have taken the heads of many men who had fine beards. The beards did not seem to help them!"

"I meant no offence. I heard that you slew the Hibernian champion. Men spoke of you and Ulf Big Nose in Dyflin."

"And I took none."

It seemed that Harold had barely made it back in time. The storms which battered our coast lasted ten days. We were lucky that the island which had housed the monastery gave our drekar and knarr more protection else we would have lost them both. Our lower stockade was breached by the stormy seas. Even our new defences were not strong enough for the gods when they fought amongst themselves. As the shortest day approached we worked to repair the walls. We repacked stones behind the wood and we added more timber to the sections close to the sea. It was as we stood back, after three days of hard work, to admire our labours that we noticed the huge amount of driftwood which had landed on the beach north of the causeway. It was fresh planks, strakes and timbers. Ships at sea had been torn apart by the storms.

As we headed in I saw Mary waddling towards me with Matildhe. Although the rains had abated the wind still whistled from the north and chilled even the most hardened of warriors.

"Why have you left the warmth of the hall? There is nothing for you ladies here."

"That is where you are wrong, husband." Mary pointed towards the island. "There used to be a church there and you and your men took it down."

"To make our homes."

She ignored me. "We now have Christians who live amongst us and we would have a church. There are those, like Brigid, who came from Hibernia. They are Christians. Morag came from Cymru and she is a Christian. They need somewhere to worship. There was a cross on the church which you did not use. Bring it and build us a church here."

I shook my head, "I will fetch the cross but I will not command my men to build a church for Christians."

"Then we will build it."

Despite my best efforts, I could not dissuade either of them from their course of action. Neither was in the best condition to be outside in this weather let alone working. "I tell you what I will do. There are materials still on the island. I will take the slaves and ask for men to volunteer to help me and I will build a church there."

# The Battle for a Home

"Why not here, inside the walls?"

"We have no room on the haugr and here your church would be surrounded by workshops." I pointed to the bread ovens and kilns which we had built well away from anything which might burn. Smoke belched from them each day for we always had bread to bake and pots to make. "You would not want to pray with that around you. You would have the smell of smoking fish too." I saw her ready to argue, "Wife, I know that Christians like to be buried by their churches. Would you want the dead to be buried inside our walls? I know that those who are not Christians would fear the ghosts of the dead and besides, if we used the shell of the church it would still be holy ground would it not?"

Matildhe nodded, "The barbarian is right, my lady. It will be more peaceful. For a barbarian he is clever."

And so I began, when the days were at their shortest and their coldest, to begin to labour on a church I would never use. As I tore my hands open on the stones I lifted I wondered if I had made the right decision to marry someone who followed the White Christ. Then I remembered the baby she carried. It made me work even harder. It was not even just the Christians who helped me. Gille, Bertrand, Bagsecg and his sons all laboured. We made a stone church. There were still large pieces of dressed stone which had been too heavy to take to the haugr. They were the foundations of the monk's church and they gave us a good start. We used those and then we used the stones which the recent storms had provided. We had the outline of the church left by the monks and we just laboured, adding courses.

When we reached the height of a man we had to use timber from our woods for the roof. We had reused the slates which the original church had had and so we used turf. It was as we were laying turf on the roof that I remembered how we used turf to buttress walls. I used the spare stone to provide buttresses to give it strength. It was midwinter day when I fitted their cross.

As I descended the ladder the Christians who had all gathered there applauded and cheered. Mary came to kiss me. "For once, husband, I will use that word *wyrd*. It is *wyrd* that you have finished the Church now so that we can celebrate Christ's birth. We may not have a priest but we can pray and sing in the church. Thank you."

Matildhe stroked my hand with her bony claw. "Thank you, barbarian, we may save your soul yet."

# The Battle for a Home

I laughed, "I need no saving. I shall die with my sword in my hand and go to Valhalla!"

While we had been labouring on the church my men had not been idle. The forests teemed with game and they had been out hunting. We did not celebrate the birth of the White Christ but we used the days following the shortest day to feast. Brigid had been brewing barrels of beer and Skutal and Sigurd had been preparing fish.

We began the feast before the actual day the Christians celebrated their god's birthday. On that day they all trooped across to the church at low tide. Gille and I escorted them and stood watch outside. We had not seen any enemies but there was no point in taking chances. Besides, it was good to be out in the chill, fresh air. The wind had changed and now came from the west. It was wetter but not as cold. Gille and I walked to the far end of the island; it was the place we had first landed. It seemed a lifetime ago.

Gille and I sat in the shelter of a rock and looked down the coast. "Life is like a circle, lord. Is it not?"

"A circle, Gille?"

"You, your wife and I, we all began life here in Frankia. You and I were not born here but we grew up here. We all went away and yet we have returned to the place where we grew up."

"That is the Norns, Gille."

"Where I grew up they were not mentioned and yet you and the others seem to think they rule our lives."

"They do, Gille. They spin their threads and webs. They tie us together even though we do not know it. They plan far into the future. When we went to find timber we did not think that we would find you, a horse master. When I spared Bertrand and gave him a horse I did not know that he would become one of us. I know not what the Norns have in store for us but, so long as we do what is in our hearts, we are doing the right thing. I know that our life here will not be easy but with the new men we have gained, we will become stronger. There are ten Franks who will become our warriors. When the weather improves you and I will venture inland and see if there are horses we can buy."

"Buy?"

I smiled, "Until we get more men we will try to buy but I am happy to take. We are still Vikings."

Just then it began to rain with flecks of sleet mixed in. "Come we will shelter by the church. It is good for that, at least."

When we reached the church the door opened and Mary led the people out. She smiled as she took my arm. "We all prayed for your soul, husband. You have built a good church."

"I am pleased that you are happy. Now let us get out of this wind and before a fire. I have an appetite!"

# Chapter 19

My son Ragnvald arrived at the end of Mörsugur. I was barred from the birth. That was the Christian way. My wife screamed and shouted for almost half a day as she fought the baby. I wondered if either would survive. Bagsecg, who had had many children said, "It is always this way, Hrolf. There will be blood and there will be tears. She will be exhausted when she is finished but there will be a red ball which will be, the Allfather willing, your son. You will count fingers and toes; you will see that his ears and nose are in the right place and we will get drunk!"

He was right. Brigid came out to me; her hands red and bloody as though she was a warrior come from a battle. "Hersir, you have a son. He is a strong one and a big one! If he grows into his feet he will be a mighty warrior. Go and see her."

I went up to our sleeping chamber. Matildhe shooed the women out and then wagged a bony finger at me, "Do not stay too long. Your wife needs her rest and the baby needs feeding. I will return with some honeyed ale for her."

I sat on the bed and looked at my son. He had a full head of hair and was a vivid colour. "Should he be that colour?"

She gave a wan smile, "I wanted him out. He could have been born any colour but Brigid says that this is normal. Do you not like him?"

I smiled, "I think he is wonderful but I have only seen horses and cows born before now. I knew not what to expect."

She held up the swaddled child, "Then take him now and speak with him. Keep your paw around the back of his neck. He is tender yet."

As soon as I held him in my hands I felt a change. He was so small and yet I had made him. He looked vulnerable and fragile as though a strong wind would destroy him. I put my face close to him to kiss him. He smelled... to me he smelled different like something strange and foreign but I liked the smell. I noticed his tiny fingers as they seemed to wave. I put my finger to touch them and he grabbed on. He had a powerful grip.

## The Battle for a Home

"You will be a warrior, my son! Do not fear your father will be there for you. I promise that I will be there to help you to fly and I will be there to catch you should you fall. I will protect you as a wolf protects a cub until you are a man and you lead this clan. That I promise, Ragnvald, and I am never foresworn."

"Ragnvald?"

"It came to me. You do not mind, do you? It will remind me of Siggi. That was the name of his father and he said he wanted a son with that name. He will be Ragnvald Hrolfsson."

As I handed our son back to her she nodded, "And I will name the next one! Hopefully, that will be a girl!"

We had our own traditions too. The Viking women took out the afterbirth and buried it. The Christian women did not understand but, as it did not appear to contravene a Christian belief, they allowed it. Then the men celebrated. I was toasted and applauded. They told tales of what Ragnvald Hrolfsson would do when he was older. Then, Karl, the Singer showed us why he was thus named. He sang Siggi's song. It brought tears to my eyes, it was so beautiful. Gille told me later that he had asked for one of our songs to learn. It was his gift to me. It was a gift greater than gold.

*Siggi was the son of a warrior brave*
*Mothered by a Hibernian slave*
*In the Northern sun where life is short*
*His back was strong and his arm was taut*
*Siggi White Hair warrior true*
*Siggi White Hair warrior true*
*When the Danes they came to take his home*
*He bit the shield and spat white foam*
*With berserk fury he killed them dead*
*When their captain fell the others fled*
*Siggi White Hair warrior true*
*Siggi White Hair warrior true*
*After they had gone and he stood alone*
*He was a rock, a mighty stone*
*Alone and bloodied after the fight*
*His hair had changed from black to white*
*His name was made and his courage sung*

# The Battle for a Home

*Hair of white and a body young*
*Siggi White Hair warrior true*
*Siggi White Hair warrior true*
*With dying breath he saved the clan*
*He died as he lived like a man*
*And now reborn to the clan's hersir*
*Ragnvald Hrolfsson the clan does cheer*
*Ragnvald Hrolfsson warrior true*
*Ragnvald Hrolfsson warrior true*

When he had finished I embraced him. "You changed the words!"
He smiled, "That is what singers do, lord. You did not mind?"
I shook my head. "Just the opposite. I know two warriors in Valhalla who are toasting Ragnvald even now." I reached into my leather purse and brought out a gold coin of Charlemagne. "Here, this is for you."
"But I wanted to give you a gift."
"And I thank you, now take my gift."
My son changed my life. For one thing, he did not seem to understand that night was for sleeping and not wailing and crying for his mother's nipple or for soiling himself with the most disgusting messes I had ever seen. I took to sleeping when I could. It mattered not if it was day or night. I just slept. After a month he began to change. He still woke in the night, but not as often and he just wished to be fed. I spoke to him each day and held him as often as possible. I wanted him to know my smell.
Mary found it amusing. "A barbarian warrior cooing over a baby; I never thought I would see the day."
"I keep telling you we are warriors and we are hard but that is for the battlefield. In our chests there beats a heart."
As the days began to lengthen so we prepared for the hard times to come. Bagsecg had worked hard all winter preparing weapons and helmets. Most of the warriors who bought one from him had the same design as mine. They did not have the golden cross as I did. Instead, they had a raven as their herkumbl. As well as my son we had two more foals born and Gerðr and Freya were now expecting two more foals. Dawn's Light and Copper had been prepared for the saddle by Bertrand and Gille. They were not yet ready to take a warrior in mail but they would bear a rider. We began to make more saddles and stiraps. Our new shields were ready. They were smaller and some, like Rurik wondered if they would be effective. The Raven Wing Clan was preparing for war.

# The Battle for a Home

I brought out my armour to show the other warriors, "See how my mail is split so that when I ride it drops down to protect my leg. The shield is smaller and lighter. I can raise and lower it quickly. It will work."

I saw them looking at the design critically. I had yet to convince them of the need to ride to war and fight on horseback but we would take small steps.

Bagsecg had also made new heads for our spears. We used ash which was an arm's length longer than a man's height. The spearhead tapered to a sharp point. I wanted a spear which would penetrate mail. On foot this was hard but with the weight of a horse and a punch from a rider, it would be easier. We made dummies and dressed them in old mail which was ready to be melted down. We put the dummies on wooden stakes on the beach and Gille and I rode at them with our new spears. They worked but, after Gille was thrown, we discovered that you had to use a special technique. You did not hit head-on but at an angle. It made it easier to withdraw the spear. We were learning and we were evolving.

Harold and Sven came to speak with me."Hersir, we need to take **'Dragon's Breath'** to sea. We have not rowed yet with a full crew and we now have new men."

I knew they were right but I was loath to leave my wife and new son. They appeared to me to be too weak to be without me. Yet I was hersir. "Very well. What do you suggest?"

"Sarnia? It belongs to the lords of Brittany and we would not have far to sail. It would give the men the chance to row and to take some slaves."

I shook my head, "We want no slaves who live close to us. But it is an idea. They will have animals we can take to breed. We will raid Sarnia. How long will it take to prepare the drekar?"

"We can leave in the morning."

The warriors were all keen on the raid. The deaths on Raven's Wing Island had been forgotten. We were warriors and my men had tired of hunting and building. We had made sure that the young Franks who had joined us could use slings and they, along with the handful of men we would leave would be responsible for guarding our walls. We would not be away for long. Sven said that even rowing we could reach it in half a day. If we left before dawn then we could be back before dark.

As we headed towards the jetty to embark I took Gille and Bertrand to one side. "Gille, you have been on raids. You watch out for Bertrand. If neither of you has to draw a weapon there is no shame. What you come

# The Battle for a Home

back with is experience and that is like gold." They nodded. "You will be at the bow on an oar together. You must keep the stroke with the rest of the crew."

I would not be rowing for I was now hersir. We had enough men in the clan for every oar to be manned. We had some oars, the ones at the stern, double crewed. Harold would come with us on this voyage to help train the five ships' boys who would swarm up the sheets and shrouds to furl and unfurl the sail. We placed our best warriors at the stern. Harold would watch the others and make adjustments to the oars as necessary. Some would work better at the bow, stern, or the mast. They each carried their chest aboard. They were empty for we would be gone a short time but a chest made a good seat. Older warriors like Arne and Rurik had the lids of their chests covered in a sealskin lined sheepskin. The younger ones laughed at them.

We placed our shields along the side for we were going to war. Sven had placed the figurehead on the prow the night before. It made the drekar whole. We rowed out beyond the island. As soon as we turned north we found a breeze from the southeast to make rowing easier. As we sailed north we felt it move as it turned with the tide and the dawn. We rowed hard for who knew when the wind might change and we still sang.

> *The night was black no moon was there*
> *Death and danger hung in the air*
> *As Raven Wing closed with the shore*
> *The scouts crept closer as before*
> *Dressed like death with sharpened blades*
> *They moved like spirits through the glades*
> *The power of the raven grows and grows*
> *The power of the raven grows and grows*
> *With sentries slain they sought new foes*
> *A cry in the night fetched them woes*
> *The alarm was given the warriors ready*
> *Four scouts therewith hearts so steady*
> *Ulf and Arne thought their end was nigh*
> *When Hrolf the wild leapt from the sky*
> *Flying like the raven through the air*
> *He felled the Cymri, a raven slayer*
> *The power of the raven grows and grows*

## The Battle for a Home

*The power of the raven grows and grows*
*His courage clear he still fought on*
*Until the clan had battled and won*
*The power of the raven grows and grows*
*The power of the raven grows and grows*
*Raven Wing goes to war*
*Hear our voices hear them roar*
*A song of death to all its foes*
*The power of the raven grows and grows*
*The power of the raven grows and grows*
*Raven Wing goes to war*
*Hear our voices hear them roar*
*A song of death to all its foes*
*The power of the raven grows and grows*
*The power of the raven grows and grows*

It was a good song to sing for it spoke of Ulf. It reminded those who knew him of his courage and helped those new to understand more of our past.

The wind turned with the dawn and swung around to come from the northwest. As we turned west we had to row harder for we were heading into the wind. When Harold and the boys furled the sail we leapt through the water. We were like a dolphin. The blue morning light was dimmed by the scudding clouds. We passed one small island to the steerboard side. There were two large islands ahead of us and they both had villages on them. We would head for Sarnia. Angia was bigger and had a high rock with a hill fort. We had not seen any such defence at Sarnia.

As we neared its eastern shore Sven headed for the smoke which rose from the fires in the huts. Where there were fires we would find men. We turned to sail south between the two small uninhabited islands and the main one, Sarnia. Siggi Far-Sighted, the ship's boy who sat at the top of the mast lived up to his name as he shouted down, "I can see fishing boats! There are huts."

I shouted back, "Any wall?"

"No hersir."

"Sven, put the helm over!" I took my helmet and jammed it on my head. Grabbing my shield I ran to the prow. I watched as the shore raced towards us. I saw villagers fleeing. A half a dozen men ran for their

# The Battle for a Home

weapons. I stood with my right hand touching the back of the prow. "Siggi, we will try to live up to your high standards."

Sven put the helm over and we headed towards the beach. The fact there were fishing boats drawn up meant that there were no rocks to rip out our hull.

Sven shouted, "Up oars!"

The warriors placed the oars in the middle of the drekar and then grabbed their shields. The ships' boys were ready to leap over the side and secure us. I jumped as the bow rose on the shelving, sandy beach and landed on the soft sand. I drew my sword and swung my shield around. There were six men facing me but I just roared a challenge as I ran at them. I shouted in Frankish, "I am Hrolf the Horseman of the Raven Wing Clan. Fear me!

I brought my sword down on the leading warrior who held a shield tentatively before him. My sword sliced down and split his head in two. The other men ran. I followed them. Without armour, they should have been much faster but they were not. I began to catch them as they snaked their way between huts. Suddenly a warrior burst out from my left and brought his sword down hard. I just managed to bring my shield up to block it. The nails and the boss caught the blade and held it as it bit deeply into the wood. As I staggered back from the force of the blow he tumbled after me. I brought Heart of Ice around in a long sweep and it sliced deep into his side. He was a strong man. I punched him in the face with my shield and his own axe sliced a long line in his face.

As he tumbled backwards he cursed, "Viking animal!"

I finished him off as he lay at my feet. As my men ran past me I took the axe and handed it to Gille who appeared with Bertrand behind me. "Here, our first trophy. The two of you search the huts for treasure. It may be buried. When you have checked every hut take the treasure you find to the drekar."

I hefted my shield around my back and followed my men. I doubted that we would catch those who fled but we needed their animals. They were less likely to try to save their animals while their lives were in danger. We stopped half a mile from the village.

"Gather as many animals as you can. Drive them to the drekar."

When we reached the village Harold and the ship's boys had come ashore to help *Gille* and Bertrand. The villages had clay dishes as well as some metal cooking pots. There were jugs of cider too. Sigurd and Skutal had not followed the rest of my warriors; instead, they had begun to collect the nets and ropes. They were filling two fishing boats. Sigurd said, cheerfully, "We now have twice as many fishing boats and four times the number of nets. This was a good raid."

While my men drove the animals back I saw that although there were not many of them they had all been kept for breeding. The four cows and six sows were all pregnant. We left the old bull but took a younger one and a young boar too. The villagers had left shellfish pots. We crammed them with fowl and killed the ones we could not cage.

After the two fishing boats were tied to the stern and we had boarded, Sven backed us out of the bay. In terms of warriors lost they had not suffered too badly. Just two men had died. They had, however, lost much of the stock. That was life.

Once we had turned we had the wind behind us and were able to loose the sail. Gudrun Witch Killer shook his head, "That was not the work of a warrior!"

I nodded, "I agree but first we secure the future of the clan and then we worry about honour and glory. Would you rather we had left warriors bleeding on this little rock? This was the first time the Raven Wing Clan raided on the new drekar. I for one take it as a good sign that nothing bad happened. The gods approve and we do that which the Norns like."

As I stood at the stern watching the island disappear beneath the horizon Sven said quietly, "That was well done, hersir. That was the way Siggi would have done it."

I nodded, "And Ulf?"

Sven laughed, "He would have smacked him on the side of his head! He was never a patient man!"

I was pleased that we reached our home before dark. The island and the rocks were dangerous for ships. It was why I had chosen this as a home and not Ćiriċeburh. We had natural defences. If an enemy tried to attack at night they risked their ship.

# The Battle for a Home

# Chapter 20

Some of the men might have been disappointed with the raid but the women were not. The pots and jugs were seen as treasure. So far we had not shared out the animals. The ones we had brought from Raven Wing Island had an enclosure. If we were attacked then we would bring them inside the stockade. Now we had to work and build bigger ones. To help keep them in and to protect them I had the slaves dig a deep ditch around it and we built a fence. The exception was the stable where we kept my horses. That was in the lower stockade. Bertrand kept calling it a baille. I asked what the word meant. I had been brought up here but had never heard the word.

He shrugged, "It means lower yard that is all."

I nodded, "Then we will use that word. It is simpler than our lower stockade."

And so our language began to change. It was subtle. I used Frank and Norse. The Franks learned Norse while the warriors often used Frankish words. The Frankish mothers used their language when talking to their children and so we evolved a new language where some Norse words were used by the Franks and vice versa. We had been two cultures and now we were becoming one. It was what had happened in the land of the wolf where Jarl Dragonheart coexisted with the old people of the land. They did not need to translate each other's words. They knew them. The difference was that there was a greater difference in our languages but we adapted.

As the weather changed for the better and the land grew greener we saw other sprouts of growth. When my two new mares gave birth my two older mares were in foal again. The sows gave birth and we had to think about the farms that some of my men wished to build. Our wood cutting had cleared much land and so I gave the ones who wished to farm, land. I gave each one an ækre. They were happy with that. As we had cleared the land close to our stronghold they could bring their families in if we were attacked. In return for the gift of land, each farmer promised one-tenth of all that they produced for the clan. None objected.

One night Mary said, "You will need to let them have animals too."

"But we have so few yet."

She was nursing Ragnvald who was sucking greedily. She winced, "I will be glad when he begins to eat real food rather than me!" As he settled down again she said, "Do as you do with the horses. Keep the bull and the boar. Let farmers bring their animals to breed and we will take one in four of their progeny. Everyone will be happy then."

I stood and kissed her, "You are clever! Where did that idea come from?"

She looked down sadly at Ragnvald, "My father used that. It made the people happy and ensured that we had animals ourselves."

We had taken all from Mary and her people. Now she was the only one left. The others were on Raven Wing Island. With their husbands dead I had no idea what Guthrum the Skull had done with them. With only two horses to ride we worked with Copper and Dawn's Light. Until the other mares had foaled we were limited. Bertrand did not wear mail and he was slight. He rode Copper and he proved to be a good rider. He enjoyed being on a horse and that helped. Dawn's Light was more skittish. Gille tried to ride her but she bucked too much. Eventually, I had to resort to riding her. I was too big for her, I knew that, but she had to get used to weight on her back and a saddle.

Each day I would walk her along the beach from Harold Haroldsson's farm on the headland to beyond the animal enclosure. After four such journeys, I would water her on the headland where Harold and his wife raised sheep and then mount her. Going down the slope made it easier for her to bear my weight and I rode her only as far as the causeway. By the third day, she had stopped bucking as much. I spoke to her while walking and while riding. I think she grew used to my voice. The trick would be getting her to bear another. I had done the hard part.

I rested her every fourth day and the three of us would ride as far south as the farmer who lived close to Valognes. His name was Alain. He knew me as Rollo. At the start of Harpa, he had a frown on his face when he saw us. "What troubles you this day? The sun is shining and soon our crops will rise from the ground."

"We have a new lord!" He wagged a warning finger at me. "He knows that you and your people have begun to farm close by Monastery Island. He will come to you for taxes too!"

# The Battle for a Home

I nodded, non committally. No one liked to pay taxes. "Does he offer protection for the payment of tax?"

The farmer spat, "When did any noble ever worry about a farmer? No, he says it is to pay for a new church in Valognes and to raise an army to fight the Vikings who are raiding the Seine. What is wrong with the church they have I say? And the Seine is far from here. Since the raid last year the Vikings have not bothered us. Watch out, Rollo. He knows of you."

As we trekked back north Bertrand asked, "Will we have to fight?"

"Perhaps but if he does come north he will have a shock for he will recognise that we are Vikings and he will not necessarily have the men to break our walls."

Gille turned to Bertrand, "It is what I told you. Our lord is clever. That is why we spent so long building our walls. We are few in number but the walls make us as strong as a mighty army."

I hoped he was right. I had not expected to be discovered so soon.

Harold Fast Sailing went to Dorestad to trade. Bagsecg and his sons had made many smaller items from some of our silver treasure. We used just the smaller coins which he formed into rings, bracelets and necklaces. Using amber we had traded in Dyflin and some jet which Ulf had left us they were attractive pieces and would fetch a high price. Mary and her women had made some beautiful dresses. They would be sold and fresh bolts of cloth bought. Dorestad was just a day along the coast and he would be back in three days' time.

I summoned all the men, the day Harold left and gave them the news about the Leudes from Valognes. "What do we do when he comes, hersir? Do we fight?"

"We will be ready to fight, Finni Jarlson, but if I can live with my neighbours then I will do so."

Gille said, "Tell them the news about the Seine, lord."

Arne Four Toes asked, "Seine?"

"It is what they call the Issicauna. Our brothers are raiding that river and they are raising an army to fight them. I asked Harold to find out more when he is in Dorestad. That port is full of gossip."

"So we prepare to fight."

"We do, Bagsecg. We make arrows. We keep the water ditch full. We make sure the ditch beneath the haugr is ready and we watch. When you look after your animals then keep an eye on the land to see if the Franks are coming. Hunters keep hunting and preserving meat. We will not kill our own animals. Skutal and Sigurd, your fish lines and nets may well be the saving of us."

"And what about our drekar? If they attack that then we are trapped and it would take a long time to build another."

"You need to find an anchorage by the island which cannot be reached on foot."

Sven nodded, "Somewhere that can only be reached at high tide by boat?" I nodded. "I will start to sleep on board with the ships' boys. There are many jobs we can do and Skutal can bring our food out on his fishing boat."

"They may not be here for months."

He smiled, "She is a good drekar and I am not unhappy to sleep aboard. I did so many times on *'Raven's Wing'* and *'Dragon's Breath'* is an even better warship. I do not mind. I will wait until Harold returns."

Rurik, Arne and I spent the next three days working with the newer and younger warriors and boys. They needed to know how we fought. We had a large palisade to protect. Even using the many boys we had who were armed with slings we would still have ten paces each to watch. So long as the enemy were on the other side of the ditch we could manage. Once they crossed then we were in trouble. Rurik had made a bull's horn into a trumpet. We would use it to signal. When it was sounded three times then we would all fall back and defend the inner ward by the halls. There we would be almost shoulder to shoulder.

Sven and his boys came up with the ingenious idea of building a cradle of wood for the drekar. Sven was pleased with the idea. "It will become a dock where we can work on the hull. See, if I build it there where the rocks from a natural hollow, we can sail the drekar off at high tide but at other times she is protected from attack by the rocks which surround her."

"That means you can only leave at high tide."

"That is when I would choose to sail anyway. I like this bay but it has more rocks than a shark has teeth!"

It took a long time for them to build their cradle as they could only work at low tide. In the end, it proved to be a gift from the gods. Whoever had placed the idea in Sven's mind saved the clan.

It was dusk when Harold's knarr edged into the bay and tied up to the jetty. While the crew fetched the trade goods he hurried to speak with us. "Your farmer was right. Many Vikings have been raiding the river they call the Seine. It is said that the Dragonheart's success began the raids and our success and Jarl Gunnar's have only increased the number of ships who attack the Franks. They cannot find a way to defeat us. Some have spent a whole seven days there raiding up and down that mighty river."

I nodded, "That was to be expected."

"Guthrum the Skull raided. He now has three drekar under his command. The gossip was that he has declared himself King of the island which he now calls Skull Island."

Rurik snorted, "King? Then I am Emperor!"

"He can keep the island. We destroyed everything that was of value there and the name means nothing. We do not relax our vigilance. Did the trades go well?"

"Aye. We fetched high prices for the jewels and the garments. I bought more cloth than was asked for. We had coins aplenty."

"My wife will be pleased."

Life should have been perfect. My son was growing and each day became more of a person and less of a mewling baby. I looked forward to the time I could teach him to ride. Our two ponies had given birth to a foal and I had already promised that to Ragnvald. He would ride as soon as he could walk. Soon I would get more ponies. If I began all the boys of the haugr riding early they would become better riders. I wanted them all to the standard of Gille and me.

Ragnvald slept better these days and I had had more uninterrupted sleep of late. It was, therefore, something of a shock to be woken up by his cries. I was not certain of the hour for it was a cloudy night with squally rain. I was awake and, as my wife saw to the baby, I descended to the hall. I would not be able to sleep straightaway. I decided to go and check on Rowan and Hazel. Wrapping my cloak around me I headed for my horses. I opened the gate to the baille and crossed the bridge to the stables. When I reached it I saw Nipper, standing, sniffing the air. His ears were pricked. There was danger.

We had two men whose task it was to walk the walls of my outer palisade each night. They all took turns. Our experiences on Raven Wing Island had taught us the value of such vigilance. This night it was Gunnar Stone Face and Rolf Arneson. I ascended the ladder to the gate and walked towards them. They were standing together looking toward the island.

"Is there danger?"

# The Battle for a Home

Rolf shook his head, "I am not certain. Perhaps it is my imagination. I thought I saw a flap of sail to the north. Gunnar thought it might be **'Dragon's Breath**."

"Sven would not loose the sail at night." I peered into the darkness. Just then I heard a whistle from the gate. We ran back to the gate. Harold Haroldsson stood there with his wife Greta.

"Hersir, there is danger!"

We hurried down the ladder and let them in. "What is it?"

"I woke to make water and I saw, to the north, three drekar. They were heading south. I did not know if they might be heading further down the coast...."

"You did right. You two go back on watch. Harold, take your wife to the haugr and wake the men. I will wake the others. Do so silently. If this is an enemy I do not want them to know we are roused."

As I passed Nipper I said, "Good dog." If he had not been alert I might have gone back to bed. Inside the hall, I shouted, "Awake and arm. There are enemies. Go to the walls." I turned to Gille and Bertrand. They always slept by the door. "Saddle your horses and bring in the farmers."

I ascended to my sleeping chamber. Mary was still feeding. "There is danger. There are three drekar heading for shore."

There had been a time when such a statement would have invoked tears but my wife had grown. "I will organize food."

"Have the younger women on the walls. Tell them to put on the spare helmets."

"You would make them think we have greater numbers than we do."

"Aye for three drekar could bring a hundred or more Vikings."

I donned my mail and grabbed my large shield, bow, and three throwing spears. By the time I was heading through the hall many of my warriors were also dressed and ready to go to the walls. As I passed Erik One Hand and Bagsecg I said, "When the last warrior has left, bar the gate. I have told the young girls to wear helmets. I want the enemy to see this inner wall manned too."

"Aye hersir."

Others had reached the walls already. They were crowded around Rolf and Gunnar. They were staring to the north. I hissed, "Spread out. I want ten paces between each man. When the boys come, put them between you."

I was already coming up with the idea of giving the boys headgear to make them look like warriors. If an enemy attacked in the dark he did not

# The Battle for a Home

make out faces but shapes. A figure with a helmet might be a warrior. The ditch we had erected gave us a good fighting platform and we were able to pass each other easily. I reached Gunnar and Rolf. It was still their watch. I knew there was no way that I could send a message to Sven. He and his boys would have to fend for themselves. Our drekar was moored over a cradle Sven had made. It was only exposed at low tide. The only time Sven could move was at high tide. As the tide had just turned he would be stuck there.

Rolf pointed to the north of the shadow that was our own drekar. It did not move much for it was anchored and had the cradle beneath it. "Look, I can see three sails."

The squally rain and wind were gusting but Rolf was right. The occasional flash of something lighter could only be a sail.

Gunnar shook his head. "They are coming too quickly."

Harold Fast Sailing had arrived and as was fastening his sword he said, "It is a lazy captain. He uses the wind which comes from the northeast. It means his men do not need to row."

"You are right. And that means they intend to land here." My mind was filled with plans to stop fellow Vikings from slaughtering us and, at the same time, I began to think about who they could be. I came up with two conclusions, either the Danes or the Frisians. Even as the thought flickered and flashed through my mind I knew the answer. "It is Guthrum the Skull. The Eriksson brothers raided here."

"Then he knows about the island."

"Aye, but does he have Ulf Big Nose with him? We almost foundered on the rocks and were only saved by Ulf. When we returned we needed a light and the fishing boats to land safely." I looked up to the heavens and touched my horse token, "Thank you Siggi and Ulf, you watch over us yet." I turned to the three of them. "You keep watch here and I will go and warn the others of the dangers." My men knew the Frisians and understood the danger they represented. Knowing your enemy was half the battle.

As I passed my warriors I told them who we faced. As I reached the gate I saw Gille and Bertrand. They had brought in the six families who lived on farms beyond our walls. I shouted down, "Gille take the families and all the horses into the citadel then come to the walls. Warn them that we fight Guthrum the Skull!"

Others might have waited until we knew but I had had the thought planted in my head. Aiden had always told me to trust such thoughts. I

## The Battle for a Home

had been chosen by the Norns and I had dreamed in the cave. Aiden told me that gave me a way to speak with the spirits of the dead. He had said, *"It can be frustrating Hrolf, for you do not choose the time but when they have something to tell you it will creep, like a hind approaching water and looking for predators, carefully, quietly. You will barely know it is there and then it will seem as though you, yourself, have conjured the idea. Welcome to the spirit world!"*

I knew now what he meant. It had taken some time for me to be comfortable with the idea of spirits in my head but now I saw that it was all part of the Norns' plan.

By the time I returned to Rolf I saw dawn beginning to break in the east. I could also make out the drekar. One was ahead of the others. The squally seas made the rocks they were approaching invisible. The telltale white was masked by waves whipped up by wild winds.

Harold Fast Sailing shook his head, "We may not have to fight, Hrolf. The rocks may defeat the drekar for us."

"Perhaps." I looked up at the sky. The rain had abated but the wind still swirled above our heads. As I looked out to sea I saw the leading drekar. It was heading for **'Dragon's Breath'**, suddenly it seemed to shudder.

Harold said, "She has struck!" Her sail had been full and the hidden rocks must have ground along the length of her keel. The mast and sail were pitched forward and then the prow rose like a rearing horse to crash back down at an alarming angle. I could not see the men being pitched into the sea but I could hear, against the noise of the wind and the sea their cries. They had been ready for war with mail, helmets and shields. If any survived then Sven and his boys would slay them with their bows. We had one less drekar to fear.

"The other two have lowered their sails, hersir. They are running out oars!" The light was improving all the time. Harold Fast Sailing knew what to look for. "They may still founder on the rocks of the island."

Even as the light improved and the two ships turned I saw oars sheer as the steerboard side of one drekar struck the rocks. They saved the ship but I knew what injuries that could cause. "That has bought us time. They will have to sail around the island and land in the lee of it." Gille and Bertrand joined me. "You two stay with me. I will need you as messengers. Harold Fast Sailing you take command here. I will go to the gate."

# The Battle for a Home

By the time I reached the gate Rurik had already put two warriors in each of the gate towers. They had bows. I laid down my spear and shield. "I want you two to make sure that there are enough stones and arrows. We need to stop the enemy before he reaches the ditch."

Eager for something to do the two of them ran off in opposite directions. Our winter work fletching had paid off. We had enough arrows. The sea had yielded us a fine harvest of stones.

Rurik said, "Do you think they will notice the line of white stones?"

We had placed marker stones to help our archers with the range. They were not in straight lines and I hoped that they would not be seen. "It matters not. If they see them what will they think? If they stop to think, then so much the better for us. A stationary target is easier to hit!"

The two drekar disappeared behind the island. I wondered if they would risk landing there. Then I dismissed the thought. If the Eriksson brothers had advised them then they would know that the causeway would be underwater. They would land on the southern beach and head towards the gates. I peered over the edge of the palisade. The bridge had been drawn up and secured. Bagsecg had made metal fastenings so that it could not be released by an axe. They would need to bridge the ditch. That would take time and they would lose men. The rain had made the sand and the earth on the far side of the bridge muddy. The horses and those coming from the farms had churned it up even more. I had contemplated putting stones down there. I was now glad that I had not.

I turned as I smelled fresh bread. Brigid led the young women, all wearing an old helmet, towards us with fresh bread and ale. They did not ascend the ladders and I shouted, "One in two go down and bring the bread and ale." As they went down I asked, "Whose idea was this?"

"Your wife said that as the bread had already risen we should bake it. She said you fight better on a full stomach! You are grumpy when you have not eaten."

I laughed, "My wife knows me well."

Their baskets empty and the beer taken they turned to head back to the citadel. Brigid shouted, "Fight well warriors of the Raven Wing Clan. Your women will reward you after the battle!"

My men cheered. My wife had been right. As I bit into the warm bread the rich smell filled my nostrils. It was a smell of home and of comfort. Washed down with Brigid's finest beer it brought it home. We fought for our families and they were worth fighting for. We would die for them! I now had a son. If I fell on these walls then the clan would see that he was brought up a warrior. Ragnvald was my future.

"Hersir, they are landing!"

Asbjorn Sorenson was in one of the towers and he pointed half a mile south of the island where the first of the ships had grounded on the sand. They were coming. We watched them pour off the drekar and gather on the beach. We had done this ourselves and I knew what they were doing. They looked for the best place to attack. Their disaster in the rocks meant that they no longer had surprise. Where was our weakness? I glanced to the east of the causeway. I saw only bodies being crashed against the rocks. He had lost one-third of his men and we had had to do nothing.

"Asbjorn, how many men wear mail?"

I saw him shade his eyes from a flurry of rain which descended. "So far I see twenty, hersir."

There would be more. In many ways, it did not matter if they had mail until they were within our walls. Until then the shields of those without mail would be as effective against our arrows as those with. The danger would come from their archers. Our boys with slings and our archers would become targets.

"I will go to the tower and see if I can pick off their archers with my bow. Archers, target their men who bear bows. They are the danger. When their warriors are close we can inflict greater wounds." Closer to us, the arrows which Bagsecg had made, with a long tapered point, could penetrate mail. Guthrum was in for a shock. When he had last faced us we had few arrows. The winter had given us plenty. Once more Siggi's gold was saving the clan.

When I reached the top Asbjorn made room for me. I strung my Saami bow. The string would become wet but I had two spares. I doubted it would come to that. Asbjorn had a bow too as had the third in the tower, Sigismund of Ljoðhús.

They were both new men and looked at my bow with interest. I smiled, "This cost almost as much as a suit of mail but it has a longer range than yours. I will try to give their archers a surprise. Yours will reach further than you think from this tower. When they near the far white stones you might be in range. I know not the strength of your arms." The strength of a bow lay in two things; how well the bow was made and the strength of the archer. Only the man using the bow knew that.

# The Battle for a Home

I saw that the mailed warriors marched in a loose line ahead of the ones without mail while the archers were at the rear. They marched confidently for they were well out of range... or so they thought. When they were forty paces from the furthest line of stones I raised my bow. With three lines of warriors advancing I did not need to aim. This was a ranging arrow. Once I knew where it would strike I could aim. With the wind coming from our left it would affect our arrows.

I released and the arrow soared high. I saw the wind begin to move it slightly right and stored that information for my next one. Then it plunged and, gathering speed, did not move as much. It struck a warrior in the second rank in the neck. He fell. My men all cheered and the Frisian band lifted their shields and stopped. I saw Guthrum the Skull turn and shout something. He was bringing up his archers. They would not have the range and, as they closed with us, we would have the advantage.

"Archers ready my command!"

"Aye, lord!"

I let the Frisian archers form a line, twenty men long and draw their bows. Four struck the water of the ditch and the rest fell short. I drew back and aimed at one in the middle. He was drawing a second arrow when I hit him.

"Archers, release!"

We, too, had twenty archers. Not all were as powerful as each other but eight arrows hit their target while twelve fell short. I loosed another and hit another archer. Guthrum realised he was losing his archers and his men were ordered forward. Even as they came another three archers were hit. One of my arrows struck a mailed warrior next to Guthrum. I hit him in his right upper arm. He could hold a shield but not his spear. The shields were locked which slowed them down. Guthrum the Skull had not yet formed a shield wall and while they came in three lines we rained death upon them. I could see as our arrows took their toll that the second drekar had landed and the warriors were hurrying to reach their comrades. Even if they had twenty archers with them too we still held the advantage for only two archers had managed to escape death or injury.

"Concentrate on those without mail until they reach the last line of stones!"

"Aye, lord!"

"Slingers begin to loose now! A silver coin for any who bring down a mailed warrior!"

# The Battle for a Home

With a sound like hailstones on a ship's deck, the stones began to strike the warriors. The stones could be deadly and could even cause damage to a head if they struck a helmet. It meant the shields were pulled up even higher. It exposed their legs. Their byrnies only came to their knees and their raised shields gave us a target. I aimed at Guthrum. My arrow hit him in the foot and, briefly, pinned him to the ground. As the line continued to move on either side of him the integrity of the shields was lost and two more warriors were hit. The wounds would not be mortal but they were effective. His foot freed, Guthrum began to march again. My archers had thinned out the line behind. The crew of the second drekar were now running. To slow them up I sent an arrow at the leading warrior. He had mail but my arrow hit his shoulder and threw him to the ground. It made the others halt and, as the warrior rose to his feet and tore the arrow from the wound, they formed their shields. I wanted a slow approach. The slower they came the more men we would kill.

They reached the first line of stones and we all switched our arrows to those with mail at the front. Their shields became hedgehogs. I continued to aim at legs and struck another four before they reached the ditch. One mailed warrior moved his shield to see the water and Asbjorn's arrow hit him in the face. He toppled forwards and disappeared beneath the waters. As a second warrior fell I heard Guthrum shout, "Back! Move back but keep your shields locked!"

As he moved back I saw a trail of blood from his foot. There were six less mailed warriors for us to fight. We continued to shower them with arrows and stones until I shouted. "Hold. Save your stones and arrows!"

Everyone cheered. I descended and Rurik shook his head. "This is not over. They will be back."

Erik Long Hair said, "Aye but they will not be as strong when next they come. We have hurt them."

"Erik is right. They might have only left twenty-four bodies on the beach but that number again is wounded. With the lost drekar crew he is down to half the men he started with."

Arne Four Toes asked, "You think he will depart?"

I shook my head, "A leader like Guthrum leads by being successful. If he fails there will be another who will take over. Guthrum will fight until he is dead or he has captured our home. We will have to battle him to save it!"

# Chapter 21

While they were regrouping, well out of range, I went around my walls to assess the mood of my warriors and to see if we had any injuries. The men were buoyant and hopeful. For the Franks who fought with us, this was good for they had not had success before. None of our warriors had been injured but some of the archers needed new bowstrings for they had fitted theirs too early and they had become wet.

By the time I had reached the gate again Guthrum and his men had reformed. I saw a band of thirty who were without armour race away from the sea towards the higher ground. I turned to Gudrun Witch Killer, "He plans on attacking the stronghold from the landward side. Gudrun, take your men and six slingers. Go and reinforce the inner ward of the citadel. There are girls there. Give them spears and discourage the Frisians. If you need help have the horn sound once."

"Aye hersir."

He only took eleven men but the effect was dramatic. There were more gaps on the walls.

"Hrolf, look, he is taking Skutal and Sigurd's fishing boats!"

I nodded. I had seen them. They carried them above their heads and it gave added protection. "He intends to bridge the ditch. When they try that then use the heavy stones. We will sink them."

I went back to the tower and restrung my bow. The boats they carried protected their heads but when they drew close we would have a flatter trajectory and we could hit their legs. Guthrum and his men marched behind. I saw that he was not in the front rank but with his hearth-weru in the third. His reinforcements meant he had a solid line of mailed warriors in the front. Behind them, I saw the wounded boarding their drekar. They would not fight us again. Further down the wall, I heard Skutal Einarsson as he shouted, "You will pay for stealing my boat Frisians! I will take payment from your worthless hides!"

We let the men with the two boats come closer but my archers and slingers subjected these new Frisians to the same treatment. I released

## The Battle for a Home

another arrow at one of the mailed warriors whose shield was not as tight to his neighbour as it should have been. It pierced his right shoulder. He kept his position but if it came to fighting then even Gille would be able to defeat him. I saw that Guthrum had come within range and I sent an arrow at him. He saw it coming and ducked. He was fast but not fast enough. The arrow struck his helmet, shattering the skull he wore and then sent the helmet spinning. I had another arrow ready and when the hearth-weru next to him raised his shield to protect his head I sent him to Valhalla with an arrow to the chest.

My archers gradually picked off their archers. Sven Siggison was struck by a Frisian arrow. His left hand was pierced. We, however, had won the battle of the arrows. The stones were a constant source of annoyance and danger to the enemy and they kept up a hailstorm for the boys were eager to impress the warriors.

"Hersir! They are nearing the ditch."

"I see them. Aim for their legs and the rest of you use stones. We will build Skutal a new fishing boat!"

My bow was the most powerful and I aimed it at the knee of the leading warrior. It smashed into it and I saw it emerge from the back. A warrior would have to be made of iron to withstand such a blow. He was not and his knee gave way causing the boat to drop at the front. Another arrow, from the far tower, hit one of the warriors at the rear in the thigh. My slingers saw their opportunity and managed to hit the legs of the warriors carrying the first fishing boat. It fell from the warriors who tried to make their way back to the safety of the shield wall and their comrades. They fell to arrows, stones and a spear thrown by Skutal.

The second fishing boat, however, was closer to the ditch for we had all concentrated on the leading one. They ran the last few paces. Arrows and stones struck the legs of those underneath the upturned boat but, although we hit them, we did not manage to inflict a telling wound. When it reached the ditch they had to stand to hurl it across. It was heavy and as soon as they raised it up they became targets. When the last four fell to spears and arrows the boat fell from their grasp and slipped into the ditch. Its bow stuck up. The deaths and wounds to twenty warriors had been for nothing. They could not use it as a bridge.

I turned to Gille. "Go and saddle Dream Strider and Night Star!"

"Aye, lord!"

As he ran off I shouted, "Slaughter as many as you can! We end this today so that Guthrum the Skull never dares threaten our walls again."

# The Battle for a Home

I loosed an arrow at the line of advancing warriors. As I did so I saw fifteen or so Frisians run from the woods back towards their ships. Gudrun Witch Killer had beaten off the attack. I looked down at this last attack of mailed warriors. The shields which had taken the arrows were now heavy. They had only lost two mailed warriors and they were close to the edge of the ditch but they were tiring. "Use the stones and the spears!"

When huge warriors like Beorn Beornsson threw a stone it dealt a blow like Bagsecg's hammer. His first stone struck the shield and helmet of a warrior in the middle. He reeled back. Erik Green Eye threw a spear from just thirty paces and with such force that it went through the right shoulder of a second. The stones and spears added to the rain of stones and arrows. There was no way across the ditch and they were dying for nothing.

I saw Guthrum turn to his standard bearer. He had stayed beyond the range of my arrows. The horn sounded twice and then twice more. The warriors began to fall back. My men cheered.

I shouted, "Archers, slingers, stay on the walls. Warriors follow me and we will end this here on our beach!" Gille had arrived with the two horses. He had brought with him our two new smaller shields. I took a spear and shouted, "Open the gate!" Asbjorn Sorenson was able to reach down and loosen the fastenings on the ditch bridge and he lowered it slowly. Rurik and Arne opened the gate and, as the bridge touched the far bank, Gille and I urged our two horses forward.

When you are on foot and you hear hooves behind you, you run faster. There is something about a horse coming at you from behind which induces fear. I had seen warriors fill their breeks when a horse came behind them. There were only two of us and had they turned and formed a shield wall we could have done little but they did not. They had been broken and left twenty men at the ditch, not counting those warriors who had carried the two boats. All that they wanted was to catch up with their leader and board their two drekar.

One mailed warrior, who was limping, turned and raised his shield. He was tired and his axe came up wearily. It required two hands to swing and he needed one to hold his shield. I stood in the stirups as I brought down the spear. It entered his chest and he slumped backwards. I let his body pull itself from my spearhead. I saw Gille do the same as I had but his opponent had no mail and his back was to him. He punched too hard

# The Battle for a Home

and the spear went all the way through. He would never be able to pull it out and he wisely let go and drew his sword.

Glancing over my shoulder I saw Finni Jarlson and Rurik One Ear leading my warriors. They were keeping together and had formed a loose wedge. Ahead of me, I saw that the lighter armed Frisians were already scrambling up the sides of the drekar. The ones before us all wore mail. Guthrum the Skull was struggling. His wounded knee was bleeding heavily and he was being supported by three of his men. I wondered if the rest would stay to help their leader. I heard the standard bearer shout, "Clan of the Skull! Now is the time to fulfil your oath!"

Twelve men turned but the rest ran. I pulled back my arm as the twelve tried to form a shield wall. I rammed my spear into the face of the warrior at the end of the line. His falling body and helmet conspired to break the head from my spear. I wheeled around, away from the waving spears and swords as I drew Heart of Ice.

"Gille! With me! Rurik! Wedge!"

My men did not take long to form a wedge. Rurik led it as they began to march towards Guthrum the Skull. They chanted as they went.

*A song of death to all its foes*
*The power of the raven grows and grows.*
*The power of the raven grows and grows.*
*The power of the raven grows and grows.*
*A song of death to all its foes*
*The power of the raven grows and grows.*
*The power of the raven grows and grows.*
*The power of the raven grows and grows.*
*A song of death to all its foes*
*The power of the raven grows and grows.*
*The power of the raven grows and grows.*
*The power of the raven grows and grows.*

It was mesmerizing. The Frisians waited to die. At the last moment, my men ran. I saw Guthrum die first. Rurik's spear took him in the throat. Finni's spear took the standard-bearer. I turned to Gille, "Now!" We rode on the right-hand side of the Frisian line. I brought my sword across the side of the head of the last warrior and his head flew through the air. As I hacked at the back of another Gille stood in his stiraps and chopped down on the head of a third.

# The Battle for a Home

It was over and the Frisians had all died. They were brave men and they had fulfilled their oath. "Take their mail, weapons and weregeld. Come, Gille let us send these drekar off!"

We had another four hundred paces before we reached them and the last men were being hauled aboard. I raised my sword and shouted, "Your leader is dead! We will bury them. They died with their swords in their hands and this is over! If ever you come back make sure it is to pay us tribute if not then we will slaughter you all. Hear my words! I am Hrolf the Horseman and this is my land! This is now the land of the Northmen!"

One white beard, with a bloody hand and a bandaged head came to the prow. "We hear you and you have my word that we will find easier prey to hunt. The Raven Wing Clan is safe from us."

"And tell any of our clan who..."

The man shook his head, "All of your clan who joined us are dead. Guthrum had a falling out."

I nodded, "*Wyrd*."

The warrior nodded, "Aye, so it would seem."

The two drekar began to back out of the bay. I heard hooves thundering across the turf. I turned and saw Bertrand. He was riding as though a pack of wolves was chasing him. He was shouting as he approached but I could not hear him over the sound of the surf and the sea.

He reined in, "Hersir!" He pointed over my shoulder, "The lord of Valognes comes. I recognise his banner. There is a column of horsemen!"

I looked to where he was pointing. Half a mile away was a column of mounted warriors perhaps fifty in total. They rode beneath a red and white striped banner. Perhaps they came in peace but they were now galloping. "Bertrand, tell my men to get to the haugr. Come, Gille, we will try to discourage them." We rode back and picked up two spears which had been discarded. We rode towards the column.

The column veered towards us and four men detached themselves and galloped towards us. Any possibility that they came in peace was removed when I saw them ready their spears. I shouted, "Gille these will know what they are doing. We go for the middle and then when we have passed, we turn!"

"Aye lord. They have no mail!"

## The Battle for a Home

"Then we have a chance. Ride as close to me as you can get." Here we had the advantage that our horses knew each other and I had trained Gille. Dream Strider was slightly ahead of Night Star. The four we charged were spread out. I was on the left and, as we neared then I stood in the stirrups and jabbed with my spear. The Frank did the same. The results were different. Mine found flesh and he flew from the back of his horse. His found shield and mail. It felt as though I was punched but that was all. Gille had not fared as well. He had also slain his opponent but the back of his hand had been scored by the Frank's spear. I turned and jabbed my spear at the back of the third Frank. It scored a deep line across the rump of his horse which reared and threw him.

"Ride hard! I will follow!"

The last warrior was brave for, having seen his three comrades fall, he still came after us. I allowed him to draw level and then, pulling back my arm threw the spear at his leg. He was little more than two spear lengths from me. My spear hit his leg and carried on into his horse. It veered and fell, crushing the Frank beneath its body. I leaned over Dream Strider and urged him on, "Now is your time. Show Night Star that you are the leader of this herd. Run, my beauty, run!"

We began to catch Gille. I looked over my shoulder and saw that the Franks were forty paces from us. When I looked ahead I saw that all my men except for Bertrand were safely inside my walls. Bertrand was too brave for his own good. "Into the citadel! Archers ready!"

As Gille clattered over the bridge I risked another look over my shoulder. They were less than thirty paces from me. Even as Dream Strider's hooves hit the turf the bridge was being drawn up. I heard shouts and cries from beyond the walls. I leapt from my stallion's back and threw the reins to Bertrand. I ran up the ladder to the gate. I saw that my archers had hit three horses and two men. I picked up my bow and aimed at the standard-bearer. He was forty paces from the ditch. His small shield was no protection and my arrow hit him in the chest. He tried to stay on the saddle but he fell.

I shouted, "Hold!" I lowered my bow and said, in the tongue of the Franks, "I am Hrolf the Horseman. This is now my land! If I choose I can slay you all as easily as I killed your standard bearer. Go and leave us alone!"

"I am Philippe, Leudes of Valognes and I rule this land by right. King Louis has charged me with its protection!"

# The Battle for a Home

I pointed to the two drekar which were now disappearing behind the island, "As you can see we need no protection. We displaced no one here and we will not harm any farmers who are close by but do not poke us with a stick! We are no tethered bear! We are Vikings and we are to be feared."

I stopped speaking and waited. I saw the lord, who looked to be little older than me, looking at the piles of bodies which littered the land before the ditch. He looked at the ditch and then at my walls. He had been chasing Vikings and now he saw how formidable our defences were. He had no chance of taking our walls. I watched as he desperately sought a way out with dignity and honour. I gave it to him.

"Send a message to your king that three boatloads of Vikings were vanquished here. That should please him." I paused to let my words sink in. "We are only a threat to you if you make us one. Do you wish to take on my men, my walls and my sword? If you do then I will come forth and you and I will try a trial by combat."

His men looked at him expectantly. They were willing him to accept so that he could show this Viking that a Frank was a better warrior. When he shook his head I knew that we had won, "This is not over Viking. I will bring more men and reduce this to kindling."

I nodded, "Your men are witness to my words. You have been warned. The consequences will be on your head!"

His answer was to turn and ride away. My men began to cheer and to bang their shields. Rurik started the song and the whole of the clan, every man, woman and child took it up as the humiliated Franks left the field.

*The horseman came through darkest night*
*He rode towards the dawning light*
*With fiery steed and thrusting spear*
*Hrolf the Horseman brought great fear*

*Slaughtering all he breached their line*
*Of warriors slain there were nine*
*Hrolf the Horseman with gleaming blade*
*Hrolf the Horseman all enemies slayed*

*With mighty axe Black Teeth stood*
*Angry and filled with hot blood*
*Hrolf the Horseman with gleaming blade*

The Battle for a Home

*Hrolf the Horseman all enemies slayed*
*Ice cold Hrolf with Heart of Ice*
*Swung his arm and made it slice*
*Hrolf the Horseman with gleaming blade*
*Hrolf the Horseman all enemies slayed*

*In two strokes the Jarl was felled*
*Hrolf's sword nobly held*
*Hrolf the Horseman with gleaming blade*
*Hrolf the Horseman all enemies slayed*

# The Battle for a Home

# Epilogue

We had waited until the Franks had left the beach before we resumed the task of burying the dead. They were not our dead but we had promised and when I gave my word, I kept it. It had been a great victory. Skutal and Sigurd's boats did not need much repair and when Sven and his boys joined us, at high tide, they also brought the bounty of the dead from the sea. We had mail, helmets and weapons. We had bracelets and warrior bands. We had coins and we even had four horses. The Franks had left us so quickly that they forgot four horses from their fallen warriors. My herd was growing. The three mares and the gelding would be valuable additions.

Most importantly my new clan had fought as one. Franks and Norse had stood together. We had faced our enemies and we had survived. We celebrated. The dead horses provided the food and Karl the singer gave us the songs. When he had finished Siggi's Song my men, well into their ale, banged their table and called for me to speak. I had had more ale than normal and I obliged.

"The clan withstood two tests today. We fought Frisians. They have Viking blood and they are fierce fighters. We stood shoulder to shoulder and did not flinch. All took part from the boys to the men. The girls played their part and stood a watch. We met our neighbours and offered them peace. If they choose war then they have a new enemy to face, us! We are the people of the north and this is our home. We are one people. If they think to shift us then they face a challenge for we will not move. We will stand and we will build. Our home will become a rock against which our enemies will break!"

As the clan cheered my wife stood. Ragnvald suckled still. Even so, she looked like a queen. "This is my husband. He will not take a title but he needs none for we all know that he is the leader of this clan. We are back in the land in which I was born. Our son will make this land even greater and I say to any enemy, if you come to this land you will have to battle for every blade of grass for we will not be moving!" She used her free hand to raise her horn of ale, "My husband, Hrolf the Horseman, Lord of the Haugr!"

The cheers and the noise touched me but above it all, I heard the voices of Siggi White Hair and Ulf Big Nose telling me that they were proud of me and that was enough. We had made a start but we would grow. My wife was right. This was our land, the land of the Northman!

**The End**

# Glossary

Ækre -acre (Norse) The amount of land a pair of oxen could plough in one day
Afon Hafron- River Severn in Welsh
Alt Clut- Dumbarton Castle on the Clyde
Andecavis- Angers in Anjou
Angia- Jersey (Channel Islands)
An Oriant- Lorient, Brittany
Áth Truim- Trim, County Meath (Ireland)
Baille - a ward (an enclosed area inside a wall)
Balley Chashtal -Castleton (Isle of Man)
Bebbanburgh- Bamburgh Castle, Northumbria. Also known as Din Guardi in the ancient tongue
Beck- a stream
Blót – a blood sacrifice made by a jarl
Blue Sea/Middle Sea- The Mediterranean
Bondi- Viking farmers who fight
Bourde- Bordeaux
Bjarnarøy –Great Bernera (Bear Island)
Byrnie- a mail or leather shirt reaching down to the knees
Caerlleon- Welsh for Chester
Caestir - Chester (old English)
Cantewareburh- Canterbury
Casnewydd –Newport, Wales
Cent- Kent
Cephas- Greek for Simon Peter (St. Peter)
Cetham -Chatham Kent
Chape- the tip of a scabbard
Charlemagne- Holy Roman Emperor at the end of the 8th and beginning of the 9th centuries
Cherestanc- Garstang (Lancashire)
Ćiriċeburh- Cherbourg
Corn Walum or Om Walum- Cornwall
Cymri- Welsh
Cymru- Wales
Cyninges-tūn – Coniston. It means the estate of the king (Cumbria)
Dùn Èideann –Edinburgh (Gaelic)
Din Guardi- Bamburgh castle
Drekar- a Dragon ship (a Viking warship)

# The Battle for a Home

Duboglassio –Douglas, Isle of Man
Dyrøy –Jura (Inner Hebrides)
Dyflin- Old Norse for Dublin
Ein-mánuðr- middle of March to the middle of April
Eoforwic- Saxon for York
Fáfnir - a dwarf turned into a dragon (Norse mythology)
Faro Bregancio- Corunna (Spain)
Ferneberga -Farnborough (Hampshire)
Fey- having second sight
Firkin- a barrel containing eight gallons (usually beer)
Fret-a sea mist
Frankia- France and part of Germany
Fyrd-the Saxon levy
Gaill- Irish for foreigners
Galdramenn- wizard
Glaesum –amber
Gleawecastre- Gloucester
Gói- the end of February to the middle of March
Greenway- ancient roads- they used turf rather than stone
Grenewic- Greenwich
Gyllingas - Gillingham Kent
Haesta- Hastings
Hamwic -Southampton
Harpa- April 14th- May 13th
Haughs/ Haugr - small hills in Norse (As in Tarn Hows) or a hump- normally a mound of earth
Haustmánuður -15th September -October 14th
Hearth-weru- Jarl's bodyguard/oathsworn
Heels- when a ship leans to one side under the pressure of the wind
Hel - Queen of Niflheim, the Norse underworld.
Herkumbl- a mark on the front of a helmet denoting the clan of a Viking warrior
Here Wic- Harwich
Hetaereiarch – Byzantine general
Hí- Iona (Gaelic)
Hjáp - Shap- Cumbria (Norse for stone circle)
Hoggs or Hogging- when the pressure of the wind causes the stern or the bow to droop
Hrams-a – Ramsey, Isle of Man
Hrofecester-Rochester Kent
Hywel ap Rhodri Molwynog- King of Gwynedd 814-825
Icaunis- British river god
Issicauna- Gaulish for the lower Seine

# The Battle for a Home

Itouna- River Eden Cumbria
Jarl- Norse earl or lord
Joro-goddess of the earth
Jǫtunn -Norse god or goddess
Kjerringa - Old Woman- the solid block in which the mast rested
Knarr- a merchant ship or a coastal vessel
Kyrtle-woven top
Laugardagr-Saturday (Norse for washing day)
Leathes Water- Thirlmere
Ljoðhús- Lewis
Legacaestir- Anglo Saxon for Chester
Liger- Loire
Lochlannach – Irish for Northerners (Vikings)
Lothuwistoft- Lowestoft
Louis the Pious- King of the Franks and son of Charlemagne
Lundenwic - London
Maeresea- River Mersey
Mammceaster- Manchester
Manau/Mann – The Isle of Man(n) (Saxon)
Marcia Hispanic- Spanish Marches (the land around Barcelona)
Mast fish- two large racks on a ship for the mast
Melita- Malta
Midden - a place where they dumped human waste
Miklagård - Constantinople
Leudes- Imperial officer (a local leader in the Carolingian Empire. They became Counts a century after this.
Njoror- God of the sea
Nithing- A man without honour (Saxon)
Odin - The "All Father" God of war, also associated with wisdom, poetry, and magic (The ruler of the gods).
Olissipo- Lisbon
Orkneyjar-Orkney
Portucale- Porto
Portesmūða -Portsmouth
Condado Portucalense- the County of Portugal
Penrhudd – Penrith Cumbria
Pillars of Hercules- Straits of Gibraltar
Ran- Goddess of the sea
Roof rock- slate
Rinaz –The Rhine
Sabrina- Latin and Celtic for the River Severn. Also the name of a female Celtic deity

# The Battle for a Home

**Saami-** the people who live in what is now Northern Norway/Sweden
**Sarnia-** Guernsey (Channel Islands)
**St. Cybi-** Holyhead
**Sampiere** -samphire (sea asparagus)
**Scree-** loose rocks in a glacial valley
**Seax** – short sword
**Sheerstrake-** the uppermost strake in the hull
**Sheet-** a rope fastened to the lower corner of a sail
**Shroud-** a rope from the masthead to the hull amidships
**Skeggox** – an axe with a shorter beard on one side of the blade
**Skerpla** -May 14$^{th}$- June 12$^{th}$
**South Folk-** Suffolk
**Stad-** Norse settlement
**Stays-** ropes running from the mast-head to the bow
**Stirap-** stirrup
**Strake-** the wood on the side of a drekar
**Suthriganaworc -** Southwark (London)
**Syllingar-** Scilly Isles
**Syllingar Insula-** Scilly Isles
**Tarn-** small lake (Norse)
**Temese-** River Thames (also called the Tamese)
**The Norns-** The three sisters who weave webs of intrigue for men
**Thing-**Norse for a parliament or a debate (Tynwald)
**Thor's day-** Thursday
**Threttanessa-** a drekar with 13 oars on each side.
**Thrall-** slave
**Tinea-** Tyne
**Trenail-** a round wooden peg used to secure strakes
**Tynwald-** the Parliament on the Isle of Man
**Úlfarrberg-** Helvellyn
**Úlfarrland-** Cumbria
**Úlfarr-** Wolf Warrior
**Úlfarrston-** Ulverston
**Ullr-**Norse God of Hunting
**Ulfheonar-**an elite Norse warrior who wore a wolf skin over his armour
**Vectis-** The Isle of Wight
**Volva-** a witch or healing woman in Norse culture
**Waeclinga Straet-** Watling Street (A5)
**Windlesore-**Windsor
**Waite-** a Viking word for farm
**Werham** -Wareham (Dorset)

# The Battle for a Home

**Wintan-ceastre -Winchester**
**Withy- the mechanism connecting the steering board to the ship**
**Woden's day- Wednesday**
**Wyddfa-Snowdon**
**Wyrd- Fate**
**Yard- a timber from which the sail is suspended on a drekar**
**Ynys Môn-Anglesey**

The Battle for a Home

# Maps and Illustrations

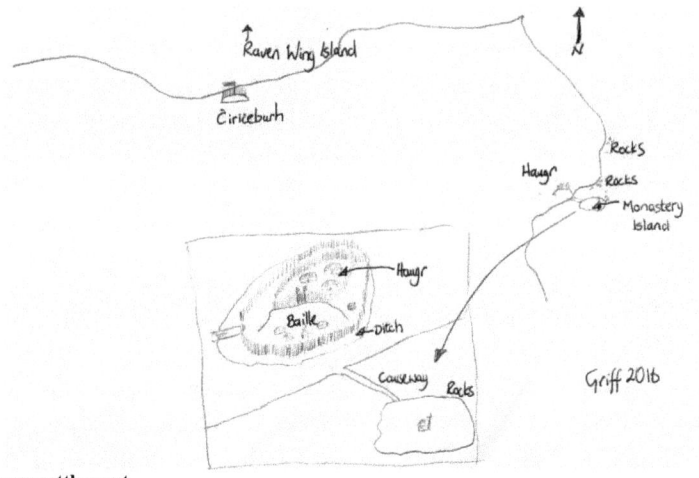

**The new settlement.**
**Griff Hosker 2016**

# Historical note

My research encompasses not only books and the Internet but also TV. Time Team was a great source of information. I wish they would bring it back! I saw the wooden compass which my sailors use on the Dan Snow programme about the Vikings. Apparently, it was used in modern times to sail from Denmark to Edinburgh and was only a couple of points out. Similarly, the construction of the temporary hall was copied from the settlement of Leif Eriksson in Newfoundland.

Stirrups began to be introduced in Europe during the 7th and 8th Centuries. By Charlemagne's time, they were widely used but only by nobles. It is said this was the true beginning of feudalism. It was the Vikings who introduced them to England. It was only in the time of Canute the Great that they became widespread. The use of stirrups enabled a rider to strike someone on the ground from the back of a horse and facilitated the use of spears and later, lances.

The Vikings may seem cruel to us now. They enslaved women and children. Many of the women became their wives. The DNA of the people of Iceland shows that it was made up of a mixture of Norse and Danish males and Celtic females. These were the people who settled Iceland, Greenland and Vinland. They did the same in England and, as we shall see, Normandy. Their influence was widespread. Genghis Khan and his Mongols did the same in the 13th century. It is said that a high proportion of European males have Mongol blood in them. The Romans did it with the Sabine tribe. They were different times and it would be wrong to judge them with our politically correct twenty-first-century eyes. This sort of behaviour still goes on in the world but with less justification.

At this time there were no Viking kings. There were clans. Each clan had a hersir or Jarl. Clans were loyal to each other. A hersir was more of a landlocked Viking or a farmer while a Jarl usually had ship(s) at his command. A hersir would command bondi. They were the Norse equivalent of the fyrd although they were much better warriors. They would all have a helmet shield and a sword. Most would also have a spear. Hearth-weru were the oathsworn or bodyguards for a jarl or, much later on, a king. Kings like Canute and Harald Hadrada were rare and they only emerged at the beginning of the tenth century.

# The Battle for a Home

Harald Black Teeth is made up but the practice of filing marks in teeth to allow them to blacken and to make the warrior more frightening was common in Viking times.

The wolf and the raven were both held in high esteem by the Vikings. Odin is often depicted with a wolf and a raven at his side.

Hamwic (Southampton) was raided by the Vikings so many times that it was almost abandoned by the middle of the Ninth Century. Egbert's successor did not suffer from as many Viking raids as King Egbert. He did have an alliance with the Frankish King.

The Vikings began to raid the Loire and the Seine in the middle of the $9^{th}$ century. They were able to raid as far as Tours. Tours, Saumur and the monastery at Marmoutier were all raided and destroyed. As a result of the raids and the destruction, castles were built there during the latter part of the $9^{th}$ century. There are many islands in the Loire and many tributaries. The Maine, which runs through Angers, is also a wide waterway. The lands seemed made for Viking raiders. They did not settle in Aquitaine but they did in Austrasia. The Vikings began to settle in Normandy and the surrounding islands in the 820s. Many place names in Normandy are Viking in origin. Sometimes, as in Vinland, the settlements were destroyed by the Franks but some survived. So long as a Viking had a river for his drekar he could raid at will.

The Franks used horses more than most other armies of the time. Their spears were used as long swords, hence the guards. They used saddles and stirrups. They still retained their round shields and wore, largely, an open helmet. Sometimes they wore a plum. They carried a spare spear and a sword.

FRANKISH HORSEMAN
GRIFF 2016

# The Battle for a Home

'KARA'
Griff 2016

One reason for the Normans' success was that when they arrived in northern France they integrated quickly with the local populace. They married them and began to use some of their words. They adapted to the horse as a weapon of war. Before then the Vikings had been quite happy to ride to war but they dismounted to fight. The Normans took the best that the Franks had and made it better. This book sees the earliest beginnings of the rise of the Norman knight.

**Books used in the research**

British Museum - Vikings- Life and Legends
Arthur and the Saxon Wars- David Nicolle (Osprey)
Saxon, Norman and Viking Terence Wise (Osprey)
The Vikings- Ian Heath (Osprey)
Byzantine Armies 668-1118 - Ian Heath (Osprey)

## The Battle for a Home

Romano-Byzantine Armies 4th-9th Century - David Nicholle (Osprey)
The Walls of Constantinople AD 324-1453 - Stephen Turnbull (Osprey)
Viking Longship - Keith Durham (Osprey)
Anglo-Danish Project- The Vikings in England
The Varangian Guard- 988-1453 Raffael D'Amato
Saxon Viking and Norman- Terence Wise
The Walls of Constantinople AD 324-1453-Stephen Turnbull
Byzantine Armies- 886-1118- Ian Heath
The Age of Charlemagne-David Nicolle
The Normans- David Nicolle
Norman Knight AD 950-1204- Christopher Gravett
The Norman Conquest of the North- William A Kappelle
The Knight in History- Francis Gies
The Norman Achievement- Richard F Cassady
Knights- Constance Brittain Bouchard

*Griff Hosker*
*September 2016*

# Other books by Griff Hosker

If you enjoyed reading this book, then why not read another one by the author?

## Ancient History

### The Sword of Cartimandua Series
(Germania and Britannia 50 A.D. – 128 A.D.)
Ulpius Felix- Roman Warrior (prequel)
The Sword of Cartimandua
The Horse Warriors
Invasion Caledonia
Roman Retreat
Revolt of the Red Witch
Druid's Gold
Trajan's Hunters
The Last Frontier
Hero of Rome
Roman Hawk
Roman Treachery
Roman Wall
Roman Courage

### The Wolf Warrior series
(Britain in the late 6th Century)
Saxon Dawn
Saxon Revenge
Saxon England
Saxon Blood
Saxon Slayer
Saxon Slaughter
Saxon Bane
Saxon Fall: Rise of the Warlord
Saxon Throne
Saxon Sword

## Medieval History

**The Dragon Heart Series**
Viking Slave
Viking Warrior
Viking Jarl
Viking Kingdom
Viking Wolf
Viking War
Viking Sword
Viking Wrath
Viking Raid
Viking Legend
Viking Vengeance
Viking Dragon
Viking Treasure
Viking Enemy
Viking Witch
Viking Blood
Viking Weregeld
Viking Storm
Viking Warband
Viking Shadow
Viking Legacy
Viking Clan
Viking Bravery

**The Norman Genesis Series**
Hrolf the Viking
Horseman
The Battle for a Home
Revenge of the Franks
The Land of the Northmen
Ragnvald Hrolfsson
Brothers in Blood
Lord of Rouen
Drekar in the Seine
Duke of Normandy
The Duke and the King

The Battle for a Home

**Danelaw**
(England and Denmark in the 11th Century)
Dragon Sword
Oathsword

**New World Series**
Blood on the Blade
Across the Seas
The Savage Wilderness
The Bear and the Wolf
Erik The Navigator
Erik's Clan

The Vengeance Trail

**The Reconquista Chronicles**
Castilian Knight
El Campeador
The Lord of Valencia

**The Aelfraed Series**
(Britain and Byzantium 1050 A.D. - 1085 A.D.)
Housecarl
Outlaw
Varangian

**The Anarchy Series England
1120-1180**
English Knight
Knight of the Empress
Northern Knight
Baron of the North
Earl
King Henry's Champion
The King is Dead
Warlord of the North
Enemy at the Gate
The Fallen Crown

The Battle for a Home

Warlord's War
Kingmaker
Henry II
Crusader
The Welsh Marches
Irish War
Poisonous Plots
The Princes' Revolt
Earl Marshal
The Perfect Knight

**Border Knight
1182-1300**
Sword for Hire
Return of the Knight
Baron's War
Magna Carta
Welsh Wars
Henry III
The Bloody Border
Baron's Crusade
Sentinel of the North
War in the West
Debt of Honour
The Blood of the Warlord

**Sir John Hawkwood Series
France and Italy 1339- 1387**
Crécy: The Age of the Archer
Man At Arms
The White Company
Leader of Men

**Lord Edward's Archer**
Lord Edward's Archer
King in Waiting
An Archer's Crusade
Targets of Treachery
The Great Cause

**Struggle for a Crown**
**1360- 1485**
Blood on the Crown
To Murder a King
The Throne
King Henry IV
The Road to Agincourt
St Crispin's Day
The Battle for France
The Last Knight
Queen's Knight

Tales from the Sword I
(Short stories from the Medieval period)

**Tudor Warrior series**
**England and Scotland in the late 14th and early 15th century**
Tudor Warrior

**Conquistador**
**England and America in the 16th Century**
Conquistador

## Modern History

**The Napoleonic Horseman Series**
Chasseur à Cheval
Napoleon's Guard
British Light Dragoon
Soldier Spy
1808: The Road to Coruña
Talavera
The Lines of Torres Vedras
Bloody Badajoz
The Road to France
Waterloo

**The Lucky Jack American Civil War series**

The Battle for a Home

Rebel Raiders
Confederate Rangers
The Road to Gettysburg

**Soldier of the Queen series**
Soldier of the Queen

**The British Ace Series**
1914
1915 Fokker Scourge
1916 Angels over the Somme
1917 Eagles Fall
1918 We will remember them
From Arctic Snow to Desert Sand
Wings over Persia

**Combined Operations series**
**1940-1945**
Commando
Raider
Behind Enemy Lines
Dieppe
Toehold in Europe
Sword Beach
Breakout
The Battle for Antwerp
King Tiger
Beyond the Rhine
Korea
Korean Winter

Tales from the Sword II
(Short stories from the Modern period)

**Other Books**
Great Granny's Ghost (Aimed at 9-14-year-old young people)

## The Battle for a Home

For more information on all of the books then please visit the author's website at www.griffhosker.com where there is a link to contact him or visit his Facebook page: GriffHosker at Sword Books

Lightning Source UK Ltd.
Milton Keynes UK
UKHW021829210622
404755UK00008B/790